ALL TRIGGERS NO WARNINGS

ALL TRIGGERS NO WARNINGS

JOHN EVERSON

Cemetery Dance Publications
Baltimore
❧ 2025 ☙

All Triggers, No Warnings
Copyright © 2025 by John Everson

"Driving Her Home" © 2016. Originally published in the anthology *Cemetery Riots*.
"The Most Dangerous Game" © 2017. Originally published in the anthology *Chopping Block Party*.
"Arnie's Ashes" © 2021. Originally published in the anthology *Beyond The Veil*.
"Sing Blue Silver" © 2016. Originally published in the anthology *Into Painfreak*.
"Forest Butter" © 2020. Originally published in the anthology *Survive with Me*.
"Ghoul-Friend In A Coma" © 2016. Originally published in the anthology *Drive-In Creature Feature*.
"Amnion" © 2016. Originally published in the anthology *Dread*.
"Watering" © 2010. Originally published in *Dark Discoveries magazine*.
"The Cemetery Man" © 2019. Originally published in the anthology *Midnight in the Graveyard*.
"Seastruck" © 2017. Originally published in the anthology *Fearful Fathoms Vol 1*.
"The House At The Top Of The Hill" © 2002. Originally published in *Horrorfind webzine*.
"Running Away From A Good Time" © 2015. First print publication. Originally published in the blog *Not Now, Mommy's Reading*.
"Dying On The Inside" © 2007. Previously unpublished.
"We Take Care of Our Own" © 2013. Originally published in the anthology *Appalachian Undead*.
"Then Shall The Reign of Lucifer End..."© 2009. Originally published in the anthology *Infernally Yours*.
"When She Was Ready" © 2023. First English Publication. Originally published in Czech as "Když je připravená" in the collection *Sešívance: Druhý steh*.
"The Last Word" © 2021. First print publication. Originally appeared as an audio reading in the special 500th episode of *Tales to Terrify* audio magazine.
"Triggered" © 2025. Previously unpublished.

All rights reserved. No part of this book may be reproduced in any form or by any electronic or mechanical means, including information storage and retrieval systems, without permission in writing from the publisher, except by a reviewer who may quote brief passages in a review.

Cemetery Dance Publications
132-B Industry Lane, Unit #7
Forest Hill, MD 21050
http://www.cemeterydance.com

The characters and events in this book are fictitious.
Any similarity to real persons, living or dead, is coincidental and not intended by the author.

Trade Paperback Edition Printing

ISBN: 978-1-964780-29-0

Cover Artwork © 2025 Kealan Patrick Burke
Ebook, Interior Design, Cover layout © by Steven Pajak

Contents

Maybe a Little Warning... Preface	xi
Driving Her Home	1
The Most Dangerous Game	17
Arnie's Ashes	39
Sing Blue Silver	55
Forest Butter	75
Ghoul Friend In A Coma	93
Amnion	117
Watering	135
The Cemetery Man	137
Seastruck	159
The House At The Top Of The Hill	189
Running Away From A Good Time	203
Dying On The Inside	207
We Take Care Of Our Own	219
Then Shall The Reign Of Lucifer End...	241
When She Was Ready *By John Everson in collaboration with Honza Vojtíšek*	263
The Last Word	289
Triggered	307
About the Author	319

For Geri and Shaun,
The center of my story.

Preface

Maybe a Little Warning…

I don't believe in Trigger Warnings.

There. I said it.

You may have guessed my stance from the title of this book, but here's the thing. I've been a constant Reader for over 50 years. I've been a Writer for more than 30. Story *means* something critical to me. And for most of my life, the ability to read or tell a story, whatever the genre and topic, was left alone. Over the past decade or so, however, I've seen an increasing flurry of hand-wringing about preparing readers with warnings to protect their delicate psyches from stumbling on something unpleasant, and pre-emptively sanitizing fiction in case something in it appears to be "insensitive" to one group or another and thus, might (*gasp*) offend someone. A few years ago, I was critiqued in a review for using an Asian name for a character in a story because it might be offensive to Asians *when I actually had named the character after an* actual *Asian guy I knew.* Step away from the red pen, friend.

With the very best of intentions, on one side of the spectrum, liberals have been telling writers what they could or couldn't write… or maybe more to the crux, *who* should and shouldn't write about things. With no doubt the very best of intentions on the other side, conservatives have taken up the Frankenstein torches to ban books that don't appeal to their sense of morality.

Our freedoms to read and write are diminishing by the day. Trigger warnings and sensitivity readers and book banning all look the same to me. They all are ways to tell us what we can read, think and put to paper. And careful, if you protest and say you have the creator's right to sketch characters as you envision them, you might be *cancelled*...

You know what? Sometimes, it's good to offend someone with an unsuspected "triggering" scene. It might make them think outside their box. The Internet age has made it far too easy to live in echo chambers of words and videos that only support the thoughts and feelings that we already have. And frankly, the value of fiction is to present a place where the reader walks in the Other's shoes. Even if the Other is bad. It's a safe space, ultimately, because no matter what happens there, it's fiction in the end.

A key power of Horror fiction is that it can shock. It can take you by surprise. A book may not be able to give you a jump scare, like a movie, but it should still be able to present a situation that makes your eyes go wide and your heart shatter like a vase of Valentine's Day roses when you walk in on your significant other naked with *another* other.

If you telegraph to the reader the nasty things that occur in your story before they happen, you subvert the impact of those things when the reader finally arrives at them in the text. You've diminished the impact of the Horror. I don't know why a horror writer would ever agree to do that, and I don't know why a reader would want it. All I can say is...

Get over it.

For generations humans consumed stories that shocked them without warnings and they survived.

Should the book's back cover or web site sales description give you *some* idea that you're going to get an extreme gorefest vs. a cozy mystery? Sure. That's a given. But that's where it should end.

I don't know if anything in the stories that follow will cause a reader to have "emotional distress" (aka, a trigger). But it's not my job to try to protect you from it either. I'm here to share the faces of evil,

Maybe a Little Warning…

the creepy twists and shocking situations that pass through my brain. I hope you'll be surprised and entertained and maybe even creeped out by some.

But I'm not going to coddle you and prepare you for what is about to jump out of the closet. And no other author should either.

What I will tell you is this.

I'm proud of all the stories that follow. Most of the tales that follow have been published in magazines and anthologies over the past 10 years since my last collection, *Sacrificing Virgins*, was released. I owe a huge thanks to Dan Franklin and Cemetery Dance for collecting them here, and I owe editors like the late Dave Barnett of Necro Publications (he published three of these stories in various anthologies), a huge debt for supporting my work in the past. Thanks to the many anthology editors who invited me to be a part of their projects over the past decade. I also owe a thanks to Honza Vojtíšek, a Czech writer and editor who has championed the translation of my work across the water and invited me to be in one of his personal collections with "Když je připravená" aka "When She Was Ready," a story that I wrote and he edited based on a short idea he had. My English text appears here for the first time.

It gives nothing away to warn you that there are ghosts and ghouls and demons and monsters in the pages that follow. There are stories of love unrequited and revenge gone very, very wrong. There are stories that stand alone, but still tie-in to other works. For fans of my novel *Siren*, I hope you'll enjoy "Seastruck," a story that tells exactly what happened to Andy, who appeared in the prologue to my fourth novel, but not in the main tale. There's a story set in Bachelor's Grove cemetery, the same real location that my novel *House By The Cemetery* was written about (the stories are not connected otherwise).

There is a story set in Edward Lee's *Infernal* world and another in Gerard Houarner's *Painfreak* world. I was honored to be a part of those projects since both authors certainly informed and inspired my fiction over the past 30 years.

And I'm excited that "The Last Word," a story written specifically

Preface

for the 500th episode of *Tales to Terrify* audio magazine, finally appears here in print for the first time.

There are stories that are quiet and stories that are extreme. The one thing they all have in common is that they all reflect core themes that we all should be able to relate to: the power of love, the dangers of unchecked desire and the crushing impact of loss.

I hope they take you on the kind of rollercoaster ride that only Horror can provide. The kind of ride that is always most effective when you have no idea what is lurking around that next curve. Horror is always best with plenty of triggers and …

No Warnings.

—John Everson
Naperville, IL
March 2025

Driving Her Home

I was drunk the first time I picked her up. It would never have happened otherwise. I don't pick up hitchhikers. I've seen the movies. They never end well.

But I'd been sitting at Teehan's Tavern in Tinley Park for one pint too many, and on the way home I decided to avoid cutting through the quiet, old part of town and instead took the long way home. It was after midnight, so I drove down the always-busy Harlem Avenue—I didn't need the local cops spotting and pulling me over on the local roads when I was the only car on the road. I didn't *think* I was going to weave… but better to blend in with a bunch of traffic. Once I reached 143rd Street though, I had to make a right and head down that lonely road through the forest preserve to reach the Midlothian Turnpike. It wasn't a long road, but it was definitely dark.

I saw her standing on the side of the road right after I turned the corner, and the landscape changed from streetlights to dark, shadowed stands of trees. She had long chestnut hair, twined in a braided ponytail, and wore a tie-dyed, cropped t-shirt and Daisy Duke frayed denim shorts; an odd outfit for the end of September. Especially since it was a chilly night. When she put her thumb out, I didn't think twice. She had to be freezing.

I pulled over.

"Thanks, man," she said, when she slipped into the passenger seat. "I'm almost home, but I appreciate the lift."

"What are you doing out here this late?" I asked. "It's not safe to be walking alone at this hour."

I saw her shrug out of the corner of my eye. "There was a thing down at Donnie's," she said. "We played some tunes, danced a bit... but now it's time, ya know?"

"Well, I'd just be careful about walking a dark road at night," I said. "You never know who you might meet."

"Like you?" she said, and laughed. I wasn't sure if I should be offended.

"Life is for taking chances, and meeting new people," she said. "Otherwise, you might as well sleep in a grave."

"Well, they always say, 'I'll sleep when I'm dead,'" I said.

"You don't seem dead to me," she said.

"Nope," I said. "And I'm not sleepin'."

Just then, WLUP-FM segued from Boston's "Don't Look Back" to CCR's "Susie Q."

"Oh, I love this one, do you?" she asked, leaning forward to bob her head.

"Sure," I said. "Hey, what's your name, by the way? I'm John."

"Marigold," she said. "But you can call me Mari."

"Glad to meet you, Mari," I said. "See—I took a chance and I'm meeting new people."

"Right on," she said. "But now you have to say goodbye."

"What do you mean?" I said.

"My house is just over there," she said, pointing to a place in the forest that looked as dark as the rest of the forested roadway.

I started to pull over, but didn't completely slow the car on the shoulder. "Where?" I asked.

"This is good," she said.

"There's nothing here!" I said, but hit the brakes. Outside the passenger's side window, the forest looked dark and foreboding.

"Sure, there is," she said. "My house is just through the trees. If you look hard, you can see the light through there." She pointed just past the bridge we'd just passed over. "See the porchlight?"

I craned my head, and damned if she wasn't right. There was a faint light beaming back there in the trees, past the small pond that the road ran over.

"Thanks for the lift," she said.

She leaned across the seat and planted a soft kiss right on my lips. The scent of lavender teased my nose. My eyes widened in surprise, and she grinned.

"Live a little," she said. And then in a heartbeat, she slipped out of my car. I saw her begin walking down the gravel embankment, but then a pair of headlights came up in my rear-view mirror. I raised my hand to shield my eyes from the glare, and when the car passed, and I looked down the path towards the trees and the overgrown pond... she was already gone.

I wiped a finger gently across my lips and took a deep breath before pulling back out onto the road.

I WOKE up the next morning with a headache and a strong memory of being kissed by a stranger on the side of the road next to the forest preserve.

"You didn't... really?" I asked myself, while brushing my beer-fuzzed teeth.

A tousle of bed-head hair nodded yes.

"Stupid," I said, and spit.

I drove down Midlothian Turnpike to 143rd Street on the way to work, just because. I'd been that way a million times, but I'd never seen a house tucked back in the forest. And I didn't that morning either. I'd have to stop and walk into the woods if I was going to.

DAYS PASSED and somehow the weekend came around again. The first weekend in October, which was a difficult time for me. You could say the beginning of October was the anniversary of the end of my life. And so, to celebrate, I played one too many games of KISS pinball in the corner by myself at Teehan's... and probably had one too many Revolution IPAs in the process before finally driving home at 1:30 in the morning. Consequently, I took the long way again.

When I turned down the dark road leading through the forest preserve, it was like entering another world. The lights of the busy four-lane road disappeared and suddenly I was snaking between the dense stand of trees on a road that shimmered with a layer of early morning frost. I felt as if I'd turned into another world.

And just as I marveled at the beauty of the silent landscape, I saw her again. She was slumped over, sitting on the side of the road. Her feet were bare, and her hands gripped her calves as she hung her head between her knees.

I don't know what made me pull over. I don't buy Girl Scout cookies and I'm not the guy that gives money to panhandlers. And I have to admit, I'm not the guy who pulls over when someone has a flat tire. I keep to myself whenever I can, and I try not to get involved in other people's problems. But a piece of me recognized her, as soon as I saw the figure on the side of the road. A minute later, I was kneeling beside her.

"Are you okay?" I asked. "Can I help?"

"Hey there," she answered, looking up from her knees. There was a tear on her cheek. "I remember you," she whispered. "The man who is afraid to live."

"I'm not afraid to live," I said. "What are you talking about?"

The side of her mouth turned up. Her eyes sparkled. Maybe it was just the tears, but her face seemed to flash with sudden humor. "Last time I saw you, I told you to live a little, remember? But here you're driving down the same old road."

"Yeah, and a good thing for you, too," I said. "What happened?"

She shrugged. "My old man's a bastard, that's all."

"Wanna talk about it?" I asked. My breath rose up in a cloud before my eyes.

"Not much to say," she said. I realized again that she was barefoot and in a thin yellow tank top, when it was something like 30 degrees out.

"Do you want to warm up in my car, at least?"

Her shoulders shrugged. "Sure, I guess."

I held out my hand and she took it. Her fingers were thin and soft. Gentle. Her nails were short and unpolished. She leaned hard on me as she got up. I realized she was limping.

"What happened to your leg," I asked, once we were in the car.

"Jackson pushed me down the stairs," she said. "Didn't like it that I was out late last night. I didn't like it that he thinks he owns me."

"Doesn't sound good," I said.

"He's jealous," she said. "He thinks he is the only one I can love."

"Are you in love with him?" I asked.

"Of course, or I wouldn't be living with him. But Jackson needs to accept that he is not the only one. I love a lot of people. Life is too short to only be with one."

"Well, if you're seeing other people, maybe you should consider moving out, if he is going to hurt you," I suggested.

She shook her head. "My baby needs a father," she said. "And he's sweet, when he's not angry."

"That's difficult," I said. I thought of the last bitter nights of my marriage, and my daughter who I almost never saw now, and of all the reasons I spent a lot of time these days at Teehan's. "If your baby grows up seeing you getting hurt, that's not good, though."

She nodded. "That is then, this is now. Hopefully, Jackson will grow up before my baby. If not...we will see."

"Want me to drive you home?"

She nodded, and I pulled out onto the empty road. I remembered I had dropped her off near the bridge rails last time. You actually wouldn't know the road there ran over a bridge if not for those rails, it was so small. It just extended the road over a drainage creek near the pond.

A moment later we were there, and I pulled the car over and killed the lights.

"Do you want me to walk you home?" I asked.

She smiled. "I'd like that."

I got out and walked around to open the door for her. She smiled and accepted my hand as she got out of the car and then led me down the shoulder of the road to a gravel path that wound through the brush and into the trees. The forest was dark, but the sky was clear, and I could see our way through the leaves by starlight. The moon's glow reflected off the pond that the path wound around. When I saw the clearing in the trees a little way ahead, Mari stopped me.

"Wait," she said.

We stopped. She slipped her arms around my neck. I responded, hugging her close.

"You're sweet," she whispered. "Thank you for being here for me now."

I didn't know what to say. I rubbed my hand on her back, and she lifted her lips to kiss me. Her touch was soft and gentle. Electric. My lips tingled as she pressed against them, and when her tongue slipped easily inside my teeth, and wrestled my own playfully, I couldn't help but surrender. My hands roved down her back, and cupped the denim curves of her ass, pulling her tight to my hips.

Her answer was to break the kiss so that she could shrug the tank top over her head. She wasn't wearing a bra. Her chest was pale and her breasts slight, but full with the milk she was making for her baby. Her nipples stood pink and erect in the cold.

"No," I said. "You'll freeze out here."

She laughed. "It's always warm in the heart," she said. And then she unzipped and pushed off my coat and pulled the t-shirt over my head. "Hold your heart to mine and you'll see," she said.

My back was cold, but she was right. As we hugged, there in the middle of the night, in the middle of a frigid forest, I felt her breasts crush against the hair of my chest and I felt as warm as I'd been in the car. Warmer, really... because my blood was pumping faster. The caress of her fingers through my hair was like magic. Every touch brought back memories of those times when I'd been happy with my wife, the only woman I'd ever really loved before or since. I barely noticed when Mari reached down to undo my belt buckle. I was lost in the feeling of her and the intoxicating scent of lavender that filled my nose when she kissed me.

We lay down on top of our clothes on a bed of crunching oak leaves. Our lips and hands explored each other slowly at first, and then with increasing fervor. Every time she touched me, I shivered with both heat and cold. She was like a live wire, jolting me with sensations I'd nearly forgotten in the past two years since my divorce. I suckled her chest and was surprised and a bit turned on when I tasted the rich water of her milk. And then she rolled on top of me, and with her hands on my chest, drew her thighs up to the place where we could truly join together. With my hands on her hips, I moved her slowly at first, easing our bodies together. And then I felt the slip and the pressure and the velvet wet heat of her, and we were truly one. She sealed us, yin-and-yang with a kiss, and together we moved, breathing together, rocking together, loving together.

When she reached her crest, our lips broke apart and she called out to the stars, "Oh yes, at last, yes!"

My own moment followed, and it felt as if my very life was draining from me in a wave that left me both full of sensation yet completely, blissfully empty. I was floating in a place between the frozen earth and the distant stars, joined to this beautiful creature with her pale features and long hair and soft hands that knew just how to touch... at last, she rolled in the crook of my arm and smiled.

"That was just what I needed tonight," she said. "Thanks for sharing your love with me."

"No," I said in a whisper. "Thank you for reminding me... how it can be."

She touched my lips with the tip of a finger. "It can always be that," she said. "But you need to *let* it be. Let it be. You have to live. Smell the flowers. Touch the sky."

She ran a finger down the chain around my neck.

"What is this?" she asked.

I lifted it and felt my face flush. "A memory," I said.

She lifted the locket that hung over my heart and with a fingernail popped it open.

"Who is she?" she asked, staring at the tiny picture of my ex-wife.

"Linda," I said. "The woman I used to love."

She nodded. "But no more?"

"I still love her. She left me."

Mari pulled on the chain until I could feel it pinch the back of my neck. "So," she said. "This is the chain that holds you down. Your anchor."

"I guess," I agreed.

"The past is past," she said, and lifted the necklace from around my head. "Let it be buried."

Something in my heart shifted at those words, and I knew she was right. As long as I wore that chain, I would never be able to move on. I would always be that lonely guy at the back of Teehan's. I tapped the back of the locket and Linda's face fell out and slipped between the brown leaves.

"Here," I said. "Maybe you can put Caitlin's picture in it."

"Yes," she smiled. "That would be nice."

I slipped it over her hair, and the empty locket settled between her breasts.

She pushed herself away from me then. "I need to go," she said. "Caitlin will be hungry, and Jackson will be angry." She fished her panties from the leaves and pulled them on. When she tugged her jeans out from under me, I suddenly felt the cold all at once. The real world returned, and I hurried to follow Mari's example. The goosebumps spread across my entire body like an ice wave.

I walked her towards the clearing, but then she put a hand on my chest. "I better walk the last part alone," she said. "But thank you."

I watched as she moved across the frosted grass towards a small two-story house tucked at the edge of the opposite tree line. There was a wooden porch in the front, but the windows were dark. I couldn't see much more than the glimmer of the moon on the windows, and the pitch of the roof as it met the sky. She opened the door and disappeared inside.

WHEN I WOKE the next day, I was worried about a lot of things. I worried about my mental state... No matter how much I'd had to drink, how had I ended up doing it—unprotected—in the leaves of the forest preserve with a stranger... when there was frost on the ground? I studied myself naked in the bathroom, wondering if in my drunken idiocy, I'd contracted something from this weird, bohemian girl. At the same time, I also worried that I'd never again feel as amazing as I had in the short time I'd lain with her. Mostly though, I worried about her. Jealousy and free love and babies didn't mix well. Just read the newspaper on any given day. What had she walked into last night when she'd gone through that door?

As I forced myself through my morning routine, my head hurt, but my heart hurt worse. This was the anniversary weekend of my divorce. October 3rd. I'd never forget that date. The day my life ended. I guess Mari had been right the first time we met... I had been existing for the past couple years, but I hadn't been alive. The first time in ages that I'd felt anything but sadness in that cavity beneath my ribs was last night – well, actually, this morning – at about 1:30 a.m. And that was with a girl who was cheating on her boyfriend. Nice.

I GOT THROUGH THE DAY, with a million conflicting thoughts running through my head. That night, I was back at Teehan's, holed up in the corner once more with a beer in my hand and a lump in my throat. I saw the couples around the bar laughing and enjoying the night. Swaying to the old school classic rock on the jukebox. I saw the singles hitting on each other, cheerful desperation lubricated by shots of Jäger. A group of three guys threw darts nearby with a cute blonde; you could see them vying for her attention. They appeared to be friends, but all in competition. Who would she decide to go home with tonight? Typical bar floor soap opera.

It was too pathetic. And in the end, they were all going to get hurt.

It just wasn't worth it.

But just as I thought that; I saw a flash of Mari's face, the memory of her intensity, as she straddled me last night. Those giving eyes and long sexy hair trailing across my cheek. It had been like she was looking into my soul. Like she had been giving everything that she was to me.

Wasn't a moment like that worth the pain and disappointment that usually grew up around it?

Maybe. Maybe not.

I slugged another pint back and sunk back into my own private pity party. Mari had given me a taste, but I wasn't likely to find it again.

I packed it in at last call. It was past 2:30 a.m. and the pint glass in front of me had been emptied too many times since 9 p.m. I'd met nobody and talked to no one but the bartender, though I *had* gotten my name into the Top 10 list on pinball. Small victory. At least until they reset the machine.

As I turned the corner on 143rd Street, part of me hoped that I would see Mari tonight. I knew it was the hope of a fool. It was super late; she'd be in bed, or if she *was* up, she'd be in a rocking chair nursing her infant. Hopefully, she'd patched things up with her boyfriend. She didn't need me to muddy those waters.

Still, as I neared the bridge by the small pond, I took my foot off the gas and stared into the dark of the forest that cloaked her house. It was warmer tonight, but the sky was thick with clouds; a misty rain had been falling for hours.

I was almost over the bridge when I saw a glimpse of pale legs moving fast against the dark prism of the forest. I veered the car onto the shoulder, stopped and got out. My forehead was instantly damp with mist.

"Mari?" I called.

The figure in the woods stopped. I hurried down the path I'd walked less than 24 hours before and finally caught up to where she was standing at the edge of the clearing, a bundle wrapped in a blanket in the crook of her arm. "Mari, are you okay?" I called.

She shook her head. Negative.

I hurried forward and she held out her hand. "Don't," she warned. "He's crazy tonight. He doesn't think Caitlin is even his. I don't know what he's going to do. I've never seen him like this."

"Don't go back, then," I said. "Come home with me. Let him cool down. You and Caitlin will be safe with me for the night."

"Are you sure?" she said. I could hear the relief in her voice.

SHE WAS quiet in the car, and I didn't want to press her. The baby in her arms held her attention, and I focused on the road. There was no way I should be driving, let alone driving a baby. I focused on the dotted white lines on the asphalt, the speed limit signs, and my own speedometer. The rain clouded the sky, and my headlights seemed to gouge tunnels through it as we sped along, the only car on the road. We were moving in a bubble through the night. Just us three. I felt a surge of protectiveness at that. Another feeling I remembered from long ago.

"You have to think of your baby," I said quietly. "You can't let this keep happening."

"I won't let him hurt Caitlin," she said.

"What if you can't stop him?" I asked.

"He's not like that," she said. "You don't know him."

I pulled into the garage at last and killed the engine.

"We're home," I said. "You can sleep in my bed with the baby. I'll sleep on the couch. In the morning, we can talk and figure out what you should do."

Mari shook her head sadly. "I know what I need to do. But what about you?"

"What about me?" I asked.

"You're still not living," she said. "I knew it the moment I saw you."

I shrugged. "I lost the woman I loved. She didn't want to be with me anymore."

She fingered the chain I had put around her neck and then lifted it from beneath her shirt to show me the locket. My locket. Now empty.

"There is more than one love," Mari said. "If you open your heart, you'll see what I mean." She smiled and shook her head. "I have the opposite problem; I love too much. Stop hiding from it and driving down the same dead-end road."

She saw my reaction and reached across to put her free hand on my cheek. "Do it for me," she said. "Let yourself love again. Live a little."

She leaned over and kissed me again, and my lips felt suddenly aglow with energy. My heart pumped faster, my mouth yearned to keep kissing her. But this wasn't the time. I had to get her and Caitlin safely to bed.

I got out of the car and walked around to her side.

I opened the passenger door for her.

Only... she wasn't there.

Mari and her baby had vanished.

I looked around the garage and called her name. But there was no reply.

A chill ran up my spine and after looking again in the car, in the back seat, and around the garage, I finally gave up and stumbled my way into the house.

And locked the door.

ON SUNDAY MORNING, after a pot of black coffee and a healthy helping of self-doubt, I pulled on my jeans and drove down to the bridge near Mari's house. I honestly wasn't sure what I was prepared to do if her boyfriend answered the door. But... I had to see her again. To prove ... that she was real. Maybe I'd hallucinated the whole thing last night. But what about the night before? Was I really that far gone?

The gravel was wet and I nearly slipped walking down the embankment from the road. The path was interrupted by puddles, but I did my best to step around them. I saw the spot on the side where Mari and I had made love; I imagined the leaves were still matted down from us, not from the rain.

When I reached the clearing, I shook my head.

And blinked.

Could it really be the same clearing? I looked behind me and there was no place where the path diverged. Yes. This was where I had stood long after midnight the past two nights, first to say goodbye, and then to drive her home.

If that was the case, what I saw now could not be real.

But as I looked across the clearing again, what I saw was irrefutable.

There was no house across the way. There was only a chain link fence that scrub bush branches grew through and that trees from the other side hung over.

On this side of the fence, there was only grass.

And tombstones.

Some of the stones were toppled, and some spray-painted with graffiti. I knew suddenly exactly what this place was. And just as I realized it, I saw a steel trashcan nearby with the name of the place stenciled on the side. I stood at the entrance to Bachelors Grove Cemetery. I'd heard about the place since I was in Boy Scouts. So many campfire stories had arisen from this hidden plot of land. I'd never been here before, never really known quite where it was. But I knew its long reputation as an abandoned cemetery, hidden somewhere inside Bachelors Grove Woods. A haunted cemetery.

And here it was.

I'd been kissing a ghost.

I walked between the broken stones, reading the names and dates where I could. Some went back to the 1920s and 1930s. There were even a couple from the 1890s. But I knew unconsciously where to go. I'd probably noticed it from the moment I'd stepped into the clearing.

On top of one low grey stone, beneath the clouded Sunday sun, shone the glint of something silver. I bent to pick it up, and retrieved the chain I'd given Mari on Friday night.

Then I stared at the face of the stone. I knew what it would tell me, but I read the engraving anyway.

Marigold Plotnik
Born, April 23, 1950
Died, October 3, 1969

There was a smaller headstone next to hers, and my eyes welled when I read it.

Caitlin Plotnik
Born, January 18, 1969
Died, October 3, 1969

I heard her voice in the car last night. Quiet but sure. *"I know what I need to do,"* she'd said.

"What did you do, Mari," I whispered. "Why did you go home that night? What happened to you?"

I knelt by the stone, and tears slipped down my cheek. Not only could I not help her, she had been dead long before I was born. Another woman whose love I'd lost.

All the things she'd said to me came rushing back. And I realized that maybe I hadn't lost her. Maybe I'd *called* her. How much of a chance was it that I saw her right at this moment in my life, the anniversary of my death... the anniversary of hers.

Maybe she had come back just for me. To give me a warning. A chance to give me a last chance.

"If you open your heart, you'll see what I mean," she had said. *"Stop hiding from it and driving down the same dead-end road."*

I picked up the chain and put it around my neck. The empty pendant dangled next to my empty heart.

"Do it for me," she had said with her last kiss. *"Let yourself love again. Live a little."*

"Thank you, Mari," I whispered, and rubbed my fingers across the rough stone that marked her grave. "I won't forget you. Rest in peace."

"Life is for taking chances and meeting new people...Otherwise you might as well sleep in a grave."

I took a deep breath and left the cemetery.

I had a locket to fill again before I slept.

The Most Dangerous Game

"Pretty impressive," Brad said, waving a hand at a long row of machines lined up against the basement wall. Lights flickered and changed colors in a series of independent patterns. From somewhere down the row, a wizard-like voice taunted, "I am the Master."

Chris nodded. "It's a lifetime collection."

"Is that a *Wizard of Oz* limited edition?" Brad grinned at the ruby slippers that served as paddles.

"Even better," Chris said. "Prototype."

Brad walked down the row of machines whistling as he went. He passed by classics like *The Addams Family* and *Gorgar* and *Dr. Who* and stopped at a machine whose backglass featured a debonair man smoking while a redheaded seductress lounged before him. "Really? An EM *Mata Hari*? I haven't seen one of those in ages."

Chris shrugged. "Yeah, solid states are easy, but the electrical mechanical versions are tough to come by. Found that one in a garage sale, believe it or not. Five hundred bucks. It was a steal, and I barely even had to shop it – the field was completely clean and it hadn't spent much time in an arcade before it ended up in someone's private collection."

Brad passed by new machines like *Ghostbusters* and *Rob Zombie* that cost thousands of dollars, his interest more in the older, classic tables. Chris must have had fifty or more pins in this game room. And all of them appeared to be in pristine condition.

"I've never even seen a *Mystery Castle* or a *Joust* before," he said. The awe in his voice was palpable.

"Well, I've got no plans tonight," Chris said. "We can order a pizza and you can play them all!"

"I don't want to impose," Brad said. He'd only just met Chris a couple weeks ago in his MBA night class. How long was appropriate to stay on a first visit?

"Not at all," his new friend said. "You said you were a pinball fan, so that's why I invited you over. You just don't run into that many pinheads anymore. Everyone wants to swipe on their touchpads."

"Too true," Brad said. "I've always preferred older games. Pinball takes more skill. Not usually crazy about the EM models because they play too slow, but anything made between 1975 to 1990 and I'm there."

They passed an *Elvira* and *Attack From Mars* and then Brad stopped short. He'd thought the room ended with the *White Water* machine, but instead, there was a doorway that led to a whole other room. And as he stared at the blinking lights and listened to the oscillating sounds, he realized that he had never seen a single one of the machines within.

"What are these?" he breathed, stepping inside.

Chris grinned. "Welcome to the inner sanctum," he said. "This is the real collection."

Brad looked at the garish backglass art around the room. There weren't as many machines in here, but they must have all been incredibly rare. He had never seen or heard of any of them. *Pitbull Pressure. Pounding The Pussy. Anger Alley. Cocktease. Politically Incorrect.* The latter had a fat naked man on the backglass, with a woman crouched between his thighs. Her lower back was inked in a tramp stamp that boasted "Daddy's Whore." As he stared at the gorgeous and often obscene artwork on the tables around the room, he realized that they all revolved around overt sexual and violent images in a way he had never seen in an arcade. Pinball art had always featured vivacious women but... he stepped closer to *Pounding the Pussy* and felt his face flush. The flippers and the ball launcher were all shaped like penises. And the entire center of the playing field was dominated by a three-dimensional nude female doll. She looked like a two-foot naked miniature of Pamela Anderson. She was preposterously stacked and her mouth lolled open, with her tongue stuck out as if in a dare. But what drew the attention first and foremost was the dark red bordered hole between her legs.

"Oh, you've gotta try that one," Chris laughed. "Seriously."

"Maybe later," Brad said, embarrassed.

"No, come on, I'll play ya."

Chris hit the button and set the table for two players. "Do it to it!" he said. "I want to see your face when you pound that pussy!"

Brad shook his head and couldn't help but laugh. Lots of guys made "mods" to games – changing the features of an existing table or completely restructuring it to a new one-off theme. But he'd never seen one so perverted.

He shot the ball onto the playing field and quietly laughed when he realized the silver ball had a black tadpole painted on it. He knocked down all four drop targets in the upper left of the field (the targets were painted to look like cartoon breasts with the spot in the middle representing nipples) and then caught the ball on his penile flipper. He held it a moment, and then let it roll a hair before launching.

"Nice one!" Chris said. "You nailed her!"

The "sperm" ball shot between her legs and into the dark cavity between.

"Wait for it!" Chris yelled.

The machine moaned in an orgasmic way through its speakers and the nipples on the preternatural breasts glowed red as the ball triggered a relay inside. The plastic woman begged "more" as a new ball entered the launch bay.

"If you want multi-ball, you have to pound her again," Chris said.

Brad shook his head in amazement and pulled back the penis to punch a new ball onto the playing field.

"By the way, if you use the ramp to hit the upper playing field and knock down all the targets there, you activate the vibrator for 30 seconds."

"I'm not sure I want to know," Brad laughed, afraid to imagine what activating the vibrator would do. But he aimed for the ramp anyway. The targets on that level all had the hole of a woman's asshole as the center circle of the target and Brad was able to knock them all down easily thanks to an unexpected bounce off the side rubber.

The machine cried out in a voice that made Brad's spine shiver. "Oh YEAH," the woman wailed. "More!"

As the ball slipped down the ramp on the other side, a humming sound began, and in the center of the table a plastic cylinder raised up where it had been inset in the wooden playing surface. An electric pink vibrator, with oscillating white lights inside. It pointed the way to the hole between the woman's legs and blocked the ball from falling into the center ball return, effectively giving the player a "safety net" for as long as it remained raised.

"Pound her while you can!" Chris urged.

The ball careened off the vibrator and Brad caught it on his left flipper, letting it roll backwards in the channel behind the paddle. When it came forward, he waited until it reached the mushroom head on his paddle, and then he smacked the button, sending the ball careening past the tip of the vibrator and right up the channel that led to the naked woman's womb.

"Yes!" she cried, and her nipples turned from red to orange.

"One more," Chris said, as the launch chute filled with a new ball.

This time, it didn't go as well. The vibrator stopped humming and slipped back beneath the surface. Almost immediately, Brad lost the ball down the middle.

"Come on, you bastard," the machine cried in a woman's voice. "Get it up!"

He grinned, and launched the next ball. This time he was determined not to "screw up." He caught it easily on the right flipper and sent it straight up. The machine responded, with an escalating series of "oh yes" moans that culminated in the plastic woman's nipples lighting white hot, and three balls suddenly launching out of her open mouth.

They rolled down her tongue back to the playing field as her orgasmic cries reached fever pitch.

"Multi-ball," Chris announced. The table exploded in a wave of lights and cries of passion. In moments, it was all over, as the balls punched into each other and shot down the side channels and center lane between the paddles.

"Damn," Brad said. He stepped back and took a deep breath.

"Gotcha worked up a bit, didn't she?"

"Fast table," he said. "But... where the hell did you get that?" He pointed at the manufacturer named on the lower left of the face. "Who is the Pinball Cabal? I've never heard of them, and obviously they never mass-produced this."

"Can you imagine?" Chris laughed. "No, this one's custom. Hardcore collectors only."

"Hardcore is right."

Chris shook his head. "That one's nothing. You should try that." He pointed at a black cabinet a few feet away. The red letters at the top of the back glass had lights strobing in a slow, steady wave behind them. The letters read JACK ME OFF.

"You're shitting me," Brad said.

Chris shook his head. "This room is for the man who's seen it all. The pin-jaded. Take that one for example."

He pointed out a machine that had a chainsaw stenciled on the side. The business end was halfway through a man's skull. Blood sprayed like a volcano. "*Blood Bath* is one of my favorites," Chris said. "The art is just killer and the table play is fantastic."

They walked closer and he pointed out the mousetrap-style mechanicals. There were ramps and steel cages and a small figure that hung from its intestines above the left upper field. The center of the table was a rivulet of blood emanating from a series of dismembered victims. Their pieces lay on two dais-like surfaces above the drop targets, which each featured medieval weapons.

"If you trigger the five times bonus, a bunch of metal spikes raise from the table and that disemboweled guy gets it again. That also opens up a back playfield room where you can see this chick being sawed in half. The models are freakin' amazing."

"What's that one?" Brad pointed to a machine with metal bars emanating from the top of the cabinet. The place where the player stood appeared to be a cage. Wires hung loosely from above, with handcuffs at the end.

"You've played *Bride of Pinbot*, I'm sure?" Chris said. "This is the next stage. They call it *The Menage: One with Pinbot*."

"What's with all the wires?" Brad asked, as they stepped closer. The center of the table was dominated by a nude, silver woman. She was pure robot porn. Her body was dotted with LED lights, and her eyes stared right at the player. Flashes of green and blue lit behind them.

"Not sure if you're ready for that one," Chris said. "That's a total couples immersion game. You cuff yourself to the 'bot and attach those electrodes to your nipples. And... well, you can guess where those go." He pointed at a hole in the front of the cabinet right at waist level. A series of wires with rubber rings and clips hung loosely.

"That... looks a little over-the-top."

Chris snorted. "Yeah, it is. Best with two players because you jolt each other. Hurts like a mother when you lose, but when you put the ball in the right hole... damn it's a rush."

"That's what she said," Brad grinned. "Hey, if *this* is the rare room, what's in there?" He pointed at a half open door. There was a machine within, but the front glass was covered in a sheet.

Chris shook his head and stepped past him to close the door. "Tournament room," he said. "Only touch those tables a couple times a year. One of a kind. I don't even let the light get at them in between plays. Speaking of which... how about actually racking up some points out here?"

Brad grinned and Chris led the way back towards the main room. "Get you a beer?"

Three hours and a handful of IPAs later, and Brad had to admit that he was long past his game. But he prayed as he stumbled out the front door of Chris' place that it wouldn't be the last visit.

The Most Dangerous Game

It wasn't.

If there's one thing you can say about pinball, it's that you can't walk away for long. The silver balls keep calling. And fans of the game stick together. So, Chris invited Brad over again the next weekend.

"Someday I want a basement like yours," he said, as they entered the main room again.

"Be careful what you wish for," Chris warned. "The overhead will kill ya!"

Brad laughed. "So, when do you hold that tournament you mentioned?"

Chris shrugged. "It depends. They're pretty sporadic, because we have to have the right players, but I'm thinking of maybe doing one soon. You interested?"

Brad nodded. "Not sure that I can keep up, but I'd love to try."

Chris extended his hand to the room. "Go then… and practice!"

Brad worked his way from *Godzilla* to *Medieval Madness* to *Stargazer* to *Attack From Mars*.

"Not bad," Chris said when he racked up a crazy points multiball bonus on *Metallica*. "But that's not what we'll play in tournament."

"So show me?"

Chris led him back to the rare room of tables he'd never seen or heard of. And he'd tried to look some of the ones he could remember up on the Internet. No dice.

"Try *Bone Dry*," Chris suggested. "I always joke that it was made out of the bones of tournament losers!" He pointed out a table that was painted on the outside in skeletal, Day of the Dead style designs. But when Brad looked at the playing field, his jaw dropped.

"That's… crazy."

Chris grinned. "Isn't it?"

The table was a maze of tubes and channels. And all of them were hedged by ribs of bone. The wood playing field was painted in garish red, while the flippers and all the bumpers and blocks and ramps looked to have been carved from ivory.

Brad pushed the start button and instantly felt how different the machine was than any of the production models he'd played all evening. The silver ball careened all over the table; with the number of obstacles, it was impossible to predict where it was going to ricochet next. But the table felt solid, and the paddles weighted just as he liked them. He slapped and cursed and lost himself in the gameplay for almost an hour. When he finally sunk the third multi-ball into the bony gullet of the skeletal man at the upper left of the field and the bonus alarms rang out in a chorus of chainsaws, Chris slapped him on the back with pride.

"I think you're ready!" he said.

"For what?" Brad asked.

"What do you think?" Chris laughed. "For tournament, of course. I think I'll try setting one up for this weekend. You in?"

WHEN HE PULLED up to 144 Golden Elm Lane on Saturday, Brad's armpits were damp. Chris's place itself didn't look like much from the street – a rundown blue frame two-story with a dandelion problem. But the outside didn't give a hint about the glory of the basement within, and he'd been thinking about this tournament all week. It was stupid to be nervous about – it was a game night in someone's basement. But... he didn't know anybody, and he was worried that he was going to be miserably outclassed. Brad wasn't social at the best of times, and he definitely didn't relish social competition.

Still, this was the chance to "get in" with a group of people who loved the same thing as he did, a rare chance for Brad. He wanted to fit in there. Maybe for once not feel the outsider.

As he walked up the concrete sidewalk to the front stoop of the house, the faint but familiar sounds of plinking scoreboards and bonus bells warmed his ears. Some of the trepidation slipped away at those comforting sounds, and he knocked on the front door with a smile. This was going to be good, he decided.

A woman in a low-V yellow tank top and loose black silk jogging shorts answered the door. Brad was taken aback for a moment, but she introduced herself as Chiana and smiled when he told her his name. The soft sparkle of energy in her brown eyes, and the welcoming lift of her lips made him feel instantly connected.

"So, you play?" he asked as he stepped inside.

"You think I'm just here to watch?" she asked with a slight eyeroll. "Yeah, I'm here to play. I'm here to kick your ass!"

She winked and turned to lead the way downstairs to where the rest of the party was audibly already in session.

"There you are," Chris yelled, and made his way across the room. "I see you've met our little dominatrix already."

Chiana slapped their host on the ass but didn't break stride, heading straight for the tables.

"You want a beer?" Chris offered, pointing towards a big blue cooler. "We are just warming up for a few minutes right now."

"Sure," Brad said.

She brought him a pale ale called simply, *Pinball*.

"Where did you get this?" he laughed.

"It's from Two Brothers, a Chicago brewery," she said. "It's not bad, and not too heavy, so you can knock down a few before your reaction time goes to shit."

She tilted back the brown neck and smiled as she swallowed. Then she waved her hand around the main room. Three men were playing various tables there, and a couple more were in the "rare" room. "What do you like to play most?" she asked.

"I love the old solid states," Brad said. "*Stargazer, Mata Hari, Meteor, Paragon*... that ilk."

She nodded. "Lemme see you go at one."

He took a gulp of his beer, and walked hesitantly down the aisle, looking for something to play that he didn't think he'd suck at. He felt put on the spot, and didn't want to come up short. He stopped at the *Mata Hari* he'd played on his last visit and decided to stake his claim there. It was a simple table – just two sets of drop targets, one bonus kickout hole, and bonus levels for tripping A-B lane sensors. Chiana rested one thin hand on his shoulder as he launched the first ball. He couldn't help but look at the bare midriff of the sultry femme fatale on the backglass of the machine and not think of the woman standing uncomfortably close to him as he hit the flippers.

The distraction proved detrimental as he missed an easy flipper return and lost the first ball down the middle.

"Tough luck," Chiana said, and brushed her hand through the back of his hair.

Brad shook his head, determined to focus. On the next ball, he managed to punch down all of the flippers for a cool 50,000 points, and then ran the ball around the A-B lanes a half dozen times and ultimately scored a free ball. When he finally lost the round, the scoring mechanism rang over and over again as it tallied up his points, finally ending at 373,459.

"I'm impressed," Chiana said.

"What do you like to play?" he asked.

She grinned. "We're not too far apart. I like the older tables too. But I'm more partial to *Addams Family* or *Dr. Who* or *Twilight Zone*."

Brad turned the tables on her. "Show me one!"

He picked up his beer from the ground and followed her to a *Dr. Who* table. He loved the Dalek augmented kickout mechanism in this machine, and Chiana made good use of it, racking up an impressive score on just two balls. But then the table sent her a gunshot right down the middle and her game was cut short.

She shrugged and picked up her beer. "That's the way the pinball bounces."

Just then, Chris called for attention and in a few seconds the dinging, ringing din of a half dozen games all scoring at once diminished into silence.

"It's time for tournament," he said. "Every table in the main room is marked with a base and a midrange score. For the first round, you have three games to prove that you can hit midrange. If you don't... you're disqualified until the final round when you'll have a chance to redeem yourself in the sudden death round. Our pinball dominatrix, and champion of the last three tournaments, will serve as score validator for this round."

A couple of wolf whistles answered that callout, and Chiana bowed.

"Pick the table you play best at," she cautioned, and disappeared down the row of machines to talk to Chris.

Brad looked around the room and considered taking the *Meteor* table, but then someone else nabbed it. *What the hell,* he thought. He turned back to *Mata Hari*. He was already warmed up on that one, and he didn't want to wash out in the first round. A handwritten sign on the backglass said that base score on *Mata Hari* was 250,000. Midrange was 400,000. All-time high score was 879,654.

"*Mata Hari* it is," he whispered, and hit the credit button.

The basement filled with the sounds of bells and balls, and he focused on the game, shooting first for the kickout hole to rack up as many bonus multipliers as possible. Then he began to focus on the drop targets.

"Not bad," a soft voice whispered in his ear a short while later. "*Mata Hari* is your bitch!"

Brad felt the press of Chiana's chest against his back as she peered over his shoulder just as the ball knocked down the last drop target. A 50,000 bonus logged, but the ball careened off the rubber in a straight line for the center. Brad nudged the table, but it was too little too late... and the game ended.

When the chimes finally stopped counting up his bonus score, the scoreboard stood at 439,332.

"You're in for Round 2," she whispered in his ear, and walked a few tables down to peer over another player's arm.

Brad took a deep breath and went to score another beer. Round one ended with everyone qualifying. Round two ran much the same, only this time, you had to change machines, and this time, one of the other players had a bad round and was knocked out until the final round. His name was Benjamin, and he didn't take well to losing.

"No fuckin' way," the guy said. He was a big dude, with kinked, curled black hair and an angry 5 o'clock shadow. "I am not..."

Chris put a hand on his shoulder and pushed him to the back of the room where they had an intense conversation. At the end of it,

Chris walked back out smiling. "All right," he announced. "We have one slot filled. Who will take the second?"

The host looked at the six remaining players around the room, and with a dramatic gesture, pointed at the "rare games" room. "Now it's time to really play pinball. Round three is... interactive."

Brad followed the group into the next room. He saw the glow of the bone table, and the laughter from the "Drain Me" machine that boasted an array of vampires on the backglass.

"I need a partner," Chiana said, suddenly at his side. "Will you play with me?"

"Sure," he said. "On what?"

She pointed at the machine with the evocative robot girl on the backglass, and a cascade of wires and clamps hanging from its front casing. *"The Menage: One with Pinbot."*

"Um..." he gulped.

"C'mon," she urged. "It's a crazy rush."

Crazy was right. As soon as Chiana made it known that she had a partner, all play in the room ceased and Chris was suddenly at Brad's side. "You might want to change into these," he suggested, holding out a pair of baggy jogging shorts. "You need to be plugged in, you know?" Chris explained.

What have I done? Brad wondered, but stepped into the back room and shucked his jeans in favor of the loose shorts. When he came out, he saw Chiana with her shirt raised up, attaching a clamp to the nipple of her breast. There were already wires leading up her thigh and beneath her shorts.

"Slip this over... well... it's obvious, I think," Chris said, as he stepped up to the machine. He held out a rubber O attached to a metal lead that disappeared inside the machine to Brad, who took the O and quickly pulled it up his thigh, beneath the shorts. It was cold as he drew it over his cock.

"Make sure it's snug," Brad urged.

Chris could feel his face turn red, but he did as demanded before lifting his shirt to attach two electrodes to his nipples.

"Are you ready to play with me?" Chiana asked. Her voice sounded rough.

"Yeah," Brad answered.

"I'll be Player One," she said, and shifted her hip to move him to the side. He couldn't go far with the wires, but he shifted to let her hands get full access to the flippers. A moment later, as she punched the ball up a chute and onto a new playing level, Brad called out in pain. As the ball ascended, the electrodes sent an escalating current of electricity through his flesh. Each time she hit a drop target, a little jolt of fire hit him in the 'nads. Oddly enough, he began to get an erection. He moved closer to the machine so nobody would see the tent in his loose shorts.

When Chiana missed and the ball dropped down a side lane and out of play, a wave of warmth washed over him. A pulse of ecstasy.

"Your ball," she said, moving aside for him to play.

Brad realized quickly that the machine rewarded the player every time he punched a ball up one of the two chutes or whenever he knocked down a target or hit one of the many sensors on the table. Gentle pulses of heat warmed and excited his nerves as the game went on, and when he moved the ball quickly across the table he almost doubled over from ecstasy as the pulses vibrated and jolted him in just the right wavelength.

Meanwhile, conversely, with every correct move he made, Chiana moaned and gripped at the table to stop herself from falling over. Soon her fingers were grabbing at his shoulder instead of the table. She was moaning slightly every time he sent the ball up the chute to the second level. Her voice squeaked slightly whenever he dropped a target. When he finally lost the ball and she took over, he found himself standing closer to her than before. While her victories were painful to him, they were also exciting... and he found himself dogging her thigh as she played. But she didn't seem to mind; her butt pressed back against him with every drop target she sunk, and when she lost the second ball, she leaned backwards with an orgasmic moan from the electricity pulsing into her most private nerves such that he had to catch and support her.

His arm went around her belly as she relaxed into him, and the buzz of sensation against his cock and nipples blinded him for a moment, so he didn't even think about moving his hand up her shirt. He felt the warmth and softness of her breasts for a second, before Chris called out from behind.

"All right, break it up, you two. Great score but... you've got one more ball before you ball... if that's what you're gonna do!"

Brad pulled his hand back with a start, and Chiana straightened herself but flashed him a satisfied smile.

When the game was finally done, it was Chiana who took home the victory, but Brad didn't even care. His body was awash in pulses of sensation, and his nose filled with the faint perfume of her, which grew stronger throughout the game. She turned at the end, as the scoreboard chimed and pulses of current ran through the wires to electrify the nerves of their sex, and pressed two warm, wet lips to his. He held the kiss for what seemed like an hour as the room spun in a kaleidoscope of red and orange waves.

"Please sterilize the equipment when you're done," Chris said, and set a jug of Windex and paper towels down on the glass of the table before the spectators moved to the next showdown match, this time on the machine made of bones.

"Damn," he whispered.

Chiana smiled. "It's not the kind of game you want to play with just anybody," she said. Her voice was low and husky. She raised her shirt, and he could see the metal clamps gripping her nipples. "Would you mind?"

He reached forward, his knuckles trailed along the skin of the underside of her breast. Brushing against that soft skin made him take a sharp breath. But he carefully released her. She reached up his shirt then, and did the same for him.

"Do you need help with..." she began, and he shook his head quickly. She laughed and bent to tend to herself.

He pulled the ring out and doused it in Windex.

The Most Dangerous Game

AS THE NIGHT WENT, Brad was surprised to find that he wasn't the worst player there. Despite not being familiar with the tables in the rare room, he ended the night fourth out of eight. The victor... was Chiana. Chris took her hand and held it up in a gesture of triumph. "Once again, she takes the prize," he said. "And as the champion, Chiana will name the player who will go up against Benjamin, our first loser of the night in the final Death Match round. The winner of that round... goes up against Chiana, at the game of her choice."

The pinball players all cheered, except for Benjamin, who stood in the corner of the room scowling. It only made his five o'clock shadow look darker.

"Who do you choose?" Chris asked.

Chiana smiled, and looked Brad straight in the eye. "I choose our newbie of the night."

Someone grabbed him from behind and the small group all surged forward, and into the "secret room" beyond. In seconds, the sheets had been pulled off the large pinball table there. Chiana pushed Brad's head through a hole in the back of the cabinet, and suddenly he found himself looking straight ahead across the wood of the table. Something clamped down across his neck, and straps were clipped to hold his wrists to the side of the cabinet. He realized he was trapped. On the other side of the table, a similar thing occurred, and he found himself staring across a five-foot space at Benjamin's face.

"You're a bastard, Christian," the other man said.

"You know the rules," Chris answered.

"The trick is, keep shooting the targets to the left," Chiana's voice whispered in Brad's ear. "That keeps the gun moving in reverse."

"Gun?" Brad said.

But then Chris was talking to the whole room. "And now for the moment that makes this Pinball Cabal special. And secret. The Most Dangerous Game. Our night's loser will play our winner's designee in the ultimate game of skill and chance. Russian Roulette!"

Brad's heart stopped. He finally saw the object of the game. To his right, currently pointed off table, 90 degrees away from his face, was a gun. It was mounted on some kind of gear-driven system and clearly could point towards either player. Presumably, the score defined who was in danger.

"The object is simple," Chris explained as the crowd gathered close. Every drop target moves the gun a little bit one way or the other. When the barrel reaches the 90-degree position and is pointing directly at one player or the other, it locks in place until it is discharged. There is only one bullet in the gun, and either player can discharge it – by hitting the trigger target."

He pointed at a blood-red drop target just to the left of center, in the middle of the playing field. It looked strange standing out there with no other targets or bumpers nearby. Like a landmine. "There's the magic, right there."

"I think I'd like to pass on this game," Brad said.

Chris grinned. "Nuh-uh! You're Chiana's knight in shining armor tonight. Play like your life depends on it. Because, my friend… it does!"

Chris patted him on the back and then reached out and pressed a button on the side of the table. A ball launched into the center of the playing field. "This is a 5-ball battle play scenario," Chris said. "So, there are no turns – you're both fighting for control of every ball. You each have flippers on your side of the table to deflect and attack. If one of you releases a bullet, the winner is obvious. If you lose all five balls without engaging the gun, the score will define the victor."

Brad realized that the opposite sides of the long table were really mirror images of each other. Each had three sets of drop targets. A silver ramp on each side took the ball up to a small secondary table field eight or ten inches above the main. Brad flipped his left flipper and realized that each player controlled a single flipper on the upper field, on opposite sides. There were over a dozen drop targets there in a semi-circle, while on the opposite side from the targets, a funnel hole in the floor led the ball to a corkscrew tube that brought it back down to the center of the main table.

Benjamin made first contact, launching the ball into two drop targets before it careened off a bumper and headed towards Brad's flippers. The gun clicked twice as its barrel moved in Brad's direction. He remembered what Chiana had said, and deliberately aimed for the targets on the opposite side of the ones Benjamin had downed. And it worked.

The gun clinked back one notch.

They volleyed back and forth twice more, each moving the gun one or two clicks forward and back. Then Benjamin caught the ramp and sent the ball to the upper level where he immediately knocked down three targets. Brad had one shot to reverse the tide, and aimed the ball at the opposite end of the semicircle of targets... but instead, he sent two more drop targets down on the wrong side of the arc. He heard the gun clicking steadily towards him.

"No way," he said through gritted teeth, and carefully waited the next time the ball came at his flipper until the last possible second. Then he slammed the button, and the ball careened on a hard angle towards the funnel and back down to the regular table playing field.

"No problem," Benjamin said, and caught the ball with a flipper that knocked down three targets in a row. The gun *clink-clink-clinked* and suddenly Brad found himself staring straight down the barrel. The last clink sounded louder, and he knew it was locked in place now. If there really was a live bullet in the first chamber, he was going to be dead in a minute. *Really*? He wondered. Was this whole deal real, or were they just shitting the newbie?

Brad tried to pull away from his position when the ball vaulted to the other side, but it was no use. His head could not move left or right, due to the walls on either side, and his wrists were bound to the machine right at the flippers... so he couldn't even pull his head back more than a few inches.

"Gotcha," Benjamin yelled, and just as Brad refocused on the table he saw the ball shoot through the lone red target.

A disembodied, but instantly recognizable voice spoke as the trigger on the gun in the center of the table notched back:

"You've gotta ask yourself one question: 'Do I feel lucky?' Well, do ya, punk?"

And then the hammer fell, and Brad closed his eyes.

Nothing happened.

"Shit," Benjamin complained, and Brad realized that he'd survived that round. He took a deep, shaky breath and focused hard on the table. He didn't intend to get put in that position again. The gun had reset itself to point 90 degrees away from his face, and he worked on sending the ball up the ramp to the upper deck. Clearly you could move the gun faster with the multitude of targets up there than you could on the main level.

What he didn't count on was hitting the wrong side of the semi-circle. The gun was suddenly pointed halfway back at him when Benjamin sent it back down the corkscrew.

It was Brad's turn to swear.

A female voice whispered from behind him. Just one word. "Focus," she said. Then a moment later, after he'd sent the ball to the other side, a hand brushed across his crotch. "I want to be *One With Pinbot* with you again."

Brad's breath caught, and he lost the ball right down the middle. The gun clicked another notch towards him. The ball reappeared in the center of the table. He heard Benjamin chuckle softly on the other side, but he refused to let that rattle him.

"If you can take him, you can take me," Chiana promised from behind.

Jesus.

Brad knocked down three targets, and then after sending the ball into a casket on the far end, a 3x Bonus light activated, and the next target he pounded sent the gun three notches forward instead of one.

"Nice," he whispered, as the gun was now better than 45 degrees towards Benjamin.

Then Benjamin screwed up and knocked down the targets on the wrong side. The gun swung and locked, the barrel pointed straight at his forehead.

"Oh fuck," he swore.

Brad didn't know what to do. He didn't want to be responsible for killing someone, if that was really what was going on here. He still wasn't sure if this was all for real, but the wrist restraints and everything sure made it seem like it was deadly serious. If he didn't hit the red target, what would happen?

The sound of a clock ticking began as Brad moved the ball around the table, refusing to hit the red target that would pull the trigger and potentially end his opponent's life. Meanwhile, the ticking grew louder.

"What are you waiting for?" someone yelled.

And then the table itself spoke. "You snooze, you lose," it announced.

The gun suddenly moved, rising out of its notch in front of Benjamin. But instead of docking at the 45-degree restart angle... it pivoted all the way around until it pointed directly at Brad.

On the other side of field, Benjamin grinned. "Thanks, pal!"

In a second, he'd punched down the red target once again.

"Oh, God damn it," Brad groaned. The trigger cocked back, and Clint Eastwood said his famous line once again. And then the hammer came down. Brad scrunched his eyes closed, bracing for the impact.

"TWO DOWN, FOUR TO GO," Chiana announced from behind.

He'd survived again.

The next time Brad got the ball, he shot it towards the coffin. And then repeated the move. But then Benjamin got the ball and rocked it towards the targets. "That casket bonus multiplier works for either one of us," his opponent crowed.

And with one target down, the gun notched five clicks towards Brad.

He swore, but sent the ball right back down the table and knocked down two targets with one glancing blow. The gun was now halfway towards Benjamin.

"Think so, huh?" Benjamin said.

He hammered it up the ramp to the upper level. Instantly he knocked down three targets and the gun pivoted back towards Brad. It looked like it would only take one more to lock at his face again.

He caught the ball on the rebound and rolled it down his paddle to the edge before punching the button and sending it.

"Yes!" he yelled out loud. The action took down four targets on the opposite side of Benjamin's field. And then it rolled down the corkscrew and back to the main table.

"Not this time," Benjamin warned, but his launch didn't connect as he planned, and Brad stole the ball, sending it quickly into two more targets.

The gun clicked into place, locked in front of Benjamin's forehead once again.

"Remember what I said," Chiana whispered close by. He could feel the warmth of her just centimeters from his waist.

Brad waited until the ball rolled right. He knocked it to the right, hoping for the rebound he needed.

And then he got the angle.

With one sharp punch of his finger, he sent the ball straight at the lone red target. The trigger switch. Dirty Harry spoke again.

"You've gotta ask yourself one question: 'Do I feel lucky?' Well, do ya, punk?"

The hammer fell. And this time, it let loose a loud explosion.

The table vibrated, and Brad saw a spot on Benjamin's forehead turn from black to red almost in slow motion. He heard a whistle and a cheer and then Benjamin's head fell forward and bled out on the other end of the table.

Hands grabbed at Brad's wrists and neck guard, and then he was standing free and shaky with Chiana's arm around his waist. She took his hand and raised it in the air. "My champion!" she declared.

On the other side of the table, two men were dragging Benjamin's body away. Somebody laughed and said, "good thing this week is free bulk item pickup day! You can put him on the curb in a bunch of bags!"

Brad felt sick to his stomach.

"You people are sick!" he cried out. "How could you do this? I'm going to…"

Chris walked over and picked up a video camera from one side of the table, and thumbed the off switch. He held it in front of Brad's face for a second before jerking it away.

"Really fucked up what you did there," Chris said. "Killing a man in cold blood like that for sport. I'm appalled."

He grinned, and shoved the camera into a pocket in the loose jacket he wore.

"Welcome to the Pinball Cabal," he said. "As soon as I met you, I thought you might be a contender. There's nothing like the rush of winning The Most Dangerous Game, am I right?"

Brad opened his mouth to retort, not really sure what exactly to say. But then Chiana pressed her lips to his.

"I promised you could have me if you won," she said. "Do you want to go to the bedroom, or the police?"

Brad only hesitated a moment. Benjamin hadn't seemed like that nice of a guy anyway, and, well, it wasn't his fault. He hadn't signed up to play Russian Roulette. Why should he risk taking the fall for something he couldn't change?

"Your room sounds better," he said.

She laughed, and kissed him wetly on the lips.

"I didn't say it was *my* room. But wait 'til you see the games we can play there!"

Chiana took his hand and dragged him up the stairs, leaving the bells and chimes behind. But the games continued on.

Arnie's Ashes

Arnie's ashes were hidden in a silver canister meant to hold flour inside a wall near Sibley Boulevard and Dixie Highway.

We never thought we'd need to worry about them being found. The building was not exactly ripe for new development. There was a quarry to the west and an expressway to the east. Weeds and scrub trees grew to the north and south. The building itself had been there since the '50s... it was made of concrete blocks and plastic siding, and I'd guess the roof leaked since it was flat and sagging and old... but nobody was going to worry too much, given its use. The place stood at the end of a row of potholes broken by occasional nubs of asphalt surrounded by an area that was about as undesirable as it got. This was a no man's land at the ass-end of three low-rent municipalities.

The sign out front along Dixie Highway read 'Adult Arcade, open 24 hours.' Carl and I knew it was a place that Arnie had frequented often, so when we decided to get rid of them, it made sense to secrete his ashes in a wall of the seedy joint. Based on the bizarre circumstances of his demise, that same joint, I assumed, was the reason Arnie was now sitting inside a canister instead of holding loquacious court at a bar on 147th Street, so... it seemed right. The place had been there for decades and was likely to be there for another century.

Nobody would admit it was there. Nobody would admit going there. Men parked in the gravel lot and walked around the side of the building as fast as they could, heads down whether in fair weather or foul.

We figured hiding the canister in the wall was a much safer way to dispose of Arnie's ashes then throwing them off a cliff or out into Lake Michigan. God knew what would happen if we did something like that.

That's what we'd thought, anyway.

Until the day they began coming home.

CARL ANSWERED the door the first time one of them showed up. I heard the brittle crack of his coffee mug hit the front foyer tile.

"What the..." he yelped. And then a moment later he called, "Darnell!!!"

I HEARD the panic in his tone and jumped up from the kitchen table we had once shared with Arnie. It had been the perfect bachelor pad for three divorced men; a three-bedroom house with a fully finished basement and a stand-up attic. We all had had plenty of space.

At that moment, it was *too* big. By the time I reached the foyer, Carl had slammed the door shut.

When he turned, his face was white. I reached for the door, but he grabbed my arm.

"Don't," he said.

"Who was at the door?" I tried to move past him.

"Seriously," he said.

Just then, a fist pounded on the door. Slow but rhythmic. I reached to open it, and Carl grabbed my wrist.

"I mean it," he said.

I turned the knob anyway. The door squealed open, and I saw the heavyset man standing just inches away from the glass of the storm door.

His body looked nothing like my old friend. But his face was Arnie's.

I did a double take, because Arnie had been skinny. This guy had to top 250.

Plus, Arnie was dead.

Minor detail.

Without thinking, I slammed the door shut.

"Did Arnie have a brother?" I asked Carl.

He shook his head.

"Maybe a cousin?" I suggested.

He shook his head again. Carl still looked sheet-white.

That's when the pounding really began at the door. The glass rattled. Hell, the wooden frame inside rattled. Dust fell from the lintel.

"Well then, who is at the door?" I asked.

Something in the doorframe cracked. It was an old house.

"I think we're going to find out," Carl said. He backed away toward the kitchen.

And then the door burst open.

Carl darted for the kitchen, while I began to back my way towards it.

"Arnie," I said. "We missed you."

The man who looked like my dead friend... with an extra 200 pounds... only grunted and lunged at me. I abandoned bravery and followed Carl into the kitchen.

OK, I didn't follow, I *dove* for the kitchen.

When I got there, Carl was crouched by the table, holding a knife.

"What are you..." I began. But I never completed the sentence. Because a second later, the football player who looked like Arnie burst into the space and lunged at Carl. I was on the floor.

I watched the unthinkable happen.

The man rushed at Carl, and Carl screamed like some kind of mad samurai and held the knife in front of him. And Not-Arnie ran right into it. Skewered like a bell pepper.

There was red. In the air. On the counters. On the cabinets.

And then Not-Arnie was down on the floor, squirming and moaning and spinning a smeary crimson pattern on the kitchen tile. A few minutes later he stopped moving, and Carl stood over him, the blade of the knife dripping the man's blood back down on his shirt.

"OK," I said. "Now what?"

There was a dead man who looked like Arnie lying on our kitchen floor.

Blood seeped from the wound in the man's chest. It quickly puddled around his arms on the floor.

"I killed Arnie," Carl whispered. The knife dropped to the floor with a clatter.

"Arnie was already dead," I pointed out.

WE TOOK the body into the basement and laid it out on the concrete floor. We didn't know what to do, really, but we knew we couldn't call the police. They wouldn't see this as a monster with our friend's face... they'd see this as a murder. So, we laid the body out downstairs until we could figure out a plan.

The problem was, before we figured out what to do, there was another knock at the door.

The two of us looked at each other in panic. "I'm not getting it," I said.

Carl shook his head vehemently. "Well, I'm not either."

The knocks on the door only grew louder. We stared at each other for what felt like an hour.

The pounding grew more forceful.

I finally caved in. "Alright," I said. "But you're coming with me." I grabbed him by the arm and dragged him along as I walked up the stairs.

It was bound to be the police. I didn't know how they'd know, but I figured someone had reported Not-Arnie's murder already. Anticipating a blue uniform and a quick ride to jail, I took a breath, held it, and turned the knob on the door.

The guy on the other side was not wearing a blue uniform.

Once again, the visitor looked exactly like Arnie.

Only this guy was tall and gangly. And dark-skinned. So... I guess, really, outside of the face, he looked nothing like Arnie. Arnie had been solid. And shorter.

But... the body is never the first thing we see. When I opened the door, I saw my friend's face. And this time, instead of slamming the door, I screamed.

While I was busy freaking out, the guy walked right past me and into the house. He turned and took the stairs to the bedrooms and disappeared.

I looked at Carl, who only cowered against the hallway wall.

"What the hell was that?" I asked. "*Who* the hell was that?"

His arm only pointed at the door.

Another guy stood there, in faded jeans and a dark t-shirt. His complexion was Latino. Yet he had Arnie's face.

Arnie had been Irish.

I stepped away from the door and pointed towards the stairs. "That way," I said.

He didn't wait for pleasantries, any more than the last Arnie had. Instead, he ascended the stairs towards Arnie's old room.

I followed him up, and saw that the first Arnie was already in the room, standing near the closet. I couldn't tell if he was looking for something, or simply frozen in place, but I didn't stick around to find out. As soon as Arnie2 entered the room, I pulled the door shut behind him. When I went down the stairs, Carl's face was white.

"What is going on?" he wheezed. I thought he might be hyperventilating. A theory had already been brewing in my head since the first Arnie had plowed through our broken doorway.

"Somebody found Arnie's ashes," I said.

His eyes screwed up, and he looked at me as if he'd just chewed a sour apple. "Huh?"

"What happened when Arnie came home that night from the smut store?"

"I don't want to talk about that."

"I don't either. But… I want you to say it. What happened?"

Carl shook his head, refusing to speak.

"You tried to kiss him," I said finally. "Because when he walked into this house that night, he had the face of a beautiful girl."

"Shut up."

"And why did he look like a girl?"

"Stop talking about it."

I shook my head. "I can't… just answer me."

"Because he did it with that girl at the smut shack? That's what you figured."

I nodded. "He admitted that much before…"

"Don't say it!"

Carl had been in denial since the day that Arnie died. But the appearance of two Arnies upstairs plus the dead one in the basement was a sure sign that denial wasn't going to cut it anymore. We had to face this thing head on. So to speak.

"Someone found Arnie's ashes," I said. "Whatever made *him* turn into that… thing… has done the same to the guys at our door."

"Why are they here?" Carl asked.

I shrugged. "Same reason Arnie took your truck and drove to that mobile home in Indiana."

Carl shivered.

"It's like salmon going home to spawn," I said.

Finally, I got the reaction I had been waiting for. It all clicked, and Carl's eyes shot open. "You mean, those things upstairs…"

Just then, something crashed in Arnie's former bedroom.

"Exactly," I said.

"Oh shit," he said. "What are we going to do?"

"Go to the utility room and grab the hammers," I said.

He shook his head. "I can't do that again."

Something screeched upstairs… a cross between a hawk's kill cry and the howl of an animal stabbed in the heart.

"No choice," I said.

Carl ran to the basement, as I took position at the base of the stairs. Hopefully, they wouldn't try to come down before he returned. I didn't know what I'd do to stop them if so. I couldn't take them both myself.

The landing filled with the sounds of things falling upstairs. The crash of a lamp, the thump of things leaving the walls to hit the floor.

Carl returned before the noises left Arnie's room. I took the small sledge from him. Carl kept the normal hammer.

"Ready?" I asked.

He shook his head, no. I took that as a yes, and began to ascend the stairs.

ARNIE'S ROOM was a disaster area. The top of one dresser was wiped clean of all his junk, while the highboy had been toppled over. The edge of it rested on the bed, drawers hung partially open to spill pairs of faded jeans and moth-eaten underwear to the floor.

One Arnie was facing the corner of the room, slowly knocking his head against the wall. The other appeared to be waiting for someone to let him out. As soon as I stepped inside, he lunged, long dark fingers scrabbling to grab at my face or neck.

I didn't wait to find out which.

With one fast stroke I brought the sledge down on top of his skull, and his body collapsed instantly to the floor.

"Jesus," Carl whispered at my shoulder.

"I don't think so," I said, not taking my eyes off the place where my hammer had fallen. The blood flowed dark and fast, but that wasn't what I was looking for. My gaze strayed to the other Arnie, who didn't appear to have noticed that his doppelganger had been felled. When I looked back at the body at my feet, I saw just what I'd been dreading.

It was tiny, at first. But then it grew, like a corn sprout captured in time-lapse video. A thin silver tendril expanded from the heart of the gore and reached past the man's black hair to clutch at the air.

I brought the sledge down and smashed the bastard.

Hot blood sprayed my face, but I didn't have time to wipe it off, because for some reason the other Arnie finally realized that it had company. He was climbing across the bed as I yelled at Carl.

"Get him!"

"I don't..." he started to complain. But then it was too late. The guy's hands had already fastened around Carl's neck. My friend's eyes bulged and instead of striking out, I heard the thump of his hammer as it fell to the floor.

"Dammit, Carl," I complained, and lifted my arm. The sledge connected with the side of this Arnie's head, just above the ear. The blow wasn't enough. The thing shifted its attention from Carl to me, and suddenly I was lying on the floor, with the angry body of a guy who looked like my best friend on top of me. Only my friend had weighed about 100 pounds less and had never tried to throttle the life out of me.

I called for Carl's help, but all that got past my lips was a wheeze.

Arnie gripped my neck like he was trying to hold on to a noodle. He lifted my head up and slammed it back repeatedly on the leg of the fallen Arnie. I pounded at his back with my fists, but it didn't seem to make any difference. Arnie was going to crush the life out of me anyway.

"Carl," I tried to call... but I still couldn't make a sound. There were stars exploding in my eyes, as Arnie's normally gentle face stared blankly down at mine.

And then... the pressure and Arnie's head suddenly disappeared. Carl's face took its place. A hand reached behind my neck and yanked me up. Carl pulled me back towards the door, and I saw that the second Arnie was now spasming on the bed. A dark stain spread across the peach bedspread.

I held on to Carl's arm and finally pulled myself fully to my feet. My vision still strobed with stars and fog, and my breath came in gasps. But slowly, I got my legs beneath me. The body on the bed stilled as we stepped backwards into the hall. But not before I saw the silver worm slip from the man's head to swim across the pool of blood on the comforter.

I could have gone back to kill it, but it wouldn't have mattered. There were dozens of them scattering across the hardwood floor already, slipping with wet plops from the wound in Arnie1's head. I knew that the tiniest ones, maggot-sized, had already slid between the cracks in the hardwood floor.

"What are we going to do," Carl asked. "We can't take all these to Fulton's!"

Fulton's was the funeral home a couple blocks away owned by a friend of ours. When he'd seen the wrong face on the real Arnie, as well as the tattoo on Arnie's arm which clearly demonstrated that the hairy body with the pretty woman's face really *was* that of the man we said it was... he'd helped us out, and put the corpse through his crematorium. But three more bodies?

No. You could only stretch friendship favors so far. And then the police were bound to show up.

"Grab whatever you want to keep," I said, still catching my breath. "And then get the gasoline can. Those things are probably already in the walls by now. We can't stay here."

MOVING out of a place you've lived in for years is definitely an easier thing when you know that there are monster worms potentially lurking in every corner prepared to turn you into a ghoul with someone else's face. And for all I knew, there were more Arnies on the way to boot.

I didn't want to stick around to find out. The first time around, I'd been careful to try to fully destroy whatever it was that had killed my friend. This time I just wanted to get away... and hopefully mask the evidence of what we'd been forced to do.

THE OLD HOUSE burned fast and hot.

Carl and I left most of the meager things we owned behind, but we took a couple suitcases. I suggested that maybe now would be a good time for us to head south, like we'd always talked about. I hated the Chicago winters, and, well... now we had no place to live through them.

I headed up Sibley Blvd. toward the I-57 Interchange. Carl sat silent beside me. But instead of getting on the expressway, I turned left and then right, into a gravel parking lot with more potholes than level surface.

"What the hell are you doing?" Carl said when he realized where I'd gone.

"I want to see what's happened to Arnie's ashes," I said.

"I think we've already seen," Carl said. "I don't want to see him anymore."

"Neither do I," I said. "That's why we're here."

I opened the door and stepped out onto the lot. Carl didn't move.

"You coming?" I asked.

He shook his head. I noticed his face looked pale. I realized that at some point in the past twelve hours, Carl had passed his limits. I decided not to push them any further. I just nodded and closed the door. Then I walked up the broken sidewalk to the old wooden door that marked the entrance to the adult peep show building. The faded red paint peeled away from the wood like old tree bark, and a sign tacked in the middle simply read 'Must be 21 or Over.'

I was long past twenty-one, and I pushed the old door open and stepped inside.

It was just as I remembered it. The place probably hadn't changed in thirty years. The entry foyer was dim and dingy; faded brown linoleum covered the floor and the walls were covered in paneling that had gone out of style in 1975. A thin man with thin hair but a solid bush of salt-and-pepper beard sat reading a magazine behind a glass counter with a cash register on one corner. The glass shelves beneath the counter featured a number of sexual aids: lotions, pills, rubber rings, rainbow-colored condoms.

I dug into my wallet for a ten dollar bill and offered it to him. He nodded, and slipped it into the drawer of the cash register. I already knew the drill, but a sign next to the cash register told the story. '$10 per half hour. Clock starts when you turn on the TV.'

I walked past the counter and turned down a narrow hallway. The walls were plastered with posters advertising porno films, and every few feet there was a door to a private viewing room. I passed two that were closed, with the sounds of human copulation bleating in exaggerated, escalating rhythms. I say exaggerated, because I don't believe regular people ever sound like that. Neighbors would never get any sleep if they did.

As I'd hoped, Room 7 at the end of the hall was vacant. I stepped inside, and closed and locked the door. The room was too dark to see anything, with no window. I fumbled for the TV switch, and the space suddenly came alive with the display of a pair of big bouncing breasts. But I only spared one glance at the screen, and then turned my attention instead to the wall above the white sheet-covered couch on the opposite side of the room.

I had stood on that couch, and lowered Arnie's urn into the wall behind it, thanks to the removable white tiles in the ceiling. The drop ceiling was low, allowing easy access to the TV wiring that snaked from room to room.

There was a jagged hole in the wall just behind the back of the couch. It looked as if someone had slammed the couch into – and through – the drywall. Had someone gotten too excited while enjoying the, shall we say, naturalistic expressionism on-screen?

I knelt on the couch and examined the gash in the flickering light of the TV. The lip of the broken drywall was covered with something dark. Dirt? Ash? I frowned. If that was what I thought it was...

I climbed onto the couch and stood on the arm to pop the drop ceiling tile. Then I pulled myself up on the beam and looked down. The silver urn was there, on the wooden ledge just a couple feet below, right where I'd left it the last time I'd been here.

Only... now it was tipped over.

A small pile of dark ash lay next to the lid, and I could see where Arnie's remains had cascaded down the inner wall to find the ragged gap in the wall. Maybe whoever had slammed the couch through the drywall had knocked the urn over and spilled some of Arnie's remains out.

Since then... it wasn't hard to imagine that men who'd sat on this couch and watched the bouncing breasts on the screen behind me had periodically bumped the wall and breathed in the resulting dust that carried the black bits of burnt flesh that had once been my friend.

Apparently burning him hadn't been enough.

I pulled out my cell phone and texted Carl. Limits or not, I needed his help.

Bring me a coat and a bottle of water. Room 7 I wrote.

Water? he answered.

From the cooler in the trunk, I texted. We'd packed some basics from the refrigerator before we'd torched the house.

A few minutes later, the door to the room opened and Carl stepped inside. He handed me the bottle of water, but looked confused.

"Arnie got out," I said, and pointed at the hole in the wall. Then I explained.

"So, what do we do?" he asked.

"We get him out of here."

I pulled the sheet off the couch and wrapped it around my arm. Then I stood back on the couch and pulled myself up into the ceiling. Hanging over the edge, I pulled out my cellphone and triggered the flashlight app so that I could really see what we were dealing with. Then I reached down with the sheet-protected hand and righted the urn. Once I had carefully pressed the lid back on it, I lifted the canister up and slid my body down from halfway through the ceiling back into the room.

Carefully I set the urn in the corner and then knelt on the couch. I blew gently into the hole in the wall... and then slowly increased the force of air. I turned away, took a breath, and blew again. Hopefully, all of Arnie's ashes were now on the dead side of the wall.

I picked up the bottle of water and pulled myself into the ceiling again. Using my cellphone light as a guide, I carefully poured the water down the wall, washing what remained of Arnie's ashes to the building's foundations.

It was all I could think to do, short of trying to smuggle a vacuum into the place.

When I was done, I slid the ceiling tile back into place, and tossed the sheet back over the couch, making sure the part that my hand had touched was in the back on the floor. I didn't think there was really any ash on it, but I hadn't been willing to risk my hand.

I pulled a tissue from the pocket of my jacket and stuffed it into the hole where Arnie's ashes had sifted through and into the lungs of some poor fools who'd come here looking for a quick, harmless release. A respite. Guys who'd looked for a private 'little death' and gotten the big one instead.

"Go back to the car," I told Carl. He nodded, and slipped back out the door. I pulled on the jacket, and then tucked the urn under my arm, draping the front of the jacket over it. I looked once at the white of the tissue stuffed into the gap in the white wall.

It seemed enough. Even if someone pulled it out, I'd washed away all that I could see of the ashes.

I followed Carl out the door.

The guy at the front didn't look up from his magazine as I passed. If he had, I wondered if he would have noticed I was wearing a coat that I hadn't been on the way in.

Why would he care? All he was here to do was to make sure there was no trouble while people fulfilled needs they couldn't talk about in public conversation. While people were actually being themselves.

Which made me smile, grimly. We never admitted publicly who we were, not really.

Not to anyone. These faces we show outside our caves... they're just masks to hide the real us.

Who were you really? I asked, as I carried Arnie's urn back to the car.

For just a second, I could have sworn I heard Arnie ask right back, "Who are *you*, really?"

CARL HELD Arnie as I drove to a Walgreens and bought some packing tape. Once I'd done that, and securely taped the lid of the urn shut so that the rest of the remains couldn't spill out again, we got on the road. It was long, and we made several stops at roadside bars, hoping to wash away the memories.

Memories of Arnie as he'd once been, loud and boisterous and funny and kind. Memories of Arnie who was not Arnie, but rather, someone else. Someone who wore Arnie's face like a curse. Someone who only existed to remind us of the person who was now gone. Shadows of a man we'd loved but probably never really known.

Who ever really knows anyone? Behind the disguise of a smile, there is really only a cipher. And the hope that the words you hear from those lips are in some way real.

You just never know.

I looked at Carl, and thought of all the things I knew of him. All of the heartaches he had confessed, and the anger and the humor, the laughter and the tears. What really lurked behind his eyes?

I would never know, even though I thought I did. But at least he looked like Carl, and not Arnie.

WE RENTED a shitty apartment in Chattanooga and took shitty jobs to pay the rent. I didn't care. It was warmer there, all the time, than in Chicago. And life was quieter. Less stress. Even though what I did every day was clean up the foul messes that people on their way out left in the hospital.

I convinced myself that cleaning up the messes was better than being on the way out myself.

Carl ended up with a job at a grocery store, bagging groceries. Something I'd done in high school to pay for the beer I wasn't supposed to drink.

Whatever.

You do what you have to do to make ends meet, and when you're done doing it, you sit back in your little manmade cave, your hideout, your mask between you and the world and think about it all. Sometimes not much at all, but sometimes a lot.

I thought a lot about Arnie. Maybe because his ashes sat on a shelf above our TV. I wondered how much I'd ever known about him, really.

What did you really know about someone beyond the expressions on their face?

When Carl and I had unpacked and moved into this little apartment, we'd found a picture of Arnie from a few years back. It showed the three of us, mugging for the camera at a sports bar somewhere, raising three glasses in the air. He'd been smiling, and looked in that moment, as happy as I'd ever seen him.

I taped that photo to his urn. It's how I really wanted to remember him.

But then I turned the urn, so that the photo faced the wall.

Because as much as I'd loved Arnie, I really didn't want to see his face ever again.

For Bob Weinberg

Sing Blue Silver

She came in a silver limousine. Stepped out onto the empty street in a black chauffeur cap, and a black formal jacket. Black hose. Heels that could be used as weapons. As she walked towards the curb, Aaron saw that her jacket hugged something a bit less formal -- a blue satin corset with silver thread. Formalwear taunting night wear. She was Asian, as he'd requested.

"Mr. Ogden," she said.

"How did you know?" he asked.

Her lips pursed in unspoken amusement. She said nothing, but glanced slowly back and forth down the broken street. There was nobody else in evidence. One streetlamp still worked a block away, though it flickered randomly, as if on the brink of extinction. None of the buildings appeared habitable. Roofs caved in, windows boarded. It was an abandoned place. A place for the lost.

His chauffeur bowed faintly, and then opened the rear door of the car for him. Aaron slipped across decadently soft dark leather seats, and sighed as he settled in. There were some comforts he could still appreciate, if not as he once did.

"There is vodka in the bar," she said. "And bourbon. Whatever you like."

He nodded, and fingered the door of the small refrigerator/bar custom fitted to the space along the sidewall of the vehicle. A cable of light illuminated the bottles from behind.

"Why are you out here," she asked. Her voice was soft... but clear as bell chimes. It reminded him...

"Just remembering days gone by," he said.

"Memories or fantasies?" she said.

He snorted. "Memories of fantasies fulfilled," he said. "Twenty-five years ago, this was the place to come to if you needed... something different."

She nodded. "If you knew where to look."

He frowned. "You weren't even born twenty-five years ago."

She said nothing. The car idled. He poured himself a bourbon, neat, swirled it around the bottom of the glass. The interior lights made the liquor glow; liquid fire. There'd been a time that he'd come here, to this neighborhood, after 10 p.m. on any given night, and waded through writhing bodies to a back room where a Japanese girl lay in wait for him, surrounded by candle flames and silver chains and finger hooks and...

"Where do you want to go now?" she asked finally.

Aaron laughed. "Places that don't exist anymore. Maybe they never really did."

"Give me an address," she said. "I'm your driver for the night. I will take you wherever you want to go."

He sipped and thought. He had taken a taxi here, because he'd wanted to walk in the past for a while. But the memories here were all dust and broken glass now. And so, he'd called for a special ride. The kind that offered a sexual pot of gold at the end of the itinerary. But first you needed to take a ride. That was part of the fun, right?

He shrugged, and spoke an address on the south side. She looked in the rearview mirror at him, as if to offer him a second chance, but said nothing. After a moment, she put the car in gear and drove. He enjoyed his bourbon in silence as the streetlights blurred by.

"You are restless tonight," she said. He didn't question her perception, or how she had it. She was right. He nodded.

"What are you looking for?"

"Things I can never have," he said. His voice cracked slightly.

"You?" she said. Her voice betrayed incredulity. "You can buy whatever you want. Go wherever you like. You have the means, or you would not be in my car."

Aaron closed his eyes. "There is only so much money can buy. At a certain point, you die anyway."

The car pulled off the main road and down a dark street. They were in an industrial district; the lights of a refinery pierced the night to the west, while the east was lined with a railyard. The car slid along the tracks for a minute and then came to a rest in a lot after crunching gravel.

She said nothing, but opened his door and stood at attention waiting for him to exit. Aaron levered his weight across the seat and used the top of the door to pull himself up. It had gotten harder to sit, stand, lay down over the years. It crept up on you. One minute, you were cracking a whip. The next, you were cracking.

"Would you like me to come in with you, or wait outside?"

"Come in," he said.

She nodded, and walked with him to the door. A sadly listing neon sign proclaimed "Adult World" above the door. The words "Beer and Boobs" flickered on and off beneath. There was scratched but legible white paint on the door itself that warned: *Nobody under 21 will be admitted. Ever.*

"This doesn't seem to be the sort of place someone like you would come to," she said. Her voice almost whistled against the low thud of a bass beat inside.

"You wear a suit, but that doesn't mean you become the suit," Aaron said.

They found the breath of old beer and a horseshoe bar inside. And a small, black, raised stage with pink neon lights along the side. A gold pole was decorated by a bleached blond with sagging breasts and a tattoo on her ass that, while stretched and jiggling, clearly said, "Bite Me."

Three greying white men sat on one side of the bar while a

Mexican couple flanked the other. The couple were as thin as the old men were fat. The young man wasn't shy about feeling up his woman in front of the rest of the bar. It didn't matter to her; she was looking at the stage, watching the gone-to-seed dancer writhe suggestively to the crooning howl of Axl Rose and "November Rain."

Aaron pulled out a stool at the hump of the bar, between the two "crowds." The chauffeur stood next to him, at attention.

"Sit," he commanded, dragging out the stool next to his.

He ordered them both a Budweiser, which appeared to be the only beer the sleazy dump offered, and then leaned back against the rounded edge of the bar to watch the dance of the fading flower on stage.

"This is not your kind of place," the chauffeur said. Her arm slipped around his shoulders, and she fingered the white collar around his neck. "I don't think what you're looking for is here."

Aaron shook his head. "Not anymore," he agreed. "But it was once. Everything's different now."

"Not everything," she said. "You're still the same."

He laughed. Bitterly. He knew better.

"Why did we come here," she asked softly. "What memory drew you?"

Aaron took a sip of his beer, and grimaced. He set it back down on the bar. "Once, there was a back room," he said. "Most people here in the strip club area had no idea. But it was a place where you could have whoever you wanted. Do whatever you wanted. In the morning, they hosed the place down, and took whoever wasn't moving down to the canal."

"Girls died here?" she said.

Aaron shrugged. "Girls, boys... it didn't matter. It was all sushi."

She looked at him with a sidelong glance. She said nothing.

"Have you ever been to Tokyo?" he asked.

She shook her head. No.

"Pity," he said. "I always ask for an Asian chauffeur, because sometimes..."

"I am sorry to disappoint," she said.

He shook his head. This time, he didn't grimace as much when he drank his beer. "In Tokyo, once, I went to an adult sushi club. Not far from the Tsukiji fish market. It was all very genteel and mannerly at first. We sat around the table they directed us to. Eight strangers, three men on either side, a couple at her feet. She was naked, but covered in slices of tuna, mackerel, salmon, crab and abalone and ... she was a rainbow of fish. Each of us ate the appetizer that covered her breasts and her belly and her thighs... but then it was time for the main course. And the waiter brought us the fileting knives. And a number."

"A number?" she said. "Did you have to eat in order?"

He shook his head. "Everyone got to have one slice from the main course... our young sushi girl. But only one could have a slice from the rarest part."

"And the numbers were a lottery?"

"Yes," he said. "The girl on the table would call a number from 1 to 8, and that was the person who was allowed to carve from between her legs."

"She chose her murderer."

Aaron shook his head. "No, no," he said. "She didn't die. She bled, yes. But she was paid well. And she went home, eventually, a piece of her, now a piece of us."

"So... you wanted to ruin her for all other men?"

"I wanted her to be part of me," he answered. "A connection like that is so rare."

"Did she call your number?"

Aaron didn't answer immediately.

"Did you eat her... sushi?"

"Not the special cut," he said. "But she called my number next."

"Next?" she said. "What did she call you for?

"To breed her," he said. His voice was quiet... nearly silent.

"You had sex with her, there on the table?"

He nodded.

"In front of a group of seven other people, one of whom was probably chewing her labia in his mouth at just that moment?"

He nodded.

"And you liked it moist and bloody, didn't you?" she asked.

Aaron blinked. And then frowned. And then nodded.

"It was the most amazing feeling I have ever had in my life."

"They don't make sushi like that in America, huh?"

He shook his head. "They didn't then."

"You brought it here, though, didn't you?"

He nodded. "That was just one of the things that happened at this club," he said. "You needed a special invite to get into the back room."

"Maybe it's still there, you just aren't invited?"

Aaron shrugged. "I don't think so."

"Why not?"

He stood and threw a $10 bill on the bar. "Come with me." He led her out a side door, and they walked to the back of the building, closer to the train tracks. His breathing grew loud as they walked. The ground there was overgrown with grass and four-foot-tall weeds. Bricks littered the weeds, and nearby, the remains of the walls those bricks had once belonged to were in evidence.

"After the fire, it was all over."

She looked at him in askance. "Fire?

He pointed at the broken slabs of concrete that once had been part of a foundation, and chunks of blackened brick that had fallen from mostly, but not fully, leveled walls. "Some people knew we were doing something different out here," he said. "And as always, they tried to stop it. There is always someone who feels you've gone too far."

He sighed as he looked at the ruins of what had once been the back room of the strip club.

"Why are you out tonight?" she asked him.

Aaron stared at the weed-covered bricks and shrugged. "Why not?" he said. "Some nights, I can almost taste it, just from closing my eyes. It haunts my dreams. My entire being yearns to taste it one more time, before I let go. But it's all over. Gone. Washed away. There are no more sushi girls."

"How do you know?" she asked. One of her palms massaged his back. "I may be your sushi girl."

Aaron laughed. "You only get to be a sushi girl once."

"Maybe I saved it for you. Your whore and yet your virgin."

He turned and pushed past her, walking back towards the car. "What's wrong with you?" he mumbled.

She managed to slip around him and was there to open the door when he reached the car, huffing with lost breath. It was harder to move now than it once had been. Harder to do most things. Some days, Aaron wondered if cancer was eating him up from inside. Colon. Stomach. Pancreatic. Liver? Things hurt. But he didn't see a doctor. He would die when his time came. He had no drive, no desire to try to extend it. When the best was behind you, what was the point, really?

When they were both back in the car, she said, "You stopped coming here. And the other places. A long time ago."

Aaron nodded.

"Why?"

"I got married," he said. "I thought I'd found that connection. I thought I'd found the one who could really go there with me. I thought I'd found her."

"But she was someone else?"

He shrugged. "She was someone. But not the someone I thought. Sometimes I thought she was someone who only wanted my checkbook. But I know that wasn't fair."

"What happened to her?"

"Breast cancer," he said. "Fitting, somehow."

"And so... you are alone again?"

He nodded.

"And looking for that connection... that special spark."

He nodded again.

"That sushi."

He laughed out loud. "I think the world of sushi has gone away."

"Nothing ever really goes away," she said. "It just waits behind closed doors."

"Whatever you say," he answered. "I just wish the reality could answer. Once I knew of a club that was so decadent... some nights they hung people on crosses at the entrance. Try finding a place that un-PC today."

"That is brave in any era," she said. "It must have been a very hidden place."

He nodded. "Only certain people knew about it. Some people who came brought others as … coin. A payment in flesh to get inside."

"I know of such a place," she said quietly. "I can take you there when you are ready."

"I'd be interested in seeing it," he said. "Though I can't imagine it is anything like the place I once knew. They called it NightWhere and it was only open one night per month. You could only get in if you were invited and you could never find it if you weren't. It was never in the same place as it was the month before. I went there for many years."

"Where there are humans, there are places like that," she said.

He shook his head. "Not like this. Sure, there are bathhouses and sex clubs and brothels in every culture in every time. But this… the things that happened there. There were perversions that I had never even thought to imagine. Sex that was the end rather than the beginning. People came and did not leave."

"If I take you to the place I know, *you* may not leave," she said.

He shrugged. "If it was anything like NightWhere, I would never want to leave again. I have no energy to search for that feeling anymore."

"Don't you still want to kill the girls and make them cry?"

He snorted. "It was never about killing," he said.

She shook her head. "No, not killing," she agreed. "Connection. A soul kiss of Thanatos. The fleeting fulfillment when two are one. Always a bitter pleasure, for you can never hold on to the passing."

Aaron's eyes widened. Nobody had ever vocalized the ghosts of his past so perfectly. Not that he'd spoken to hardly anyone about the violent pleasures of his past.

"You're too young to know such things," he whispered.

She lifted her cap and bent her head low, so that he could see the roots at the top. There were traces of grey there. "I am older than you think," she said. "And I have desires of my own."

She replaced her cap and settled into the driver's seat once more. "Where would you like to go next?"

"You loved her," the chauffeur said. She stood behind him in the night. The moon slipped in and out of clouds above, lending an eerie light to the gravestones below.

"I gave it all up for her," he said.

"You loved her," the chauffeur said once more.

He nodded. "I did. But still, we never completely connected. She never understood me. Not really."

"Nobody ever really does," she said. "We are all separate in the end."

"I put myself in a box for her," he said. "Tied it up, and hid it on the top shelf of a closet. Always there... but always hidden."

"Is that when you stopped going to your club? Your NightWhere?"

He nodded. "She humored me, and went a few times. She enjoyed the attention, but never understood that the bar and dance floor at the front were just window dressing for the real reason people were there. She tried bondage play there a few times, but she never had an interest in going through the inner door to The Red. When she said she didn't want to go anymore, I stopped. And soon the invitations stopped coming."

"Is that when you began to go to the secret room at Adult World?" she asked.

He shook his head. "No. That was before. That was actually where I met her. That was why I thought we were truly one mind. But her need was different than mine. She needed to be seen, to be desired. Nothing more. I didn't understand that at first."

"And when you did?"

"I tried to go back, but it was too late."

"Why?" she asked. Her hands massaged his shoulders from behind.

"You just saw," he said. "The places I knew are gone. Rubble. There is nothing left of the past."

"Time moves forward, not back," she said. "Say goodbye and drive with me."

The gravestone in front of him looked much the same as those in the rows all around them. But Aaron read his dead wife's name on it; spoke it out loud. He let the *Born* and *Died* dates linger on his tongue as he remembered the times when he had been inside her, and the times when he had paraded her for others to envy. And the times when he had sat right next to her on the couch, arm around her shoulder, and still felt as if he were alone in the room.

He touched the smooth edge of the granite, and nodded. Then he turned towards the small Japanese woman in her "fuck me while I drive" chauffeur outfit. "Take me to the place you know," he said. "I am ready."

She turned and walked ahead of him to the car, opening the door for him once more.

They drove in silence, and Aaron poured himself another bourbon. The streetlamps and traffic lights turned into blurry trails as his eyes filled with tears. Once he'd given away a part of himself, hoping to be filled in turn. But all that had happened was that his emptiness grew larger, deeper... until he was nothing but a gulf. A vacant man in a false skin. He had pretended to be something he wasn't for so long, he no longer knew what he was. He wasn't the man he'd pretended to be, but he wasn't the man he once had been either.

The car left the main road behind and slid through an alley. He didn't recognize the neighborhood, but the rent was definitely declining by the block. Apartments were flanked with pawn shops. Windows were boarded, but people moved on the sidewalks outside. The buildings were not deserted, only desolated. They pulled down another alleyway, and then the car rolled to a stop. His door opened, and when he stepped out, he saw there were entryways to a couple of bars, as well as an old neon arrow that pointed from the second floor down at a doorway. The sign above the red glow proclaimed, "Peep Shows 25 Cents."

She motioned for him to head that way. "What you are seeking is there."

Aaron shook his head. "I don't think so," he said. "It's degenerate, sure, but not exactly the kind of place…"

"Did they keep your secret room on a bright, busy street?" she asked.

He couldn't argue that point, so he stepped forward, and she opened the blacked glass of the door for him.

The place smelled like mildew and ammonia. It was small, dingy, close. Something sexual occupied every space the eye could roam, from vibrators to dildos to Spanish Fly pills to crotchless panties. There were only three rows of shelving units crammed into the narrow room between the four walls, all of them overflowing with porn DVDs and each section labeled with the particular kink catered to: MILF, Lesbian, Bondage, Gay…

An old oriental man behind the counter leaned forward as they stepped inside. The chauffeur approached him and extended her hand. The cashier took it in his own, and appeared to study it for a moment. "I'd like a coin," she said.

He said nothing, but reached below the counter, and then placed something in her hand.

She turned to Aaron, her dark eyes strangely bright.

"This way," she said, moving down the aisle towards the back of the shop, where a sign read "Adult Arcade." She led the way down dirty tile steps into a lower level. At the bottom, a line of wooden booths had been constructed out of plywood, and painted black. Thin doors opened into the booths, and next to each was a small glass display window that featured the DVD covers of the movies that presumably played in each booth. The hall smelled of old urine, and Aaron shook his head when she approached one of the booths.

"No," he said. "I don't think so."

She stood impassively at the entryway to a booth and waited for him. The DVD covers next to the door showed a line of naked men, all holding their cocks out with their hands. A big-butted brunette was kneeling at the center of the line, both of her hands as well as her mouth occupied.

Aaron sighed, and stepped past her into the booth. She pulled the door closed behind them. This was it then. All of her talk would amount to a blowjob in a seedy peep show booth? He felt his body deflate. This was worse than he could have imagined.

The chauffeur pushed a coin into the slot next to a video screen mounted in the ragged plywood wall. But as soon as the screen came to life, she turned around and pointed to the door they'd just entered. Her arm brushed his as she did; they could both barely fit in the space at the same time. He trembled at her touch. Maybe a blowjob wouldn't be the worst thing.

"Open the door," she said.

"Huh?" he said. They'd just stepped in. The movie had just begun playing on the screen behind them.

"Open the door."

He did; confused before he turned the knob, and even more confused after.

The dingy hallway outside the peep show booth was gone.

Instead, there was a long corridor in its place, leading away from the door. It was blindingly white, though he could discern no actual light fixtures. The walls themselves seemed to glow.

"Come with me," she said, and led him down that long walk. He followed, and eventually the door behind them disappeared. When he glanced back, there was nothing to see but white.

"I don't understand," he said. "How did we get here?

She extended her hand and showed him the tattoo between her fingers. "The man at the front of the store gave me the coin… because I have this mark. Nobody can enter Painfreak without this," she said.

"Painfreak?"

"It's the place you've been searching for," she said. "It's a place known by many names and there are many doorways, though all of them are well hidden. You've seen an aspect of it before, in your Night-Where. Once, it was all you needed. Now, it is all you need again. And that needing… that's the only time one can find entrance. The need must be strong enough. Yours was."

The corridor ahead changed. With every step, the white dissolved, giving way to strobing colors and laughter. And throbbing music and moans. Aaron could see motion, figures dancing; the vibration of a bass drum made the hair on the back of his arms shiver. Rhythmically.

"I don't understand how we got here," he said.

"You called," she said. "I came."

Before he could answer, they were there, in the club with the others, the long white road behind. She shed the cap and jacket, tossing them to the wall. Then she stood in front of him, corset shimmering in the moving club lights, the black hose of her thighs catching the colors and sparkling darkly with the rhythm of the beat. She slipped her arm around his waist and drew him close to her, rocking her small pelvis to his. He smiled and gave way to the motion, though he didn't know the song.

A blond girl in pigtails danced her way next to them; she wore black leather boots and red panties, and nothing else. Her breasts were pendulous, bouncing with every beat of the drum. She jiggled them against his arm, and tried to cut in. He resisted, and the girl shrugged, leaving him with a wet kiss on the cheek.

"You should go," the chauffeur said, pointing at the throng of people. "Dance and lose yourself here."

He shook his head. "I'm not looking for emptiness. I have that already."

"You want more?" she asked.

He looked around, acknowledging the titillation factor of the sex-on-the-dancefloor gyrations, and then nodded his head. This drunken debauch did nothing for him anymore. It never really had; he had always gone quickly to the next level. The level that toyed with pain. The level that put life itself on the razor's edge.

"Follow me," she said.

She led him through rows of half-naked dancers. They passed an area where men and women were chained to walls and racks, as others took turns making their marks with whips and flogs. They passed couches where men mounted men and women smothered men with the deltas of their thighs.

When they reached a wooden door so large and old it looked medieval, she turned to him and cautioned. "If you pass through this, there is no turning back. In Painfreak, every person must find their level. If they go too far, push too deep... some never return."

"What is beyond the door?" he asked.

"Pain," she said. "And pleasure. Dark lusts fulfilled. Thirsts quenched. Souls bled... what do you desire?"

"Something more than this," he said, gesturing to the revelers in the room around them.

She nodded, and lifted a round iron ring pinned to the front of the door. It was surrounded by four heads carved into the ancient wood. Each featured a different expression – one laughing, one crying, one screaming and one blank – the absence of all emotion or expression.

The door opened and they stepped into a dark hallway lit by glowing red embers on either side of a stone path. The waves of heat were palpable. The chauffeur turned and placed her hands on his shoulders.

"Are you ready to leave it all behind," she asked. Her eyes were wide, and serious. "There is no holding back here, no reservation. To get it all, you must give up all."

He nodded. "There is nothing else for me now, nothing more to hold me back."

She nodded, as if she had expected that response. "Then remove your clothes. Shed your false skins and inhibitions at this door. Carry nothing of your society in here. This is the place for primality. For indulgence. For violence. For transcendence. Bring no binds that hold you back."

She removed her hands from his arms then, and reached behind her back to loosen the ties of her corset. After a moment, Aaron began to remove his shirt. As the chauffeur removed her hose, he undid his belt. When he hesitated, she was there, and pulled down his zipper for him, dragging the pants down his thighs, and then loosing his underwear from his hips with her thumbs. The wilted slug of his manhood slipped free, and her face moved past, so close he could feel her breath on his testicles as she dragged his pants down, down, and off.

When he was completely nude, she stood, with both of their discarded garments in a pile in her arms.

"No turning back," she said, and then threw the clothing onto the coals. They smoked, and then quickly caught flame. As they did, she slipped her arms around his back, and raked it with her nails. "Welcome to Painfreak," she said. "This is the place you have dreamed of all your life. The place you tried to create in your secret room."

She leaned up and kissed him. Her tongue was hot, and sharp in his mouth, and he felt his entire body stiffen, rising to life. Waking from a sleep of years.

Her hand slipped down his side and found his own. She turned and led him down the path of fire, and into a room of blood.

Screams erupted from every side as they walked through the room. There were beds made of leather straps, the straps tight enough to support the weight of a body, but with enough gap to allow the blood to seep through freely. Because this was where those who wanted to feel the pain in their pleasure came. And those who wanted to give it.

Aaron stopped near one bed where a woman lay on her back, wrists bound together above her head, ankles tied apart to force her thighs to remain open. A hirsute, brown-skinned man straddled her. At first glance, it was a typical bondage scene. Until you looked at his fingers. Which each wore a steel cap on their ends... and each cap was tipped with a tiny barb. As he shoved his cock inside her, he drew his fingers down her body, opening red ribbons of feeling across her breasts and arms.

She screamed, and yet moments later, wrapped her arms around him, drawing him down to a hungry kiss. When he raised himself up, his chest hair glistened with her blood.

Aaron walked past orgasmic women with breasts stretched taut by hooks and men with testicles weighed down by heavy chains or cocks impaled by metal skewers. At one bed, three women held a man to the bed, as a fourth dragged a knife across his inner thighs. She stifled his screams with her crotch as she fellated his obstinate erection.

They left that room, and entered a strange mechanical place that whined with sound. The scent of hot metal and oil permeated the air, and bodies bound by chains and iron rods moved back and forth, pulled and stretched by engines that revved and sighed. Men with skin burned red pulled against the chains, desperate to gain just one more foot, to reach the prone bodies of the women waiting just out of reach. Like the men, the women were bound and naked, streaked with black machine grease, but they appeared desperate to welcome the bodies of the men. Every few minutes, the men would gain a foot on the chain and mount one of the women, fast and hard before being eventually yanked back to the line. It was a strange sight, a half dozen naked men, cocks sprung, pulling against the machine to reach the nirvana of glossy vaginas that lie tauntingly just out of reach 90 percent of the time. A bell sounded, and chains went slack, and all of that muscle suddenly released. The entire line of bodies slid into gear and slapped together wetly; the clank of the machines now augmented with a chorus of groans.

"Farther in," she said. And he nodded.

There were other rooms they passed, and scents of boiled flesh and excrement and the sounds of steel and wetness.

And then they came to an empty room. With an empty bed.

The chauffeur reached down to a small table and came back with her fingers curled around the haft of a thin, silver blade. She presented it to him.

"You have waited long enough. I have waited my whole life."

She lay down on the bed, and slipped her wrists into round leather hoops. Aaron saw what he needed to do, and bound her ankles with the restraints that dangled at the foot of the bed.

"You are sure," he asked.

She nodded.

He bent over her and kissed her, and she filled his mouth with urgency. He answered, kissing her eyes and cheeks and breasts, covering her with his bites and licks. The memory of the girls he had once had in the secret back room of the club came back to him. He remembered the things he had done to them with his knife, and his cock. Only in those moments, had he ever really felt complete.

"Take me," she urged him. "Eat me," she whispered.

He chewed on the gummy tips of her nipples and bit her belly until blood flowed. But when she whispered once more, he could restrain the knife no longer.

"Sushi," she said.

He lay between her legs and touched the blade to the thin petal of flesh trembling there. It seemed to breathe, gasping open and closed, desperate for fulfillment. Longing for completion. Aaron fingered her flesh, tantalizing it, letting it moisten. The longer he toyed, the more she glistened. And when she'd reached what he felt was the perfect flush of pink, he drew the blade down, and carved.

The chauffeur screamed, and tried to close her legs. But they were locked in the stirrups he'd fastened.

Aaron stood. Naked. Paunch sagging. Cock fully erect, rubbing against the hair near his bellybutton. Blood dripping from the flesh between his fingers to splatter and run down the silver hair of his chest.

He held the petal of her sex up to the light, where she could see, and then let it slide into his mouth.

Warmth. Salt. Perversion. Desire. Dream.

He lost touch with the world in that moment, floating on the wave of taste and texture and the audible music of faraway screams. He shivered with lust and laved her broken flesh before crushing it with his teeth.

The nerves of his mouth burned with a fire that he could not have explained. Pleasure. Perversion. The taste of her flesh.

Aaron bent and gripped and brought the knife down again, and the chauffeur cried out again in a note of agony that only made the taste of her in his mouth even more exquisite. Only in violation could he feel fulfilled. He brought the sliver of sexual flesh up and held it above his lips before letting it fall, like fiery sugar to his tongue.

Rapture.

The space between her legs flowed in a red tide. Release.

Aaron tasted heaven. A dream so long denied. So darkly wished for. And yet still...

... as the initial taste and electricity in his nerves eased... he found it wasn't enough. It was a taste of heaven, but not what he truly sought. What he yearned for. He didn't want the feeling to be fleeting.

"Lie down," the chauffeur demanded. While he had savored the forbidden taste of her, she had released herself, and undone her ankle restraints. Now she stood before him with blood-streaked thighs and bruising, well-bitten breasts.

"Lie down," she said again. Aaron complied. He laid down on the thin leather straps of the bed, and felt the warm wetness of her blood stick to his skin.

The chauffeur locked his ankles in place, but then also reached up and brought a chain across his wrists. He had left her wrists free, and she had held herself back, as he'd carved into her most intimate flesh.

She did not give him the choice. His wrists were locked.

And he didn't care. He gave himself up to whatever she wanted, whatever he had left. He had tasted her and...

She raised the blade so that he could see. "My flesh to you, your flesh to me," she said. And then she brought the blade down to slice just below the head of his penis.

The pain was hideous.

Aaron screamed. And strained against his bounds.

But to no avail. The blade moved against him, as her fingers gripped the mushroom head of his manhood between them. He felt both the frisson of penetration, and the ripping as flesh separated.

And then the chauffeur was leaning in, over his chest, with a bloody sliver of skin and flesh hanging above her mouth. She had peeled the skin off from around his shaft. Degloved his penis.

"Your flesh for mine," she said. "A communion." And the skin of his manhood disappeared into her mouth.

She undid his wrists then, and his ankles. Aaron looked down to see an angry red stake where his cock had once been, and part of him laughed, while part of him cried. The pain was excruciating. And yet... somehow distant.

"You have looked for connection all your life," his chauffeur said. "I have looked for the same. That's why I took your call tonight. Together we can reach that place. Your blood in mine."

She slipped one leg over his lap, and bent to kiss him, the iron taste of him still fresh on her lips.

"Will you be mine?" she asked.

Aaron looked into the brown, endless eyes of her, so exotic. So erotic. He nodded. "I will," he gasped.

She moved her pelvis over his, and let his mushroom head find purchase in the slippery gore he'd made of her sex. When she was sure, she let go, and allowed herself to be impaled by his bloody spear.

Both of them screamed, as he slipped home.

The pain and blood only lubricated their orgasm, which came quickly, violently, a series of wild waves on a shore of fire.

Aaron opened his eyes and saw hers looking back at his, both of them haunted and aghast.

Afraid and amazed to have finally found...

"Yes," he said. Only that.

She nodded, and smiled. And closed her legs with him still inside. Their wounds kissed and wept. And he held her close, arms locked around her back, pulling her as tight as flesh allowed.

WHEN HE AWOKE, the next morning... or night – there was no division of time in the depths of Painfreak – she was there still, hips pressed to his, breasts wet with sweat against his own. The room flickered with the shadows of fires unseen, and the chauffeur's arms remained around his neck.

"Hey," he said.

She smiled, brown eyes pools of beauty and need and desire. He didn't want to ever look away, but he did try to shift, to separate himself from the heat of their long embrace. But she came with him. As his thighs moved, they dragged her along.

"What?"

He looked down the brown silk of her waist and saw the place where his flesh entered hers. His cock somehow, unbelievably anchored inside her. Aaron pulled his hips back, and shifted his weight. Instead of leaving her, he saw her pubes stretch and move with his own. The skin of her groin lifted with his motion, skin pulling, but not letting go.

"We are one," she whispered. "Just like you always dreamed. Completed at last."

"I don't understand," he said.

"Your flesh to mine," she said. "We ate from each other… and gave back to each other. We are connected, for eternity. Two now one. Truly and deeply."

He tried to shift his hips again, and her waist and legs moved across the bed. It was going to be difficult to walk this way.

"This is fucked up," he whispered. She only smiled and he realized that he could actually feel the emotion that surged behind her lips. Her thoughts were in his head: wave of relief. The pure excitement of knowing that a lifelong, terrible emptiness was finally filled.

He realized the feeling echoed the surge of his own bitter heart. He was suddenly, strangely completed. Content. He stopped trying to pull away, and instead kissed her deeply, and wondered if they could simply stay that way, lips and groins locked forever. Aaron closed his eyes and saw through hers. He looked old… but younger than he'd felt in years.

We won't be leaving Painfreak will we, he thought.

A warm surge of bliss served as her answer.

He realized in that moment that while she was inconceivably part of him, he didn't even know her name. But she read his mind.

"My name is Aaron," she said. She moved her arms up and around his shoulders, and pulled him even closer. "And I won't ever leave you," her mind whispered inside his own.

"I will always love you," he said.

Or she said.

It didn't matter anymore.

Forest Butter

"I told you not to take a shortcut," Evelyn said. Her voice was shrill. I was used to it. There had been a time when her chattering treble had been attractive. She was a woman with a girl's voice. Once that had been sexy.

Not anymore. Now it was just grating. And she had a daily habit of using it to berate me. When she opened her mouth, I had fantasies of stuffing the end of a baseball bat in it. The image actually made me giggle sometimes... her eyes all huge and surprised... this big cone of wood sticking out between her teeth... and silence. She wouldn't be able to say a damned thing. For once.

Yeah, that would be hilarious.

"You tell me a lot of things," I answered. "How am I supposed to know which ones to listen to?"

I know. I suck. I'm an asshole for thinking about stuffing a bat into the mouth I used to kiss. Especially a woman. Because, you know, girls are sacred. Doesn't matter if they're stupid, self-centered, nagging bitches, they should still have doors opened for them. Because they have a womb and I just have a penis. All hail the holy cervix. Doesn't matter if they're dumber than rocks and meaner than a viper. A guy should bow down and hold the goddamned door.

Whatever.

At the moment, all I cared about was finding some place to pull over. We'd been on the road for 11 hours, and it was dark and raining and I was wiped-out-tired. That's a new word, by the way. Wipedout-tired. Mine. I coined it.

We'd been driving down an empty snaking road lined with a solid line of trees on either side forever it seemed. The only thing that broke it up were the white canopies dotting many of the trees and dragging the branches to hang lower. Tentworms. I remembered them from the last time I'd driven through Missouri. The things created huge tents of silk in the trees to serve as their homes. And nurseries. They ate the trees alive. If you punched a stick through one of those white cocoons, a thousand wriggling worms would fall out.

I know. Because I stopped along the side of the road once and did just that.

Not tonight. I wasn't getting out of the car again until we got somewhere. It was crappy out there, though the rain did seem like it was finally beginning to subside.

And then, just like magic, I saw the neon light through the dark twisted grasp of the trees reaching for the sun that was gone.

Pink and blue neon, calling out through the forest to a weary traveler; "Vacancy," was the word I could read a few seconds later. *Kind of like the space between Evelyn's ears*, I thought. When we cleared the tree line, I pulled on to the gravel road that led over a small bridge and up the hill to the three-story wood-sided country inn.

"This better be a decent place," Evelyn warned. "I don't want to stay in some roach motel."

I turned the key in the ignition and the engine died.

"At this point, I don't really care," I said. "I need to sleep."

"I'm not staying in there if it's a dump," she said.

I shrugged. "Then you can stay in the car."

I pocketed the keys and got out. I hadn't gotten to the front door of the Deep Woods Inn before I heard the door slam behind me. I smiled. She wasn't going to give up that easily. I didn't see her sleeping alone out in the back seat of a car in the middle of nowhere.

The place looked like an old backwoods' mansion, fronted by a wooden porch with pillars that supported an overhanging roof. When I opened the screen door to step inside, it was like entering a whole other world.

The lobby was a long room with dark wood plank floors and gnarled wood paneling. A dim orange light hung from the ceiling. Deer and boars' heads were mounted strategically on the walls around the room. Along with some bucktoothed creature I couldn't readily identify. Beaver? Ground hog?

I approached the front desk, a small rough-hewn counter behind which hung a collection of room keys, each on separate, numbered hooks.

The screen slammed behind me.

"There's nobody here," Evelyn said. "Let's just go."

A voice instantly refuted her from a small doorway behind the counter.

"Y'all need a room?"

The man looked as old as the forest. Lines crossed his face like veins on an oak leaf, and when he crossed his arms, his wrists were gnarled as bolls.

"Yes," I said. "We've been travelling all day. I can't go another mile."

He nodded. "I think we can set you up for the night. With the weather the way it's been, not many folks have come out this way lately."

The man turned to the wall of keys and put a hand to his chin. After a second, he pulled the set from the hook labeled 4. "This'll do ya," he said. "Do you have any luggage to bring in?"

"Just one bag," I said. "I'll get it in a bit."

"Follow me, then," he said, and led us down a hallway. The lights here were so dim I could barely read the numbers on the doors, but he walked unerringly to #4 and slid the key in. The door creaked open, and when he flipped a switch on the inside wall, an old, yellowed ceiling light cast illuminated a room that appeared frozen in time. The carpet was a thick brown shag, and the walls looked dingy and yellowed.

A single bed with a pale red comforter took up much of the space. You could see the valleys worn in the mattress by previous tenants. There was an old bureau next to it, with a black and white photo of an aged woman in a frame on top. There was an odor. Something stale and old. A little like dog.

I started to step inside, but Evelyn didn't follow.

"I'm not staying here," she said. Her words were clipped and firm.

"It's just for a few hours."

She shook her head. "It's dirty and smells. I won't sleep in there."

I closed my eyes and shook my head. "It's the middle of the night and we need some rest. It will be fine."

The old man said nothing, but stepped aside when I followed Evelyn back down the hall to the front lobby. I heard him close the door behind us.

"What's the matter, Earl?" a woman's voice called.

Its owner stood in the lobby and barred Evelyn's flight towards the exit door.

Earl came up behind us and answered.

"Little lady says number four is too dirty to sleep in," he said.

"That so?"

"I'm sorry," I began, but Evelyn raised her palm and cut me off.

"Do you have a nicer room," she said. "Something that doesn't smell like a bear's den and has a soft bed that doesn't look like an elephant slept in it?"

The old woman raised a white eyebrow.

"They're all much the same," Earl answered.

His wife, however, looked at the keys on the wall and nodded.

"We can set you up in the special suite, number eleven," she said. "It'll cost ya a lot more though."

Evelyn shrugged. "As long as it doesn't smell. Let's see it."

"Show them upstairs, Earl."

The old man lifted a key from the appropriate hook and led us towards a small stairway at the end of the back hall. Each stair creaked as we ascended the narrow passage, and I could see Evelyn's lips pinching tighter with each step.

"This better be good," she hissed.

I frowned. Nothing was ever good with Evelyn anymore.

But when she stepped over the threshold at the top of the stairs, she gasped. Earl followed her and nodded. The attic room was beautiful. The A-frame ceiling was built of heavy, varnished timbers. The floor and walls were much the same. It was like walking into a hidden cave inside a tree trunk.

The bed was huge – king-size with an ornately carved headboard. The comforter looked almost like cotton candy; it was thick and fluffy with delicate pastel patterns... but the surface didn't look solid. It was almost as if someone had taken the padding out of the inside of a blanket. He stepped next to the bed and patted it and raised an eyebrow. It might look as easy to tear as a giant ball of cotton, but it was solid.

"Is this more to your liking?" the old woman asked.

Evelyn shook her head in violent agreement. "Yes," she said. "I can stay here."

"Glad to hear it," the older woman said. "We want to make sure our guests are comfortable."

Evelyn walked to the double doors that presumably opened onto a balcony and tried to look outside. But the darkness with the forest tree cover was absolute.

"You'll get some sunlight through there in the morning," the old man said. "But we're in the heart of the forest here; the branches wrap around this place like a million arms. It makes it hard to see the stars."

She turned away from the black glass with a yawn.

"We'll leave you to settle in then," he said. The couple turned and disappeared out the door and down the stairs.

"Satisfied?" I asked, and Evelyn nodded.

"They never said how much this room cost," I noted.

My wife shrugged. "It's worth it, whatever it is. I was not going to sleep on those bedbug infested mattresses downstairs."

I opened my mouth to say something but then thought better of it. No need to start another argument before midnight.

"I'll go grab the suitcase," I said instead and headed back to the car.

THE LOBBY WAS ALREADY empty when I reached the landing, and I hoped they hadn't locked the door. It hadn't been locked when we'd arrived, though. I put my hand on the knob and it turned easily. There was no padlock above it. I stepped out onto the wood porch and into the humid night. The faint sound of locusts whined from somewhere far away, but it was soft; the rain had smothered most of the night sounds of the forest. There was an odor to the air, a pungence that was almost sweet. The scent of rotting wood and damp fungus. And something I couldn't describe. Whatever it was, I liked it. It was the smell of being far from home.

I walked across the front gravel drive and popped the trunk. It sounded absurdly loud in the heavy quiet of this place. When I grabbed the suitcase out, I tried to shut the lid as quietly as possible.

The innkeepers had clearly gone to bed. They did not reappear when I walked back through the lobby. I lingered there for a moment, looking at one of the display cases hanging on the wall near the main entrance. It reminded me of high school biology class – there were three brown moths pinned inside, each with a different complex pattern of tan and white mottling on their long fuzzy looking wings. The mouths were triangular, almost like a bee's. They were beautiful creatures.

The faint scent of the forest followed me as I walked quietly up the stairs. Now that I'd noted it, I realized the entire inn smelled of that faint, but very specific, scent. When I stepped into the attic room, I realized that it was strongest here. It wasn't unpleasant... but it was a little funky. I raised an eyebrow and after setting the suitcase down, walked across the room to close the glass doors. It was one thing to let the night air in, but who knew what else might decide to come inside.

Evelyn was already in bed. She'd laid her clothes out on a wooden chair next to the nightstand. I had assumed she'd want her nightshirt from the suitcase, but apparently she couldn't wait. Some husbands might look at this as an invite to slide in naked next to their wives for a bit of hide the insert-favorite-euphemism-here. I knew better. Pushing at that envelope could only bring trouble right now.

So, I popped the suitcase, pulled out my pajamas, grabbed my toothbrush and a tube of paste and stepped into the small bathroom. I realized we were lucky here – I'm sure the rooms downstairs were just sleeping rooms that shared a communal bath. Evelyn would have flipped out about that.

When I finished up, turned out the light, and slipped beneath the soft sheets, I moaned with pleasure. I think it had to have been about the most comfortable bed I'd ever laid down in. Evelyn didn't even stir. I stared up at the ceiling thinking about the day for about 90 seconds before sleep crashed over me like a wave.

I DIDN'T WANT to open my eyes. Morning had come; the morning light glowed through my still-closed eyelids. I felt like I'd slept for 12 hours, but still, I just wanted to lay there in that crazy comfortable bed. The funky smell I'd noticed the night before was heavy now, almost a forest earth floor perfume of sweetness and decay all in one. I breathed in a deep breath and smiled at the way it made me feel. Enveloped in something good. Something organic. Something...

Something was holding me down.

My eyes opened and I struggled to look around, but my head wouldn't turn. I was lying on my side, facing the window, with my arm beneath my cheek. I could see the morning light dappling the wooden floor near the bed. But when I tried to lift my head and move my arm... I felt nothing.

"Evelyn," I croaked.

She did not respond.

"Evelyn," I called louder. But she still did not answer.

I focused on trying to move. My eyelids were blinking, and I could speak, but my whole body felt unnaturally warm... and almost numb. It was like I was floating in nothingness. Pleasantly heated nothingness.

I looked at my left arm, which hung across the mattress, the fingers clutching at the edge of the bed.

Something was moving across the back of my hand. I couldn't feel it, but I saw the motion.

It looked like an inchworm. It was cream-colored, maybe almost flesh-colored. Its back arched up and down as it moved across my hand. Before it reached the other side, two more moved up on my pinkie.

I tried to move my fingers and saw the index finger tremble. That was encouraging. Especially since there were now six worms moving on my hand.

"Evelyn," I said again.

A worm moved across my lips. I felt it as I opened them to speak and something dropped into my mouth and wriggled on my tongue. That much I could feel. I tried to spit it out, but instead, it slipped down the back of my throat. I could feel it squirming as it slid past my tonsils. I stifled the urge to vomit, since I really didn't want to lay here with that in front of my face. There were things worse than worms.

Not a lot. But that was definitely one of them.

I decided to focus on my fingers. Moving them. It took my mind off the fact that there was a worm on its way to my stomach.

If I really tried hard, I could make each of my fingers twitch. Not much more. But I kept working on it.

I was still working when I heard footsteps across the wooden floor.

"Ah, Mr. Naper, you're awake."

It was the old man.

"I see the tentworms have decided to come in. It's that time of year. We don't typically sleep people up here in the summer 'cuz of that, but yer missus seemed pretty set on it."

I saw a pair of overalls move into view, and a hand touched my forehead.

"Ah'yep. You've got the fever. I can see yer missus has it without even touching. Yer wearing some clothes to protect ya, but she musta gone to bed bare-ass nekkid from the looks. And that's a lot of easy skin for them to nibble on."

"Get them off of me," I begged.

"Too late for that now," he said. "They done come in overnight and spin their cocoons on ya both. Filled you up with their poison so's you cain't go running off while they finish their work. Once enough of that stuff's in ya, you won't never move again."

"I can still move," I said, twitching my fingers to prove it.

"Might take them a bit longer with you with your night clothes protecting ya some. I'm pretty sure yer little woman ain't gonna say boo again."

"What will happen?" I whispered.

"Oh, they'll finish up that cocoon so's none of you is sticking out, and then they'll lay their eggs. Then... just a matter hours and you'll be tentworm teats. Millions of those little critters all sucking from yer skin. That stuff they pump into you will make you all soft by then. Always amazes me how fast the whole process goes. I've seen it here on this cocoon bed I dunno how many times and it always makes me wonder how we even got to have any trees left out there where they normally live. I guess trees just take longer to digest."

"Please," I said. "Pull me out of this bed."

The stained denim in front of me stepped back, and then away.

"Not once the process has begun," the man said. I heard his footsteps moving around the bed and then a low chuckle.

"She didn't seem so sweet when y'all came in last night, but my word, the tents do seem to think so."

The jeans came into view again and he crouched down so I could see the deep wrinkles in his face and the spark in his gray eyes.

"You know what the main thing is that these hills're known for?"

I tried to shake my head, and I did feel my chin move a little. I don't know if it was enough for him to see.

"Probably not, seeing's you're not from around here. It's a thing called forest butter. It's the best thing there is for spreading on day-old bread or a muffin. And it only comes from here 'cuz it's only produced by this particular breed of tent. They don't produce much of it at all from just the tree nests you probably saw driving in. But when they capture a rabbit or a deer or like what we found, a man or woman—oh my, there is a lot of it once those babies grow up and move back out to the forest."

He stood up. "You know, I should let you try it. Least I could do before you make a batch."

With that, the old man trod with heavy feet out of the room.

"Evelyn," I called again, but there was no response.

I focused on moving my fingers and was encouraged to see that now I could make each one of the knuckles bend. It wasn't a lot, but it was more than I could do when I'd first woken up. Maybe some of the poison was wearing off.

One of the worms was inching its way up and over the middle of my thumb. I crooked my index finger and used it to flick the thing to the floor. I saw now what they were doing. An almost invisible thread of white followed each of the worms across my hand. The things I'd seen earlier on the back of my hand were gone, but more moved across my wrist and fingers to take their place. Their backs arched then fell. Arched and fell.

And I could see the faint down of cocoon – liquid cotton – beginning to become visible all across my arm.

"So you're looking for a last meal, huh?" The old woman's voice came from the doorway. It startled me, and I felt my shoulder actually shift when I jumped at the sound. So, I wasn't completely immobilized yet.

I heard her cross the room, and a moment later a broad, yellowed smile grinned into view. She wore a faded pink housedress decorated with white flowers. And on a small plate she held a piece of toast. It was slathered in something that looked like curdled cream. Almost the texture of peanut butter, but lighter.

"I'll have to help ya with this, see'n as the babies have set you on their table."

She picked up the toast and held it to my mouth, and the scent I'd smelled throughout the Deep Woods Inn last night filled my nose. Pungent as the smell when you've picked at the lint between your toes, but sweeter. I'd thought it was funky the night before, and that's the best description I had for it.

Forest Butter

When the butter slid across my tongue, my mouth instantly filled with saliva. It wasn't sweet or sour... I don't know how you'd describe it, but it sent an alarm through my nerve endings. In a good way. I chewed the bread hungrily and could hear my stomach growl, begging for more. Faster.

"I thought you'd like it," the woman said. "Ain't met nobody who didn't. And this batch is fresh; we just had a couple up here last month. Made enough butter to last us fer weeks, even with selling it down at the grocery."

I was eating the worm-digested remains of the last people who'd foolishly slept in this bed?

The thought almost made me spit out the toast.

Almost.

But the butter was too good to deny. Instead of spitting it out, I opened my mouth and chewed another bite. And another. With each movement of my teeth, it became slightly easier to take another bite. It was almost as if repetitive motion made the paralysis wear off.

When I finished the bread, the old woman patted my head.

"Now you understand," she said. "I hope ya won't hold it against us that we let the little babies do what they like up here. How can ya say no to forest butter like that?"

She stood up then and walked around the bed.

"Yes sir, they sure is likin' yer wife. Probably gonna take them a bit longer to get around to finishing yer tent. But they'll get it. Don't you worry. Most of 'em go out to the trees for the sun during the day, but come night time... my lord these things are busy. I don't know when they ever sleep. Not that I sleep so much these days myself. It's hell on a woman to get old. Anyways. Me, I got my chores to do now. I'll check back on you a little later. If ya still can, I'll even bring ya another treat for dinner, maybe. Could be yer last supper. We'll see."

The sound of her feet diminished, and I heard the boards of the old stairway creak.

If we had slept in one of the old bedrooms downstairs, we'd be on the road right now, miles and miles away from here.

Instead, we were hours from being worm butter.

I flicked another worm off my thumb and noticed the finger moved a little easier than before. I fanned my fingers and forced them to contract in a fist and expand. The more I did it, the easier it got, and soon I could move my wrist back and forth.

If I could get enough muscle motion reinstated before nightfall…

I MOVED my fingers until they were sore. I chewed air until my jaw hurt. As the morning turned to afternoon, I could turn my head and move my arm at the elbow. It only flopped up a couple of inches and then fell back to the bed but… it was a lot more than I could do when I woke up. It felt as if I could shift my spine a little bit now too. It was hard to tell, since my whole body still felt as if it were suspended in a thick liquid. But I did not dare to rest.

If I could work enough of the poison out of my muscles, I might be able to roll myself out of this bed. I understood now, too, why the bed was so comfortable.

It was a mattress made of cocoons. As I laid there staring at my fingers, I could see the intricate white threads that wove the top of the mattress and the sheets that covered me. The threads were tiny, but dense. Layer them enough, and you got a lattice as strong as steel.

I saw fewer worms as the afternoon went on. Maybe my motions were driving them away, or maybe they just were all outside, feasting on leaves. Either way, I pressed for some advantage, using every minute to try to move.

It was exhausting, and several times I found myself pausing to rest, only to begin slipping into a drowsy sleep.

The room had turned largely to shadows when I heard the innkeepers next. The stairs creaked and a pair of heavy shoes stepped across the floor.

A low whistle sounded. It must have made my head shift because a hand suddenly felt my forehead.

The knuckles were thick, and I saw the grey curls of hair on the fingers when the hand lifted. The old man.

Forest Butter

"Still awake, eh?" he said. "Shouldn't be long now. Yer missus has been enjoying a whole host of new suiters this afternoon, looks like. But you? They'll come back to nest tonight and you'll be able to sleep sound."

Another set of steps sounded in the room, and the old woman's voice asked, "He still fighting it?"

"Yep," the man said. "You wouldn't have thought he'd be a strong one, but maybe the babies just don't like him so much."

"I promised him a Last Supper," she said.

"Waste of good butter."

"That ain't very Christian of you at'll, Earl."

I heard the old man grunt and then his steps head out of the room. A moment later, she knelt in front of me and winked. "I knew you was gonna hang on for one more bite o' the butter," she said. "I could tell this mornin'."

With that, she began feeding me another thick hunk of homemade bread slathered in forest butter.

The taste again made my mouth water uncontrollably. I gulped and chewed at the bread and the old woman laughed. "Yer appetite ain't gone still, that's fer sure."

She stood after I finished the last crumb. She walked to the window and looked out on the coming night. "It's just the way of nature," she said. "You won't feel nothin' bad, I promise you. When tomorrow comes, you'll be in another place, that's all."

Then she walked away.

I HAD no intention of being here when tomorrow came. The forest butter had awakened my mouth, and now I redoubled my efforts to move my fingers and arm. I tried to shift in the bed and could feel small spots of my skin slide against the inner "cocoon" of my pajamas. My clothes were stuck in the worms' silk, but I was not completely immobile any longer inside them. I swiveled my arm and slapped my fingers toward my face.

For the first time all day I could touch my lips and face. There were sticky spots on my cheeks, and I rubbed them off. Then I felt along my neck and realized there was a thick skein of cotton there. I dug my fingernails in and pulled.

My arm fell back to the edge of the bed with a tuft of worm silk that looked like five balls of cotton.

I repeated the motion. This time, when I opened my hand to release the cocoon to the floor, I saw a handful of gyrating, angry worms.

Little by little, I freed the area around my neck and ripped a slice through the silk that bound the sheet (and me) to the bed. The stuff was easy to rip in very small tufts, but if I tried to grab a big handful, my fingers couldn't budge it. So, I worked carefully, pulling layer upon layer of it away. It was like stripping cotton candy one fingerful at a time.

I still couldn't feel my legs, but my upper body seemed to be coming back to life.

The room was now fully in darkness, and I could hear the sounds of running water and voices in the kitchen downstairs. It was after-dinner chore time. At some point, I heard a clock somewhere chime, and I realized the room was now in total darkness, except for the blue-white light of the moon.

And then I smelled it.

The heavy scent I now knew came from the worms rolled into the room on the breeze. And more than the breeze. As I looked at the window, I could see them inching across the sill. Dozens of them. Hundreds of them. There were soft sounds as worms tumbled across each other to the floor and moved towards the nest.

My bed.

The first wave crawled up and over the mattress with determination. A wave of inch-worming shapes, intent on coming home to feed. And to spin.

They were not going to cover me again.

I swatted my hand and arm back and forth across the area of the bed I could reach, shoveling them back to the floor. I could see them wriggling in the midst of my arm hair when I raised my arm.

And I could feel the sudden pinches of warmth.

There were probably only minutes before I would be overcome.

I grabbed at the head of the bed with my good hand and pulled. I could feel my body move, but then stop.

My pajamas – which had protected me from bites – were now keeping me locked inside the cocoon. I shook my head. No way. Not after a day of peeling off cotton. No.

I slipped my arm down my chest and began to unbutton my shirt. My fingers fumbled and struggled, but one by one, I got the shirt undone. And then I used my arm to push my body up from the bed. My shoulders slipped free of the shirt which remained stuck in the skein of silk. For the first time in almost 24 hours, my entire torso was raised up from the bed. My other arm was still a little numb, but I'd been working my fingers beneath the sheets all day, and I forced them to push and help drag my upper half forward. Then I reached beneath the sheets again and pulled the drawstring on my pants. I forced the waistband to loosen, and tried to wriggle my ass to shift up and out of them.

A tide of worms meanwhile had crawled up the bed and were now squirming across my bare belly and disappearing under the sheets. I felt things crawling amid the warmth of my privates and grimaced. Maybe that's what gave me the last burst of strength I found. Or maybe it was seeing the bizarre tunnel of cotton that protruded from Evelyn's open mouth. Worms shifted inside it, moving quickly in and out and around that tube of silk. She'd never known when to keep her mouth shut and the tentworms had apparently burrowed their web deep inside her over the course of the night and day.

I threw myself off the bed.

My feet stuck inside the cocoon and my head struck the floor, smashing a horde of tentworms at the same time as sending stars across my vision. The pain woke something in my spine, and I was able to twist my middle. With both hands, I clawed my way across the floor until my lower half finally toppled over the side of the bed. I felt the warmth of tentworm venom from new bites moving through my body. I only wanted to lie down and sleep.

But not yet.

I couldn't stand. I couldn't even feel my feet. But I pushed myself up with my arms until my legs moved at the knees. I moved like a tentworm myself, inching and arching my way away from the bed and across the floor. I moved until my shoulder met the wall near the stairway. And then I pulled myself up to sit.

My suitcase was still there, and I leaned an elbow on it as I looked back at the bed, which was now alive with worms. They shifted and writhed and spun. Waves of heat moved across my body and at one point, I couldn't help it… I peed right there where I sat. Maybe that helped release some of the toxins. Or maybe just the adrenaline of escape coupled with the physical exertion of moving did it. But after I sat there drifting in and out of consciousness, maybe for a couple of hours, I finally came to myself enough to grasp that I had to get out of this room. The worms were focused on the giant cocoon of the bed, but I had been smashing any that moved across the floor in my direction.

I reached into the suitcase and pulled out a t-shirt.

It took me ten minutes or more, but I finally got it over my head.

My jeans were folded inside, and I stretched them out next to me before trying to slip my legs inside. I could feel the hard metal of my keys in the pocket when I inched my hips into the denim. I flicked several writhing white things out of my pubic hair to the floor and used a fist to smash them.

The room smelled thick of forest butter.

I didn't worry about my shoes. I didn't think I could possibly bend over that far to get them on. Instead, I crawled to the bed and pulled myself up on the nightstand to stare one last time at Evelyn's face.

Her eyes were open. They didn't blink, but at one point, her pupils did move. She stared in my direction with a demanding look. *Get me out of this,* her eyes said.

"You got yourself into this one," I said. "And this time, I can't get you out of it. In fact, I don't even think I want to."

Saying those words lifted a weight from my heart, and I smiled at her and shook my head. It was good to be able to shake my head. Especially at her.

"Goodbye Evelyn," I said. Then I used my hands to hold myself up against the wall, and staggered, slow plodding steps to the stairs.

It took a long time to work my way down without falling.

THE LOBBY of the inn was empty, with just one dull orange light shining near the front desk. I used the desk to prop myself up, half walking, half dragging my feet around the room from the stairway.

There were a stack of small jars there near the cash register, and I stopped to read the sign in front of them.

"Forest Butter, $7.95" it read.

I grabbed a handful of them and shoved them in my jean pockets before moving carefully around the rest of the room and opening the front door with a creak to let in the night air.

It was redolent with the scent of worms.

I took a deep breath and staggered across the porch, down the wooden steps, and out to my car. I levered my way into the driver's seat of my car and turned the engine over.

The innkeeper had been right – the room upstairs had come with a high cost. But as I took a deep breath and smiled at the quiet seat next to me, I realized that I was glad to pay it.

Ghoul Friend In A Coma

You know, whether they're dead, alive, or somewhere in between... all girls are the same. They want your undivided attention. "Love, love me do." There was never a better four-word phrase written to describe girls.

Maybe that's why I started to notice Regina. She seemed so quiet and shy. So totally NOT like the other girls. She was pretty, I guess, in a quiet way, too. But she didn't really let you notice. She always wore loose jeans and t-shirts, usually with some kind of longer shirt over them, sleeves half-rolled up. Except when it got really hot. She didn't do much with her hair, but it was snow-blond and looked full and glossy despite her lack of effort; she wore it curled loosely over her shoulder. Mostly, she let strands of it hang down half over her face, which hid her eyes much of the time. The guys in class didn't pay her any attention; they were all focused on the spandex and lip gloss girls.

Maybe that's why I noticed her. The cheerleader mallrats just annoyed me. I couldn't stand to listen to them. And certainly none of them ever talked to me.

Don't get me wrong though, that's not to say I didn't have a girlfriend. Amy planted herself next to me at the lunch table every day, and I had learned a long time ago not to try to walk home from school without her. I can't say that I ever actually asked her out. And most of the time she was around, I'd frankly have preferred to be by myself. But... she was useful when it came to working on term papers. And my mom loved her. That alone made it worth keeping her around. Mom left me alone when Amy was over.

So, anyway... you can imagine that I had to be careful of my eyes for Regina. I'd never even really talked to her. I figured she was pretty smart though, because she took more sick days than anyone I knew – and she still managed to pass her tests, at least in the classes I had with her – English Lit and Calculus.

Today was one of those days that I noticed her seat was absent a body. Normally I wouldn't have worried, but then right after 7th period, the principal came on the overhead with an announcement.

"This is a reminder that the Renfield Meadows curfew remains in effect. Please make sure if you are walking or bicycling to go straight home today. Be safe, not sorry. Thank you."

The bell rang then, and everyone jumped up to head for the door.

Shit. The last time they made one of those announcements, there'd been a freshman missing. That was almost a month ago, and they still hadn't accounted for the body.

"Who do you think it is this time?" Amy said, latching onto my arm in the hallway. I resisted the urge to yank my arm away when she wrapped her fingers around it. Every day I reminded myself that she gave me a cover. As long as she was my "girlfriend," I didn't have to deal with a bunch of other shit. I wore Amy like a security blanket. That sounds lousy, I know but hey... she was happy... I was, mostly, happy. It worked, okay?

"Another dorky freshman who wandered into the forest preserve, you think?"

I shrugged. "Maybe."

She laughed, and leaned her head on my shoulder as we walked. I blew a ringlet of her black kinky hair out of my mouth.

"Will you walk me home and keep me safe?" she asked.

I shrugged again. "Maybe."

I was a real catch of a boyfriend, I know. But she never seemed to notice.

"C'mon," she said, yanking me forward. "I want to stop at Burger Palace on the way. I'm starved."

Nobody was ever going to look at Amy and worry about her being starved, but I knew better than to argue. At least when she had food in her mouth, she shut up for a minute. OK, maybe only 30 seconds, but I took what I could get.

THE NEXT MORNING, I saw Regina walking down the hall and it's weird to say, but when I saw her, I instantly felt better. I still hadn't heard who the latest kid was that was missing, so I guess part of me had wondered if it was her. But no, there she was, head down with an armload of books. And just as I noticed her, and felt better knowing she was okay, I saw one of the spandex girls pull a typical mallrat move. Sandra Tolley held one arm out, right in front of Regina. A second later, that arm connected with Regina's stack of textbooks, and that carefully stacked pile was suddenly up in the air. You could barely hear it above the noise of a hallway full of kids, but I heard the books hit the tile with a sharp *slap, slap...slap*. A couple pieces of looseleaf flew into the air and disappeared in the rush of milling teens. I saw Sandra stifle a laugh just before she gave the most unauthentic apology ever. "Oh, I'm *sooo* sorry," she said to Regina. "You really should watch where you're walking, though."

With that, she disappeared into the crowd to join her friends as Regina scrambled to reclaim her stuff.

I bent down to pick up her History book, and grabbed a couple assignment pages that already had shoe marks on them. "Here you go," I said, when we both stood.

She looked at me through a loose lock of hair the color of fresh cream. "Thanks," she whispered. "You didn't have to."

I shrugged. "But I wanted to."

Her lips seemed to smile, just a little, and I realized for the first time that her eyes were blue. Pale, piercing, ice blue.

"Well, thanks then," she said. I could barely hear her voice above the din around us. And then came a voice that I could hear above every other.

"There you are!" Amy said. She slapped a mitt full of fingers around my biceps and pulled me to the side a step. "I waited for you at your locker, but you never turned up."

I shrugged. "I got here a little early and was heading to class when I…"

"When you decided to chat with Weirdgirl? What did she want?"

I looked away from her and saw that Regina had already vanished.

"Nothing," I said. "Someone pushed her and I helped her pick up her stuff."

Amy smiled and ran her hand across the back of my head. Kind of like she was petting a dog. "Well, aren't you just a Knight in Shining Armor. Maybe tonight you can carry my books for me, huh?"

The warning bell saved me, and after a perfunctory kiss we separated and went opposite directions to class.

IT WAS ONLY a week later that we got another one of those "watch your back" announcements over the loudspeaker. Joe Watson groaned behind me and said out loud what we were all thinking. "Holy shit, another one?"

"Joseph!" Mrs. Powers yelled, but it didn't matter. The final bell went off and we bolted like a stampede for the door. Curfew or not, killer or not, we all just wanted to be out of that school.

"You think it's someone from Heller High?" Phil asked, falling into step next to me.

I shrugged. "Doesn't really matter. It wasn't us, and they still haven't caught the guy."

"How do you know it's a guy?" Amy asked. I could hear the breath catch in her throat; she'd obviously run to catch up, not wanting to miss a minute of *my* conversation with *my* friend. "You know there are female serial killers too."

"She's right," Phil said. "Girls can be more nasty than guys."

"Gotta agree with you there," I said.

"What do you mean by that?" Amy said, and punched me in the shoulder.

"Hey," Phil said, changing the subject. "Do you guys want to get together tomorrow night? Watson got a 12-pack off his older brother, and we were going to drink 'em out by County Line."

"What about the curfew?" I asked.

"We'll stay hidden. You know that ditch we used last month? It's perfect. It's unincorporated, so the cops don't patrol it, and it's deep enough that you can't really see it from the road."

"And the killer?"

"That bitch is not going to fuck with a group of us."

I took a glance at Amy. She was no longer happy with the female killer idea, I could tell.

"I'll have to see if I can sneak out."

"You could come study at my house," Amy said.

"That's a good excuse," I agreed.

"No... I meant, you really could come over."

"What time, Phil?" I asked, ignoring her point.

"Probably get there around 9, after it's dark."

"Perfect," I said. "See you then."

Phil nodded and took off towards his block. Amy was irritated that I was choosing beer in the ditch over an evening at her house. It was refreshing. She didn't say anything for about three blocks. And then finally...

"So what time are you picking me up?"

WHILE YOU COULD HUNKER down in the ditch and not be seen, Phil and Joe and Larry were not exactly trying too hard. Amy and I rode our 10-speeds out to the spot, because it was only a couple miles. We'd just passed the Rollin Pesticide plant at the end of the industrial park when I spotted them up ahead. Their flashlights bobbed back and forth from the side of the road and occasionally caught on the undersides of the trees nearby.

Two minutes later, we had dropped the bikes at the bottom of the grassy gulch. Joe held out a bottle to each of us. "Happy hoppy Saturday!"

I held it up. The bottle was brown, and the label was dominated by a frog with an enormous belly. HopOrtunity, the label said.

"Is it any good?" I asked.

Joe shrugged. "Who cares? It's beer and it's free."

There was some wisdom in that. Something along the lines of, "Don't look a gift horse…"

I took a swig, and the bitter metallic taste slapped me across the face. When I breathed out, I could taste it in my nose.

I raised an eyebrow and took a breath before looking around. The road behind us was empty, but I could see the parking lot lights from the industrial park just a quarter mile down the road. "Where did you park?" I asked. I knew that someone had driven; there were no bikes in the ditch but ours.

Phil pointed to the trees. "Right back there."

There was a small gravel drive just a few yards away that cut across the ditch and wound back into the scrub trees beyond.

Next to me, Amy started to cough. I turned to look, and her mouth was crinkled up in a horrible grimace. She held the bottle out in front of her like it was poison.

Phil laughed, and took the bottle from her hand. "Not Hoppy with it?"

"That tastes like kitchen counter cleanser!" she said.

"No worries," Joe said. He rooted around in a duffel bag for a minute, and came up with a clear bottle with a plain label. All I could read on it was the word "Vodka."

"Always have a fallback position," he explained.

Amy smiled. "You're the best," she said. I could see her sneaking a glance at me to see if I was noticing how happy Joe had made her. I suppose she wanted me to feel guilty. I just took another swig of my beer. I reached out a hand to Phil and took back her abandoned bottle. "I can take care of that for her," I said.

Amy shook her head, visibly annoyed that I wasn't reacting. "You wouldn't have a Coke by any chance, would you?" she asked.

"I'm a boy scout," Joe said.

"You're the best!" Amy purred, and kissed him on the cheek. She glanced back with a "look at me" grin, and I raised my bottle to toast her.

I could tell that wasn't the reaction she was going for. But jealousy? She wasn't going to get that from me.

"Don't chug all of that," a voice came from the ground beyond Phil and Joe. Lydia propped herself up on one elbow, taking a break from roto-routing Larry's tonsils. "I want some when I'm done here."

With that she buried Larry's face in her hair again, and Phil snorted. "By the time she's 'done there' we're going to be on the way home."

He turned on a boom box and pretty soon the ditch was rocking with both laughter and guitars. It was a good Friday night in the Middle of Nowhere U.S.A.

About an hour later, as Amy lay with her head in my lap and Phil was going on about the godlikeness of his newest favorite guitarist (he had a new guitar hero every month), Joe suddenly stopped in mid-sentence and barked, "kill the radio."

Phil slapped his hand on the volume, and everyone was quiet. I understood why a second later, as the sound of crunching gravel came from nearby.

I was staring in just the right spot to see the car, as it turned off the two-lane and crept towards the trees. And I could see the driver clearly as the car crossed over the ditch. There was no mistaking that pale face and even lighter hair. It was Regina.

She was driving an old beat-up Toyota. I'd seen her in it at school, so it only took a glance and I was sure it was her. She didn't seem to see us in the ditch below as she crossed over and then began to speed down the lane to disappear into the trees.

"What's back there?" Joe asked, just before he turned the radio back on.

"Might be an old farmhouse or something," Phil said. "There aren't any subdivisions this far out."

"Huh," Joe said. "Never had anyone go down that road while we were here before."

Amy piped up. "Well, that's it, party's over. Guess you'll have to find a new ditch to drink in!"

Joe shook his head. "Seven bottles left. We've got a while to go. You'd better just talk to your vodka."

Amy smirked and put the bottle to her lips. She'd already downed the Coke and hadn't asked for another. After a minute, she squeezed my hand. "Take a walk with me?"

I knew better than to refuse. "OK, but let's not go too far," I said. I looked at Phil and said, "Be back in a bit."

We stood up and Joe tossed a bottle cap at my head. "Where you guys goin'," he drawled. "Don'tcha wanna get nasty down here in the ditch like Lydia and Larry? They'll make room!"

"We'll be back," I said, and crawled up the steep incline towards the trees. We followed the gravel road back a few yards until the mix of oak and pine branches obliterated the stars overhead. And then suddenly Amy was pushing me against the trunk of a huge rough-barked oak, and sticking her boozy tongue down my throat. Her lips felt warm and moist and swollen, and I have to admit, I enjoyed having her chest pressing against mine. I could feel the hard cup of her bra through my t-shirt.

Her hands were around my neck and then grabbing at the zipper of my jeans. "Mmmm, I have missed you all week," she whispered as she slipped one hand inside my briefs to grab the tip of my quickly expanding manhood. Okay, maybe teenhood. But... right then, I felt man-ish. That's for sure. And all of my bitching about Amy's annoying controlling ways disappeared when she got my belt undone, and I pulled her shirt over her head.

She could be a bossy bitch, but she knew what to do when she was naked. Or half-naked, anyway.

And after drinking a quarter of a bottle of vodka, she was even more energetic than usual. I did my best to reciprocate, because I definitely appreciated what she was doing.

A while later, she rolled over on the forest floor and swore. "Ow, there's a pine needle up my ass!"

That, I assumed, signaled the end of our little field trip, and I grabbed for my shirt and pants and stood up. Her bra was in my jeans, and I fished it out and tossed it to her. I had to stop and watch as she slipped one arm through, and shrugged her breasts into the white lace. You could say a lot about Amy, and a lot of it not very complimentary, but you could not deny that she was stacked.

"Quit gawkin' and get dressed," she said. "I want more vodka. If you're a good boy, maybe I'll let you peek again later."

I doubted that. She was about 15 minutes from being thoroughly trashed. I hoped she was going to be able to ride her bike home.

"Thanks for bringing me," she said. "I'm having a good time."

"Me too," I said, as she took my arm. Just at that moment, something like a scream sounded from deep in the forest.

"What the fuck?" Amy said.

We stepped onto the gravel of the winding road and peered down its length into the depth of the forest. I could just make out the faint light of a house back there.

Something shrieked again, but fainter this time.

"Owl?" I said.

"That was not a fuckin' owl," Amy answered. The more she drank, the more she swore, I had noticed.

We stood there for several minutes, breathing quietly. Listening.

But the sound didn't come again.

"Come on," Amy said finally. "We should get back with the others."

A few minutes later, we were back in the midst of laughter and a pounding bass beat. "I hope *you* were a boy scout," Phil laughed. I took a beer from him and only answered with a smirk. An hour or so later, we all staggered out of the ditch, and headed home under the light of a million stars. It was way past curfew.

On Monday, I noticed Regina's seat was empty in English class. Normally, I wouldn't have thought too much about it; she was gone at least a day every week it seemed like. But... it occurred to me – much belatedly – that she had driven down that gravel road on Saturday night... the same road where we'd heard something a little later that sounded like a scream. What if she had gotten home and the Renfield County Killer had been waiting for her?

The thought bugged me throughout the day; I had Calculus class, too, where I was also confronted by her empty chair.

After school, I decided to go for a bike ride. Mom was still at work and Amy had softball practice, so I was on my own.

I headed out onto the two-lane towards the industrial park, and pulled off the road at the ditch where we'd been drinking Saturday night. The telltale frog labels stared at me from the deepest edge of the dropoff. I laid the bike over them, and crawled up and out of the ditch to walk down the gravel towards where Amy and I had made out. Towards the house I assumed was hidden back there.

And my assumption was correct.

The road wound around and suddenly I was standing in a small clearing, with a two-story cedar-framed cottage tucked at the edge. A stand of oaks and maples climbed into the sky behind the green-mossed shingles of the place; I could see the gutters were overflowing in pine needles, leaves and acorns.

I stood there looking at the place, assessing the sagging screens and the weathered wooden porch that stood four steps up from the gravel drive. And suddenly I didn't know what the hell I was doing here. I was just assuming this was her house. If Regina answered the door, what was I going to say? "Hi, I thought you might have been killed two days ago so I finally decided to ride out and see." Or what if her mom came to the door and asked if I was a friend of her daughter. "Um, well, not really..."

I almost turned around right then. But I'm stubborn. Hell, I've stuck with Amy this long, haven't I? I don't let go of things when I should.

So, after fidgeting in place for a while, I walked up the warped wooden steps and stood in front of the old wooden door. I almost knocked. And then something made me walk to the family room window instead. I wanted to see what I was getting into. I leaned past the drapes on the side windows until I could see in through the glass to the room beyond.

It took a minute for the scene to register.

I saw a brown couch, sitting right beneath the window, and a beige carpet that extended across the room to end where another room and a stretch of tile began. The family room led straight into the kitchen. It looked like a big kitchen, with dark wood cabinets that stretched to the ceiling, and an old white refrigerator on the left side of the room next to a stove.

All of those things registered before my mind allowed me to see the elephant in the room.

Well... not an elephant exactly.

A dead body.

Two, actually.

From the color of the hair, I was reasonably sure that one of them was Regina.

Oh, mother fuckin' shit.

It was her that had screamed on Saturday. I'd been just a few yards away and I'd done nothing. And now...

I started to back away from the window, ready to run to my bike, truth be told. And then the faintest voice whispered in the back of my head, *"what if she's still alive and just unconscious and you leave her yet again... maybe then she'll be dead by the time someone comes back here."*

I didn't want to know. But I *had* to know.

I put my hand on the front doorknob, assuming that my white knight's efforts would easily be rebuffed and I'd have no choice but to leave.

But... the knob turned.

I could hear my heart pounding in my head as I stepped onto the carpet.

What if the killer was still here?

Two days later?

I tiptoed across the carpet and then knelt on the edge of the tile just a couple feet away from that otherworldly blonde hair. Both bodies were naked, and a pool of dried blood extended across the tile all around them, but most of it seemed to stem from the neck of the body next to Regina. It was another girl; from what I could tell, she looked about our age. Her brown hair was twisted and matted in blood, but her face was down towards the floor and away from my view. Regina's face lay in the same direction, as if she was staring at the girl's back. If they'd been in a bed, they might have been cuddling. Their hips were cupped together. The creamy curve of Regina's butt gave me a hard-on in spite of the hideous situation. The girl was… had been… beautiful.

I extended my hand slowly. It shook as I held it over Regina's head. Gently, cautiously, I laid it down on that white-blond hair and stroked it, gently.

Poor girl. She'd barely ever talked to anyone, and someone did this to her and her friend. I was actually kind of surprised to see her with someone… I didn't think she'd had a friend in the world.

Her hair was soft under my hand, and I ran my fingers down it all the way to her shoulder.

My breath caught, as my fingers touched the soft curve of her arm. *Too little, too late, chicken-shit*, I thought. *If you ever had a chance, it's gone now.*

Regina suddenly moaned and rolled onto her back.

My eyes must have bugged out of my head as I saw hers open. Her face was splattered with dried spots of blood, and where her cheek had touched the floor, it looked like a solid bruise of dusky red.

"Hi there," she said softly, blinking a couple times, and then adjusting her jaw back and forth. I could see her chin shift. "What are you doing here?"

"You're alive!" I said.

"Yeah, I guess so," she said, and sighed as she pushed herself up to a sitting position. Her breasts were small, but perfectly smooth. They were also streaked in dried gore.

"What day is it?" she asked.

"Monday," I said.

"Damn," she said. "I missed school again, huh."

"Um, yeah. What did he do to you?" I said. My voice was a church whisper.

"Who?" she asked.

"The guy who did this," I said. "It was the Renfield County Killer, wasn't it? How did you escape?"

"I didn't escape," she said. "Nothing to escape from."

"I don't understand," I said. "Then what happened?"

Regina put her hand on my shoulder. "You know how you guys were partying in the ditch on Saturday?"

"You saw us?" I said.

"You weren't trying too hard not to be seen."

I shrugged.

"Well, I was having my own party up here."

She held one arm across her chest, covering herself, but raised the other to touch my cheek.

"You were worried about me, weren't you?" she said. She sounded surprised.

"Yeah," I said. "I..."

"You shouldn't have come," she said. Her voice sounded sad.

Suddenly I had a strong suspicion that all those announcements of missing teens and Regina's frequent absences from school might be connected.

"There is no serial killer, is there," I said.

Regina shook her head. There was dried blood on her lips.

"Did you drink her blood?" I asked.

She shrugged. "Some."

Regina began to move, and I jumped to my feet. Standing, I could see now that it wasn't just the dead girl's neck that had been opened. There were gory holes in her belly, and her breasts had been turned into hamburger.

"You ate her," I said.

Regina didn't answer me. It occurred to me in that moment that it was probably in her best interest to make sure I didn't leave the house alive. And from the look of the body on the floor, she had no problem whatsoever with killing.

I turned and ran for the door.

I was across the carpet and back on the old wooden porch in five seconds, but it was the sixth second that fucked me up. My shoe caught on a raised plank just before the stairs to the gravel road. I grabbed for the wooden banister, but missed, and then there was spark of white light as my forehead hit the flagstone path at the base of the stairs just a second before the rest of my body hit the ground.

"I PROMISE, I'm not going to eat you," were the first words I heard when I woke up.

I was in a bed, tucked in beneath pink sheets and a fluffy sea-green comforter. My head was throbbing. I put my hand to my forehead and felt a lump there. A thick, gauzy bandage. Regina sat on the side of the bed. She'd washed her face and was wearing a loose yellow cotton tank top. Part of me still managed to notice that she hadn't put on a bra.

"That was quite an escape," she said. Her voice was soft, with a hint of laughter rolled up inside it.

"Not very effective," I admitted.

She shook her head. "Do you want some aspirin?"

I nodded and groaned as I did. It hurt to move.

She got up and walked out of the room. She hadn't bothered to put on shorts. I wasn't sure whether to be excited or scared.

A minute later she was back with three pills and a glass of water. "Take an extra," she said. "I think you need it." I downed them and laid my head back. "Ow," I said.

Regina slipped her legs under the covers and slid in beside me. She propped her head up with one hand, while stroking mine with the other.

"I really appreciate it that you came out here to check on me," she said. "Though, of course, I also wish you hadn't."

"Because now I'm a problem," I said.

"Maybe," she said. "I guess that's up to you."

I couldn't help but close my eyes when she ran her fingers across my hair.

"No problem," I said.

"Good," she said, and pushed herself closer to me. I put my arm around her and drew her close. Her skin was cool, but her eyes were electric. My heart skipped when her lips touched mine, but she didn't bite.

LATER, when the light began to wane, I sat up in her bed. "I have to go," I said. Part of me hated to call the question. Would she let me leave?

"I know," she said with a yawn. "But could you give me a hand first?"

"Sure," I said. "Whatever you need."

A minute later we were in the kitchen, and she pointed to the body. "I need to move that downstairs."

"Um..."

"Come on," she said. "I do it by myself usually, but you could make it easier."

"Usually?" I said. "How many times have you taken bodies downstairs?"

"Just grab the feet," she instructed.

And just like that, I was helping Regina carry a body down a flight of stairs through a concrete room to another set of stairs that led to a damp, horrible earth cellar. The stench almost made me lose my lunch.

We laid the body down at the end of a row of corpses. It was a small room, but she had nine bodies laid out there, most of them missing large amounts of flesh. I assumed that was from her hunger, not from decay, though the first bodies were just blackened husks. The buzz of flies filled the air.

"Thank God dad put a door on that room," she said as we stepped back outside, and she pulled the door closed with a snap.

"Where is your dad?" I asked.

"Oh, he's in there. First row on the left," she said, and walked away from me towards the stairs.

"You promise you won't tell anybody," she said. "I mean... not anyone."

I nodded.

"And your head?" she asked.

"I hit a bad pothole and fell off my bike."

She smiled. "See you in school tomorrow?"

I shook my head. "Yeah."

The whole walk down the gravel drive to my bike, I wasn't sure whether to puke, or dance.

I'd just made out with the girl of my dreams. In her bed. Only problem was, afterwards, I'd carried a dead body down to a cellar. The body of a girl she'd eaten.

On Tuesday, Regina was back in class, and I caught her eye in English. She smiled, in that quiet, don't-notice-me way which guaranteed that nobody else in class even knew she was there. But I knew. I saw the glint in her eye beneath that frost blond hair. And part of me... a growing part of me... yearned to be back in her bed, letting her stroke my hair... and anything else she wanted.

I caught her later at her locker and when nobody was in earshot, I thanked her.

"For what?" she said.

"For letting me go."

"Thank you, for helping me pick up my books... and other things," she said. "Can you come over today?"

"After school?"

She nodded.

"Sure."

IT WAS DICEY. Amy always wanted me around to do homework with. And she managed to sneak in some other activities when her parents weren't around. I excused myself, saying my mom needed me to help clean out the garage, and maybe I could come by after dinner. Instead, I made my way from the garage to Regina's house.

The next day, Amy had softball again after school, but on Thursday, I had to tell Regina 'no' so that Amy wouldn't get suspicious.

And so it went for the next few days. I was a ping pong ball between the girl I wanted to be with, and the girl who was my cover.

The hard part was the weekend. Regina wanted me to come over.

I wanted to be with her.

Amy wanted to go to the movies. There was an outdoor showing of *Star Wars* at the Park District on Sunday night and I agreed to take her... but I promised Regina that I'd come over afterwards. Tuck Amy back home, show my face to the parents, and duck back out to spend a couple hours with her. After all... she didn't have any parents to worry about a curfew. I just needed to convince mine that I was home and tucked in for the night.

It all went fine... except that I almost barfed when Amy put her tongue down my throat in the middle of the attack on the Death Star.

I realized at that moment that I couldn't keep the charade up anymore. I had to let her go. I didn't know if Regina would want to be seen as a couple – that would only draw attention to her, and she definitely worked hard not to do that.

But I wasn't going to hide under the protection of Amy big boobs anymore. I was done there. She had to go.

After the movie, I practically threw her at her front door and hurried down the street to my house. A half hour later, I was on my bike and heading towards that by-now-familiar gravel road.

What I didn't notice, or count on, was Amy being at her bedroom window and seeing me ride by.

Girls have a sixth sense when their guys are slipping away. Some of them are more possessive than others.

Amy... was pretty possessive.

THE RED LED on the alarm clock in Regina's bedroom said it was 1:24 a.m.

"I gotta go," I said. "It's Monday already." She stirred next to me. She'd been almost asleep.

"Mmm, no," she murmured.

"It's late," I said. I ran my hand across her cheek, and then down her neck and shoulder. She slipped her hand up my back and pulled herself closer, daring me to stay.

"No," I laughed. "Seriously... it's crazy late. If the cops catch me on the way home, I'm totally dead."

She shifted and brought her lips to mine. "Come back to me?"

"Always," I promised.

Five minutes later, I was pedaling hard past the Rollin Pesticide Plant, praying that I'd reach my house before anyone saw me on the road. The curfew was still in force.

What I didn't know, was that before I'd picked my bike out of the ditch, there had been a knock on Regina's front door.

REGINA WASN'T in school the next morning.

That wouldn't have phased me in the past, but now that I knew the score... I wondered what she'd done after I left.

The day seemed to drag forever, and I couldn't stop yawning. But then during the last period, we got that oh-so-familiar announcement once again.

"Students, this is a reminder that the Renfield Meadows curfew remains in effect. Police are investigating a new disappearance from the area. We do not want to alarm our students, but we want you to be safe. Please make sure if you are walking or bicycling to go straight home today. Be safe, not sorry. Thank you."

I was definitely not going to go straight home. Luckily, I'd ridden my bike to class this morning, and so I dodged Phil and Joe and high-tailed it out of Renfield Meadows High towards the industrial park. The sky was overcast, but I didn't care if it rained. I wanted to know what trouble Regina had gotten into in the past 12 hours.

I dropped my bike and hustled up the steps of her deck. I pressed the doorbell a couple times, but when she didn't come, I tried the doorknob.

As usual, she hadn't locked it.

I let myself into Regina's house. This time, I didn't worry about myself. I was worried about her. I crossed the thick carpet of the family room and saw her lying down on the kitchen tile. She was wearing her nightshirt... the same one she'd been wearing when I left her. Only now, it was soaked in blood.

On the floor next to her, was Amy.

There was no mistaking those kinky black curls.

"Oh, Jesus fucking Christ," I whispered.

I knelt down at Regina's side and pulled her over until she lay on her back. Her lips and chin were still sticky with blood.

Amy's neck had been torn out, and I could see the yellow slabs of fat that Regina's teeth had exposed on her sides.

Those nicely cushioning boobs were no longer looking so inviting. Regina had chewed the hell out of them.

"What did you *do*?" I said.

Regina's eyes fluttered open.

"Huh?" she asked. She put her hand to her mouth to stifle a yawn.

"You *ate* Amy!" I screamed.

She scrunched her eyes together a moment, and then looked at the body beside her, then back at me. "Yeah," she said. "She was pretty good."

"Seriously?!" I said. I really didn't know what to say.

"She showed up after you left here," Regina said. "She was really angry."

"So, you… ate her."

"It had been a week; I was hungry. You should be happy. She was a pain in the ass to you all the time anyway. Problem solved."

I face-palmed myself.

"I assume since you're here that I missed school again. What day is it?"

"Monday," I said.

Regina nodded. "She put me into a food coma. The good ones always do."

"Speaking of which," I began. I faked a grin and pointed at my teeth.

"Huh?" she asked and then understanding dawned and she poked a fingernail past her lips.

"A little more to the left," I said. "You've got a piece of Amy stuck right… there."

She swallowed and then showed me a clean grin.

"I suppose you're going to want me to help you move her downstairs."

"Yes," she said. "But not yet."

DIGGING Amy's grave was one of the most difficult things I've ever done. Aside from the putrid stench of the cellar, Regina wanted me to make it extra deep.

"It's time for me to start planning for the future," she explained. "This is the best place for them; close to the kitchen and totally private and contained. No suspicious outdoor graves. But this room is pretty small. So we need to go down far so we can stack them."

I dug down until my head was level with the ground. Then Regina helped me climb out. I was drenched in sweat and my arms were trembling from the effort.

"I don't know if I can do this," I said when we went back upstairs to the kitchen.

"She was a chunky one, wasn't she," Regina said, nodding as we stood over Amy's chewed up torso. "Not sure what you saw in her."

"That's not it," I said. "I was just thinking about… her parents. I know them and all, and they'll wonder what happened to her. They'll never know."

"You think it would be better if they saw that somebody *ate* her?" Regina asked. Then she shook her head. "Let them live with the hope that she's still alive somewhere."

Five minutes later, my bossy ex-girlfriend was at the bottom of a deep hole. And my bossy new girlfriend was handing me a pair of rubber gloves.

"Let's get my parents in first. They've been here the longest; we're going to need these."

Digging the hole may have been the hardest thing I've ever done. But grabbing onto the rotten flesh of Regina's mother's legs was definitely the most disgusting. A good chunk of her guts stayed stuck to the ground when we heaved her body up. They just kind of… ripped.

After I threw up, we picked the body up again and tossed what we could into the hole. Her dad followed, and I used the shovel to move the pieces that had grown a little too sticky with the ground.

"Why did you start doing this," I asked, after dropping what may have been her father's kidney onto his blackened chest at the bottom of the hole. Amy's white and gory flesh was still visible in spots beneath the grey and green and blackened flesh of Regina's parents.

"You mean, eating people?" Regina asked. She stifled a yawn and rubbed her belly. It stuck out of her otherwise thin frame. "I blame the pesticide plant."

I shot her a querulous look.

"Remember when they had that big explosion a few months ago, and they shut down the highway for hours while they cleaned up the mess?"

I nodded, and she pointed at another body. This one looked to be a teen, but the chest and guts were so gnawed on I wasn't sure if it was a boy or girl. That and the skin had taken on the dark colors of rot. I picked up the feet again, as Regina grabbed the arms.

"Well, after that, we all got really sick. Dad thought Mom was going to die at one point."

"Did you go to the hospital?"

She shook her head, and then we heave-hoed the body into the hole. It was getting pretty full.

"Couldn't afford it. Neither of my parents had worked in months. So... we rode it out. They got better, but it wasn't long after that when I lost my appetite. Like... completely."

Regina pointed at the next body, and we picked it up together. This one wasn't so quick... mushy.

"My mom would call me to breakfast every morning, and I just sat there and couldn't eat it. Or if I did, I'd go to school and puke it right back up. One morning, she called me and when I came into the kitchen, I'll never forget it. She gave me a hug and asked if I was hungry. And that's when it hit me. Like... I can't explain it. I realized that, yeah, damn right I was hungry. I was *starving*. And she smelled like the most delicious thing I'd ever smelled in my entire life."

"And so, you... ate her."

Regina nodded. "The next thing I remember, I woke up and mom was lying on the kitchen floor with blood everywhere. I didn't know what to do. But I knew my dad would be home soon. So... I dragged her body down the stairs and hid it here."

"What about your dad?"

"When he got home, I told him mom had gone out. When she didn't come back, he figured she'd finally just given up and run away. She never liked living out here in the middle of nowhere, and he blamed himself. He got all gloomy."

I started filling in the hole with the loose dirt as Regina finished her story.

"That was the worst week of my entire life. I wanted to kill myself, but I really didn't want to die."

"So, what did you do?"

"I realized that I just couldn't eat normal food anymore, so I tried eating raw hamburger, and even a steak."

"No luck?"

"Barfed it right back up."

"So, what did you do?"

"A week later, I ate my dad."

I COULDN'T BELIEVE that we got all those bodies into two really deep holes. I couldn't believe that I dug holes that deep, actually. And I really couldn't believe what Regina did to me in the shower when we went upstairs to clean up. She did have a way of taking a boy's mind off the stench of rotting bodies and burial of his ex-girlfriend. She said she always got horny after a good meal. I told her that the image of her eating Amy might not be the best foreplay.

Later, lounging in her bed after one of the most enjoyable hours I've ever spent, I told her that she really couldn't keep feeding so close to home.

"I know," she said. "I was thinking the other day and kind of hoping you could help me... um... find new sources. From out of town."

Great. First, I'm her undertaker, and now I'm her cannibal delivery boy.

I couldn't go any further down that road, not right then. I'd had enough that day. But I did finally ask the question that had been plaguing me for days.

"You're not going to get hungry one night and eat *me*, are you?"

Regina's face fell. She looked positively hurt. Then she rolled over and lay on top of my chest. That beautiful white-blonde hair hung like mist over my shoulders.

"Just don't make me mad," she said. Then she winked and added, "And don't let me get hungry."

PEOPLE AT SCHOOL figured that Regina and I became an item because she showed me sympathy after Amy disappeared. Kind of a rebound romance. My parents were concerned at first, but they liked it that I actually had date nights every Saturday night, especially once the town lifted the curfew, after a few weeks passed without any further disappearances. I think my parents liked it that Regina was quieter than Amy, at least around other people. It wasn't so obvious that she had me under her thumb. But oh, she did. The difference was, I didn't mind being under her thumb as much as I had Amy's. If only my parents had seen what we did on our road trips to find what Regina called… new takeout food.

I'M with her every day now, except for Sunday mornings, when typically my ghoulfriend's in a coma, thanks to the food I helped her lure home the night before. It's like I said at the beginning. Whether they're dead, alive, or somewhere in between… all girls are really the same. They want your undivided attention. They want your love.

And they want you to pick up dinner.

And you know what… with Regina, I'm okay with that.

I just make sure she's never hungry.

AMNION

Brod's skin tasted salty. Not surprising, given the workout she'd just given him. What was strange, though, was the silky-smooth feeling of his sweat-slicked chest against her lips. His normally wrinkled, leathery skin felt firm. Tight.

"Mmmm," she whispered in an ear that had somewhere lost its tuft of trademark white hair. Perhaps he'd taken his razor to new old places. "Your skin feels smooth tonight."

Brod seemed to have recently taken a refresher course in personal hygiene. She had her suspicions about why already, but they were confirmed when he rolled on top of her and cracked the cockeyed grin that had always told her he was keeping something in reserve. Secret. His left eyelid drooped and winked with its decade-old chronic twitch.

"Must be my new workout routine," he said. "I feel forty again."

Elizabeth smiled and accepted him inside her—with feigned interest—for the third time. Not because she didn't enjoy the fact that he was actually up to the task, but because she knew he wasn't spending time at a spa, or improving his muscle tone by working out with weights at the gym. He was doing pushups on some hopeful resident or ditzy nurse at the university hospital. Some*one*—not some*thing* —else was getting him in shape.

When she drew her fingernails across his back to mar that taut, newly unblemished skin—laser treatments? she wondered—it wasn't because she was passionate about his embrace. She wanted to let the slut know that someone else owned this piece of meat. This piece of lying, aging, always-working-late meat.

ANGEL LONGED TO BE A REDHEAD. Don't buy that bullshit about blondes having more fun. Any real man knew that while blondes looked good in a tan, redheads looked hot on their man. Angel, unfortunately, was a real blonde, at least in her mind. The kind that made men slip off the curb as they were walking, or stumble over the hood of oncoming taxicabs. She wore it long and calculatedly unkempt, so that it waved and weaved across her shoulders and cheeks like a shredded mass of corn silk. Beneath those wild tresses, her eyes beamed like a cat's, slippery, green and cool.

Despite the heads she turned, and the bed partners she lured, Angel wanted nothing more and nothing less than to live red. "If you haven't had red, you're worse than dead," went the motto. But she didn't want to *color* it red. She wanted to *be* red. She wanted to live it. There was a subtle difference between faking it on the surface and actually being red to the core. There were plenty of ways to dye and electro-excite hair into virtually any color of the rainbow. The kids lately were having the down on their bodies slicked with a bleaching gel that colored all of the hair into patterns of Day-Glo green and yellow. Walking through any mall was akin to stepping through an obstacle course of human-shaped caution signs. A parade of babbling snow cones.

But Dr. Brod had reluctantly promised her a cure, as if being blonde were a disease. He said there might be a not-quite-legal way to grant her desire. Not that she hadn't had to pry the promise from him. Actually, pry probably isn't the operative term. Ride would be a better descriptor.

Angel had met Brod at the university medical center. He was a professor, running clinical trials on a new bone treatment or some such. She'd answered an ad looking for research guinea pigs and agreed to waive all rights to a lawsuit if whatever gunk they fed her made her sick instead of...well...whatever it was supposed to do.

Angel did it for more than the money. She had answered because the university was the home of the GeneX research. Angel thought if she could get on the inside, she might find out if there was a way to genetically change her hair. She hated dying her eyebrows every couple of weeks. And forget about coloring the carpet. Angel wanted an actual metamorphosis, not be dipped like the kids.

The funny thing was, when she met Dr. Brod, the first thing he told her was that he needed her to take a dip.

In a pool.

She'd shrugged. "I didn't bring a hair dryer though."

"We'll have one for you."

"Or a suit."

The doctor had peered at her over the tops of his wire-rimmed glasses. The man was an anachronism. Nobody wore glasses anymore. Hell, most people didn't even keep their boring old blue or brown eye color. Angel, born with cow-brown eyes, had chosen cat-eye green. But many of her friends were more provocative, staring down potential suitors with pink irises shaded and carved to resemble twin vaginas. The theory went that if a man could stare down a woman who exposed herself to him with every gaze, he could handle anything the woman desired.

But the doc didn't seem to have gone for body mods or dips or eye-art. He was just a craggy old man in a stained white jacket. An errant white hair in the bushy granite of his right eyebrow stood straight up in the air, like a flag. His left eye shivered and blinked with a tic.

"I'll need you to strip and immerse yourself completely in the tank for a few minutes," he advised.

"Will there be anyone watching?"

"Just me," he said. His voice was cool. Completely devoid of emotion.

Disinterest wasn't a comfort; it only brought out the worst in Angel.

She loved a challenge. She stood and began to unbutton the white cotton blouse.

"Lead me in," she said, pulling the shirt open to reveal a frilly, pink lace bra.

The doc had only nodded and pointed to a black door. "It's through there," he said. "There's a dressing room, if you like."

"I'm fine here," she said, wondering what he'd say as she stepped out of her sateen Shelvi's to show off her thong. Baby blush pink and edged with the lace of Take Me, the latest libidinal-enhancing gimmick that had generated one of the most popular ad campaigns on the net.

Spanish fly was history. Now you could buy the emotion-twisting Take Me fabric, stitch it into your date outfit unseen, and guarantee end-of-night success, so long as your chosen partner made physical contact with the fabric. Or, if your use of Take Me wasn't a secret to the person you wanted, it could be semi-hidden from public view but blatant to the lover, its shimmering rainbow surface immediately obvious if one got one's hands down the wearer's pants to find the panties. If the amorous partner wasn't already overwhelmed by desire from being in close proximity to the broadcasted allure of the fabric, when his hands slipped across the lace he'd get a neural charge that often brought men to a premature...beginning. Not an end, since that first excited masculine spill was quickly erased from the emotional mind by continued proximal exposure to Take Me.

The manufacturer was currently involved in a class action lawsuit, so Angel had stocked up on the panties. Apparently, the use of Take Me in the workplace by thousands of exploitative co-workers had all but brought productivity in many companies to a wet, panting, back-on-the-desk—or copier—humping halt.

"Your choice," Dr. Brom said and turned away from Angel to pick up a measuring tape and a notepad. He stepped close as she dropped her bra to the floor and stretched a tape from the middle of her breastbone to the tip of her right nipple.

"I'll need to record some specifics to provide a baseline," he said. And without another word, he began tracing the wrinkles in her sun-browned skin and counting off numbers as he scribbled data down.

Angel had kept herself in shape—and in tan—over the past 20 years, and she was used to having an effect on men. But Dr. Brod was giving her zero. She needed to break through that cool exterior. Not that she actually wanted him, she just wanted to prove that she *could* have him. She rubbed her crotch against his thigh, and then, just as a test, she rubbed her hand across the shimmering material hugging her privates tight, experiencing the jolt of pussy-wetting pleasure that she'd expected. The fabric was working. But Take Me hadn't raised a smile, let alone a hard-on, in the doctor. She dropped the useless thong to the floor at his calm direction and turned, completely nude, to face him again.

Since this approach wasn't working, she tried another method that had always worked for her. "Can you turn me into a redhead?" she asked, as he stretched a cold tape measure from her left knee to touch the dewy flesh of her private area.

"Use dye," he said, looking up at her. His eyes seemed silver in the harsh light of the fluorescent fixtures. He nodded at the well-groomed thatch now warming his hand. "It should take easily on you. Clearly, you're a real blonde."

"Isn't there something more permanent that you can do?" she moaned, putting on her best schoolgirl act. It still worked on guys, even after 39 years. "You're a researcher. Can't you do something with genetics?"

"Let me think about that," he'd promised. "For now, I'd like to finish this bit of research we're about to start. Let me show you to the tank."

ELIZABETH HAD LIVED through Brod's indiscretions before. She knew all the signs. While normally a distracted, yet strangely neat man, when another woman managed to obscure the endless flurry of numbers, formulas and projects on his radar, he would take an even greater interest in his personal hygiene, perhaps try a new haircut, buy new clothes. Not just a shirt or pants but a whole new wardrobe. He'd begin lifting weights, going to the gym. Start a diet. All counter to his usual obsession with working in the lab, sleeping in his clothes and getting up, hair standing twisted and coiled from four hours of restless slumber, to disappear back to the university and closet himself in the basement labyrinth again.

When Brod cared about his personal presentation, he was once again trying to live up to someone else's dreams. He never had vanity for her.

After all this time, it didn't surprise her, but she couldn't pretend that it didn't disappoint. Elizabeth had given her life to this self-centered, obsessive man. And when he looked up from the intellectual orgasms of his work, on those few days that he resurfaced to the reality of lips and breasts and sweat-slick desire, he invariably turned to someone else for physical explosions of passion. Never her.

She lifted a glass that he'd left on the kitchen table and held it in the air above the sink. For a moment, she was a student of Brod's again, thinking about physics. If she let go, would it withstand the shock of impact? Could glass be as resilient as her heart? She dropped it into the sink. It shattered, and even though she'd known it might, her shoulders flinched at the noise. Their house had actually rung with something like emotion. Loud, unpredictable and dangerous.

Elizabeth sifted through the shards and lifted a long, steel carving knife from the dirty dishes. She didn't know if she could withstand the impact anymore. But she wasn't going to stay safe and unnoticed in the kitchen anymore.

Flipping a strand of hair that had recently shown a new, undyed interest in silver, Elizabeth decided it was time to check in on Brod's latest research project.

"This is the Amnion," he told her.

Angel took two steps down the ladder and her feet and ankles were immersed in warmth. She leaned toward him, hoping the position accentuated her naked breasts. Not hoping. She knew the position showed her off goods. Her hope was that it would have an effect on him. She needed to own him if she was ever going to get what she wanted. She stared as much at his crotch as his face, looking for an answer. And stepped down another rung.

"And the Amnion is…?"

"I can't explain much without jeopardizing the experiment," he claimed. "Let's just say, I'd like to see it have an effect on those little wrinkles I measured. And perhaps take away some of that weight that gravity has given you over the years."

Was he actually saying, all polite-like, that she was a sagging old bag? Angel's heart went cold. She'd never had a problem enticing a man, and here this one, who was probably old enough to be her father, was critiquing her. She worked out. She went to the skin-shade salon. Yeah there were some sunspots, some wrinkles, maybe her breasts weren't quite as perky as a 19-year-olds, but…

"Just dip yourself under the water for as long as you can," he said. "Come up for air, and do it again. I'll let you know when you can get out."

Angel let herself go then. Her heart sank as fast as her body, and she slipped beneath the warm water of the dark tank. She closed her eyes and put two fingers on her nose to keep the water out. Then she let the black liquid bring the cover of night over her.

"Do you feel any difference in your body?" Dr. Brod asked a few days later. This time, when Angel came back to the university research lab, she wasn't quite as cocky as she had been the first day. She had stripped and strutted, and the old man had ignored it, taking her measurements like she was a farm animal, making her step into a tall, narrow barrel of water.

"A little," she said. "I feel like…I don't know, maybe I have a little more energy this week or something."

Dr. Brod nodded and pointed at her clothes. "Let's take a look, shall we? Do you want to change in here again, or should I show you the dressing room?"

Angel pulled the t-shirt over her head and dropped her jeans in a flash. He may have shot her down, but she still wasn't shy.

"Diminished, yes," he murmured, holding the tape measure to the crease beneath her breast. As he held the tape to her eye and instructed, "Blink and hold," Angel stared hard back at him, hoping to drill through that cold steel to the hungry man that had to be hidden somewhere inside.

"What is the Amnion?" she asked when he was done marking things on his chart.

The doctor paused and put the eraser tip to his lips.

"The Amnion is, I hope, a way to reverse the effects of aging," he finally answered.

"Like the fountain of youth?"

"More like a rejuvenation spa," he said. "At least, that's what I'm hoping the research will prove."

"Have you tried it?" she asked.

"No," he shook his head. "That would hardly make my research objective."

"Are you afraid?" she asked.

"Of the Amnion? No, of course not."

She stepped closer to him and wrapped her fingers around his forearms. "Then I think you need to give it a try."

"Absolutely not," he exclaimed, pulling away.

Angel pressed on, slipping her arms around his neck and pressing her "sagging" breasts to his white-shirted chest.

"If you want me to get into that tank again, you'll have to come with me."

"Don't be absurd," he said, but Angel locked her feet behind his and pressed her body forward. She hadn't bothered wearing her Take Me today, but he was interested. He might pretend otherwise, but she could feel he was hard. "Who will time the experiment?"

"There's room for two," she insisted. "And I won't go in without you this time."

"Absolutely not," he complained. And then she whispered in his ear.

In the end, he went. Angel unbuttoned his shirt, pulled his undershirt over his head and was working on his belt before he knew it. Then she pulled him, naked, by the hand to step on the ladder of the dark oval chamber filled with what he called the Amnion.

"Let me get a good look," she said, rubbing her hand along the white-haired pelt of his chest, cradling the low-hanging fruit of his manhood in her palm as she gave his body a critical eye. "I want to be able to make my own assessment of this experiment."

"Hardly objective," he commented.

She pulled him down the ladder and into the water. As his neck slipped under, she whispered, "I don't care."

ON HER FIFTH VISIT, Angel didn't want to talk to Brod. After their first dip together in the Amnion, she'd stopped calling him "doctor." Before the door had fully closed behind her, she was shucking her T-shirt and shorts. She hadn't worn undies beneath them, so impatient she was to get in the water.

"Come on," she laughed, grabbing his hand.

"I need to measure y—"

"I don't have any more wrinkles," she said, cutting him off. "And my tits haven't stood this tall since I was in high school. Now come on and let's see what this shit will do for your dick."

She giggled and pulled him from behind his desk. "I want to do ten minutes this time."

"I don't know what that will do," he said.

"I bet it makes you ten years younger," she said, slipping her hands into his briefs to pull them down. "And it may make me jailbait!"

When he was naked, his interest was undeniable.

"I want you to do it with me in the Amnion," she breathed, running her fingers across his interest.

"I'm not going to be able to publish this," he complained. But he followed her to the ladder.

"You're not going to perish, either," she laughed.

They disappeared into the warm swirling waters of the Amnion, where their wrinkles dissolved, and Brod's interest increased. In no time he was locked inside her, and her gasps echoed like small explosions in the hollow nose of the chamber.

Angel's pride was back.

And so was her girlish figure.

ELIZABETH TOOK the Fifth Street Tube to the university district. The car shook and trembled as it rounded the bend past GeneX canyon—the explosion of corporations and research firms that had grown up around the university's key discovery: a process to manipulate the genome of virtually any living thing. The results were far-flung. Butchers were replaced by MeatGrinder houses that simply grew their meat on walls of shivering, exposed red flesh. Steaks and roasts were carved from the prolific flesh on an hourly schedule. Dogs and cats were no longer so much bred as manufactured to order. A litter of pups could produce a pre-programmed Doberman guard dog alongside a frolicking collie, if the pregnancy was reprogrammed early enough.

But there were unforeseen side effects. The streets of many a city were now overrun with wild pets that had been abandoned in favor of the new, made-to-order animals. Who wanted a mutt with a lazy eye, or a weak bladder, or a big white spot across its face when you could paint your pet by the genomic numbers? Herds of cattle starved in Midwest forest preserves and southwestern deserts after they wandered unwanted from the farms that had imploded with the explosion of the MeatGrinder industry. Only a few houses still bought and packed food made from living, grazing animals.

While the cures had been worked out for cancers and AIDS and other endemic diseases, the gene tailors were prohibited by law from offering or experimenting with anything other than treatments for disease in humans. Factories were beginning to be staffed by mindless armed and legged drones to do repetitive tasks that required more finesse than a machine could handle. But the remaining human workers in those factories were still prohibited from using the same technology to enhance their own breasts, erase a tumor or cure any number of non-life-threatening issues that would no doubt form a cottage industry the likes of which had never been seen.

There was a black market, of course. And it was no secret that if you walked past the silver and glass towers and sea-green blockades of GeneX row, past Thomas Avenue, you came to a backwater beach of quieter, more distressed buildings that housed nondescript mail-order businesses and headchip manufacturing firms. They harvested memories for a dime and sold them for a dollar.

Elizabeth walked past the Thomas Avenue sign and immediately the gutters began to reveal cracks and gaps, and the buildings decayed from shining carapaces of ornate industry to paint-peeling shacks crisscrossed with black iron bars. She came to Jeffrey Street, where the memory-leaching Cross-Poll Industries squatted inside a converted warehouse, and then Scott Street, where a headchip manufacturer kept a three-story distribution depot. These were still the mostly legitimate offshoots of GeneX. But Elizabeth wasn't here for black-market genetics. She walked down the beat-up street of false dreams to the darker heart of Slipstream.

Elizabeth could easily have masked her premeditated deed with a genetic soup that turned bones to rubber or dissolved the nerves in an excruciatingly slow fire trail through the body. Given Brod's line of work, such an accident would be eminently explainable. A genetic experiment gone awry. But Elizabeth didn't have the mind for games or dodges. She was a direct kind of gal. She walked up the weedy sidewalk of End, Inc. and nodded in mute agreement with herself.

She had come to Slipstream to buy a plasma gun.

"TALK TO ME ABOUT RED," Angel insisted for the fiftieth time, rolling off Brod onto the floor of his office. They had spent ten slippery minutes together, clutched and bucking inside the tank and another twenty on the sandpapery weave of his carpet. When he stood, his back was a rash of red dots and, Angel noted with pleasure, smooth as silk, as if his skin had just been formed. The hair that speckled his shoulder blades had, over the past three weeks, turned from silver to a wiry black. She'd seen a similar change in her own body; all the spots and wrinkles from years of skin-shading had sloughed away, leaving her a hide of coppery cream. She shivered when she rubbed her skin. She felt hot.

"Just use the goop the kids do," he advised for the umpteenth time. "It soaks into the skin and changes the hair at the root. Takes weeks before you really need another treatment, and you can make yourself whatever color you want, all over."

"I want it to *be* me," she insisted. "Not a paint job. You can change me, I know you can."

"You know that would be illegal," he said, running a long finger across her forehead, tracing the line of her scalp. "And why would you want to be red?" He slipped a hand between her legs and she started at the jolt of pleasure. "Blondes have more fun."

"If you haven't had red, you're worse than dead," she retorted.

"You're hopeless."

"You're stubborn."

Something clicked inside the room.

"You're dead," a quiet voice announced.

Angel looked up and saw the silvering woman standing in the dark of the office door frame. A blanket of shadow crossed her face but didn't completely obscure the creases of aging love lined there.

"Elizabeth!" Brod said, leaping from the sweaty carpet to his feet. As soon as he did so he realized he'd only exposed himself more, and held a hand between his legs to protect the shiny, wet turgidity that proclaimed and evidenced against him. He actually managed to blurt, "It's not what you think!"

"Oh no?" she said, lips unwaveringly straight. "Do enlighten me."

"It's an experiment," he said, nodding, as if the excuse convinced him of his own inculpability. "The effects of the Amnion—"

"The Amnion?"

"Yes, yes!" he grinned and beckoned her to follow. He bravely turned his back and walked towards the hall.

"Wait."

Angel lay still, a frozen mannequin beneath the gaze of the blaster. For once, the green of her eyes did not say go. When Brod turned back to see Angel about to be snuffed, he quailed.

"Eternal life!" he shouted.

"For who?" Elizabeth asked, weaving the gun sights back and forth from one frightened green eye to another.

"For anyone who enters the Amnion."

Elizabeth almost laughed as she saw her husband's penis slap his left thigh, and then his right, as he jittered back and forth, motioning for her to follow.

"Explain," she said, motioning for Angel to stand and precede her.

He led her to the tank and pointed at the ladder. "I've been working with a rejuvenation treatment," he said. "I never intended to use it on myself, but…"

"But she made you do it?"

He nodded hurriedly. "Yes, exactly."

"And it made you feel so young and horny you just couldn't resist, right?"

Brod rolled his eyes back and held out his arms. "You are the most perceptive woman I've ever met."

"So you decided to make the blonde bimbo young and leave me to rot?" she replied. "Some reward."

"No," he said. "It wasn't like that—"

"Get in."

Brod looked from the black O of the blaster muzzle to the piercing gaze of his wife.

"No honey," he tried. "I've already been in today. I'm not sure what more exposure could do."

"Get in."

"I still need to measure what today's treatment has done."

"Get in."

"It could be dangerous."

The orange tongue of the blaster licked the floor to the left of Brod's feet and leapt into the air to carom off the ceiling and end in a sizzling twirl of smoke on the floor a few yards away.

"So could this," she answered.

Elizabeth didn't waver. Step by step, she forced Brod to step down the rungs of the ladder into the black mirror of the Amnion's watery soup. When his hair spiced the surface no longer, she turned to Angel and gestured with a nod. "Get in."

It was all Elizabeth could do not to blast the perfectly taut cheeks of the slut's derriere as the blonde slipped haunches and hooters into the liquid to join her submerged husband.

"Bitch," Elizabeth whispered, as Angel disappeared into the dark well of the cylinder. She saw the cover that hung over one side and reached out to pull it up and then down to cover the mouth of the chamber.

She fastened its latches, ensuring that the guilty could not escape, and grinned. There was a gap for air if either of the little adulterers cared to breathe. They could smother in each other's arms for all she cared. Elizabeth stepped away from the black, silent oval and decided to try to find out exactly what her husband had been up to.

"IT'S GENETIC MANIPULATION, to be sure," exclaimed the twisted scrawl of Brod Scottsdale in his handwritten notebook. Elizabeth hadn't had to look long to find it; she'd met him two decades before as his student, and later served as his secretary.

"But if diluted enough, it may pass the FDA as a wrinkle reducing treatment. All they need to see is that it works, and that after some clinical trials, it doesn't damage the epidermis, but rather, refresh it."

She followed his notes through the discovery of the genetic nanoprobe trick that told dying cells to slough off a particular decrepit enzyme and encouraged the resuscitation of epidermal cells. The life of the probes was extremely limited, which resulted in a slow, gradual devolution of the scourges of time. Elizabeth shook her head at his notes about his own first descent into the Amnion. It had been more than a month before, and only last night had she realized that his skin was smoother, his hair less gray.

Sneaky bastard. He was going to slip a genetic treatment through the FDA while slipping his own rejuvenation past her. All the while leaving her to wrinkle and shrivel like a goddamned prune.

Elizabeth slammed the notebook shut with a low squeal that resembled the building call of a boiling teapot. The steam was invisible.

ELIZABETH WENT out to grab a sandwich after the noise of fists echoing on steel grew too much for her. By the time she returned, full and suffering from just a touch of remorse—or was that heartburn?—the pounding had ceased.

She turned the cylindrical lock of the lid until the latch clicked audibly open. Her stomach clenched as she looked down into the black pool, searching for a hand, or a head, or some sign of life. Had she drowned them?

Something white bobbed just below, and then the bob turned to a finger.

"'Sbeth!!!!" called a high squeal of laughing delight.

Brod's face peered up at her from the shadow near the ladder. Only, it didn't really look like Brod's face. It was long, stretched like taffy. Gaunt. And the hair that had rimmed his lips was gone. The silvering crown of his forehead had fallen out to leave him bald as a pool cue. The blue of his eyes was certain, though, and the wizened—yet at the same time youthened—Brod climbed up from the depths of the water, crystal-black droplets raining from the creamy, hairless knots of his shoulders and forearms. He looked like an ancient teenager.

"We thought you'd never come back," he said.

But his voice sounded strange. Flat. Or high. And the thin, balding body that housed those too-familiar eyes looked strange; like a boiled corpse. Or a bloated baby.

He reached for her as he stepped over the ladder and onto the carpet of the lab floor. Elizabeth shivered with apprehension and repulsion.

"Stay back," she whispered, but Brod didn't stop. Long, whitened fingertips reached for her, and she held the blaster at the pale, hairless chest of the man who'd decomposed to an aged boy and said, "Stop."

But Brod had never listened to anything she'd said and he certainly didn't now. Instead, he grinned and his hairless cock pumped to instant readiness as he held his arms out and cried, "I want you—"

The blast of the plasma gun echoed in the long room, and the wizened, youthened remains of a man-boy collapsed in a muddled red heap. Elizabeth stepped back from the shivering mess and cried.

From the eclipse of the Amnion chamber, another thin hand reached up and out, pulled against the steel of a rung to launch her body back from the black of rebirth to the sandpapering scour of now. An almost piercingly blonde head with cat eyes surfaced from the water, wet as a drowned duck. As long, thin limbs pulled her taut flesh from the water, two pale pink lips grinned, and a long tongue licked.

Those cat eyes spied the bloody mess left by the blaster and whispered, "Red."

Elizabeth watched as the girl-whore reached bone-thin hands into the gory cavity of her dead husband's ribs and then pulled back from the carnage to massage the remains of him into her scalp. Coil by coil, strand by strand, the wraith-thin girl-woman bathed and coated, rubbing her head in his belly in quiet ecstasy. With her fingers she teased the excess of his blood from her hair and slicked the slime of his life temporarily from her eyes as she dipped, again and again, like a bird in a pool of his flesh.

At last, she stood, arms at her sides, proud breasts jutted out as if she were a freshly pubescent fourteen-year-old in plaster relief. She squealed and licked crimson lips as she held up dagger hands to Elizabeth and cried, "Red. I am red."

"Dead," Elizabeth answered, shaking her head in disgust before firing five blasts directly into the unnatural youth of the girl's bloody breasts. The creature collapsed, quivering, to the floor.

Elizabeth then aimed at the floor and kept shooting until the flesh of her husband was indistinguishable from the flesh of his whore.

When the mutated, adulterous pair were nothing but a crimson gel on the floor, she stripped herself and took a long swim in the black waters of the Amnion. She got out every five minutes, rested awhile and then measured the span of her crow's feet. She was careful and waited an hour between each immersion. She left the room each time and walked down the street to have dinner at midnight and breakfast just after dawn before she was through. When the wrinkles were nearly invisible, and Elizabeth was satisfied with her revitalized form, she put on her clothes one final time and picked up the blaster once more. With one shot, she cracked the base of the reservoir and was gone from the building before its final splashes had hit the floor. She was eager to start a new life, free from the chains that Brod had locked around her.

"Red, my ass," she mused, as she strode away from the still-waking university and towards The Tube, twirling a strand of formerly-silver—now golden—hair between her fingers. "Everyone knows blondes have more fun."

Watering

Aaron shook his head in disgust at his front lawn. He'd barely dropped his bags in the front foyer after returning from his vacation before going back outside, turning on the water and picking up the hose.

Early in the season, his care and the rains had painted his yard a lush green. But now that the summer sun had burned hot day in and day out while he'd been lying alone on Caribbean sands, the weak spots showed through. The spring's golf course-perfect carpet was now marred by the dead brown circles; spots where either Aaron had dropped too much fertilizer or where his neighbor's dog had relieved itself.

"Damn dog," Aaron grumbled, pointing the hose at the nearest of the circles. "No matter how you try to keep things nice, somebody always comes and shits all over it."

He sprayed the dead spots – circumscribed in accentuating rings of deep green – with the hose over and over, and then moved around the side of the house to water the backyard. His wife Celine had always ragged on him about keeping the grass looking good, driving him out to water before the sprinkler curfews at 7 a.m., and pushing him to spread fertilizer at night after work, before he could sit down to dinner. While she was no longer with him, since she'd seen fit to shack up with someone else, he still felt strangely obliged to continue the work, just as he'd felt obliged to use the plane tickets they'd bought together for St. Thomas.

"Bitch was good for nothing *but* fertilizer," he mumbled. "Don't know what that asshole ever saw in her; all she ever did was lie there."

The spray of water suddenly sputtered and coughed, and Aaron threw down the nozzle in disgust. "Damnit!" he cursed, and stomped to unkink the hose from where it had caught between the brick and the gutter downspout at the corner of the house.

Yanking it free and dragging the excess loops of green rubber around the house, he again picked up the nozzle to begin watering the lawn at the back of the house. It was then that he noticed the new spot of brown. A spot much larger than the dead circles in the front of the house. While most of the grass leading from his patio to the back fence still retained a healthy sheen of chlorophyll, at the back corner of the yard a browning blemish extended fully five feet in length and two in width.

Aaron's mouth dropped open at the sight. An image sprang to mind; it was late at night, the cold chill of a spring breeze coaxed goosebumps from his bare skin – skin that gleamed in the moonlight with a sheen of sweat. He'd tried to forget the scene while drinking it up on the beach, but now the dead grass brought it all back to him in a flash. He was digging a hole in the back corner of the yard, and with the dull orange light of the flash, he peered down to see its bottom. Celine's sea-green eyes stared up at him from the dirt, but she did not see him. Nor did the thin carmine line of her lips betray a word. "Just lie there, like you always do," he'd said as he lifted the shovel again.

Shrugging away the image of dirt scattering across her still face, Aaron focused his hose on the brown patch in his grass.

"You always were a piece of shit, Celine," he whispered. "This just proves it. You don't even make good fertilizer."

He sprayed and sprayed at the spreading evidence of his wife's grave, until the dark cracks in the gray dirt drowned in the glut of water that seeped all the way down to her cheating heart and the dead, burnt grass swam like a hula skirt cast aside to the depths of the ocean.

The Cemetery Man

If a girl ever tells you that she thinks it would be hot to have an intimate date with you in the cemetery, I'd recommend walking steadily away. I didn't.

I wish I would have.

KENDRA JENKINS WAS A QUIET GIRL. The sort of wallflower type that blends into crowds better than blue into gray. But she had this thing about her. Maybe it was the crease in the corner of her eyes. Maybe it was the slight tremor in her voice when she talked; not of fear, but of nervous excitement. Her voice wavered and dove as she'd softly talk about the things that really got her going. I remember meeting her at an adult education class I was taking on film noir appreciation. Her feet would twitch whenever the instructor played a clip of an old black and white movie. Especially at the parts where the film showed a pair of black shoes striking the pavement in an increasing rhythm, as the focal character realized that he or she was being pursued by something in the shadows.

After watching her calves tremble with excitement during one too many Hitchcock films, I had to ask her out one night after class. We had coffee at a little Bohemian place, and I knew she was having difficulty saying the things she wanted to say. Or maybe she just didn't know what to say. Her eyes blinked nervously whenever I looked directly at them. She looked away and played with her hands.

Finally, when the conversation got really awkward, I asked her if she wanted to take a walk. She nodded, and I paid the bill quickly. Minutes later, we were walking down a sheltered street and passing a cemetery. It was an old one, the grounds well sheltered by a forest of trees. Kendra's feet slowed, and I could see the now-familiar signs of excitement in her body.

"Do you want to go in?" I asked.

I FELT REALLY weird about undoing a girl's bra while I had her bent over a gravestone. That said…weirdness didn't stop me. A guy has to have priorities. And tits beat propriety hands-down any day.

Kendra moaned as my fingers fumbled with the clasp across her spine, and when she decided I was taking too long, my hands were suddenly joined by her own fingers and the clasp snapped open. I don't know why they make those damn things so hard to open; it's like they're protecting gold or something…well, on second thought…

My hands slipped under the front of her bra, and, in seconds, she'd shrugged out of it so that two brown nubs begged me for kisses beneath the moonlight. How could I say no? Trust me, I didn't. And Kendra didn't either. For all her shyness and awkwardness earlier, once we were inside the wrought iron gates of the cemetery, she lost all inhibition.

"Did you ever see Jean Rollin's *The Iron Rose*?" she asked me as my lips suckled her ear.

"No," I whispered. "Is it a noir?"

"Not as such," she gasped. My fingers had slipped beneath the belt of her jeans. "Rollin was a French director who experimented in the '70s with a slew of movies mixing eroticism and horror. *The Iron Rose* was about a couple lost in a cemetery. At first, they're playing with the forbidden and making out in a tomb...but then, they get spooked, and they can't find their way out of the graves."

I looked up from sucking myself a good mark of new ownership on her neck and saw the pointed spears of the fence posts just a few rows of graves beyond us. "I don't think we'll have that problem," I suggested. "The gate is just over there."

"Yes," she said. "But what if it wouldn't open when we tried to get out?"

I trailed my tongue across her neck up to the underside of her jaw. "Then we'd climb the fence," I said.

She rolled her eyes. "You have no sense of futility."

"No," I agreed. "Because what I'm doin' right now is definitely not futile." With that I closed my teeth on her left nipple and rolled it around on my tongue and teeth.

She moaned appreciation as my fingers fumbled with the clasp of her belt with just about as much success as I'd had with her bra.

The lights of a car flash across the landscape of the cemetery, and we both pressed ourselves low to the stone until the dark came again. Kendra pushed herself off the flat surface of the broad cemetery stone and pulled me down to the grass before it. "Let's lie with the dead," she said, and then giggled self-consciously.

I couldn't believe this was the same girl who couldn't maintain a steady conversation at the coffee shop just an hour before. When we'd crossed the border into the cemetery at night, she'd seemingly switched personalities. Not that I was complaining.

"I love the dark," she said, as if reading my mind. "That's why I love the old movies so much. They're all about shadows. I'm not real comfortable in the daylight."

"I don't know why," I said, trailing my tongue down from her breasts to circle the thin dark pit of her navel. "You're beautiful."

She snorted. "Uh huh. While the lights are out."

My tongue slipped lower, and she stopped protesting. And then I heard a moan. Normally, that would be something to make a man proud, when his tongue was making her talk...so to speak. But in this case, that moan wasn't coming from the throat just a couple feet above me.

I looked up, and her eyes flickered wide at the same time. "What was that?" I whispered.

She shook her head silently.

I twisted my neck, craning for a glimpse at what had made the noise. All I saw were tombstones. Gray-white stone silhouettes against the black of the sky as far as the eye could see. "I don't see anything," I whispered.

Her hands slipped first down my back, and then up along my spine. I shivered.

Then the moan came again.

I rolled off Kendra and into a crouch. With my shirt off and my pants half down my thighs, I must have looked like an ass. Like some guy crouched down about to take a shit. But I wasn't worried about how I looked. Someone was interrupting my enjoyment of tits, damn it. And it was not making me happy.

"Come on," I said, pointing at a stone crypt not too far away. "Let's get out of the open and away from the road."

Kendra nodded and held her shirt up against her bare chest with one hand as she held my fingers in the other while we sprinted together between the tombstones. When we arrived panting at the crypt, I read the name carved into the stone over the door. Tchichovesky, it said.

"I can't pronounce that," I said.

Kendra snorted. "I think it's Polish," she grinned.

"That doesn't help."

"Try the door," she suggested.

I laughed. "Right, like that's going to be left wide open." I reached out to test the iron grate that locked the Polish dead within this Chicago cemetery and oddly enough, it gave. Unlocked.

"After you," I suggested, when the heavy steel door to the inside of the crypt creaked open.

"Such a gentleman," Kendra said, but she also didn't wait for me.

By the time I'd stepped all the way inside and turned, she'd dropped both her shirt and the rest of her clothes.

"Have you ever wanted to fuck in a tomb?" she asked, as her arms slipped around my waist.

"I gotta be honest..." I started to say. But then her tongue was in my mouth, and there really wasn't much point in trying to finish the thought. I quickly forgot about whatever noises I'd heard outside, because well...there was a naked woman underneath me. And her breasts were...do I really need to explain myself here?

At some point, she rolled me over, straddling me and rocking on my hips like I was some kind of decidedly non-puritanical carnival ride. Carnal ride, is what I was. In the dim light of the moon that lit the mausoleum we were in; I could still read the names of the tombs that were set in the wall behind her. The last name all read Tchichovesky. But there was one, closer to the floor, where the stone marker had been removed, and you could see the glint of a coffin just beyond.

I tried not to look, because seriously, coffins and erections? Guys—trust me on this, they don't generally mix. And I did not want to lose mine at that particular moment.

Nevertheless...when I heard the moan again from just outside the door of the tomb, I pulled out and away from Kendra.

"Something's out there," I whispered.

"So, stick with me here," she said.

My eyes must have bugged out of my head at that, because she laughed. Out loud.

"What's the matter," she whispered. "Am I scaring you?"

I shook my head. "No, the fuckin' noise outside is creeping me out."

She laid back on the cold dusty stone of the crypt and looked up at me with clear intent. The spark from the darks of her eyes still shone in the shadows. She arched her back so that her tits stood up and demanded attention.

"Haven't you always wanted to fuck in a tomb?" she whispered again.

You know...in all honesty, I have to say that my answer to that was a big no. But at that particular moment, the mounds of her breast and the dark shadow of her pussy and the husk of her voice all pretty much cancelled out the fact that we were naked in middle of a house of bones. I found my erection again and briefly forgot the sounds from the graveyard outside.

Everything was great (if a little weird), until the screaming began.

This time when I pulled out, it was over.

"What the fuck was that?" I said. My cock withered wetly between my thighs like a limp weed.

Kendra sat up, hands suddenly eclipsing her chest. "I don't know," she whispered. The sex was out of her voice now. Her hand grasped for her shirt, and, in a flash, that amazing chest was covered in cotton.

Together, we trembled our way to standing and moved toward the door to the crypt. The noise from outside came again.

"Ohhhhowwwwwuhhhhhh!"

I forced myself to be the "man" and poked my head partway through the opening in the door. Just as I did, something cracked like a rifle shot outside.

The moaning stopped instantly.

That's when I saw him. A white face moving slow and deliberate amid the white stones. His eyes were black pocks in a head that seemed to glow on its own in the moonlight. Silver hair and white skin so pale it hurt.

He moved across the graveyard like a wraith himself, but I knew in a heartbeat that he was real, not made of shadow and fear. I knew in that moment this was the man to avoid. If you were in the graveyard and not dead...this was the man who would haunt you.

I did not want to be haunted.

"Get dressed," I hissed, and I could hear Kendra adjusting her clothes behind me as I watched the figure stalk the darkness between the stones. I buckled my own belt and pulled a shirt over my head.

"We need to go," I whispered. "Someone's out there."

'Someone,' was not really what I was thinking. More like...some *thing*. I held a finger to my lips and cautiously stepped out of the door of the crypt and back out and into the night. It's weird how you can "hear" the air move. While we'd been in the tomb, everything had been dead silent (no pun intended, honest). But as soon as we stepped outside, the world felt broader, and I could hear the thin movement of air across the rocks. From somewhere far down the row of headstones, I heard that tortured moan. And then again came a sharp report. It probably sounded louder than it really was, given the lack of any other noise. I thought it was a gunshot.

I took Kendra's hand, and, together, we dashed between the headstones toward the exit. We both hunched halfway over, trying not to be seen by whatever lurked deeper in the grounds. I don't know if it really helped us to be unobtrusive, but it did slow us down. Have you ever tried running and crouching at the same time?

Nevertheless, we skulked our way stone to stone until the exit gate was in sight. I was just starting to breathe a little freer and straighten my running posture a bit, when my foot struck something soft and I stumbled.

Kendra's hand abruptly left mine, and I heard her stifle a shriek.

"What's wrong?" My whisper came out more like a strangled yell. Kendra wasn't looking at me though. Her eyes were locked on the thing that lay on the ground between us.

The thing I'd stumbled over in my stagger to the gate.

The thing whose mouth gaped open beneath a pair of empty black eyes that stared sightless toward the moon.

"Holy shit," I whispered, and knelt on the ground next to her. "I think he's dead."

"Yeah," Kendra said. Her voice was low and soft...but completely lacking in fear.

"That guy must've shot him," I said. I could hear the panic edging into my own voice. "We've gotta get outta here!"

"I don't think so," she said.

"What do you mean, you don't think so? There's a guy walking around here shooting a gun, and there's a dead guy right in front of you. I can put two and two together, and I don't think we should be here right now."

"I meant, I don't think that other guy is what killed him," Kendra said. "Look at his face. Closely."

I leaned closer and shifted to stop my shadow from blotting out the moonlight. The guy looked...old. His face was dirty white and covered with creases and scars. His hair was greasy and unkempt; at a quick glance, he appeared (and smelled) like a street bum who'd been lying here for the day. Or the week.

But Kendra was right. It was more than that. His skin wasn't just dirty and creased...it was discolored. The skin appeared to be flaking off like dandruff. His teeth were yellowed and cracked. The closer I looked, the less human the dead man appeared.

"Look at his hands." She nodded at the arm closest to me.

I followed her gaze and saw fingers gnarled like claws, blackened nails grown long enough to warp and twist. Tufts of hair curled out from below his knuckles. All I could think of was an article I'd read once that debunked the myth that when you're dead, your nails and hair keep growing, feeding off your rotting flesh...

"OK," I agreed, "He looks creepy as hell. But I still think the guy with the gun killed him."

I pointed at the blackened hole in the corpse's chest. You could see bone beneath the ragged opening in his tattered shirt.

"See any blood?" Kendra asked simply. I opened my mouth to argue—maybe to suggest the lack of splatter was due to cauterization?—but from somewhere not too far behind us, I heard another moan.

"Let's go," I demanded, grabbing her hand. "Now."

I pulled her to her feet, and, together, we ran the last few yards to the cemetery gate. We rounded the corner of the gate, and, when I looked back, I swear I saw the pearly white head of the guy I'd seen from the door of the tomb stalking toward the gravesite we'd just vacated. Was he coming back to get rid of the evidence, or was he coming for us? I didn't want to stick around to find out. I forced Kendra to run for the next five blocks until the cemetery was completely out of sight.

"Are you scared of a dead body?" she asked when we finally came to a halt, and I leaned down to clutch my knees as I gasped for breath. Kendra, interestingly enough, barely seemed to have broken a sweat. I made a silent vow to start working out again. Clearly, I was in piss-poor shape.

"No," I wheezed. "I'm scared of *becoming* a dead body. And sticking around the cemetery when some guy's walking around shooting people seems like a good way to become one."

"I'm not sure I want a guy who's that easily freaked to walk me home," she said. I turned to look at her in surprise and saw her eyes staring hard at me, unblinking. She was hungry for something and completely unshaken by what had just happened.

"Oh, am I walking you home?" I asked.

She shrugged nonchalantly and began to walk ahead of me. Gunfire, a stalking killer, dead rotting corpses...they all disappeared from importance as I remembered the feel of her breast in my hand.

"Which way do you live?" I asked, as I hurried to walk by her side.

KENDRA LIVED JUST a few blocks from the cemetery, in an old brick apartment building that had not seen a facelift since the '70s. The hallway inside was paved in tight weave orange and gold carpet, and the stairway rails were painted utility green. But the feel of the building instantly changed when we stepped through the door of Kendra's apartment.

"Welcome to squalor," she said, as she flipped on the living room light.

It was hardly that. It was more like a museum of light and dark. Kendra had covered most of the apartment's bland beige carpeting with long black and gray carpet overlays. The passionless walls were nearly obscured by the array of poster-sized frames. Her apartment was a mosaic of black and white photography. Some of it was instantly recognizable. She had displayed movie stills from classic noir films like the haunting *Laura*, and the gleefully twisted gaze of Robert Walker as he outlines a murder in *Strangers on a Train*. There were several Hitchcock stills actually, including one provocatively deadly image from Janet Leigh's fateful shower in *Psycho*. And even without any actor's faces in the frame, I instantly recognized the opening running feet and trench coat from *Kiss Me Deadly*.

She saw me eyeing the art and smiled. "I like noir," she said. "A lot."

I nodded. "I see that. Gives the place color," I joked.

She raised an eyebrow, but didn't laugh.

"Do you want a drink?" she asked.

"Bourbon on the rocks," I said. "Hold the rocks."

She grinned. "Now you're just fuckin' with me. Although, I have to point out, you forgot to wear your private dick hat. But you know what, I can do that. Are you okay with Knob Creek?"

"It's not my favorite," I said. "But it'll do in a pinch. Just don't call me a dick again."

"Then don't be one."

She disappeared into a galley kitchen and left me alone to explore the two gray couches and four black and white walls of the living room. The place was small, but definitely comfortable. Especially if you loved old movies. I sat down on one of the couches and stared up at the wall, trying to name all the different films the photos and posters came from. They didn't all announce themselves. Her tastes ran deep. As glass clinked on the counter in the kitchen, it occurred to me that Kendra was a ringer in our film class. I'd guess from the look at her walls that she knew more about noir film than our professor.

I don't know when she slipped into her bedroom, but when she came back with my glass of amber "bad judgement" she was wearing a black silk robe. From what its silky thin material revealed, she wasn't wearing anything beneath it.

"Can I buy you a drink?" she asked, feigning a noir bad girl throaty husk.

"I think you already did." I took the glass and tilted it back, enjoying the burn of bourbon in my throat. The faint scent of lavender caught my nose, and I grinned as the liquor threatened to make me cough.

"Drink fast," she advised, plopping down on the couch next to me. I could see the pale curve of her calf as she rubbed it suggestively against my own.

"Why?"

"Because we got naked a little while ago in a cemetery," she said. Her voice was a rough whisper. "And that just makes me hotter than hell."

"You don't care that we also saw a dead guy?" I asked.

She took my left hand in her own and slipped it beneath her robe to a place both prickly and warmly wet.

"Clearly not," I answered my own question.

It was the first time I ever fucked someone beneath the leers of both Janet Leigh and Lana Turner, I have to say that. And probably the most energetic exercise I've ever had as well.

Let's just say when I woke up the next morning, things hurt that I didn't know I had. And that's probably enough said about that.

I WATCHED the local paper the next couple days, looking for news of a corpse discovered in the cemetery. Which, as I write this, sounds like a stupid thing. What else would you find in a cemetery but a corpse?

Still, usually the stiffs are buried behind those iron gates, not lying around on the grass.

No "murder in the graveyard" stories appeared.

Kendra didn't seem interested in talking about the dead guy, but she lit up every time I mentioned the cemetery. It seemed to be about the only thing that could get her to talk, though. She turned out to be something of a cemetery buff and had pictures from all sorts of famous cemeteries around the country. Green-Wood Cemetery in New York. Resurrection Cemetery in Chicago. St. Louis Cemetery in New Orleans and a hundred less famous places in between...Wherever she travelled, she said she always found the local burial grounds. She was one of those people who took gravestone etchings, so it made a lot more sense to me how hot making out on a gravestone had been for her.

We went out a few times over the next couple weeks, but none of our dates were quite like the first. That shy girl came back for long, uncomfortable stretches. Frequently, she'd look distracted and stare over my shoulder when we were having a conversation. Or, more like, I was having a conversation. She really wasn't saying much.

I was starting to think that maybe this wasn't going to go anywhere. We hadn't gone back to bed since that first, bizarre date. Maybe that had been "heat of the moment" for her, and she really wasn't that interested in me. I wasn't sure what to make of it.

Then one week in class, we watched the classic 1949 noir film *The Third Man*. I was sitting behind her since I got to class late. When the nighttime gravedigging scene began, her calves started rocking. She was wearing a summer skirt, and I grinned as I watched the hem shifting and shivering back and forth around her anxious legs. I swear I think she wanted to take one of the shovels and dig up a coffin herself.

After class, I asked if she wanted to go out for a drink.

She shrugged. "Maybe?" she said. "I've got some stuff I need to get done tonight, though."

I don't know what made me say it...probably her reaction to the graveyard scenes in the film. Grabbing for something to bring her attention back, I blurted, "We could stop at the cemetery afterwards?"

She paused. Her lower lip trembled; not much, just enough to show her thoughts were turning.

"It's a date," she said. "Pick me up in an hour? I need to change."

"Don't go changing..." I said, but she shook her head.

"Don't make me change my mind."

"Got it," I said. "See you at nine-thirty."

WHEN I PRESSED the button to ring her apartment, Kendra didn't buzz me in and invite me up. Instead, her voice came over the tiny intercom speaker. "I'll be right down."

A moment later, I could see the elevator open just beyond the foyer. Kendra appeared, wearing a slinky off-the-shoulder black dress with fringe trailing across the top of her knees. She also wore black fishnet stockings and leather ankle boots. She'd pulled back her hair tight and wore red lipstick. She could have walked out of the movie we'd just watched earlier tonight. I felt like a bum in jeans and a brewery t-shirt.

When she stepped outside, I whistled.

"I believe I'm underdressed," I said.

She smiled but shook her head. "You promised me a cemetery," she said softly. "I just wanted to be ready this time."

I TOOK her to The Penultimate Stop, a late-night bar on the edge of downtown that featured some fine mixology, but also had an impressive couple dozen taps. She ordered a Negroni, while I tried an obscure IPA. We talked a little about *The Third Man*—she was a big Orson Welles fan, but admitted it was the cinematography, not the actor, that really made the film.

When the bartender refilled our drinks, she made a point of saying "that's the last for me." She didn't talk much after that as we drank; her eyes roved the room, "people watching." The Negroni disappeared quickly.

"Care for a walk through the tombstones?" I asked when I noticed there were only cubes of ice left in her glass, and her gaze had stagnated to stare out of the bar window to the dark empty street beyond. Her eyes quickly met mine for the first time in several minutes.

"I thought you'd never ask," she said.

The cemetery was just around the block from The Penultimate Stop. I sometimes wondered if the place had gotten its name because of the graveyard. One last drink before you die? Kendra's step quickened the closer we got to the entrance.

The night was quiet; a faint breeze rippled the hair on the back of my neck as we slipped past the black wrought iron gates and down the main path through the cemetery. Stars pierced the blanket of night above like faint Christmas lights. The moon was only just beginning to rise.

Kendra's hands clenched my arm.

"I'm so glad you're here with me," she said.

I realized it didn't matter that it was *me*—she just needed someone who would humor her gravestone fetish. But still, I was glad to be the guy. Part of me knew she was damp already, just from walking into the place after dark. I intended to make her sopping wet before the night was through.

Her hand moved up and down my arm as we walked down the asphalt path that twisted and wound around the gravestones. At one point, I felt her massage the curve of my butt, and I began to look for a place that we could duck off the path to do what we'd come here for.

"Want to sit down?" I asked, pointing beyond a few rows of grave markers to a small clearing near a tree. There were bushes that hid part of the area from the path, which seemed ideal for what I had in mind.

But Kendra had other thoughts.

"Can we find that crypt we were in last time?"

She gave me one of those looks—you know, the pouty mouth, big dark eyes, "if you really love your baby doll, you'll do this thing for me" look.

"It's over this way," I said, and we began walking toward the older section of the cemetery, where there were larger stones. And eventually, full-fledged small stone houses.

I led her across the grass, winding between the granite stones toward the old gray tomb. There were several in this area, but I recognized the one we'd been in last time. A guy doesn't forget when he makes out in a mausoleum.

Somewhere behind us, a night bird shrieked. At least, I hoped it was a night bird.

"You don't think that guy is wandering around tonight, do you?"

I shook my head instinctively. But then, of course, began to wonder if he was out there somewhere nearby. Maybe shooting someone. Causing distant shrieks that weren't birds at all.

"Let's get out of sight anyway," I said and pulled her to the door.

It opened like the last time, and we stepped into the heavy smell of must. I hated to think of the reason. There were small doors where I knew the coffins of this family lay in state. I turned my back to them and took her in my arms. Kendra's eyes sparkled with excitement. Her tongue moved with urgent excitement against mine. As her hands roamed my back, my own slid down to move up and under her dress. I could feel the silk of her hose and the garters that held them. And I was about to pull her down to the ground when she broke our wet kiss with words I didn't want to hear.

"Can you open one of the crypts so we can see the coffin?"

She was breathing heavy and her eyes looked desperate. I wanted to, but I couldn't say no.

"I'll try," I whispered.

There were six doors in the wall behind me, and I reached down to the lower middle and turned the silver handle.

The small door creaked open.

"Let me see," she whispered. She pushed around my shoulder to peer into the dark opening.

"Can you pull it out?" she asked.

"I don't think that's a good idea," I said.

She rubbed against me, shifting her thighs to scissor my leg. "Please?"

I reached into the darkness until my hands found the cold surface of hard wood.

Going against all my instincts, I grabbed hold of the thing with both hands and pulled. The coffin shifted and moved easily out of the hole. Part of me was disappointed at that; I'd hoped it would stay put.

Kendra gasped audibly when the surface of the coffin came into view. A moment later, her tongue was in my mouth.

Seconds after that, and I was stripping the dress from her shoulders.

As the call of the night birds echoed eerily from outside, I laid Kendra down on the cold marble ground and uncinched her bra.

She didn't wait for me to work on the rest. In seconds, I was shirtless myself and sucking on her chest as her black stockinged feet wrapped around my waist.

I tried to slow us down, but this was going to go fast no matter what. Her wetness coated my skin as I moved from her mouth to her nipples and back again. I slid inside her without a thought.

Something creaked nearby, but I couldn't take my mouth from hers to look. I honestly didn't care at that moment. She was hotter than ever before, her fingers clawing my back, her legs dragging me, locking me deeper.

Without warning, she shifted her weight and rolled, pressing me down to the ground. She was grinning as she began to ride me cowgirl style, black garters easing up and sinuously down against and above my hips.

"Don't pinch," she complained, and I barely heard her.

"I said stop it," she said again.

"I'm not doing anything," I gasped.

Kendra's eyes opened. They stared at me, then at the position of my arms—which made it impossible for me to be the one pinching her.

She looked down at the blackened nail kneading at her soft white skin.

That's when I saw the face *behind* Kendra.

It was a ghastly, pasty face. A mask of frozen skin and blue veins. And a mummified hand reached around her ribs to rub and pinch a nipple.

Outside, something shrieked. This time the sound seemed much closer.

"I don't think we should have touched the coffin," I whispered.

Her eyes grew very wide. To her credit, she didn't scream. Instead, she moved her own hands until they encircled her breasts, and the blackened things that massaged them. And then slowly, carefully, she eased the hands back and away from her.

Then she turned to face the dead man who had taken advantage of her. I thought she'd finally let loose and scream when she took in the hideous visage that had crept out of the coffin to feel her up.

"Not so hard," she said instead.

I couldn't see the corpse's reaction; her body blocked his face from my view. But I could see his gray arms reach around her back, and those dark, wrinkled fingers dig into the skin near the slope of her ass and drag their nails upward.

I heard her moan in excitement instead of fear, and I finally found the courage to sit up.

"Kendra?" I whispered.

I leaned to the side and saw something I hope that someday I'll be able to forget. Though I doubt it.

Kendra had her lips on the pale dark lips of the corpse. And as I realized this, I saw her arms reach around his shriveled back and pull his crypt-cold skin close to hers.

The dead guy made a sound like gravel in a grinder, and suddenly he stood up, and yanked Kendra with him. She squealed with surprise, but didn't escape his grasp as he pulled her into the coffin he'd vacated. Kendra struggled then, a flash of white skin on gray, black garters on purpled veins, their bodies sliding against each other and the silken cushioned sides of the inside of the coffin. And then the dead man reached up and pulled the lid of the coffin shut with a loud slam.

It sounded final.

I leapt up from the floor and grabbed at the lid of the coffin, scrambling to pull it back open so I could get Kendra out.

The lid wouldn't budge.

I strained against it, my fingernails bending with the force, but nothing happened.

"Kendra!" I yelled. I thought there was a thump from inside. But she didn't answer.

"Kendra!"

Shrieks and high-pitched cries came from just outside the crypt now. A minute ago, I would have cowered and stayed inside. But I couldn't anymore. I had to find something or someone to help me open the coffin.

I pushed open the creaking metal door and stepped out into the graveyard. Night covered the ground in a cloak of dark shadow, but the stars gave enough light for the tops of the gravestones to reflect in a blue-white gleam against the night.

Something moved to my right. A flash of white against the shadow.

I turned and saw a woman's face heading right toward me. Her mouth was open in a silent scream. Her arms were raised, reaching out to me as if begging for help.

Behind her, a man gave chase. His arms raised in the air behind her. I saw the barrel of a gun silhouetted for one second against the stars.

"Stop," I cried, and moved to intervene. In a heartbeat, they had passed me by, her feet pounding fast between the stones.

Then there was a sharp pop, I assumed from the gun, and she gave one sharp, pitiful screech, and fell to the ground. The man followed her down, disappearing between the stones.

Without thinking, I ran to where they'd disappeared. But when I arrived, the man was already raising himself up from the ground. The woman—an older, wrinkled thing with a pallid complexion—lay still on the earth. For a moment, I thought she looked like an image from one of Kendra's noir films. Bleached of all color, her cheek a stark contrast to the black ground.

"Why did you have to kill her?" I gasped.

The man shook his head.

I realized in that moment I had seen him before. This was the same man who had stalked the cemetery on the first night Kendra and I had come here. He had deep-set eyes, silver hair, and a hawk nose. We'd dubbed him, The Cemetery Man.

The man shook his head and slid his gun into a holster on his belt.

"I did not kill her," he said simply. "She was already dead."

My confusion must have shown visibly on my face, because he smiled and reached out a hand to touch my shoulder.

I flinched, stepping back.

"I won't hurt you," he said. "I *can't* hurt you."

"You did a pretty good job on her. And I saw one of your other victims here a couple weeks ago."

"I don't hurt anyone," he said. "I'm just the guardian. I put those who should be slumbering back to sleep."

"You killed her," I insisted.

He shook his head and pulled the gun from his belt. Aimed it at me.

"No," I cried, putting my hands out in surrender.

That didn't stop him. The gun exploded at short range and a cold finger drove through my chest.

I knew I was done. He'd fired at close range, and this had to be the last few seconds before my brain registered the fatal hit...

...but I didn't fall over.

"I told you, I can't hurt you," he said. "Because you're alive."

"I don't understand."

The Cemetery Man pointed to the woman on the ground. "She died months ago. But sometimes the dead are restless." He gestured with one hand around the graveyard. "It's my job to send them back to sleep."

I put a hand to my chest, where the bullet from his gun should have lodged. There was no blood.

"This gun is for the already dead," he explained.

I couldn't quite process the fact that this man wandered the night with a gun that "killed" the dead. And so, I moved on. The reason I was out here by myself flashed before my eyes, and I forgot about the dead woman before us.

"I need your help," I said. "I know of someone your bullets can hurt. And I need you to use them. My girlfriend is in danger."

The words *grave danger* actually ran through my head in that second.

"I must put this one back where she belongs," he said.

"There's no time. I need your help now," I insisted.

I could see a spark in the depths of those black eyes, and then he nodded.

"This way," I said, and began to retrace my steps to the crypt. The Cemetery Man made no sound behind me, but when I looked over my shoulder, I confirmed that he followed.

I led the way through the stones and into the small house of death where I'd last seen Kendra. The dark outline of the Cemetery Man waited silent in the doorway, as I reached down to pull open the lid to the coffin that now held Kendra as well as a dead man.

Like before, I couldn't raise the lid.

After watching me struggle for a minute, the Cemetery Man stepped forward and pointed for me to move out of the way. And then, with sure hands, he reached down and grabbed at the lips of the wooden box.

The lid creaked open.

Inside, the mummified remains of a man lay erotically entangled with my girlfriend.

They didn't appear to be moving.

"It's time to return to sleep," the Cemetery Man pronounced.

At his voice, the ashen head of the corpse turned slowly, until its teeth gaped at both of us standing above.

I swear it shook its head in denial before it began to extricate its decaying limbs from the creamy legs of Kendra.

Wasting no time, the Cemetery Man drew the gun from his holster, and with the flick of his finger, fired off a spectral shot.

The dead man's eyes widened, and then he lay back down abruptly, his dirty tangled hair draped across Kendra's naked shoulder.

I reached down and grabbed her by the arm, pulling her away from the corpse.

But she was dead weight.

"Kendra," I whispered, as her head lolled. I had raised her shoulders above the top of the coffin, but she didn't move.

I slipped my arm under hers and propped her up as I pressed my head to her chest, listening for a heartbeat.

There was none.

"She made her choice," the Cemetery Man said. "And now she sleeps with the dead."

"No," I said. "That thing took her...please, you have to do something. Help me. Help *her*."

The Cemetery Man gazed at me, dark hooded eyes like entryways to the place beyond where the gravestones led. The place where Kendra had gone. I felt the truth beaming from them in the dark.

"I can do nothing for her but help her remain asleep," he said. "I must go now and finish my work of the night. I'd suggest you put the coffin back as you found it, and leave her and this place. This is no place for the living."

With that, he disappeared back through the door and into the night.

I was left holding the lifeless body of my girlfriend, her legs still in the coffin tangled with the desiccated legs of a dead man.

What did I do? Drag her out and tell the police that a ghoul had killed her? I could just imagine how that interrogation would go.

After some consideration, I kissed her cheek and laid her back down in the box. It's where she had wanted to go, I realized, after all. I reached behind me and grabbed her boots and dress from the floor, draping them over her naked body.

She looked peaceful and happy there, with her lips facing the wrinkled gray lips of the original occupant. It occurred to me that I'd been cuckolded by a corpse.

I let the lid slam shut and pushed the box back into the chamber. Then I grabbed the silver handle and secured the door.

When I was sure I'd left nothing else around to give evidence of our liaison here, I stepped out into the night and shut the mausoleum door behind me. I walked back to where I'd seen the Cemetery Man kill (okay, put back to sleep) the old woman, but her body was gone. Somewhere in the distance, a night bird cried, and I peered into the shadows, struggling to catch a glimpse of a ghostly white man skulking amid the stones.

"Here I am," a voice said from behind me. I must have jumped a foot in the air.

"You scared me to death," I gasped.

He shook his head. "I don't think so."

"Will she wake up?" I asked.

He shrugged. "It's impossible to say. None of them should wake up, but lately, my nights are busy more and more."

"How long have you been here?"

He shrugged again. "A year? A decade? A century? The nights

bleed into one, and every dawn it all slips away. All I know is that I'll be back again tomorrow to keep them asleep."

"I can't believe she's gone," I whispered. The finality of it all had hit me.

The Cemetery Man nodded. "Life is fleeting. A fickle gust of air that comes and goes without warning."

There was nothing I could say to that.

"Thanks for your help," I said, and extended my hand.

He reached out to take it, and his fingers passed right through mine like a chill breeze.

"Enjoy it while you can," he said.

And like the end of a film reel, his face suddenly dimmed and melted away, leaving behind the background of the starry night sky.

Seastruck

Be careful what you look for... it might find you first.

The hair rose on the back of his neck, and Andy suddenly had that creepy feeling that he was being watched. He did a slow 360-degree turn, staring down the empty, rock-strewn beach, and up the winding path of dozens of crooked stone steps that had led him down from the tiny French village to here. There was nobody around... and no place for anyone to be hiding. The sea moved and moaned ahead of him as a gull screeched somewhere just offshore, long and plaintive. Then again. The bird sounded anxious, but there was no reply. Although the sun still hung strong at the edge of the horizon, the place was grey, foreboding and lonely.

It was a familiar feeling for Andy. He'd been feeling that way since the night he left Cassie lying lifeless beneath the waves near an empty beach in California.

But that was years ago, and he was far from there. *And that hadn't been his fault!* He told himself that same thing every time he thought of her, but it didn't make a difference.

He felt as if he stood at the edge of the world. There was something different about this place; he had walked the beaches north of San Francisco a thousand times, and while it had always felt isolated... he'd never felt this remote.

But he had flown halfway around the world to be here because... well... this was where the map had led him.

He pulled the photocopy of the ancient parchment out of his pants pocket and unfolded it. The edges were so creased the thing was in danger of falling into four separate pieces. Evidence of his attention; he'd stared at it a lot. In his apartment. On the plane across the ocean. In the cab on the way to his hotel.

The map had been very specific. It plotted coordinates using old school sailor methods that, with a little work, Andy had been able to match up with Google maps. The Internet was a wonderful thing. And the old rum-runner captain who'd stuffed that map into a bottle and kept it corked and stowed in his cabin trunk had probably seen a very similar scene when he'd been on this beach a hundred years ago to what Andy was seeing now. The tiny village at the top of the stone steps most likely had fewer people living in it now than then. When he had passed through it to find the steps to the sea, he had barely seen a soul... most of the buildings seem to have fallen into disrepair.

Andy walked down the beach and traversed the arc of a long rocky finger that jutted out into the ocean. While, in the scheme of things, this was a small inlet, it still took him 10 minutes to reach the tip of the finger once he'd rounded the corner.

When he did, Andy stopped and stared out at the ocean. The waves were moving slow and steady. According to the old map, the reason he was here was just beneath his feet. But the white crash of saltwater on the rocks three feet away didn't lend confidence to that. It felt as if this bank was a solid wall of stone and sand leading steadily down to the ocean floor.

Andy set down his backpack, kicked off his sandals and stripped off his shirt.

He wasn't going to wait another minute to find out if the map he had studied – literally for years now – was true.

This was the moment of truth.

Seastruck

As he set his shirt and sandals and pack in a pile, Andy again had the feeling that he was being watched. But when he looked up the hill towards the dying village... he saw nothing but browning grass... and old rocks.

Andy turned and dove into the ocean.

The water was cold... enervating... and quickly dark.

Andy swam down into the surf, struggling to keep from being slammed against the wall or pulled out to sea. The old pirate's map had basically said the thing he was looking for... was here. At the apex of the apex.

He slipped through the waves and a pang of uncertainty overtook him. More than uncertainty... pure, depressive panic.

He had been fingering and dreaming of the treasure at the end of this rainbow for years. All based simply on just a map that he'd found in an old wreck at the bottom of the ocean. A jot from a rum-runner stuffed in a bottle. Who was to say that it hadn't been false from the start? And if not... who was to say anything was left of the treasure stowed at the red X a hundred years ago?

A hard slosh of waves pushed him forward and then sucked him back from the edge of the rocks.... And then Andy saw it.

The dark hole in the rock that said... there was no rock there. It was *too* black.

He struggled to keep his aim, and kicked to move forward. His head slipped through the gap, and he grinned.

The map had not lied. There was a buried passage here, a cave-like opening, meters beneath the waves. Andy kicked to push through. He had a flashlight clipped to his belt for just this reason. The undertow threatened to drag him back, but he pushed forward, grabbing at the slick rocky edge of the wall with his hands. His fingers scraped and slipped.

And then Andy got a push from the current as the water slid back. It allowed him just a small grip on the rocky edge, but it was enough. He pulled himself through.

The world grew strangely silent. Not that he could hear in the water before he'd entered the divide but... still... things seemed to get even more quiet. The rush of the waves behind him was gone... he was hanging in a wall of dark water. It was like floating in limbo; he wasn't moving forward or back. He swept his hands out and pushed ahead.

Andy's head moved past the lip of the entry, and just beyond, he saw the slope of the ground moving up and away. He already felt his breath getting thin and he kicked to launch himself towards what he hoped was an internal opening where there would be a pocket of air above the waterline... otherwise, he had to double back quickly.

Something brushed against his back... something soft and cool. Andy shivered. Probably a fish... or seaweed. His head broke the top of the water, and he inhaled sharply, gasping for air. His eyes couldn't see anything at first, but he could breathe. The air smelled fishy, and stale... but there was air. The cavern vented to somewhere.

But he couldn't see any light indicating where.

Andy swam until his knees cracked the silt. And then he stopped swimming and climbed up on the sloping shore. When he crawled up into the darkness, he took a breath, and closed his eyes. Something brushed against his back again, and Andy jumped. He looked around sharply... but his eyes couldn't make out anything in the blackness. He reached down and felt for the flashlight he'd stashed in his belt on a loop. Found it and flicked it on.

As the room flashed painfully into view, a white explosion on his pupils, he could have sworn he saw a gray form slip off to his right.

Andy flashed the light back and forth, exposing a deep cavern of hanging stuff (seaweed?) and distant walls. He didn't see anything that might have brushed against him.

And then again, at the edge of the cavern... something almost grey... not quite white... something like a flash.

It was gone.

In its wake, Andy spied the wood of ancient chests. Seven of them, lodged against the back rock wall of the deep underground cave.

This was the place. He had really found the end of the rainbow. The X on a pirate's treasure map. How unlikely – and amazing – was that?

Andy crawled over to one – the ceiling was too low to stand – and after setting the flashlight on the ground, put both hands on the edges of the wooden trunk.

Ever since he had found the map while diving off the shore near Gull's Point in the wreck of an old rum runner, Andy had wondered if its description was real… or if it remained still undiscovered.

And now…

He knew the map was true. There were chests from ages ago, still sitting here, in a hidden cave near a tiny shoreline town. But what did the chests actually contain?

He pushed against the lid to try to find out.

The wood creaked, and he strained to break the seal of decades of salt and warping and decay. Andy swore as his hands slipped up the side of the wood, and a sharp pain jabbed his palm. Splinter. He held his hand in the middle of the light and could see the dark spot in the skin of his hand. He grimaced as he pried it out with two fingernails.

"Damn it," he murmured again. The hand stung.

The light of the flash lying on the ground next to the chest was faint, but he could see the lid clear enough to know that it hadn't budged. Andy picked up a rock lying nearby and took aim. He slammed the rock against the corner of the chest. His shoulder stung with the impact; the chest was solid. He put his hands on the corners and shoved upward again, and this time, there was a sharp squeal as the lid lifted; the rock had loosened the seal.

Andy grinned as the heavy top rose. But as his eyes rose with the old wood, he saw that there were two legs on the other side of the chest. And attached to those was the pale V of a female crotch. And the fish-white pucker of a bellybutton. And above that a pair of small but clearly feminine breasts, tipped by dark, coin-sized nipples. And above that…

A face that made Andy gasp.

She was beautiful.

Her eyes were a piercing sea-green; her mouth small, lips a cupid's bow of bee-stung pink. Her nose rose thin and proud; her cheekbones high. Ringlets of glossy black hair swooped across her cheeks and down her shoulders.

Andy fell back from the chest to land on his butt. His heart was pounding a hundred beats a minute from shock at seeing her... and from excitement at seeing her.

But who was she?

Before he could ask, she cocked her head, opened her mouth and let out a high ululating scream. Andy put his hands to his ears as the sound pierced his head; there was a pain in the back of his eyes, but then it faded, and instead of pain, he suddenly yearned for the sound. It wasn't a scream at all, he realized. It was a song. A high-pitched trembling note of sadness that began to change as she moved. His hands dropped from his ears and he stared at the beautiful naked woman in front of him. She stepped around the chest to stand over him, as he still sat clumsily on the damp stone. Her mouth remained open now in a perfect O, as she sang in a weird operatic soprano. The notes shivered and shifted, sounding both exotic and ancient, moving down a scale as their effect moved down his spine. He could feel his body relaxing, his groin warming. She pushed against his chest with two hands and somehow suddenly she was straddling him, her mouth inches from his own as she ran gentle fingers across his cheeks and neck. Her nails were long and dangerous. Her eyes looked into his, and he felt pinned; a butterfly on a board.

She sang a strange, entrancing melody that had no words.

He could do nothing but listen.

Andy looked into her eyes and saw the flecks of brown and amber that shifted as her pupils grew wider. He was drawn into her gaze and as she sang he saw nothing but green... her eyes were inches from his; somehow she had laid him down and he couldn't remember his head touching the stone but he didn't really care; her lips were centimeters from his own and her breath blew across his mouth as she still sang to him, a sensual, ululating melody that played him like a harp; each note touched a nerve of pleasure; his body moved of its own accord now, he had no will, his waist shifting with her song. He thought he saw her lips curl upwards in a smile, but that couldn't have been right because her mouth was open and her song did not stop, she never took a breath, she just kept singing and her eyes kept staring and...

Andy was naked and engulfed by a strange naked woman in a foreign cavern and that thought came and went as quickly as his own orgasm; he wanted to ask her for her name but then everything was black...

THE SKY here was full of stars. So many stars you could drown in their light. Endless constellations of faint and brilliant light. A myriad milky way of endless eloquent glamour. Glimmer. Grandeur...

Andy realized that he was lying on a beach and mentally babbling.

He sat up with a start.

Why was he lying on a beach in the middle of the night staring at the stars?

And... he realized with the heavy movement of his erection as he shifted... why was he naked?

It came back to him with a flash; the swim to the hidden cavern, the trunks of treasure, the naked woman who had never said a word to him yet somehow had stripped and taken him.

Holy shit.

But how had he ended up back here and where were... He stopped asking the question as he turned and saw the dark outline of his swimsuit crumpled next to his waist. Andy shook his head and yanked one leg hole over his foot. It was almost painful to pull the waistband over his manhood... which remained throbbingly, painfully erect.

"What the fuck happened tonight," he whispered, as he began to walk, a little unsteadily, back up the beach towards the faint lights of the town above.

ROLLIN-DE-CALLAIS WAS A DEAD TOWN. When Andy woke up the next morning, and walked through the empty lobby of his hotel, he realized that while there were a lot of buildings, nobody really lived here. There had been an old stone sign upon entering the town. And a long row of buildings, classic, long-standing stone structures that had clearly been constructed long before Andy's great-great-grandparents had been conceived. The buildings were hundreds of years old, and there was a hotel and nearby bar... but really, when you began walking around... it was quickly evident that there were very few structures that were actually occupied. Most had glass that was not only spider-webbed with cracks but frosted brown with the age of disuse.

Andy left his hotel and walked a few blocks, noting that all of the facades seemed well-aged. More than "well." Cracked stone. Dirty, spider-webbed windows. Closed doors. The place was a museum of dust and age. As he walked down one block, Andy wondered if anyone had been there in months. Maybe years.

It was depressing.

Eventually he found a block where there was a fruit market, and another hotel, and a café that was serving breakfast. He found a table and sat down, ordering a coffee and some eggs from a dour-looking old waitress who may or may not have spoken English. He honestly wasn't sure if they'd communicated or not when she nodded and walked away from the table.

But she did come back with a steaming cup of something black... so he had hopes for his plate.

It had scrambled eggs, and a biscuit... and a brown, dried out thing that could perhaps be called bacon. He chewed it and determined that no bacon had ever tasted so poorly. It was burnt and crusty.

He drank his tiny bitter cup of coffee and stared at the pictures on the brick walls. Black and white stills of people who he did not recognize, and brands of food (or beer) that he had never tasted.

There was only one other patron at the place, at a table in the corner near a window. Andy stole the occasional glance in her direction, but she did not appear to share his curiosity. He worked on his breakfast in silence, and then, when the sullen waitress took his credit card for the bill, he finished his last bitter, salty bites of food, and then left the depressing restaurant to walk around the rest of the seaport town.

Andy wandered the next few blocks, where the town still seemed to have some life. A small news and sundries stand seemed to still be open, along with another small restaurant. There was a tiny grocery (which appeared to pull in no patrons at 9 a.m. in the morning), and a fish market, where an old Chinese man was still stocking the tray with fresh caught. It was early... and eerily still.

But the quiet was not the sleepiness of a town just before waking up. It was the silence of an abandoned place. The silence of loss.

Andy passed the tiny fish market and a small café, and then walked another three blocks past shuttered buildings before finding a corner with another open door; a small tavern called The Gentil which advertised "rooms available" on a small placard sign above the tall wooden doors. He looked down the street that ran along the edge of the cliff that led down to the ocean... and didn't see any other buildings that appeared occupied. Everything appeared grey and eaten by the salt and wind. The wood facades showed wide dark cracks; the windows were boarded and broken.

He looked over the edge of the cliff to the ocean, which surged grey and green against the shore below. It looked like a long fall down. The wind gusted against his chest and he rocked with the force for a second before stepping back. If he fell, he suspected nobody would find him before the birds or crabs picked his bones completely clean below.

Andy turned away from the ocean and walked back towards The Gentil behind him. He was curious about the place. It was like a last outpost before the wastelands. And when he walked inside... it was a different world. The air smelled warm, full of smoke and onion. The bar was long; heavy, dark wood stretched down one wall and angled 90 degrees to jut against the other. Two golden taps stretched up from the center of the bar, and behind it, the wall was covered in mirrors and glass shelves; Andy could make out a long collection of bottles of scotch – McCallan and Old Pulteney 21 years – on the second shelf, most of them dusty with age.

"How kin I help ya?" an old man's voice came from the back of the room. Andy walked deeper into the room and saw the man finally, far to the right, sitting on low wooden chair just behind the edge of the bar. The man was portly and old; his head was nearly bald, but there were long tufts of white at his ears, and a strap from his glasses that hung behind his ears.

"Just looking around," Andy said.

"Where ya from?"

"San Francisco," he answered. "Just got in last night."

The old man nodded. And raised a thick-tufted eyebrow. "And what in the serpent's name would make ya come to these parts from there?"

Andy shrugged. "A death wish?"

The old man stifled a grin and nodded.

"Might have some truth to your mouth there."

Andy walked across the creaking planks to rest an elbow on the bar. "What happened to everyone here?" he said. "It looks like the whole town closed up shop and walked away."

"They didn't walk away," the man said. "They swam."

"Did the fishing dry up here?"

The man shook his head. "The fish are just fine. It's about the other things that swim in those waters."

"What do you mean?"

The old man shrugged. "The ocean giveth, and the ocean taketh away. Some of us leave… and some of us have stayed."

Andy stepped closer to the man. "How long have you lived here?"

"All me life," the man said. "It's where I was born. But that don't make it a place that's safe. That don't make it a place where people can survive and thrive. Take a look outside, and you'll see what I mean there."

"That's my point," Andy said.

The man put a hand on the edge of the bar and pulled himself upright, with a grunt and a moan.

"I will tell you this," he said. "The faster you get out of this town, the longer you'll see the sunset."

With that, the man turned his back and hobbled to a doorway behind the desk. He disappeared through it and never looked back, leaving Andy in an empty lobby.

"Well," he said aloud. "I guess it's a good thing I don't need a room here. He should be in sales."

Andy looked around the old room and shrugged. Then he pushed open the door and stepped back out onto the street.

He'd learned nothing. Apparently, he had been dismissed.

Andy shrugged, and walked back to his own hotel as he considered. He was here to swim to the pirate's hidden chests. He wasn't going to accomplish that by diving into the waters that other people told him not to.

He walked back through the mostly mothballed town and decided to change clothes and head back to the cave he had been in yesterday. When he walked into the lobby of his small hotel, he heard a couple speaking vehemently in French in the sitting room... and an old man demanding something at the front desk in German. To him, it felt as if the town had decided that the tourist was gone, and the real people had taken over again. And the real people didn't speak English.

He walked past them all and walked up the creaky back stairs to change and get the things he needed from his room. After the previous night, he thought what he really needed was a pepper spray that worked underwater. A woman had stopped him from getting what he'd come for yesterday, and while the flashes of memory he had of the event made him feel both warm with excitement and queasy with guilt, he didn't need her to get in his way again. This had been an expensive journey... and he needed to walk away with something to show for it.

Andy walked down the creaky back wooden stairs with a backpack on his shoulder that he hoped to fill with some shiny things from an old, abandoned pirate's chest. But first he had to swim there again... and after yesterday, it was not looking like he could bet on being there alone.

Andy stripped down to his trunks on the beach and dropped his clothes next to the grey and listing lifeguard station that remained (and appeared to have been long relegated to abandoned status). He pulled the straps of the backpack onto his bare shoulders and walked down the cool sand and into the breaking waves.

He hoped that in the middle of the day that he wouldn't run into whatever force he had yesterday. With a deep breath and a leap, he was heading down into the shadow of the waves.

THE DARK SPOT in the wall underwater was easy to find after yesterday... it came up quickly as he swam along the rocky finger in the water and Andy pulled himself up and through it. When he stepped onto the dry area above the water level, Andy's heart began to beat double time. What if the woman who'd found him yesterday was still here?

The best thing he could do would be to work fast.

Andy flipped on the waterproof flashlight that he'd packed and looked around the cavern. He quickly found the chests he'd seen the day before. He shone the light all around the underwater cavern, but other than grey walls, there was nothing to be seen. It was silent here, and dark.

Andy held the backpack open next to one of the chests and began to move the gold chains and coins from the treasure chest into his own holder. The pirate's chest didn't need these things anymore. It wouldn't care if he divested them. He worked fast. But tried in vain to do it quietly. With every clink of metal on coin, Andy shivered. And looked around. He saw nothing moving in the shadows, but he felt as if a hundred eyes were watching him. He was a beacon in the middle of the dark.

The backpack filled slowly, and Andy lifted it several times to make sure it hadn't grown too heavy. It would be just his luck to strap it on his back and end up sinking to the bottom of the ocean and drowning because he couldn't carry it and couldn't get it off his shoulders.

He hefted it when it was about three-quarters full and decided that that was the limit. Then he swung it onto his back and stood. Holding the flashlight out in front of him, Andy started walking deeper into the cavern. He knew the safest course of action would be to dive back down the hole that he came in through... but he was curious. Where did this cavern lead... was there anything else to see?

The floor was grey and glossy when he shone the flash across it. The walls around him looked the same and grew narrower the farther he walked from the entrance. Andy stepped carefully across the damp surface, and after just a few yards the room narrowed to a small corridor. He held the flash ahead of him and looked at the space beyond. The corridor narrowed, but on the other side, he could see that it opened out again into a wide space. And in that space... there were things that should not have been there. Things that would not normally being in a cave that was only accessible from a doorway beneath the mark of low tide.

The flash moved across a latticework of wooden walls and something that looked, from a distance, like rumpled blankets. Andy took a breath. He knew now that the woman who'd pressed him to the ground (now there was a euphemism) wasn't just someone else who had happened on the cave at the same time he had. People *lived* down here.

A chill went down his back when he realized that the booty in his backpack was not just lost goods. If people lived down here, then the chests were not abandoned. And that made him a thief, not a scavenger.

Andy stepped back from the corridor and moved the flash back from chest-high to focus on the floor. He was not putting the stuff back. He'd waited years and flown halfway around the world to find it. So, he could not be found here.

Something slapped, wetly, on the floor somewhere nearby. He didn't wait to see what it was. Andy ran to the small open pool that led back out to the ocean. He jumped in feet-first, and as his head slipped below the surface, he thought he saw something move in the cavern he'd left behind. It could have been the shifting shadows, but to him it looked like the shifting curls of a woman's hair.

Whatever it was, it vanished a second later as his face slid beneath the steadily churning saltwater.

He panicked at first, as the water sucked him and the backpack down; he didn't float in the waves, he sank ... like a stone.

He imagined arms parting the water behind him, following him down into the blue. The thought propelled him to action; he kicked hard and cupped his hands and swiped them to his side. A moment later, Andy stopped sinking and instead began moving slowly away from the rock ledge and towards the shore. Every feathery touch of seaweed fronds on his feet made his heart jitter.

But he walked out of the surf unchallenged. One large heavy backpack dripped water slowly but steadily down his back as he began the walk back up the sand and stairs to return to the town above. Or what was left of it.

Every few steps he turned his head and looked behind. But all he saw was the empty, untenanted sand of a lonely beach. No angry seawomen were chasing him down. He was alone on an empty beach.

Andy left it behind as fast as humanly possible.

The dining room of the inn was all but empty that evening, and Andy ate a bowl of soup and homemade bread alone in the back corner of the room. A fireplace blazed on one wall, throwing flickers of uncertain light against the wall of trophies. Large, glossy-scaled sharks and other large fish were mounted across the room. Their eyes seemed to stare and watch the room with the shifting of the light. A shiver ran down Andy's spine as the open eyes of the four-foot long, blue-gilled monster nearest to him seemed to swivel and stare straight at him.

He looked away, refusing to hold eye contact with the dead. Instead, he downed the last remnants of the bland but filling stew of beef, potato and leeks in a brown gravy, and then emptied the flagon of lager the waitress had offered.

Waitress was probably a misnomer – she was likely the owner or wife of the owner, he thought. She had checked him in yesterday and was the sole person moving in and out of the kitchen. For all he knew she had cooked this dinner as well.

An older couple sat in the other corner of the room talking in whispers. Every now and then he caught one of them staring directly at him. They quickly looked away when he met their gaze. Between them and the fish... and the guilt of having a backpack full of treasure sitting unguarded upstairs, Andy decided not to stay for another lager. He put two foreign bills into the holder and pocketed a receipt. Then he pushed back his chair and went upstairs.

There was nothing to do here but turn out the lights and go to sleep – the room had no television and was just a long and narrow space carved into the attic. The ceiling slanted down nearly to the floor on the side where his bed was shoved up against it, a tiny window broke the darkness of the night just to the other side of his headboard.

Sleep came quickly in the tiny room. But it was a troubled sleep.

Andy dreamed of that night so long ago; sex on the beach with Cassie, rough sex. And the darkness that spread out across the sand beneath her head when he realized too late what he'd accidentally done. She had brought him out to that empty stretch of beach to help her cast a sex magic spell... and her implements of magic or voodoo or whatever you wanted to call them – candles and stones and a book of spells – he'd left them buried in the sand when he'd walked her body to the edge of the California precipice and dumped it into the black waves. It was a memory he'd dreamed and relived a thousand times, only this time, as her limp body splashed into the ocean below, he suddenly felt himself pulled along. He was yanked off the cliff and sailed down the rocky bank behind her, splashing into the whitecaps just behind her feet. He could taste the salt on his lips and the burn in his eyes as he opened them to see her floating just below, a naked white cruciform, arms spreadeagle, hands reaching out, it seemed, to touch the bottom of the sea.

Reaching out to touch skeletal fingers outstretched from the ocean floor.

ANDY WOKE WITH A JOLT, his heart pounding.

His forehead felt wet, and cold.

He had come halfway across the world, but he would never escape the horror of that terrible, deadly night. The guilt weighed on him like an anchor. And right now, that anchor was making him feel suffocated. He wiped the water off his face; it covered his hand and he wiped it clean on the bed. Too much. He couldn't have sweated so much. Crazy. He wiped it again and felt how damp his hair was. Andy sat up, threw the covers off and stepped out of bed.

He stepped across the room to reach the lamp on a small table just beyond the window. His right foot stepped in something cold.

Something wet?

The light clicked on, and he looked at the narrow passage that led from the bed to the hallway door just 12 or 15 feet away.

There were footprints in his room.

Wet footprints on the old wooden planks. They led to… and away… from his bed.

"What the fuck," Andy breathed.

He sat down on the bed for a moment, gaping at the evidence. Someone had been staring at him sleeping. The footprints near the bed didn't even look like prints… they were small pools, the water there had dripped and spread, while someone stood there, staring. The prints nearest the door had nearly evaporated.

Who had watched him sleep?

He knew without question.

The woman from the cave. Probably here for his gold. Her gold. His heart leapt and he jumped up and went to the backpack, still wet from the ocean. He'd set it on a towel in the corner. But his panic was unfounded. It remained undisturbed.

Andy pulled on a shirt and some jeans, and stepped out of his room to the hallway. The faint, drying prints continued out there and led down the stairs to the open room of the main floor. They were harder to see now, but he followed them almost to the front door before they disappeared.

"Something you need?" a gruff voice said from behind.

Andy jumped, but it was only the innkeeper woman. She stood like a tank in the center of the room, her hair in a net, her nightgown covered in a thick blue robe.

"Someone was in my room."

"What do you mean?"

He pointed at the faint smudges of wetness that led up the stairs.

There were footprints in my room," he said. "Wet footprints that come all the way down here."

The old woman's eyes widened. "*Sirena*," she hissed. "What have you done?"

"What do you mean?" he asked.

"How dare you lead them to this house. In the morning, you will be gone."

"But…"

"In the meantime, lock your door," she said. And with that, she disappeared back down a dark hall behind the innkeeper's reception desk.

He looked once more at the steps that led to the front entry of the inn and saw something glimmering in the light from the one orange lamp that remained lit on a table near the front window. Andy walked over to see what it was and knew before he reached it that the woman had left it for him to find. He picked it off the floor and pocketed it after turning the wet coin over and over in his hand. A piece of the treasure.

Andy opened the door and stepped out of the inn onto the stone steps. Before the door closed behind him, he caught the glimmer of another coin, just a few steps from the door. He bent over and picked it up with a frown. Was this what he thought it was?

The harsh light of the moon grew stronger as he stood there, contemplating. A cloud slipped to the horizon and he could see now almost as clearly as in daylight. The grass sparkled with early dew, and the walkway was too damp to see any individual footsteps. But he did see another coin just a few steps away. He picked it up, and continued to play the game, walking along the path. He had a feeling he knew where she was trying to lead him. When he reached the steps down to the beach, he hesitated.

But then he heard a voice from below. A beautiful, unnerving, nakedly sensual voice. A woman had begun to sing. High and tremulous notes that seemed comprised not so much of lyrics, as emotions. With every lilt of melody, his heart seemed to pump harder, and his legs moved forward almost of their own accord. Absently he shifted his pants and realized that he had an erection.

Andy put one hand on the rail to start down the stairs to the beach, following the voice. But then something smacked him against the leg.

"Ouch!" he cried out. Another one hit him in the chest.

"What the hell?"

The pain broke his attention from the song for a second, and then he saw the innkeeper standing just a few feet away, gesticulating wildly to him. She'd thrown rocks!

"What the hell?" he said.

"Get back to your bed now or you will never sleep on land again," she yelled, and then turned and ran back to the inn.

Andy realized that his legs had completely answered the call of the song, and for the moment, the old woman had broken the spell. A violent tremor overtook his legs; for a few moments, he had completely lost control. Andy turned and staggered after the innkeeper. He felt sick... and drawn to the song that continued to echo from the beach below. He covered his ears and screamed, refusing to allow his mind to hear the beautiful melody. He vaulted up the steps to the inn, pushed his way through the door and then slammed it shut, holding both palms against the wood as if he was holding back a force pressing on the other side trying to get in.

When he finally turned around, the innkeeper stood near the front desk, holding a crucifix aimed in his direction. "What did you *do*?" she hissed. "Why have the *Sirena* come to my house?"

She shook her head. "Don't tell me, they will want my soul as much as yours. They have taken too many here already. I should throw you out into the night right this moment. But I am not so cruel. At the dawn..."

She let the phrase dangle and shook her head at him, as if he were a son who'd proven a huge disappointment to her. And then she disappeared, presumably back to her bedroom.

Andy didn't sleep well. His dreams were plagued with a woman who smiled at him and sang – a beautiful, horrible, entrancing song. When the sun began to lighten the old orange and yellow threaded comforter on his bed, he rose and packed up his few belongings, slung the backpack over his shoulder, and walked out into the hall.

There was a faint murmur of talk coming from the great room below, and he leaned over the rail to look down. The innkeeper was pouring a small cup of coffee (he hated the coffee cups here, they were *all* small!) for two older men who sat in dark coats. Seamen, by the look of them, ready for any weather, though it was supposed to be a nice day today.

As Andy began to descend the stairs, the chatter stopped. He had the unnerving sensation of three sets of eyes following his feet on the steps. When he reached the bottom, one of the older men cleared his throat, and whispered something to the other. The innkeeper walked to the desk and waited for him.

Andy walked over and pulled out his billfold to pay for the two nights he had stayed. She told him the amount, with no preamble or apology for kicking him out, and a moment later he was signing a receipt.

As he pocketed his copy and began to walk towards the front door, one of the men called out to him.

"She'll never stop, you know. She'll follow you wherever you go."

Andy looked at the man. He looked like the sort who'd been on a fishing boat since he was seven years old. Now he was probably 50 or 60, his hair a tangle of grey waves and his eyebrows just tufts of salt and pepper fuzz.

"I live on the other side of the world," Andy said. "I don't think she'll swim across the ocean."

"Don't be so sure," came the response.

Andy shrugged and stepped out of the door.

As the door closed behind him, and he took a deep breath of the salty mist of morning, Andy realized that he didn't have a plan. He should probably have called for a cab from the inn... but he hadn't really intended to be leaving town immediately.

Andy walked away from the inn on the lonely road into the center of town. There were precious few businesses that still were *in* business here, as he'd already noted, but none of them were open now. It was too early. He wandered for a bit, and then made his way to the road that bordered the descent to the beach. The water looked grey and cold this morning, the sky still overcast as the sun burned sullenly orange on the horizon.

Was there really such a thing as a siren? He wondered. He hadn't truly believed in the sex magic that Cassie had tried to craft with him as her "donor" a decade ago, and he didn't really believe superstitions about sexy, toothy women who lured men to their deaths on the rocks of the shore. But he *had* met a strange, silent woman in an underground cave who'd left him confused and breathless and wondering if it had all been a hallucination.

And he had been drawn like a puppet to the sounds of a woman's voice just a few hours ago. Was that proof of a siren? Or proof that he was still suffering from jet lag? He had to admit the events of the night before had left him spooked. The wet footprints next to his bed even more than the intoxicating lure of the song that had caught him in its hook. Andy walked down the broken steps that led in a winding path down the hillside to the beach. The scent of the sea was strong as he stepped over froth-covered brown fronds of broken seaweed until he stood on hard packed sand, still wet from the last large wave.

He looked out along the promontory that extended into the grey-blue expanse of water. Did Sirens live there, tucked out-of-sight below the waterline? Or, more likely, a band of gypsy squatters?

The beach gave no answers.

Part of him longed to swim back out there with his backpack and unload the treasure to return it to where he'd found it. Then he could at least alleviate himself of that guilt. If the gold belonged to that woman, who was he to fly across the world, walk into her home, and steal it from her?

On the other hand...

Andy shook his head. He would not give up what he'd come so far to find. Tonight, he'd sleep miles from here, and tomorrow he'd be in a plane flying halfway around the world. The gold was now his. Simple as that.

He turned away from the endless horizon to walk back up the stairs and out of this forsaken town.

And found that he was no longer alone.

A woman stood on the first step leading up, blocking his way.

A woman with long, kinked black hair, and startling eyes.

A familiar, naked woman.

Andy averted his eyes in embarrassment for a moment but then looked back at her once more. He was not spying; she blocked his way.

It was the woman who had seduced him in the underwater cave. He would not fall for that again. Andy began to walk towards her. She remained stationary, a perfect carving of flesh and beauty. A signpost between the strange world of the sea, and the human world above. A tollkeeper? He had a feeling he knew what she wanted. It was in his backpack.

Andy drew closer, and as he did, he felt his heart pump faster. She was beautiful. And dangerous. There was something about her stance that told him she was no frail flower. She may have been naked, but she was not helpless.

"Hi," he said, when he was just a few steps away. "I was just leaving."

She shook her head at that, very slowly. And then opened her mouth to let loose a piercing cry. No, not a cry, a song. That initial note drew his attention and then turned into a quivering, baleful note that shifted and dove, changing emotions and pitches without notice. Andy felt his bones weighed by sadness and then buoyed by joy. Erotic longing, and then desperation. He realized as she stepped towards him, still singing, that he could not move.

Literally could not move. His legs were locked, his fingers frozen.

She slipped her arms around his shoulders, and he felt the hard points of her nipples press against his t-shirt as she drew him close, all the while, still singing. The sky behind her grew faint and his vision blurred. All he could focus on were her eyes… sea-green and hungry, staring deeply into his own as her voice drew him into her.

Then her lips met his, and the sound shifted inside him. Andy felt his feet moving; cold slipping up his calves. Part of him wanted to scream, as the chill of water reached his waist, but her eyes held his and the vibration of her song filled his mouth. Then her face pushed his beneath the water, and Andy tried to scream. She only stroked his back and drew him with her through the waves. He closed his eyes to block the salt and found that he couldn't reopen them. And why would he want to? He was held safe in her arms, drew breath from her song, moved forward on her kicks...

ANDY LAY in a bed of moss. He didn't know how long he'd been there and couldn't tell whether it was night or day; there were no windows here, though there was a faint light. The walls held what looked like faint flames; patches of phosphorescent green and orange glowed atop golden torch holders. Sea lights.

Something warm and soft covered him; a blanket of some kind, though not made of cotton. It felt thin as paper but held in his heat. And a good thing, he realized, as he shifted to roll on his side and realized his clothes were gone.

A rustling nearby. Cool thighs slid into the small bed beside his own.

The woman from the beach. She rolled atop him. In the faint light, her cat-green eyes seemed to glow with their own energy. Her heavy lips parted, and with a thin pink tongue, she traced the edges of his lips. He felt himself respond beneath her, and she spread her legs to meet him, shifting slowly, sinuously across his hips until his eyes widened, and her breath hitched. She lowered her sex and her lips onto his simultaneously, drawing him into her from both ends. Andy's eyes almost rolled back in his head as the pleasure of her washed over him, animal-pure and amazing. His tongue wrestled with hers, and then he jumped when he caught his tongue on what felt like a hook. She opened her mouth and he withdrew his tongue, just barely catching a glimpse of the teeth within. They looked too numerous... and shark sharp.

It clicked in his brain then that she truly was not human. Not exactly. But that didn't stop his hips from moving faster to meet her own, or his cry of release when he couldn't hold back anymore and he let go, encouraged by the sharp bleats of her own orgasm. His head rolled back then, and he struggled to catch his breath. His mouth held the faint taste of iron, from his own blood, and his waist felt nearly numb.

Her long nails trailed across his forehead and down his chest, slowly, exploring him without a word. And then she pressed a kiss to his lips and slid away.

Andy felt sated and strange... and slipped easily back into sleep.

The next time he woke, she brought him food; fresh slabs of fish, and green fronds of something he knew grew from the ocean floor. He was tempted to refuse it; but his stomach growled and she pushed a cube of the white meat to his lips, nodding her head. He accepted it finally, and saliva burst throughout his mouth with the first taste. It was rich and creamy and wonderful.

He didn't need her encouragement to finish the rest.

When he was finished, she led him out of the bed to walk around the shadowy expanse of her home. The phosphorescent torches lit their way, as they stepped through a small path between two large boulders and into a larger space which clearly was where she spent most of her "home" time. And clearly, she didn't do it alone. Seated at a long driftwood table were three other women. All of them lithe and attractive. Andy was acutely aware of his nakedness now. But the women were as bare as the siren who'd led him to them.

They spoke to each other in a language he could not fathom; it was high-pitched and fast, and one of them, a pale blond-haired girl with ice blue eyes, looked directly at him at one point and laughed. The girl nodded quickly and laughed again.

"Do you speak any English?" he asked, and the women only looked back and forth at each other blankly. Then they continued to jabber amongst themselves. At one point, one of them walked across the room to an old chest and opened it to rummage around within. She pulled something out and then walked across the room to present it to him.

He took it and marveled at the ancient leather. The front cover read simply, *The Bible*.

He didn't believe in *The Bible* any more than he believed in Sirens, he thought. And then raised an eyebrow at himself given the change in his situation. Perhaps he would have to reconsider *The Bible*.

He shook his head and pushed it back across the table. The woman frowned and then went back to the chest. She pulled out two more books and dropped them on the table in front of him. They were of different vintages, one with a black cover, one of red leather.

The Bible, they both read.

"So that's the way it's going to be, huh?"

He leafed through one for a while, before settling back in his chair to stare up at the dark ceiling of the cave. He didn't know what was expected here, or how long he was to stay. But he was not going to memorize the "good book" as he waited to find out.

Someone had gotten up from across the table.

The blue-eyed girl. She was the tiniest of them all, a thin waif with an almost boyish chest, her small nipples only raised slightly from the plain of her tummy. But she was gorgeous, he thought. Her skin was pale and covered in a faint down, and her smile contagious.

She was smiling at him now.

She drew him to his feet with one slender hand and led him down a different hall then he had entered this room by. They ducked beneath a low ceiling and then they were in a tiny little side cave. It was decorated in pink – pink tapestries and flowers and beads. When she pushed him towards the small cot against the wall, he saw it was draped in pink sheets that clearly were not woven underwater... these had been taken from the mainland. While his captor lived naturally, this Siren was clearly entranced by human things.

And apparently, he was one of the things she was taken with, he thought, as she pressed him to the bed and straddled him without any foreplay.

She drew his hands up to cup her nascent breasts and once again he was ready for a woman's need in a heartbeat. She wasted no time in making use of him, and grinned a sharp-toothed smile when he broke that tight boundary and slid inside her with a wet jab. Her jaw yawned back and then she slammed her chest down against his own, and rolled, drawing him to his side and then pushing him to take her from the top, missionary. Her fingernails dug into his back like tickling knives and he gasped and thrust faster, urged on by her wild desire. It should have been over fast, but she milked him for what seemed like an hour, shifting and turning and scratching him until they both screamed together, her eyes and mouth wide and sexily inhuman.

When they were done, she draped herself over him. Without saying a word, she went to sleep with her head on his chest.

The next time he woke, there were bodies on *either* side of him. Neither appeared to be the women from before. But when the one with long straight black hair saw he was awake, she put her finger to her lips and hissed "shhhhhh," before slipping that same finger between his legs to prod and tease him awake once more. He didn't think he could possibly go again so soon, but this girl teased well, and... bit; his chest was bleeding in three different places when she finally finished grinding herself to happiness.

But she fucked him silently, and when she was done, and he was empty, she put her finger to her lips again, and slipped back out of bed to disappear back out of the hall.

Andy waited a few minutes but the other girl next to him didn't stir. Slowly, he slid a foot out of the low mattress and tiptoed out of the room. He thought he was going in the direction of the main room, but instead he found himself at a set of stairs carved into the stone. Shrugging, he decided to explore, and walked down. The walls provided enough illumination to see a few feet in front of him, but it was the smell that ultimately reached him before the source.

He rounded a corner and found himself in a cave of death.

A literal boneyard.

The air stank of rot and dank fish and decay. Stacked against all the walls were piles of bones. Leg bones, rib cages, hands. Stacked like a tower in the center of it all were a hundred human skulls, all of the eyeholes aimed at the doorway. As if they were watching.

"Oh hell," Andy whispered. Lying near the doorway were four

bodies that were clearly waiting to be disassembled to join the rest. While most of the bones had been picked clean, there was still some yellow fat and red gristle hanging from the joints, and the legs and arms were all still connected to the core. That was what the smell was, he realized. Not-so-old remains.

Andy backed away from the room, his heart pounding.

He had a horrible suspicion that if he didn't find a way out of here, that his recent pleasure would quickly be turning to pain.

"No fuckin' way," he said, and stole back along the corridor, listening carefully to make sure he didn't stumble on one of the Sirens. This was their lair, and he had no idea *where* he really was... but he knew one thing – he was not going to be caught. That said, he probably didn't have much time until someone realized he was missing.

The open room with the driftwood table was still empty when he finally found it, and he stole across the center, back to the hallway where his captor had originally led him in here from. He passed the place where he'd first awoken in her bed and moved fast down a corridor that he hoped led back to the outer room where he'd originally found the gold. He couldn't afford to be cornered now.

The corridor opened out on a familiar space. Andy smiled. Home stretch. He'd found it easily.

The chests were just across the room. And so were his backpack and clothes. He ran to them, and pulled his cold, soggy jeans over his legs with difficulty. His shirt was still soggy too; it made him shiver, but he got it on. And then he picked up the backpack. He could leave it... but to hell with that. After all of this? No. He had earned his reward.

He slung it over his shoulder and moved to the small pool in the corner where the ocean exit was. Andy put one foot in the water and grinned. From here to the beach before they woke. He could do it.

That's when the song hit him.

A quartet of painful harmony. The most beautiful thing he had ever heard. He turned slightly and saw them, four naked Sirens, all singing in unison, a song that echoed in his mind with inhuman screams and angelic sighs. A song that brought his cock to erection, and his eyes to a leaden droop. A song that made him feel like puking and gorging at the same time. A song that brought every emotion he had ever had back at once, a fury of dreams and nightmares.

His captor, she of the curled black hair, strode forward ahead of the others, and gripped him by both arms. She continued to sing, but shook her head at him in disgust. Then she lifted the backpack from him and tossed it easily back to the chests. With one palm she slapped him across the face.

Between that and the force of the song... Andy fell. The melody rose louder and angrier until he felt his ears grow hot with pounding blood. He was sure his brain was leaking out onto the floor, but he couldn't move a muscle.... He could only lie there and tremble as they took out their anger on him in song.

When the pain in his eyes grew to be more than he could bear, he let go. The waters of unconsciousness washed the sound away.

ANDY WOKE NAKED ONCE MORE.

The bed was soft, softer than any bed he'd ever slept in.

Not only hadn't they killed him, but they'd made him even more comfortable than before. So... that was something. But what did they *want* from him? Why had she brought him here and why wouldn't they let him leave? Surely they weren't just going to play musical beds with him until he finally got a bad case of erectile dysfunction?

He opened his eyes and stretched.... There *were* worse ways to be held prisoner, he thought. And then realized he couldn't move his arms. Or his legs. *Shit.*

He craned his head and confirmed that he'd been tied, spread-eagled, to the bed.

And it wasn't really a bed, but a thick mattress of something downy soft on the floor. As he looked across the room, he could see two small toddlers hunched over something in the corner. He looked around and saw that the ceiling was very low here, and mobiles made of the white bones of fish heads and colorful seashells twirled and spun. He was in a nursery.

Something tickled his foot, and he twitched, trying to push whatever it was away.

There was a faint noise. A baby's cry.

Something soft and wet covered his big toe. The wetness was followed by a sound. A coo. Tiny hands on his thigh. Grasping fingers, tickling near his belly, reaching lower to his groin. Touching something that shouldn't be touched, not by a baby. And then he felt something wet suck down on him there too. Testing. Tasting.

No, he panicked. *Wrong. No.*

He shook, trying to dislodge the babies, but instead, he only attracted the attention of the two toddlers across the room. They both turned from the toy they'd been playing with, and squealed in delight when they saw what was going on in the bed. They stumbled towards him, and he could see now what they had been playing with.

Bones hung from the low ceiling. It looked like a ribcage.

The wet suckle on his toe turned from mildly pleasurable to a sudden bolt of white-hot pain, as the baby's tiny shark teeth bit down. "Ouch!" he cried, and at the same moment the wet gnawing on his cock turned from teasing to teething. He writhed against the binds, trying to shake the babies away, but it only had the opposite effect. More teeth bit down on his thigh and his belly. On one of his nipples. And then the teeth began not just to bite, but to bite and pull.

And rip.

"Stop," he cried out.

"Shhhhhhh," a voice said nearby.

The woman with the black hair.

She crawled into the bed next to him and patted the head of the babe latched onto his chest. He felt blood running down his ribs.

She kissed him, and shook her head. A cascade of curled black hair fell over him. It trailed down his chest as she shifted. She gently disengaged and moved the child that had bitten him where it counts the most. She bent lower and took the child's place. Her tongue traced the tooth marks; he could feel the sting of the tiny wounds as her tongue moved across him, soothing him.

Despite the pain of all the bites, he responded yet again to her provocation. But before he got fully hard, he felt a horrible, sharp stab. His middle went cold, and then the pain came in a nauseous wave. The Siren raised her head from his middle, the remains of his manhood bleeding between her lips.

She chewed him with razor teeth as he watched, and then swallowed before she bent down to kiss his lips. The blood from his lost cock dripped down her chin to pool on his throat which had finally begun to scream. She put her fingers on his lips, encouraging him to close them.

Then she slipped off the bed and moved away, out of his sight as he wailed and swore. He could feel the blood pumping out in a steady heart rhythm between his legs and he cried in desperation, "No, no... please no..." over and over.

The babies didn't care. Some of them screamed right along with him as if it were a game... tiny howls that made his spine jerk and his arms twitch uncontrollably. Whenever one of them made a sound, it was as if invisible nails drove into his nerves. Untrained Siren talent.

One by one, all of the babies in the room climbed onto the bed, drawn by first blood. There were seven of them. The oldest looked to be about four. She hovered over his face for a moment, studying him. She had the curly black hair and wide sea-green eyes of his captor.

At first, the children simply pinched and poked and prodded him, like a human toy. They laughed and gurgled and squealed as they explored his captive body.

Then a piercing heat burst from his left shoulder as the oldest one bit down. He felt – and heard – his flesh separate from bone.

Presently, the sounds of play stilled, as the younger children followed the lead of their older sister. Playtime was over.

The Sirens all began to feed.

The House At The Top Of The Hill

The house at the top of the hill was haunted. Everyone in town knew it. Everybody said so. But, boys being boys, and a dare being a dare, that naturally didn't keep Tommy and Bret from climbing its steps on a cold, darkening afternoon in October.

October 31, to be exact. When else would you dare your friend to put both feet inside the threshold of a haunted house?

It had started earlier that day in the cafeteria.

"Chicken," Bret had accused, and he wasn't talking about the mystery meat hidden in the disturbingly garish orange Halloween sauce. He was taunting Tommy.

"Not," Tommy quailed, looking around the lunchroom to see who might be listening.

"Are too. Balk, balk balk," Bret continued, raising his voice. "You're a big chicken, afraid of the boogie man."

Some of the other kids were starting to lean in towards their table, and Tommy could hear conversations all around them dying out, as his classmates tried to hear what was going on.

"I'm *not* chicken," Tommy said. "I'll do it under one condition."

"What's that?"

"You've got to do it, too."

Bret bit his lip and looked about to back out. But then he nodded.

"Deal."

AND SO NOW THEY CLIMBED, step by creaking wooden step up the long grey stairs that led from the cracked cement sidewalk up the brown dead hill to the tall grey doors of the haunted house. The doors that seemed to reach up and up into the very rafters of the high thin roof, which seemed to lean and pitch and grasp at the darkening clouds themselves.

Bret sneezed as the cold October wind gusted by, moving the dead weeds in a swishing hiss all around them.

"We could go back," Tommy said. "If you're getting a cold."

Bret wiped his nose with a sleeve. "Chicken?"

"Never mind."

The two boys continued their ascent, 23 steps in all, and at last stood, breathing heavy and chilled from more than simple cold, at the weathered door of the haunted house.

"Well, go ahead," Bret announced. His voice seemed to catch, just a bit. "I dared *you*. I'll go with you, but you've got to go first."

The windows to the left of the door, looking into what had once been a living room, were shattered, and Tommy could see the shredded yellowed curtains swaying in the growing October wind. A storm was blowing in.

"What if it's locked?" he said, stalling.

"What if it's not?" Bret countered.

Tommy reached up and turned the tarnished brass knob.

It wasn't.

Locked, that is.

The door opened with a long, slow, high-pitched creak.

"Well, that should have woke the dead," Bret tried to joke. Tommy didn't laugh.

The door leaned against the inside wall, letting the fading light of the afternoon stretch across the dust-covered wooden floor inside. Tommy could see a stairway leading up just in front of the door, and the tickle of whispering shadows created by the blowing curtains moved across the walls of the room just to their right.

"Well?" Brett said after a moment. "You going in, or are we going to stand here and look at the door all night? Come on, before someone sees us."

At that, on the street below, a car went motoring by. Tommy could hear a Beatles song fading in the background. "Get back, get back, get back to where you once belonged..."

He lifted his right foot, closed his eyes, and stepped inside.

THE HOUSE WAS OLD, one of the oldest structures in town. Some said it had been built by pilgrims. As long as Tommy could remember, nobody had lived in it. Inside, he could smell mildew and dust, and his feet echoed hollowly on the bare wooden floor. It felt colder inside than it had out. Bret sneezed again, behind him. *He* was still outside.

"Well," Tommy hissed. "I'm in, what about you?"

His friend finally followed him through the open door, and the two boys stood in the dingy front room of the haunted house.

"Doesn't seem very haunted to me," Bret announced bravely. He kept his voice low, however.

Tommy nodded. After all the buildup, the empty room almost seemed a let-down. He didn't feel anything here but neglect.

"Let's look around," Bret said.

They walked through the front room, every step telegraphing itself throughout the house with the clomping echoes of abandoned space. The kitchen was in the back, a small, depressing room. The floor was dirty linoleum that once might have been white, but now looked orange with age. A small, steel-rimmed table leaned crookedly against a wall peppered with nail holes, their nails and hangings long removed. One white shellacked cabinet door hung open, and Tommy could make out the bright orange and yellow mottles of sunny flowered shelf paper inside. There were gaps in the cabinetry and blackened spots on the floor there where a refrigerator and stove once stood. One globe from a five-armed light fixture lay shattered on the floor.

"Come on," Bret said, and they stepped back from the kitchen to walk down a dark hallway.

There were three empty bedrooms at its end, and the boys peered quickly into each. The bare windows leered back at them like laughing mouths. There were shadows and holes on the walls where people once had hung their shelves and pictures and posters and more.

All gone.

They passed a door on the way back to the front room, and Bret stopped them.

"Open it," he said.

"Why?"

"See what it is."

Tommy shook his head. "Not part of the deal. Come on, it's getting dark outside. Pretty soon we won't be able to see anything in here."

Bret sneezed again. "Chicken."

"Won't work this time," Tommy said and started back to the front room.

Bret reached out and opened the door himself. Tommy stopped when he heard the creak.

"Halllooooo," Bret called out, his voice echoing weirdly. "Ghosts, where are you? Come out, come out wherever you are..."

Tommy felt his heart stop.

It was one thing to sneak inside a haunted house. It was another to tempt the haunts, if there were any.

"This must be where he killed them," Bret whispered.

"Huh?"

Bret was pointing into the blackness beyond the door. The smell of mildew and decay -- the smell of age -- had increased.

"Downstairs. They say the father took his kids down into the cellar, tied them up and chopped their heads off, one by one. Then he went upstairs and hung himself. That's why they say you can hear kids crying sometimes late at night. And you can hear the creaking of a body dangling from a rope."

"Why would he do that?" Tommy said.

"His wife ran off with another guy and he freaked out."

"Where'd you hear that?"

"Everybody knows," Bret said. "Where've you been?"

"I just heard it was haunted," Tommy said.

"Yeah, well, get tuned in. Wanna go down?"

"Yeah sure, after you."

Bret closed the door, and the two boys started back to the front room. But then, Tommy put his hand on Bret's shoulder and stopped him.

"Shhh. Did you hear that?" he whispered.

The curtains rippled across the room, but it was getting harder to see them in the gathering gloom of a blustery Halloween night.

"What?" Bret hissed.

"Something creaked upstairs."

"Just the wind," Bret said. "Cut it out."

But then he heard it too. It came from just above them, in the room beyond the ceiling.

Creak, cronk, creak, cronk.

A steady push and pull rhythm. Rope sawing board.

"Still think it's the wind?"

Creak, cronk, creak cronk

"Does it matter? Let's get out of here before the whole house caves in."

Thump.

The creaking stopped.

Clomp.

Bret and Tommy started towards the door, but before they reached it, Bret held up a hand. He put a finger in front of his lips and pointed, up, in the direction of the stairs leading to the second floor.

Thud.

Tommy listened. A new creaking had begun, but this one sounded more like the creak of feet on boards. Like the creak of someone walking.

Clomp.

Like the creak of one stair after the other, slowly being trodden down.

Thud.

And they had to pass in front of the stairs in order to get out.

Clomp, thud. Clomp, thud.

How many stairs were there? Tommy wondered.

"Come on," Bret hissed, and the two boys started towards the door again, but just as they reached the foyer, the owner of the feet stepped into view.

"Can I help you boys?"

His voice was molasses and nails, dark and sharp. His face was long, and pallid, his nose a crooked hook, his lips like two thin worms come to nestle atop an endless chin. He wore a black jacket that hung low, past his thighs, and pants that hung in folds and wrinkles atop dull, dark shoes. Graveyard shoes.

Brett screamed, and dove beneath the man's arm, making for the door. It was still open, and he hit the stoop in a roll, calling out "Come on, Tommy, come on!"

Tommy sprang to follow, but it was too late. The man flung the door shut with a crack, and stood before it, arms folded. Face drawn.

Tommy noticed that while the man's complexion seemed pale overall, his neck was ringed with an angry red and purple bruise.

"Not so fast," the man said. "Why are you in my house?"

"I'm sorry," Tommy stammered. "We were...we were...just... looking around. We didn't mean any harm."

"Nobody ever does, do they?" he said. "Come, sit down with me a minute before you go. We'll talk. I so rarely get visitors anymore."

Tommy backed away from the man, thinking that there was no place to sit but the floor. But when he turned slightly, trying to keep the man in view as he stepped back into the front room, he sucked in a quick breath.

The dusty, empty, wind-tattered room was now full of furniture. Its floor shone in a deep mahogany gleam and a Chinese rug covered its center. The man gestured to a deep red velvet couch.

"Sit."

Tommy hunched his backside up to the edge of the couch, and pushed backwards, not really believing that anything would be there to support him. The room had been empty a minute ago. He'd walked through the spot where the couch now was.

But the couch felt solid, and he tried to relax into its fuzzy embrace.

His heart was pounding, and in his head he cursed the name of Bret over and over and over again.

The man paced the center of the rug and put the fingers of each hand together lightly, as if praying. Then he touched one skeletal finger to the white dome of his forehead and said, "They say I'm crazy, don't they?"

"I want to go home," Tommy answered.

"Yes," the man said. "We all want to go home, don't we? But sometimes, we go where we don't belong, we get just a little too far, take just one too many steps…and we can never go home again, eh?"

"Please?" Tommy said. "I promise I won't bother you again."

"And maybe I won't let you go unless you promise that you WILL bother me again," the man said. He chuckled then, a low, creaking sound, like the settling of a house. Or the sound of a man on a noose, swinging slowly in the breeze.

Tommy looked behind him and saw that the curtains were no longer moving. The curtains were no longer stained and tattered. They were brilliant white and reflected the colored shadows of the tiffany lamp in the corner. It was rose and orange and emerald, and stretched to ragged points where dragonflies struggled to fly out of the glass and away from its edges. Trying but always trapped in the ornamental glass. Trapped in this room, like Tommy was now.

The man stepped closer, and Tommy shrunk back into the couch that couldn't exist.

"Three chances," the man said. "Three chances to go home. If you miss them all, you stay here with me. Here is your first."

The man held up three hairs between his fingers. Two dark. One light.

"Choose the long one, and you must seek your exit upstairs. The short one, downstairs. The middle one…and you can walk out the door right there."

He stood in front of Tommy and held out his hand.

"Choose."

Tommy sucked in his breath. Which hair meant home? And which meant the cellar? In his head he began to chant "eenie, meanie, minie moe…"

"That one," he said, pointing to the blonde one on the right.

The man separated the blonde hair out and nodded. His nose seemed to touch his lips as he bent down to show Tommy the other two. The one Tommy had picked was the longest.

"Upstairs," the man said. "Your first chance takes you upstairs. Don't mind the mess, I haven't cleaned much since my wife's been gone."

Tommy didn't move.

The man pointed. "Go now. Or stay with me here forever."

Tommy slipped off the couch and walked to the door. When he looked back, the man was gone.

He stood between the door and the stairs and saw his chance. Grabbing the knob, he twisted it hard to the right and pulled.

The knob came off the door and lay cold and useless in his hands.

"Nooo," Tommy cried and stomped his foot. Tears were starting to trickle down the left side of his face.

"Upstairs," came the voice of the long, thin man from out of nowhere.

Dropping the knob, Tommy started up the stairs. They creaked and groaned under his weight, but at last he reached the top landing. There was light here from the room at the end of the hall. He walked toward it, heart beating in his chest like a jackhammer.

He stepped into the lighted room and gasped.

In the corner was a dark chest of drawers, and in the far side, a wide bed with a pink, lacy comforter. In the center of the room, hanging on a rope from the bronze-based light fixture, was the man.

"Hello again," the ghost said, eyes bugging madly as he swayed from the rope around his neck slowly, to and fro. The creak of his passage echoed through the room.

"If you'd gone the other way, you could have slipped out the back window and down the trellis to meet your friend. But instead, you came right to me. Not so good at hide and seek, I bet. Ready to take your second chance?"

Tommy nodded.

"Good. This time, let's try a little riddle. If you guess the answer, you will be allowed to leave. If you don't, you must go to the basement for your third and final chance."

"What always moves at the same speed, but no matter how hard you try, you can never get ahead or behind it?"

Tommy thought. Cars moved at different speeds, and so did buses. But you could get around them.

"A train?" he guessed.

The ghost's head shook slowly, the purple bruises on its neck twisting like angry veins. "Time," the dead man answered. "And now, it's *time* for you to head downstairs."

The ghost choked a little, and a thick discolored tongue poked through his lips.

"All the way downstairs."

Tommy turned away and went back down the stairs to the front door. He stood for a moment, wondering if there was some way to pry it open without a knob, when he heard the voice from behind him.

"Allllll the way...."

He walked through the front room and down the hall, stopping at the door Bret had found. It was already open. The stairs were lit from the glow of a bare bulb.

He put a foot on the first step and froze as it creaked.

"Alll the way down..."

He was crying now, crying hard and free. He didn't want to go downstairs, he hadn't wanted to come inside a haunted house. He didn't want to die here. What if he chose wrong the third time? What then?

"Allllll the way," the voice echoed again.

Shutting his eyes to force out the tears, Tommy grasped the handrail and stepped down again and again and again.

The basement had a cement floor, painted grey. A washer and dryer stood against one wall, the tin flues and box and coils of an ancient furnace took up another. When Tommy walked to the center of the open room, he saw the reason that the man was swinging from a rope upstairs.

Planted in a row across the center of the floor were the heads of three boys. Their eyes were open, and blue. One had blonde hair, the other two dark. They were young. And bodiless. Their necks bled streams of ghost blood across the cement.

"Hi" said the blonde one. "Playing with dad, are you?"

"If he asks you anything about squirrels, he hates 'em," said one of the brunettes.

"Have you seen my ma?" asked the third. "My neck hurts."

The stairs behind him creaked.

"And now for our third and final challenge," the gravelly voice said. "Remember, if you miss this one, you get to stay here and keep the boys and me company."

The man walked away from the stairs to stand behind the heads of his three sons. In his hand, he now held a long, wood-handled axe. The steel of its blade was spattered with red and rust.

"One of these boys knows where the key to the back door is. You'll need it if you're going to leave here. Listen to the right head, and you leave here with *your* head still on your shoulders. Pick the wrong one, and you'll join my boys."

Tommy looked at the dark-haired third head and asked, "Do you know where the back door key is?"

The boy stared blankly at the wall behind him. "Ma will come. She's probably just upstairs. Would you get her?"

He looked at the other brunette. "Do you know where the key is?"

"Squirrels," the boy said. "My dad hates squirrels. You don't have a squirrel do you?"

"Enough," the man growled. "Quit stalling. Choose the head that knows where the key is."

"How can I be sure any of them know where the key is?" Tommy asked. "They don't even know where *they* are."

"Because one of them has it in his pocket," the man smiled.

"They don't have bodies!" Tommy said.

"Sure they do. They're just laying over there." The man pointed to a far corner of the basement, where what looked like a bundle of old bound-up rags or laundry was piled. Tommy saw now that it wasn't rags, but feet and arms piled in the corner.

He stared again at the boys and wondered which to pick. The only one that seemed to have any sense was the blonde boy. And just as he thought that, the boy winked at him.

"I choose…" Tommy began and raised his finger to point at the boy with the blonde hair.

But just as he did so, the blonde boy widened his eyes and crinkled his brow. Then with a twitch of his eye and a squint, he seemed to indicate the squirrel boy to his left.

"That one," Tommy said, pointing at the squirrel-obsessed kid.

"Dad loves to play games," the blonde boy said again, and then faded out of sight.

The ghost's wicked grin slipped away. His haggard face sagged, as his blackened fingernails clenched.

"Looks like you've won," he said grudgingly. "This time. Don't be a stranger, now."

"And don't forget the key." Then he vanished as well.

Suddenly, the bulb went dark, and Tommy was trapped in the basement in pitch blackness. Laughter sounded from somewhere above in the house.

Tommy almost ran back towards the stairs, but then stopped. The bodies had been over there, in the far corner. And the man had said he'd need the key that had been in the clothes of one of them. Did that mean when the bodies went away, the key would still be there?

Tommy crawled in the direction of the "rags" he'd seen a moment ago and stopped when he felt the cold hard concrete of a wall before him. Then he moved his hands back and forth across the floor, hoping to slip across a cold piece of metal.

He'd almost given up hope when his fingers nudged something across the floor that went *ting*.

In seconds, he'd found it again. And then he scrambled back towards the stairs, where the tiniest bit of light was still leaking down from upstairs. Grabbing the wood banister with both hands he launched himself up and clambered up the wooden steps till he got to the hallway. Then he stood and felt along the wall as he stepped towards what he hoped was the kitchen.

It was. There was the front room, curtains swaying drunkenly in the broken window breeze. Through there, that blackened threshold, was the kitchen, and a back door. The house was silent. And empty again.

He took the step, and heard the crunch of glass beneath his feet.

Then his hand was on the door, and he fumbled the key into the padlock that held the door closed from the inside. It clicked open, and he turned the knob.

From upstairs he heard a steady *creak, cronk, creak cronk*

From somewhere outside, he heard his name. "Tommy?"

The door came open with a screeching complaint.

He pushed past the screen door and stumbled down a stand of concrete stairs to find himself in the overgrown backyard of the haunted house.

A harvest moon shone a bloody orange over the yard as he looked back at the tall, slanted structure. The windows stayed black.

Tommy ran around through the tall weeds and found his friend in the front of the house, tears streaming down his face.

"Tommy" he cried once again, staring at the tilted shutters but not daring to go inside again.

"I'm here." Tommy said, and fell to the ground at Bret's feet.

"Are you ok? I thought you were never going to get out."

"Do I look like I've seen a ghost?" Tommy said.

"I saw him too," Bret said.

"Yeah, but I met his kids."

"Whoa," Bret said. "Better you than me. I think I've seen just about enough up here."

"Yeah, me too," Tommy said, fingering the key in his pocket. He looked up at the 2nd story window where he knew the ghost of a man was even now swaying from a ghostly rope. Was there just the hint of a shadow moving to and fro up there now?

Bret started down the 23 stairs to the sidewalk. Moving fast.

"Feel like Trick Or Treating?" he called over his shoulder, aiming himself at a band of short witches and devils and ghosts parading down the sidewalk just ahead.

Tommy hurried to follow.

Running Away From A Good Time

"You're the worst," Trevor said. "Always running away from a good time." He looked at me with that disgusted look that reminded me more and more of mom – the downcast right eye, the puckered lips, the flared nostrils. When mom – or Trevor – wanted you to do something, they put their whole face into letting you know.

"I'm sick of trick or treating," he said. "I've taken you all over the neighborhood. Now let's go get in on a game of two-on-two with those guys and give the candy a rest."

I looked across the clearing at the two boys running back and forth on the old, cracked basketball court and shook my head. "I'll stay here," I announced, and scooted back on the old wooden slats of the sagging park bench. "You go," I said.

"You can't play doubles with three people," he grumbled.

"They're half your size, so it'll be even."

Trevor liked pushing other people around; I figured he was so adamant about playing because he'd get his kicks out of creaming a couple kids in funny dweeby patchwork clothes who barely looked my age. Kids who probably didn't even know how to play basketball. They were dashing around the court and throwing a ball back and forth, but they never dribbled. Eventually it became evident why not -- when they stopped and actually shot at the rusty basketball hoops with the forlorn nets, the ball slipped through and fell to the ground like a stone. It never bounced.

"Suit yourself," Trevor said, with obvious disgust. He hated having to cart his little brother around, and this was his way of rubbing my face in it. He knew I didn't like sports.

I settled back on the bench and dug my hand into the overflowing bag of candy. It was so full that I wasn't sure if I could carry it all the way home. Trevor hadn't lied when he'd said we had walked all over the neighborhood. This park was at the dead end of a street I wasn't even sure I'd ever seen before. It emptied out onto this clearing that was surrounded by a stand of towering old pine trees and browning oaks. Trevor went jogging across the gravel and crabgrass to the basketball court; I turned away and looked out at the old houses on the other side of the street. They seemed grey and dark in the gathering dusk. Colorless. Maybe they were actually grey; it was hard to tell in this light. I didn't think Trevor's game was going to last long; nobody would be able to see the ball soon.

I focused my attention on a Twix bar and a couple of Reese's Peanut Butter cups. For a few minutes I couldn't care about anything more than the amazing sensation of each sweet bite. It had been a long afternoon, and this was my reward at last. When I finally got up to find a trash bin to throw the wrappers in, I realized that I couldn't see Trevor out on the court. The two kids were still playing, shooting a ball back and forth between them. Every now and then, one of them gave out a high-pitched laugh. At least, I thought it was a laugh. But instead of making me smile, it made me wince. I could literally feel the kid's voice in my spine.

After tossing the wrappers in an old, rusted can, I sat back on the bench and watched the basketball court. Trevor didn't reappear.

After a few more minutes, I began to grow worried. It was now so dark that the two kids were just shadows, ghosting back and forth against the dark curtain of the woods beyond. Other than the occasional screech of the one kid's donkey laughter, the neighborhood was completely silent. I picked up my candy bag and walked down the weedy path towards the court. The two kids didn't seem to notice my approach, but as I got closer, I could see that the clothes that had looked odd from a distance were actually patchwork quilts of mismatched colors – squares of red and gold and blue and plaid all jammed together with no obvious pattern. They seemed chubby and squat and strange in their weirdly random clothes and somewhere in the back of my brain, a warning bell went off. Actually, I'd begun to feel odd about this a while ago, but now I had to admit that there was something not so normal about these kids who were out playing with a ball that never bounced in this court that seemed to have been abandoned long before I was born.

I stopped and watched one of them shoot the ball into the net across the court. The moon was beginning to rise, peeking out over the edge of the oak trees, and I could see in its cool light how the ball hung in the dark fringe for a moment, before dropping to the pavement with a faint splat. One of the fat little kids ran to grab it, and before I knew what was happening, the other called to me with voice that lilted and sang like a calliope that had wheezed flat.

"Do you want to play, too?" he said, just before the ball sailed through the air and into my arms. I dropped my bag of candy to catch it, and as my hands closed around it, I noticed a couple things right away.

The ball hadn't bounced because it wasn't really a ball. It was heavy. And wet and sticky. Something like a Brillo pad rubbed on my palm, and I lifted the thing up to look at it.

The wide blue eyes of my brother Trevor stared back into mine. Only, his were simply wide and lifeless while mine were bulging out of my skull.

I shrieked and threw the head back into the air. One of the creepy kids darted forward to catch it, and with one arm lofted my brother's head behind his back and up towards the listing net. Trevor's forehead smashed into the backboard and then dropped through the net in a perfect swish.

"You can be on my team," the kid announced. He pointed at a stack of dark logs to the right of the broken asphalt. I thought I saw a dark stain spreading out on the pavement next to them. "Those guys were all on his."

I realized that the logs were actually a stack of bodies. Decapitated bodies. With squares cut out of their jeans and shirts. I suddenly understood where the patchwork clothes had come from.

"No way," I cried, and took off running towards the silent grey houses.

"Don't run away now, we'll have a good time," one of the boys complained. "And we can take you back to our house later. We've only got one night to play; you've got all year."

I thought I saw faces in the windows of the grey houses across the street, but I just turned and kept running down the center of the street, in the direction I hoped was towards home. I didn't slow, even when I thought of my brother, and the huge bag of candy I'd left behind.

Trevor had been dead wrong. Sometimes the best thing you could possibly do was to run away from a good time.

Dying On The Inside

The first time it happened, he was at the water cooler. The moment was unremarkable in every way. Nobody was around; the office was quiet. He pressed the lever to allow the cool processed water to stream into his cup. One minute he was fine, albeit a little sleepy, and the next, as the stream threatened to overflow his plastic Brookfield Zoo cup, something tickled the back of his throat. A second later, and he was doubled over, coughing. The roof of his mouth burned as he passed what felt like liquid flame through clenched teeth. He struggled not to make a scene, praying inwardly that nobody heard his gasping, retching cough.

Josh grabbed for a paper towel from the counter of the kitchenette and blocked the damage from hitting the floor. He coughed again, feeling the fire move out of his lungs, and again. After a couple more spasms passed, the attack subsided, and someone called from down the hall, "You alright, man?"

Josh called back a weak "all clear" and then looked at the center of the paper towel at the phlegmy goop he'd spit up. He stared at the mess for a good long time, and even held it up to the light see better. He wasn't sure what to think.

The center of the paper towel was spattered in black. As if he'd coughed up a ball-full of ink.

JOSH LOOKED at the IN basket and his heart sank. When he'd finally pushed away from the desk at 8 p.m. the night before, it had been almost empty. But this morning, thanks to an over-aggressive mailroom staff, an over-enthusiastic management team and a dozen glowing yellow envelopes marked "Interdepartmental / Confidential," the basket was already overflowing. And he hadn't even turned on his computer yet. Once the spam advertising Viagra and Cialis were trashed from his e-mail box, he knew he'd have a long list of requests with little red Outlook "urgent" flags next to them.

Everything was urgent. Nothing could wait.

Throwing his jacket behind the door (he didn't even try for the hook), he slipped into the too-familiar chair and hit the computer 'On' button. Before the familiar startup chime rang, he was already shredding envelopes and planning all the phone calls for the day that he didn't want to make. Mentally, he crossed off the fleeting idea of going out for lunch. Neither his waist, nor his schedule could allow it. A tear threatened to escape from the side of his left eye, but he disguised it with a sneeze. After wiping his face with a tissue, he picked up the phone and began to dial the first call-back. In his head, he could feel his consciousness wither. He heard his voice begin speaking when the line picked up, but even he didn't listen to what he was saying. In his mind, he was imagining a life somewhere far away. Where maybe he worked on a farm, or as a handyman -- someone who didn't push numbers and memos through a computer, but who did work that actually produced meaningful life-sustaining products. In his imagination, he'd meet a smiling, cheerful girl who loved to joke, and they would go out to movies and make out in the back seat on Friday nights. There would be no suits and high-pressure meetings. There would be no ridiculous mortgages or country club dinners filled with hot air. There would just be the two of them, having honest fun after an honest day's work. Maybe he'd even change his name to something more real than "Josh." Something like Frank, or Chuck...

AFTER WORK, Josh stopped at the health club for his obligatory workout; he'd been working too late the past two nights to fit it in and he didn't look forward to the knowing glances of his wife, or her not-so-subtle pats on his belly. Not that he really believed if he got into shape that she'd slip her hand lower than his spare tire. Sometimes it seemed as if the last time they'd had sex was 1999. After an hour, he climbed in the SUV and drove the 2 miles home. Moments later, after an endless day, he was walking through the door from the dusty shadows of the garage to the glare of the front room lights.

"Hi honey, I'm home!" he called wearily as he pulled the heavy oaken door shut behind him. The shutters outside rattled every time the door closed. Corrine had insisted they tack on an ostentatious wood door on their weathered old house...as if that made the rest of the house look younger. Whatever.

"Daddy!" yelled Agnes, his six-year-old.

Here's the marker of the last time I had sex, Josh thought as he hugged the toothpick-thin bones of his daughter close.

"Your dinner's cold," were the only words he heard from the other denizen of the house.

Work late = trouble. Work out = trouble. Don't do either one and be fat and broke = trouble.

A giant grin took over Josh's face as he considered his plight. "I'm screwed six ways from Sunday," he thought, and gave Agnes a last squeeze. Then he considered, "exactly what does that phrase mean?" Before he could answer his internal question, a tiny hand dragged his into the kitchen.

THE SECOND TIME IT HAPPENED, Josh was lying in bed next to his wife. He rolled on his side and kissed the side of her neck. It was silky cool, and a strand of hair stuck in his lips. He was promptly backhanded. "What do you think you're doing?" Corrine hissed.

"Jesus," he railed. "You could at least try once in a while."

"Why would I want to with you?"

"Maybe because I'm your husband, and the father of your child?"

"Yeah, well, those were two of the biggest mistakes I ever made," returned a voice he hardly knew, muffled and soured by its proximity to the pillow. Or maybe by its proximity to him.

"Yeah, well, you were the worst tax deduction I ever married," Josh countered, instantly knowing that it was a stupid thing to say. Retorts were not his specialty.

The other side of the bed returned...silence.

And that's when the tickle came again. He tried to hold it in, but the heat slithered around his tonsils and choked the back of his eyeballs. He could feel the pressure build from his chest up the back of his throat like oily flame. Soon he could feel it fuming through his nose and he gave way, his entire body contracting as he coughed, hard, into the smothering palm of his hand. The tickle grew and the cough repeated, *hack, hack, hack.* His palm grew warm and wet and he choked back another cough, only to have five more rush past it to spew something past his lips and into his hand.

The light clicked on as his eyes watered and his nose ran and he tried to swallow back any further explosions. And then the nightstand light flicked painfully on, and in the midst of a flaming cough that seemed to carry a piece of his soul with it into the room, Corrine's voice suddenly rose like a banshee in the midnight.

"Jesus Christ, Josh, you've ruined the sheets."

Her attention to his health was touching. But she was right. The sheets were spotted and stained with something ugly, oily and brackish black.

Dying On The Inside

THE NEXT MORNING, Josh felt the gurgle in his gut. He'd just finished his coffee and was ruffling his little girl's hair with his fingers, when something shifted in his middle. Corrine walked through the kitchen just then, slippers padding loudly on the floor and hair as tangled as a squirrel's nest. She had black rings around her eyes and Josh found himself stifling a laugh as he imagined her to be, not a middle-aged housewife, but a giant squirrel in a flannel nightgown.

The humor was short-lived, as he felt something shift, painfully, in his bowels, and suddenly excused himself from his daughter to run to the bathroom. The details are unimportant, and frankly unenticing. But when he finished his business and stood up to look in the bowl, he found himself staring at a murky mirror of shadow and silt.

"Oh shit," he murmured, and wondered if that was what was really in the toilet. He'd sat and purged, but things had never looked so black to him before.

He didn't have long to think about it, because at that moment, the tickle started again at the back of his throat. Quickly he bent to pull up his pants, flush the toilet and stumble out into the hallway, trying to hold down the tickle in his chest, but failing miserably. He spattered the walls with inky sputum as he went.

"Goddamn it, Josh!" Corrine yelled behind him. He crumbled to his knees, still coughing. His wife of 20 years never looked at him, only stared at the trail he'd left and cried. "We just had these walls painted. Can't you use a tissue?"

"I'M GOING TO DIE," Josh thought, as he drove to his doctor's office. "I'm puking and shitting out black tar, and that's no good. I'm going to die."

He tried to consider any conceivable reason that he might be expectorating black goo other than death and came up with nothing. The Black Plague and tuberculosis came to mind, and though he thought both had been cured by medical science, he was sure that, in fact, he had contracted both.

His doctor took a pulse, spied up his ears and with a wooden popsicle stick pressing his tongue down invoked him to say, "Aaaaaah."

"You've been watching your diet?" Dr. Ababu said.

Josh shrugged. "Been watching it go down my throat, yeah."

The diminutive Indian doctor shook his head and clarified. "I mean, you've been exercising and eating good food, vegetables, you know?"

"I haven't been doing chasers of rat poison, no," Josh said.

"Hmmm."

The doctor listened to his breathing and heart again, then asked him to cough. When Josh tried, he achieved only a thin, hollow "chkkk, kkkahhh."

"I think you get some rest, and eat your greens, and you be just fine by next week," the doctor pronounced.

Josh didn't buy it, but he was halfway to the exit when a spasm hit him again. This time, it was so intense, he went first to his knees, and finished with his ribs rubbing the carpet. Two nurses were holding him on either side and suggesting that he "calm down."

When the spasms subsided enough for him to answer, Josh responded with perhaps the most eloquent retort of his life.

"I'm calmer than fuckin' death," he rasped, before spitting out a new gobbet of black on the carpet.

The doctor by now had come out of the back appointment rooms and hovered over him, not finding a place to kneel between the two nurses and a jerking, spasming Josh.

"Perhaps we should do an x-ray," the doctor suggested.

"Yeah," Josh said, collapsing with his face in a puddle of black. "Perhaps we should."

"You're welcome to seek a second opinion," the doctor said a short while later. He pointed at the grimly colorless x-rays glowing from the lightboard on the wall. "But if you're going to, I advise you to seek it quickly."

He pointed to the shadowy mass that filled the center of Josh's midsection, below the throat and above the pelvis. The entire area seemed smoky.

"We need to take a look at this," the doctor said. "Up close."

"You mean you need to operate."

The doctor nodded. "Yes. Only then will we be able to tell what we can do for you."

"I'm going to die, aren't I?"

The doctor nodded again. "We all are." And with that, he walked out of the room.

OVER THE NEXT THREE DAYS, Josh collapsed twice from coughing fits that left gobs of oily ichor clotting on the carpet next to him. And despite his wife's complaints at the fumes, he also spent a good deal of time in the bathroom, literally feeling his insides dissolve and slip from his body to the sewer.

He wasted little time in scheduling the exploratory procedure.

"We are just going to use the endoscopy this time," the doctor said. He explained that the tiny tube with a camera on its end would enter Josh through the throat and slip down past his lungs to see what was going on inside. Only then would the doctors know what they were facing, and what they could do to stop it.

They gave him an anesthetic, and Josh closed his eyes as they readied the metal snake to plumb his insides.

"Roto-Rooter to the rescue," he mumbled.

The doctor bent over him and began to slide the tube down his esophagus. Josh couldn't feel a thing, but still felt the urge to cough. A nurse stood by as the doctor stared into a small screen and guided the tiny telescope further down. The doctor grunted once, and then again. He sounded surprised.

"What do you see, doctor?" the nurse whispered.

"Nothing," the doctor said. His voice held a mix of surprise and awe. "I don't see anything at all."

JOSH LAY for an hour in the recovery room. He slipped into dreams of oceans and beaches beneath the white walls and sterile ceiling lights alone. Corrine had stayed home to watch Agnes.

He wasn't awake long when the doctor entered the room.

"Do you love your wife?" the doctor asked, holding up an x-ray to the light.

"Sure," Josh said, unconvincingly.

"Do you love your job?" the doctor pried again, still brandishing the x-ray.

"It's all right," he answered.

"Do you love your life?" the doctor tried a third time, and threw the x-ray aside.

Josh shrugged. "Sure, I guess."

"Lies!" the doctor spat, walking across the white room to peer down close to Josh's face. His eyes were so brown they seemed black. As if they reflected the stuff that Josh was coughing out. They didn't blink. "If you are not honest with me, I cannot be honest with you."

Josh paled. "Doc, what's wrong with me?"

The doctor looked up and stared a moment at the white wall behind the patient. Then he looked back at Josh's face, and bent to whisper, inches from his face.

"You do not love your wife. Or your job. Or your life."

After the silence stretched out from seconds to minutes, Josh shook his head slowly, in agreement, under Dr. Ababu's black gaze.

"Mmm," the doctor nodded, finally breaking the silence. "I've seen this before."

"Seen what? Is it TB? Cancer?"

"Worse," the doctor said. "You're dying inside."

"What do you mean?" Josh began, and then, as if on cue, a tickle began in the back of his throat.

"Do you get a thrill of adrenaline each day, when you go to your work?" the doctor asked. "Do you feel like what you do *means* something?"

Josh shrugged.

"What do you do for fun after work," the doctor pressed. "Watch TV?"

Again, a shrug.

"What is the most important thing in your life…the thing that if you lost it, you feel as if you would die?"

Josh thought, but before he answered, the doctor posed yet another question.

"When was the last time you made love to your wife and felt like a man?"

Josh didn't answer. The tickle had started again in earnest. He was coughing out the black, slimy ichor that was his soul onto the sterile paper sheets of the bed.

"That's what I thought," the doctor said. "You are just the shell of a man, a skin with no heart. You died a long time ago, you just didn't know it."

THEY KEPT him at the hospital that night for observation, but Josh used the sterile hours for introspection. He thought a lot that night. He considered the pathways of his dead-end job. He considered the cold hands of his empty marriage. And he mourned the bright smile of his beautiful daughter, who would never understand why her daddy had slipped away, into the black, black ink of a loveless night. Would it really be better for her to watch him waste away right there in front of her?

He packed his bag in the dark of twilight, as down the hall the nightshift nurse played Sudoku on the computer. He stood, uncertain, in the shadow of his hospital door at 3 a.m.

"I'm ready," he said, to himself as much to the dark.

"Too late," came the reply from inside his heart. "You can't escape the life you made." The tickle started then, and grew.

"I want to live again," gasped Josh, as the coughs began.

"Too late," came a voice in his head, which sounded strangely like the doctor. It didn't matter.

"You've already died inside," the voice said. "Now lay down. And accept death like a man."

Josh fell to his knees and coughed. The blackness came.

"Why?" he gasped.

"You're hollow inside," the doctor's voice said.

"Fill me up again," Josh begged.

"Only you can do that."

"I can't move," he complained.

"Then you have your answer."

Josh cried out once, then again, as black decay spilled from his lips and he cursed his wife, cursed his job, cursed his life. But mostly, he cursed himself for his weakness. He heard the doctor's voice whisper in his ear, and Josh nodded his head slowly. Then he began to cry. His tears left inky trails across his cheeks. He climbed back into bed, returning, as he always did. Not leaving.

IN THE SMALL hours of the morning, Josh woke again in his hospital bed. The doctor sat by Josh's side. The bed sheets were sodden with black tar. The refuse of a lifetime of broken dreams and unfulfilled promises. When Josh lifted his arm, a sticky film of blackness tacked his skin to the sheet. It parted with a gummy snap.

"Are you ready yet?" the doctor asked, pressing a stethoscope to his throat.

"Yes," Josh gasped.

"There's no going back," the doctor said, and Josh nodded, accepting a ream of paperwork on a clipboard. He signed his name to the will at the top, and then the birth certificate at the bottom. When he stood up from the bed, he looked at the sewer-dark stains and closed his eyes.

"You're dead," the doctor proclaimed, peeling off the top sheet from the clipboard. "And newly born," he added, handing Josh a copy of the birth certificate from the bottom of the papers. "Don't look back."

Just before dawn, Josh exited the hospital. He carried nothing on his back, and left his car parked in the hospital garage. It was no longer his. He was no longer him.

When he walked into the Safeway two days and two states away, he struck up a conversation with the saleswoman in the aisle. It was unintentional, but there was a spark in her eye that captured him. And the sarcasm in her lopsided smile made him feel instantly warm. After a few minutes and a couple of mutual laughs, she asked his name. Josh smiled and held out his hand.

"Hi," he said. "I'm afraid I lost my manners. My name is Chuck. What's yours?"

"Nothing lost, nothing gained," she said. "My name's Marie."

In his chest, Chuck felt an empty space begin to fill again.

We Take Care Of
Our Own

Let me just state right from the start that I didn't want to go. I had a comfortable apartment in Chicago and there is nothing like a jog by Lake Michigan at 6 a.m. on a pleasant morning in June to start your day. Moving to the sweltering backwoods was not my idea of a good summer. But not having a paycheck was a worse idea. So, I took the assignment, packed my back seat with clothes, a stereo, and some DVDs and my trunk with as much Goose Island as I could fit, and I drove eight hours to the foot of the hills. According to the boys upstairs at Lietzner's Prime Food Additives, productivity seemed to be suffering at one of our main plants hidden out in the boondocks of Appalachia. It also seemed that the boys thought that I could be easily repositioned to investigate this supposed lapse. I was expected to pack up my life, drive across country, and spend my summer away from Wrigley Field to find out why. You might be catching the drift that I wasn't particularly pleased about this situation.

You'd be right.

Their one acknowledgement of the difficulty that such a move might pose to their loyal employee was a rather pathetic gift. They gave me the digital Dictaphone I'm recording this on, to help me record my reports while I was walking the factory floor. I could slip it easily in my pocket and spit out whatever intelligence I found for the tiny microphone to catch. Never mind that I'd still need to transcribe my words later if I was going to send them a useful document of my findings. But whatever.

The company had rented me a small house near the food additive factory which I eventually found after several wrong turns down roads that ended in tall stands of gnarled trees and brush and the occasional ramshackle white frame house. The rent-a-house I eventually ended up in had five times as much space as my apartment and probably cost half as much, but there was something about it that made me uneasy as I unloaded my car.

It was too quiet there.

The gentle but persistently lulling sound of the rush of cars or busses or the El was missing. After I piled all of the food I'd brought on the white tiled kitchen table and dumped the clothes on the sheetless bed to put away later, I sat down on the rented couch (nondescript brown, but surprisingly comfy) and stared at the sliding glass doors that led out of the family room to the wilds of the back yard.

The house creaked and the faint wind whispered.

From somewhere far away... or maybe closer than I thought... I heard something scream in pain. A nighthawk's dinner?

The hairs on the back of my neck stood on end. I wasn't afraid of street noise, but this backwoods shit creeped me out. It took me a long time to get to sleep that night in my large bed in my large room in the middle of a very large freakin' nowhere.

MY FIRST THOUGHT at a report to Chicago: This factory has poor productivity because it is staffed by morons.

I made this determination without spending more than 5 minutes on the first morning tour. I was met at the door by Jameson Tal, a big man with a flannel shirt and a strong need for a lifetime supply of Listerine.

"I'm sorry they made you come all this way," he explained when he met me at the aluminum screen door that opened on the parking lot. "Things have been a little slow here, but we've had some folks out sick. Now that Mel and Tracey Lou are back, you should see the same kinds of numbers you're used to."

I nodded and tried to smile at his unease. No plant manager ever wanted headquarters sending someone in to look them over. But I wasn't going away. The company had paid my rent for the next 90 days.

I smiled and nodded and held out my hand. "I'm sure it's all good," I said, "but they gave me a summer vacation to hang out with you. So ... I'm going to get to know Mel and Tracey Lou and everyone else before I go home. I'm sure I'll be out of your hair before you know it, with a great report."

Actually, I wasn't sure of anything of the kind. I was pretty sure this was going to be one of the longest, most torturous summers of my life. And whether I thought the slugs working the floor were performing up to par or not, I *was* telling Jameson the truth about one thing: I wasn't going home for a while.

THE PLANT WAS one of those places that made you feel grey and hopeless as soon as you set foot inside. The kind of place where life wasn't what you lived, it was how you died. Slowly, and painfully. This wasn't the sort of place where people yelled out the lines to The Who's "Teenage Wasteland" with glee as it played over the stereo. This was the place where they laid down and died silently, with their fingers ground in the machines that they fed for 8 hours a day. The machines that had no regard for their humanity.

Tal introduced me to the aforementioned Mel and Tracey Lou, and I was less than impressed. They stared at me with empty eyes and barely answered a question when I posed it. The humanistic side of me suggested that they were just scared. Cowed into silence.

The cruel part of me shrugged them off and said they were dumb.

Neither was the case.

I didn't know that then.

And so, I asked Mel out for a beer after work. I wanted to know what was going on. What better strategy than to get a man drinking if you want to get to the truth?

Mel didn't offer the truth I wanted.

I took him to the local bar, bought far more rounds than appetizers and got from him that the reason Lietzner's was producing less was because ... there was less to produce.

This was not the answer I was looking for.

But I didn't give up. I had the whole summer to burn, whether I liked it or not.

I didn't like it. But I wondered about Mel.

He came to work with bruises on his face. And a silence in his shoulders. He didn't talk easily. I knew in the base of my spine that something was up, whether it related to the plant or not. But I couldn't get it out of him.

"You look pretty beat," I said at one point, thinking that the double entendre was definitely intended, and hoping he would answer.

"Nah," he answered. "Just a bad day."

I didn't believe that, not for a minute. But how do you pry?

I watched him. And I watched the others. For the next few days. The factory worked, as a factory does. People pulled switches and pushed packets from the conveyer to small trollies that took them to other places to be packaged and sold. There was not a problem with the system. If there was a problem, there was a problem with the people.

All I could see was that the people worked slowly. Like machines themselves.

Hands moved left. Bodies shifted in tandem. Legs stepped left... hands pulled product back from the belt and after a quick addition, placed them back on the belt. Alarms sounded, stopping the line. And then readjustments happened, and the conveyers creaked into motion again.

I couldn't see anything going on here that was any more or less productive than any other plant I'd been to. People were bored and they performed like dull automatons. That was factory life, right? I knew what it was like. I'd worked on a line when I was younger. You got into the rhythm, checked your brain out, and prayed for the 5 p.m. bell.

The place smelled like every food you've ever caught a whiff of… only, magnify it by 100. It wasn't a pleasant fruity smell then… it was an overpowering, chewable stench. I hated the days that they made the flavoring for beef stew.

"How is your wife?" I asked Mel at one point. We were sitting in a bar a few blocks from the plant after work.

I hadn't counted on the fist that connected with my jaw as his response.

When I picked myself up off the floor I searched his eyes for a reason. But all I saw was fear.

"Leave her out of this," he said. His voice shook.

"Out of what?" I asked.

"You're here to shut down the plant," he said. "Don't ask how she is. You're going to kill her."

I was still shaking the sting of his knuckles off my jaw, so I just shook my head faster. "I'm not here to do anything of the kind," I promised. "I'm here to get the plant working back at the level it used to but I'm definitely not here to kill anybody doing it!"

He didn't look convinced. One of his dark eyebrows slanted down to meet his scowl.

"If this plant closes, she *will* die," he said again.

"You need the health insurance?" I asked, trying to sound comforting.

Instead of the reaction I expected, he laughed. "Insurance," he nodded. "I gotta go."

THAT WAS when things got weird.

I'D WALKED through the plant – but just down the middle aisle on the first couple days. After that, I stuck to watching the floor from the offices overhead and talking with the managers.

But I knew something was wrong when I decided to walk the floor during a regular shift and talk to the workers as they were running their machines. That threatened to interrupt production, but I thought it might be worthwhile. Mostly, they just ignored me. But sometimes, they acted as if I'd set them over the edge.

They screamed. They lunged at me. I shrunk back, but there was really no need. I hadn't seen the chains that held them to their machines until then.

Chains!

Holy crap. This wasn't just a factory. It was a hidden fortress of white slavery. Part of me said to march immediately to Jameson and demand an explanation. But the other part said to talk to the workers while I had the chance. Once I confronted the boss, I wasn't sure I'd be allowed back on the floor again. On second thought, I realized that if I confronted him, I wasn't sure he'd let me out of the factory alive. They may still keep slaves here in Appalachia, but they sure didn't let on to the outside world.

NOTE TO HEADQUARTERS: perhaps a gun would have been more useful than a Dictaphone?

I STEPPED CLOSER to a woman in a denim shirt and pants. She fed the machine slowly, methodically.

"Excuse me, ma'am," I began.

She didn't answer. Her hand moved slowly, forward and back, forward and back. It was almost hypnotic.

"Excuse me," I said again.

Nothing.

I reached out and touched her on the shoulder.

And then I got a reaction. Almost an explosion.

The woman's head jerked around and she lunged at me, mouth wide open, eyes bugging out of her face in rage, bloodshot and yellow. She screamed something unintelligible, and I leapt back. Seconds after her arms left the levers of her station, an alarm rang out and a red light began flashing overhead.

I had barely begun to take all of this in and react when two strong hands grabbed my shoulders and pulled me away from the crazed woman.

Jameson.

"What the hell are you doing?" he yelled. "You can't interrupt the line. You of all people should know that!"

He dragged me down the aisle of workers (none of them even glanced at us) and up the stairs to the management offices.

I waited while he gave me a tongue-lashing filled with vitriol so heavily accented, I could barely understand him. And then quietly, I asked my question:

"Why are you holding these people prisoner?"

I'm not sure what reaction I expected from him, but it wasn't laughter.

That's what I got. A big belly laugh. His eyes rolled back and he shook his head at me as if I was the rube, not him.

"Why are we holding them *prisoner*?" he asked, still stifling laughter. "Because they are prisoners. There's a group of people down there who are working off their debt to society. We partnered with the state prison to get some cheap labor. We pay them minimum wage, and they work the line every day. But we can't afford to have them go running off and we can't stand behind each one. So, they're in leg irons while they do their shifts. They're not always terribly happy people, as you found."

It definitely wasn't the answer I was expecting, and that must have showed. His dark brown eyes lit suddenly with humor, and he raised an eyebrow as he said, "What did you expect, that we still keep *slaves* here in the south?"

I got out of his office quickly, before I let my Barney Fife out with an "Uh, yep."

I DIDN'T CARE what Jameson said, there was something going on there that wasn't right. And I intended to find out exactly what it was from Mel. But so far, he hadn't been exactly talkative. I needed to know a little bit more about him.

Maybe I'd watched a little too much "Maverick" when I was a kid, or maybe I was just bored. But when Mel left the plant that night at the 5 p.m. siren, I followed.

He drove a rusting Ford pickup through a maze of backroads through the small grey town outside of the factory and then through forest and swamp. I followed as far back as I could while still keeping the back of his truck in sight – I focused on the numbers at the end of his license plate: 252.

I drove past the driveway he went down and eventually pulled my car into the ditch on the side of the road. Then I walked back to where I'd watched him pull off. I stood on the edge of the driveway, a long, curved gravel road through a stand of overgrown trees.

I could see the hint of the mountains through the breaks in the trees, and the interruption of a white-frame house down at the end of the gravel drive near where the red lights of the Ford flickered and died.

I waited a few minutes, to be sure he'd gone into the house, and then cautiously began walking down the gravel path. The air was heavy with the end of a summer day; I had to give this place that – it was hot and humid, but the air tasted unlike anything we ever breathed in Chicago. It smelled rich with the scents of life. Organic, heady... clean.

Right now, I could smell the heavy scent of some kind of flowering tree. I didn't know what it was, but the perfume was thick, and not completely sweet. There was a cloying aftertaste of rot somehow, deep within the smell.

Death within the sweetness. So much like life itself—death always growing in the heart of the light.

I breathed it in, and exhaled. And then stole towards the house as dusk slipped through the trees.

The house looked beaten and old... kind of like Mel himself, I thought. I was walking along the side when I heard the screen door of the front of the house crash shut.

My heart stuck in my throat and I flattened myself to the siding. I could hear the creak of a car door, and then the slam as it shut again. Slowly, I pushed myself to step forward, until I was at the corner of the house, and could peer around.

Mel was walking up the three steps of the front porch, carrying a bag of something.

The screen door slammed again, and he was gone.

I slipped around the corner, daring myself to creep along the front of the house. If he came out at this point, I was dead. Nowhere to run.

But the front door remained silent. I moved closer to the picture window that looked out over the wooden porch. The ledge was lower than my waist, so I carefully knelt down, and tried to stare inside without being seen.

Mel lived in the aftermath of a tornado.

Inside, I could see a couch and old tube television. And in the next room I could see a kitchen table, some half-open dark brown cabinets and a refrigerator that, from the rounded edges on its door, may have been as old as me.

And then I saw Mel, dashing into the kitchen from some other room in the house. He threw a white package onto the counter and then pulled open a drawer. I watched him slice open the package and then rip open whatever was inside.

From somewhere deep within the house, I heard a sound.

It reminded me of a heavy door closing. And a sigh. And a tortured scream.

All in one.

Mel turned away from me and vanished down a hallway into the depths of the house. I crept across the porch and moved in the same direction.

The next window I came to looked into a bedroom.

A woman (I assumed Mel's wife) was there, standing near the bed.

I watched as he held her, his arms tight around her waist. She moved against him, jaggedly, and I saw his hands slide up and down her back, grabbing her in passion, pulling her close to him.

Part of me wanted to pull away... this wasn't something I should be seeing. But the voyeur in me bade me to stay.

I was almost getting turned on when they turned to the side, and I could see her in profile. And that's when I saw the black leather strap tied across her cheek and mouth.

As they turned, I saw that her hands were not completely free either. They were bound in white cloth. Almost as if he'd tied a dish towel around them.

I watched as he hugged and pulled her close and they twirled around the room. And I began to realize that his hug was as much of a struggle as it was an embrace.

When they reached a certain angle, I could see her eyes.

They were not lit with love.

She looked hungry.

That's when I saw that her hands were not pawing his back in amorous-ness... she was clawing at him in violence. If her hands weren't wrapped in cloth, she'd have shredded his back in short order.

"I know, I know," I could hear him say through the window. "I brought it. Don't worry."

He pulled back from her and picked up a white paper package from the dresser behind them. He pulled a red piece of bloody meat from the paper, and his wife's gaze followed it. She lunged forward, and then I could see the chains holding her taut to the bed.

Mel reached around the back of her neck and released the gag. It fell to the floor as her body surged forward. And then he held the meat up over her mouth and she leapt up for it, like a dog. She groaned and pulled against her chains, and when he released the meat, she swiped it into her mouth with her "mittened" claws in a heartbeat.

I'M NOT sure what I thought at that moment. I couldn't do anything but watch as Mel reached behind him and fed her strip after strip of raw meat. When it was gone, he went back to the kitchen and returned with more.

I watched as Mel fed his wife until she appeared sated. After a while, she stopped grabbing for the meat and turned to lie down upon the bed. I could see clearly then the chains that held her ankles and waist.

And I could see the love in Mel's eyes as he inched forward and slowly, tentatively, reached out his hand to stroke her hair as she slipped into a meat coma.

She was hunger, and he was her slave.

I understood now why his face was sometimes bruised, and marked.

Something was really wrong with Mel's wife.

The weird thing for me was, this was the second time I'd seen a woman in chains today. Somehow it had all gone from strange to stranger.

I SLIPPED AWAY from the window, and back down the gravel driveway. I didn't want to face Mel right now to ask any questions. I wasn't sure what to ask, exactly. "Why does your wife like raw meat so much" didn't seem to be the right entrée. And "why do you keep your wife chained up like a dog" wasn't the best leading question either.

THAT NIGHT, I lay in my bed and kept seeing Mel's wife lunging for the blood steaks in his hand. I didn't think she cared a whole lot whether she latched onto the meat he held or the meat he *was*. She was hungry. That was all.

Nearby, I heard a too-familiar hum. It closed in, the sound of its hunger growing louder, nearer.

I slapped at it with one firm, fatal, smack.

The mosquito died on my arm. Hunger incarnate. Hunger overcome.

I couldn't help but think that Mel needed to do something similar. Though I didn't expect he'd be open to the idea.

I CONTINUED to delve into the plant's production and personnel records. And it didn't take too long to see a trend.

Something had happened in January. The first week of the year, the rate of factory sick days suddenly doubled. You could shrug that off, at first, to recovery from over exuberant New Year's Eve celebrations. We saw the same problems in Chicago, but it was a minimal event. A few days of heightened absenteeism, and then things dropped back to normal.

Here however... they'd increased.

By February, an eighth of the workforce was absent on any given day, and the trips to the company infirmary had skyrocketed. Six months later, that hadn't changed. And when I looked at the company doctor's appointment records, I saw that he was solidly booked every day of the past month.

I decided a visit to the doctor was in order. Impromptu. I didn't want to wait until July to get in. I set off down the stairs and across the main floor of the plant and down a hallway that led alongside the shipping dock. The company physician's office was all the way in the back of the factory.

The sign on the outside of the glass door said Fagan McLeod, MD. I stood outside for a moment, peering in, and as I did so, the door to my left that led out to the parking lot wrenched open.

A white-faced, gaunt man shambled inside, pushed along by a disheveled woman. Black strips of hair clung to her face, which was beaded in sweat. I saw why instantly. She was having difficulty herding the man forward. She had his arms chained, and prodded him with something in the back, but he kept trying to turn on her, and from deep within his chest, moans of anger trembled. They were contained, however, by the rubber gag around his mouth.

"Kin ya git the door," the woman begged of me.

I did. And once they were inside, I followed them.

The waiting room was small, and two other couples were seated along the longest wall. In each case, one of the two was gagged and restrained. Their "keepers" struggled to keep them in place, and I quickly understood why the walls were completely bare of decoration, save for numerous dents and cracks.

This was a holding pen, not a waiting room.

"Can I help you?" a woman called. She poked her head out of a small receptionist's office. I stepped up and introduced myself. "I'm from the home office," I explained. "I need to speak to Dr. McLeod for a moment."

She led me through a white door and into an examining room and gestured for me to have a seat. "He's with a patient right now," she said. "But I'll make sure he stops in before his next appointment."

He didn't keep me waiting long. A brief knock on the door, and a broad-shouldered man in a white lab coat entered the room. His silver hair curled in a thick wave across his forehead, and his mouth was nearly obscured by a salt and pepper beard and mustache. Behind his glasses beamed two strong, if slightly sunken blue eyes. He looked like a retired lumberjack wearing a doctor's garb.

"How kin I help ya?" he asked. He didn't sit, choosing instead to lean against the closed door.

"Your schedule has gotten pretty full these days," I noted.

He nodded. "We take care of our own."

"What's wrong with your own?" I pressed.

"Lots of things," he said. His expression didn't change. "Meningitis, the flu, head colds, congenital problems... I treat them all."

"You didn't mention anything that would require chains and ball gags," I pointed out.

He nodded. "We do have some psychiatric cases as well," he admitted.

"And you see them all on Tuesday, or what?"

The doctor shrugged. "I have patients to see," he said, putting his hand on the doorknob.

"What's going on around here really, doctor?" I demanded. "What's wrong with the people in your waiting room really? Is there some kind of epidemic?"

"Everything's fine," he said. "As long as they come in for their shots every week, everyone stays healthy."

He opened the door and held his hand out, motioning for me to leave. "Go back to your production reports," he said. "We're taking care of the workers and their families down here. You go take care of the numbers and spreadsheets up there."

With that, he disappeared around the corner and into a treatment room.

I started to walk towards the exit and then thought better of it. Instead, I followed the doctor. I ducked into the room next to the one he'd entered and quietly closed the door. Then I pressed my ear up to the wall. I could just barely hear him speaking in the next room.

"... the raw meat has been workin', then?" he said.

Muffled response. A woman's voice. I wondered if it was the woman I'd opened the door for earlier.

"We'll keep on with this dosage," McLeod said. "As long as you can handle him? Otherwise, I can give a heavier sedative to use?"

Muffled response.

"No bites?" McLeod asked. "Good. Keep it safe, and you can keep him home. Now hold his arm for me if you can, and we'll give him his dose."

A sudden crash and McLeod yelled. "Hold him!"

Something pounded against the wall, as if someone had just beat a fist, or a bat against it. Then more thumping sounds, and a woman's voice, screaming "No!"

I hung against the wall, frozen. What was going on next door? Should I break my cover and help? But then it quieted, and I heard McLeod say one word. "Good."

A minute later, he laughed and said, "He is a big one. Better get him out on the line now."

I heard the door next door open, and then the doctor added one more caution. "Watch yourself, Elly. We don't want to lose you too."

I waited until the noises next door had been quiet for a few minutes, and then I poked my head out of the door. Seeing no one, I walked back down the hall towards the reception area. The waiting room looked much the same as when I left it: three couples sat there, with one partner of each pair bound and gagged.

"Meningitis, the flu, and head colds my ass," I said to myself.

WHEN MEL GOT HOME from work that night, I was waiting for him on his front porch.

"Evening," I said with a smile. I didn't stand up.

"What are you doing here?" He stood halfway down the sidewalk, clearly uneasy with my presence. His eyes shifted back and forth, peering over my shoulders to take in the house. Wondering if I'd somehow been inside? Or looked inside?

"What's wrong with her?" I asked.

"She's fine," he said. "She just needs medicine."

"And meat," I added.

"What do you know about it?" His voice raised, and he stepped closer, angry.

"Why is your face bruised?" I asked. I kept my voice quiet. "Are you having problems controlling her?"

"Mind your own business," he growled. "Get off my property."

"I'm not leaving until I know what's going on here," I said.

"Get outta here or I'm gonna take out a couple a' yer teeth," he warned.

"You want to keep your job?" I asked sweetly. "You want to keep your health insurance? She needs those injections every week, just like the others, doesn't she?"

His eyes widened.

"Yeah, I've seen McLeod's waiting room," I said.

Something in his shoulders slumped at that moment. He stepped onto the stairs and brushed past me to step onto the porch.

"You want a drink?" he asked.

"Sure," I said. "I been waiting here for a long time. Been waiting for an answer for a long time."

"You're not going to like it," he warned.

I nodded. "I pretty much expect that."

HE LED me into the house, and to the kitchen. "First things first," he said. Then he pulled a white paper package out of the refrigerator and unwrapped it. I followed him down the hall and to the room where she was chained. I watched him tenderly kiss her forehead and cheeks as she beat her bound fists against his back. Then I watched him loosen the ball gag and feed her strip after strip of raw meat until she could take no more. Sated, she didn't struggle as he refastened her gag and laid her down upon the bed.

Back in the kitchen, he pulled out two tumblers and poured two fingers of bourbon into each. He emptied his in one gulp and then refilled.

I sipped mine slowly, waiting for the story.

"It all started at the company New Year's Eve party," he began.

"I've always said they should stop spending budget on that," I said. "Nothing good ever comes of them."

Mel nodded. "Yeah. Well, certainly not this year."

"What happened?"

"One of the girls from the Shipping Department, Plutina Wade, found a new experimental flavor from Dr. McLeod's laboratory, and decided to use it in moonshine shots."

"Wait a minute," I interrupted. "McLeod is the company doctor, isn't he?"

Mel nodded. "Sure, he is. But first and foremost, he's in charge of developing new flavors. He had been working on a new one called Huckleberry Pie, mixing some local berries with some other compounds. And Plutina thought that'd make for a great moonshine mixer. And she was right. She and a little group got snockered on the stuff before the clock struck midnight on New Year's Eve. And then, when they called for everyone to claim a place beneath the mistletoe, she picked out Fin Kinnane and led him under the red berries of one of the plants that they'd tied to the rafters.

"He gave her a kiss… apparently a pretty good one, probably 'cause he saw she didn't look like she could barely stand up straight anymore. Problem was, when the kiss was over, Fin didn't have no tongue anymore.

"He still managed to make a lot of noise though. But he wasn't the only one. Seemed that everyone at Plutina's table had somehow gotten a bad hunger for their dates that night. There was a lot of blood beneath the mistletoe. And a lot of people got themselves bit trying to bring Plutina's party down. In the end, we got 'em all into the company infirmary and locked up 'til the doc could figure out what was going on."

My eyes must have looked pretty large at this point, because Mel gave me a thin-lipped laugh. "Yeah. Sounds ridiculous, doesn't it?"

"What was in the flavoring?" I asked.

Mel shrugged. "Only Doc knows. All I know is he was experimenting with some kind of wild berry. It wasn't ready for anyone to taste it yet. But once they did, it changed them, and he couldn't come up with a cure. He's been trying for months now."

"What does he inject them with every week?"

"That's just a vitamin shot, with a time delayed tranquilizer. Gives 'em nutrients to keep up their bodies while putting 'em into the quiet zone for three or four days, usually."

"And in the meantime, you chain them up and have them run the assembly line?" I said, my voice rising with incredulity.

Mel looked at me like I was a lunatic.

"What kind of people do you think we are?" he asked. "Those are prisoners from the jail. When we had too many workers out, we started the work program with the prison. Gives them a way to work off their sentence and fills in the places where we've lost workers. You came here wondering why productivity was down? Well, mainly because for a couple months there, we had a couple dozen spots open on the line while Doc was trying to find the cure."

"Doesn't seem like he's been too successful."

A step creaked behind me. "He's working on it."

I felt a pinch in my arm, and just as I turned to see Doctor McLeod's face grinning over my shoulder, he pulled the needle out of my arm. I could see that the syringe was empty.

"What did you..." I began.

I didn't finish. I slept.

WHEN I WOKE UP, there were chains on my ankles. I noticed them when I pulled myself off the cold floor on my elbows, and heard the clink-clink-clink of the metal drag across the floor when my legs shifted.

"What the hell?" I mumbled. The world still seemed blurry and warped.

A door closed behind me, and I shifted to see who it was.

The tall jeans and heavy boots of Jameson Tal stepped across the white tiles towards me.

"Ya shoulda stuck to your sales reports and quotas and whatnot," he drawled. "Thing is, you stuck yer head where it don't belong."

Jameson sunk to a crouch and shook his head at me. "People don't like that, ya know."

"I was sent here to find out why productivity was down," I said. "You could have just told me that you had 20 or 30 people out with some local epidemic."

"And you woulda had us replace them instead of take care of them."

"Not if you'd told the company that it was an illness related to our products."

Jameson grinned and shook his head. "You think we want a parade of you people down here, putting us all under the microscope?" Jameson shook his head. "We take care of our own."

"You can't hold me prisoner here forever," I said. "And if you let some of the folks from the lab in Chicago or Michigan come down here, they might be able to help Dr. McLeod isolate and cure whatever this thing is that he's unleashed."

Jameson smiled and shook his head. "I'll be honest with ya," he said. "I'm not so sure everybody wants this thing cured. I know Jed Boucher says he's never had this much fun with his sister before. I've seen the cat scratches on his face, and I gotta believe him there. In any case, you're not bringing the roof down on us. You're going to send some positive interim reports over the next month or two, while we get the prisoner program workers fully trained. They don't cost nothing extra, so payroll don't know the difference. And pretty soon the line will be running as good as it ever was. Chicago will be happy, and wonder why they sent ya. The bean counters won't ask no more questions."

"I'm not sending any such report," I said. Bravado sounds great, but it's almost always a foolish exercise.

Jameson nodded. "No, I suppose technically that's true. *You* won't send those reports, but I will. With your name at the bottom. Nobody's going to miss you back there, and when you stop sending your updates, and they finally get around to asking where you are…I'll just tell 'em that I thought you went home 2-3 weeks ago…"

My stomach clenched. Was he really suggesting…

"Just remember," Jameson said. "I didn't want to do this. You brought it on yerself."

Just then, the doctor stepped into the room and motioned for Jameson. "I called for an assembly this afternoon," he said. "Everyone's excited."

"Zombies can't live on steaks alone, eh?" Jameson said.

Dr. McLeod shook his head. "No," he agreed. "They need man."

With that, they both left the room. That's when I pulled out my dictation recorder and decided to record my last report. I *did* discover why productivity was down, even if nobody will ever find out. I had to document it, even if this recorder will simply get smashed and thrown away.

Click

The door just opened. The doctor held it for Mel, who led his wife in on a chain. A line of others are now following him through the door.

"I'm sorry man," Mel said. "But she's hungry. She needs you."

He's releasing the gag from her mouth, and her teeth look stained. Hungry.

The sound of chains dropped to the floor.

She's moving towards me.

"Don't fight it," Mel warned. "It'll go faster then."

I DON'T WANT to die. I've moved as far back into the room as I can, but the chains won't let me move anymore. Mel's wife and somebody's husband and a dozen other shambling creatures have entered the room. Their gags are off. My own personal death race is on.

I never wanted to come here.

"Ow! Shit, motherfucking bitch…"

"We take care of our own," Jameson Tal called from far away. "And soon you'll be one of us."

Their hands are all over me. Their teeth…*Shit!*

I'm going to turn this off now. My legs are bleeding, and I can't kick much more. You don't need to hear my screams.

I'm the one "taking care of their own" now.

And they are hungry.

Then Shall The Reign Of Lucifer End...

Rhi kissed the dust on the wooden floor and tasted the rancid spice of age. Brett and Charlie had brought her here to dispose of. She had no illusions about their motives. After they'd drugged her, tied her up, beat her and then raped her repeatedly, she had known hours ago why, after a week in hell on earth, they had finally driven her out to the most remote location in the county. They were frightened by what they'd done to her over the past few days in that locked room, and knew they would never get away with it if she went free. She was used up now, and they wanted her to die. Only trouble was, from what she could tell, they were too scared to actually take care of the deed themselves.

For days they'd kept her locked in a room in the city. They'd chained her, abused her and used her like an animal. She had swallowed their sour cum and even more sour piss, as they had laughed and pulled her hair to force her to nod yes every time they asked "mmm, you like it?" But through all of the degradation and torture, they had always fucked her with condoms, as if afraid that they might get her pregnant. They had been very intent on learning her cycle when they had first picked her up and brought her to the torture room.

She had taken that as a good sign that they intended to let her go eventually.

So, when they both used her on the dirty planks of the abandoned house and, for the first time, both rode her bareback, Rhi knew it was over for her.

End of the line.

This time she just laid there, without protest, as they filled her up with so much hot spunk that it oozed back out over her swollen distended labial lips. Their orgasms burned like rough sandpaper on a fresh wound as their sperm coated the bruised and bleeding flesh inside her. The rash on her thighs burned from the chafing of their hairy, anxious legs and a smell like dead fish filled the room as they pummeled her again and again, knocking her head on the boards. She hadn't showered in a week, and Rhi cried as she smelled the rank scent of herself and their stale sweat mingle while the pain spread again all across her belly and legs.

Afterwards, they punched her in the gut and kicked her in the back and laughed at her until she had staggered away from them and then fallen over to lie trembling on the bare floor like a drunk with the tremens.

She figured they had originally lugged her to the old farmhouse thinking she was dead – she'd blacked out at some point back in the city, in the torture room. They probably had thought she was gone for good. From the red-searing pain in her back and neck, she wished they had been right. But instead, after they muscled her from the trunk and tossed her here on the floor of the abandoned old house, she had started to moan. She supposed that only then had they realized she was not dead. Not even close. That's when they decided to take advantage of the situation to plant one more fuck in her. Actually two, for the price of one. It was no bargain for her.

Fuck, it hurt. The pain rolled over her brain in waves of awful surf. She could taste the iron of her blood and the acid of her pain and defeat with every swallow. She'd done nothing to deserve this but exist...sometimes existing was a condemnation in and of itself.

After they'd done their business, they'd left her there, bleeding and dying on the floor of the old house. Rhi kept her eyes closed and relished the quiet. The house was silent as death without her rapists in the room. She could feel the warmth of her blood and their foul sperm leaking out of her to stain the floor beneath, but she didn't dare try to move. The room may have been still, but everything screamed too loud inside.

Maybe she *would* finally die here, she hoped. She'd never wanted to live anyway. Not because anything unusual had happened to her. She'd been dumped last month, again, by another shiftless loser who'd fucked her and run. And her mom had met her match this summer in the big C. The docs'd tried to saw off mom's boobs to save her, but it didn't do any good. In just a few months, Rhi had watched the poor woman go from a robust, brassy take-no-shit-from-anyone woman to a carved-up shell of zombie without any fat, hair or spirit.

But Rhi knew her mom's death and her own chronic disease of getting dumped were not reasons to give up; everyone goes through shit like that. The problem was, Rhi had never felt all that committed to life anyway. She never had her mom's spirit, and couldn't just fuck and be happy like so many of the guys she met...and lost. Maybe she just didn't have the energy to keep them. Lately, she hadn't had the energy to care whether she lived or died. Why else would she have been stupid enough to answer an ad that had read simply, *"Female test subject wanted. Must be over 18, and willing to pose nude. E-mail photo and bra size to demonx@inferno.com."*

THEIR VOICES WERE RETURNING. They were chanting and the odor of something like October burning leaves filled the air. Rhi had a flash of Easter mass at church when she was a girl, and it occurred to her what the smell was. Not autumn leaves.

Incense.

The strange words grew closer. More intense. Rhi's toes clenched as she waited for the inevitable. And then it happened. Charlie's hairy fingers clenched her shoulder and pulled Rhi up to her knees. Something shiny glinted in Brett's hand.

That's when the pain really began.

WHEN RHI CAME TO AGAIN, it was night. Blackness blanketed her body. Muscles screamed in agony when she lifted her head. The memory of why replayed in vivid agony behind her eyes. Charlie and Brett had walked around her in a circle chanting strange words and spreading incense; then they had knelt and begun to carve her alive with a flimsy serrated steak knife, there on the floor. When the cutting began, she'd found one last burst of energy she didn't know she even had. Maybe she didn't totally want to die after all? She had punched and kicked and tried to escape, but was too weak from a week of fighting ropes and beatings. Charlie subdued her easily with a couple hard fists to the jaw and a tight chokehold around the neck.

Through the haze of pain, Rhi thought that they still did not seem intent on killing her…they hurt like a bitch, but none of the blades bit deep. They stung more than stabbed, crossing and crisscrossing the surface of her back, drawing lines of pain in her shoulders and ribs and then, when they flipped her bloody body to face them, they carved her breasts and belly. Maybe they were trying to draw her pain out? These were not the shrieking buffoons who had raped her and laughed at her for days. Charlie and Brett looked deadly serious, as they held her down and drew designs on her in permanent ink; blood.

SHE FELT EVERY CUT NOW, and stared at her naked chest – her chest whose nipples and breasts those apes had pawed and twisted and sucked for hours – to see what horrible words they had finally decided to etch into her indelibly, flesh graffiti. They had to be words, she thought. Their knives had cut her for hours it seemed, slowly and deliberately, in curls and straight lines. They had skipped space and sliced again, splitting the skin dozens of times to free rivers of liquid fire that left her hoarse from screaming. She couldn't move through it all, as one of them always pinned her hard to the floor while the other drew bloody notes in her skin. Her throat now felt too swollen to speak. As she stared through the shadows at herself, desperately afraid of what scars they had forced her to wear for life, she realized that it was not all black around her. She could make out the curves and twists of ornate tattoos of blood that connected her nipples to her bellybutton and arrowed down to that crusted thatch between her legs. Everything wept tears of blood, and the air itself seemed to cry with her. The faint glow in the room was of red, horrible light.

When Rhi tried to move, her back threatened to explode. And her left leg felt numb...probably from where they had kicked it, again and again, like a soccer ball.

Why? Rhi whispered....*What did I do...*

Fuck you! A voice answered from the darkness. Taunting. *What did any of us do? Yet here we are. Just fucking deal with it, like everyone else. So your daddy fucked you? Well, you're a big girl now, kick him in the balls. So your boyfriend dropped you for someone else? You're a big girl now, fuckin' cut out his heart and eat it. Don't you know, eating your pain gives you strength?*

Rhi tried to swallow the hot iron leaking in her mouth and choked.

Would you rather go to hell with me? Huh? The voice taunted. *Follow me to the Mephistopolis...the city of the dead. Try petting a Ghor-Hound and we'll see how much you whine about a little beating.*

Rhi could see the owner of the voice now, a shadowy imp in what seemed to be a doorway. The crimson light bled through its oval border, and she raised a hand toward the figure, pleading for help.

Wait a minute... the thing said, scratching its chin. It laughed nervously, just before it turned and ran away.

...you're not dead...

THIS IS GONNA SOUND STUPID, but the thing I love about hell, is the chairs. You go into a restaurant, order some soul soup, and more often than not, you prop your burnin' ass down in a literal throne of a chair carved with intricate barbs and spines and inlaid with dozens of silently screaming skulls. Think about it – every time you sit down, you're planting your ass cheeks on some poor fuck's brainpan, some schmuck who screwed up so bad he didn't even succeed in hell! Screaming skulls are a dime a billion here in hell, but I still love the artistry. What else is there to do in eternity, but carve horrible beauty from bone, artful utility from death?

I was sipping a virgin Bloody Mary – which had as much virgin in it as vodka, thanks to Satan and the pulping stations – when she came through for the first time. The wall behind the bar just exploded, bone and gluey blood spraying everywhere. Through the breach she came, hair a wild spray of brambles and weed, face a smooth complexion of creamy death, body etched in bloody symbols and writhed in the weeds of the cemetery, only her bluish white belly button poking obscenely through the cover. Her feet disappeared in a skein of twisted muddy roots.

As she fell in a muddy, crimson heap to the ground just in front of the bar, the sky opened up outside, and rain coated the windows in sheets of red. The air in the bar thickened, and in moments the floor of the tiny oasis was overrun with crimson foam, as some new slaughter from above overflowed the sewers below.

The woman rose from a crumple of limbs on the floor and shook the dirt from her hair. The roots, however, still wreathed her in organic clothes. She opened a dark, terrified mouth and screamed until the glasses rattled dangerously behind the bar, and then she ran for the door, into the blood storm, like a banshee.

"What in eternity was that?" I whispered.

"What difference does it make?" someone else griped. "If we don't hit the road, it's gonna drown us..."

He was right. The blood had risen several inches already. You hardly noticed it at first because it was warm and relaxing – a hot salt bath. But spend a long enough bath in a blood rain, and you'll die forever regretting it. The shit was like acid on souls – it ate away at your skin until you were nothing but bleached bone. And unlike most punishments in hell, you didn't automatically grow your skin back after a bloodbath. Sometimes it took long, painful years. Sometimes, I'd heard, your body never grew back at all...but the pain – akin to having your flesh continually, repeatedly scoured with a dull cheese grater – never dulled.

WE COVERED our heads with whatever we could grab – flesh napkins, newspapers, Zap-heads who'd passed out on the floor -- and ran out of the bar with our shields into the blood. All around us a siren wail of the less fortunate, burning dead went off. The blood raged like fire as it ate into your post mortem body, eager to dissolve the spirit beneath, and I raised my voice to join the chorus. My condo was only blocks away, but I could feel the rain eat into my skin like the growing warmth of an acid burn.

I nearly broke the lock off my door and dove through my bedroom and into my bath to rinse the acid rain away as fast as possible, but I could tell that I'd be feeling the destruction of this desecration for days to come. My skin burned like the very real fires of hell.

But I'd get over it. I hadn't been caught in a while, but I'd lived through blood rain before.

What bothered me more than the pain though, was what had started it all. Aside from the usual genital-rending shrieks from the johns near the wall of flesh of the red-light district, it had been a quiet night until she was suddenly, violently born from the bar's wall. And then, to coin a bad phrase, all hell had broken loose. Who was she, and why was she here?

RHI STOOD naked on the street, a rain of rust lathering her body like pig's blood at a prom gone cruel. She'd pulled the roots away from her skin after falling to the floor from…she had no idea where. One minute, she'd been following the shadowy form of a taunting imp, and the next she was lying on the floor of a strange, hellish place with strange, hellish people and pulling out the barbs of roots and vines and stems she'd gotten entangled in during her fall.

The sky screamed at her in vicious wet curses. She ran.

Everywhere she went, the blood followed.

THE WORD SPREAD QUICKLY. How could it not…after the girl fell into our bar, the blood rain continued for 6 days and nights. The helevision declared that this much pain and suffering had not descended on the Mephistopolis since before the last visit of the Etheress. After her last incendiary attack on Lucifer's citadel had reduced his prized armies and plans to rubble, the Morning Star had retreated deep inside the ruins of the Mephisto Building, his warren of suffering. As Lucifer licked his wounds in silence, the atrocity level in hell had actually dropped. Oh, make no mistake – it was still hell. But it seemed as if some of the heart had gone out of the suffering. Some theorized that the travelling rain of blood was Lucifer's latest strategy for releasing the power of the damned to use for his own ends.

But I knew better. I'd seen the girl's eyes as she fell through into the realm. She'd been shocked and scared and lost. And I'd seen the warmth of her aura…she was no lost soul. She was an offering of the River Gods sent through to hell in a sieve from earth. A creature of blood and bone that would soon find her end here in the place where such things could never, ever exist.

At least that's what I thought at the time. But then the blood rain came near again, and I realized that the girl was still here, somewhere…and on the move. This time, instead of hiding in my apartment, I decided to find her. It hasn't hard…I just followed the weather (and stayed out of it).

I stopped at a scalper's and bought the skin of some poor pathetic lover who'd lost it during a sexual encounter in the Ampitheatre and set out into the epicenter of the storm. You could smell the iron everywhere…it was like breathing a menstrual cycle; the air was humid and spoiled with the endless stream of dying blood.

No one else lurked about; even the Constabs and Bonecrushers stayed in from the rain. I wondered what Lucifer thought; surely even in the depths of his despair, he was aware of the spreading stain.

"Who are you?" I asked when I found her. She stood in the center of the Slaughterhouse Square like a waif in invisible thrall. Her eyes shone bright with vacancy. She wasn't fully here. Maybe the enormity of the atrocities of the Mephistopolis had left her in denial.

"It won't stop," she said. Her belly swelled like a blue-white gourd. I realized in a horrible flash that she was pregnant with death.

"You brought through the blood of fertility with you," I said. "But there is not fertility in hell."

"They were beating me," she said. "they beat me to death…"

I reached out to touch her, and couldn't quite connect. My hand passed through her skin and she flinched. My skin crawled.

"You're not dead," I pronounced.

"Then why am I here?" she asked.

"Because you always wanted to visit the city of the dead?"

She shook her head.

Something screeched nearby. The telltale gleam of death steel shone from the alley just beyond. "Come on," I said. "They've had enough of you."

"And you haven't?"

"I'm curious."

"I'm dead."

"Tell me a better one. I'm the one without a corporeal body here."

I dragged her into a stairwell and forced the door to the storeroom beyond.

The Cockomite grinned salaciously at us when we slipped inside. The thing guarded the door with its large sacks of flesh and opened a dark maw wide. A glint of jism drooled to the ground. The room smelled like salty seaweed and piss. The cockomite gurgled expectantly.

"Come to cum?" it gasped. Instantly its fat, blue-veined torso began to grow, a grotesque mushroom threatening to drown us in a coming eruption of its diseased clumps of rotting sperm.

Rhi's mouth dropped as she watched the cockomite elongate to its full 12-foot length. The cankers on its belly glistened with pus and the rhythmic throb of the veins in its concave, glans-like chest were audible in the small room.

"What's a' matter?" the thing laughed. More saliva dripped like pearly, yellowed hand cream to the ground. "Haven't you ever seen a dickhead before?"

"Yeah," she said. "One killed me. Two, actually."

"You're not dead. You just haven't been laid right. Come closer and let me help."

The girl squealed and I pushed her ahead, and away from the cockomite. The damned things were a pestilence in an ocean of foul. And like any plague, their numbers seemed to be growing exponentially. One heckled you from almost every dark corner. They couldn't stand the firelight of hell in the outdoors – shriveled up and dissolved -- but lately no shadow seemed safe from the wretched things. I'd heard speculation that they were the souls of human child molesters, but I never stuck around one long enough to ask.

When we found an empty spot deep within the basement of the building, I grabbed her shoulder and forced her to stop. "Enough," I said. "Why are you here? Who sent you?"

The black beneath her eyes rippled like waves. "I don't know why. They tied me down, and fucked me, both of them. They kicked me a lot, and then cut all these designs into my skin." She gestured at the intricate pattern of cuts that crisscrossed her body, some gashes still weeping pale plasma and pus, some scabbed over. She looked as if she'd run into a very deliberate barbed wire fence. "They filled the room with incense and said all sorts of weird things…"

"What kind of things?"

"Some of it I couldn't understand… But I heard them talking about making me the mother of hell…and fucking me to the other side."

A cold spot grew in my gut as I stared at the unnatural blue tinge to her belly. "Did they say anything else about hell?"

"They said a lot of shit. I couldn't understand most of it. For a while one would chant something while the other one got between my legs and … you know. They traded off."

"What kind of chanting?"

"It sounded like another language. Then Charlie cut me, and everything got blurry. The next thing I knew, I woke up in this hot, shadowy place where some little gargoyle was making fun of me. When I tried to follow him, I fell through all this dirt and mud and roots – like I was slipping through a tunnel. When I hit the floor, I was here. But there was blood everywhere, and horrible creatures. I ran, but no matter where I went there was blood. So much blood."

"Deadpass," I said. I knew now how she'd gotten here. And I had a suspicion of why.

"Huh?"

"They performed a ritual over you, and then dropped you on a deadpass."

"What's that?"

"A place where the walls between hell and earth are thin. They beat you to within an inch of your life, performed a ritual, and prayed that you were close enough to death to slip through the deadpass to hell."

Her mouth wrinkled up, as if she was going to burst out crying. I gripped her shoulder tight. Crying here would only make matters worse. It would lead all manner of pain sycophants.

"Why?" she whispered. "I didn't do anything to them."

I placed a hand over her belly and sensed the angry, twisting infant within. "Were you pregnant before they raped you?"

"No," she said, confirming my suspicion.

"I think I know why. Though it was a huge longshot. I'm not sure what they hope to gain."

From the other room, I heard footsteps. Things clinking and rattling...as if someone was searching for something...or someone.

"We have to go," I hissed.

She held my arm, refusing to move. "Why did they do this to me, tell me?"

I leaned close and whispered my suspicion in her ear. "Because if a living woman conceives and bears a child in hell, she becomes the Mother of Hell. And her offspring, the prince. She would unseat Satan himself."

"Then I need to get home and have my baby there," she said.

"That's even worse," I said. "Then you will unleash Hell on earth."

Something crashed at the doorway, and I scooped her up like a doll and began to run deeper into the dark labyrinth. "We have to go, now!"

The noise behind us grew as we ran through the building, knocking over chairs and glasses and who knows what.

I pushed through a set of doors and entered a milking room, and cursed myself for not realizing where we were sooner.

"Shit," I moaned, as I ran through the long lab and the heads of a score of demons turned to take us in. In the center of the room, an insanely bloated woman lay prone upon a table. She was naked, and the well-used flesh of her gut and thighs hung over the edges of the table like great gobs of melted cheese, but her enormous breasts were encased and held in place atop her in sucker-like cups. Tubes of bubbling liquid ran from those suckers to a hissing, vibrating machine nearby. The juice seemed to flicker and swirl in the tubes in ribbons of both snow cream and cherry red. The woman's screams echoed and rebounded through the room like the amplified cries of a cornered mountain cat.

Some of the demons monitored the equipment while others brought additional tubes around from an octopus of a machine to connect to her mouth and sex.

"What are they doing to her?" Rhi gasped.

"The same thing that will happen to you if I don't get you out of here. She came here through a deadpass too, and now they're milking the blood of human kindness from her. As long as they can feed her, and titillate her and keep her alive in hell, they can extract gallons of it from her every day. Enough to heal half the wounds of hell."

"She's alive?" Rhi asked.

I nodded. "You two may be the only living humans in hell right now. It's a very rare thing for a living soul to get sucked through a deadpass. But when it happens...well, hell has its uses for humans. You're more valuable here than any fortune you've ever imagined."

As the demons pressed the tubes to the woman's mouth and vagina, she shuddered. Silver-strong tendrils slipped like hungry snakes inside the fat woman's soft wet, pink parts, and a jarringly mechanical whirring sound filled the room as a dark fluid flowed through the tubes to pump liquid inside her. Whatever it was, it rendered her euphoric. In seconds, her screams from the suction of milking had quieted and we could hear ecstatic moans shuddering through the tube.

Five demons flexed and adjusted their dark leathery wings menacingly, and began walking toward us.

"They can see your aura," I hissed, and lofted her to my shoulder again to run. When I found a door back to the street, I took it. As soon as we stepped outside, my feet went ankle-deep in puddles of steaming blood. The blood rain had not stopped while we were inside.

Shaking it off, I dragged her up a flight of stairs and found our way blocked. An army of Constabs waited across the street. They stood stock still, long scimitars and violet eyes waiting for their quarry.

Us.

"Let's end this now, before it goes any further," a demon captain demanded. It stepped forward from the mob, approaching the curtain of blood rain that surrounded Rhi like a hideous umbrella. It ran down the outside of the stolen flesh I wore, and even with the protective curing agent I'd applied to the skin, it was still dissolving my "raincoat" layer by layer, a poison death to the dead. A poison that threatened annihilation just centimeters from my own skin.

It was the only thing that kept the army of lost souls from charging us right now. No one wanted to spend the next two months regrowing their flesh from the seeds of bone. They waited for her to make a mistake. We were all cowards here. Sadists and cowards.

"Let us pass," I demanded, and pressed her to step sideways down the street. As the curtain of blood rain moved, so did the line of Ushers ripple and retreat, anvil-like heads bobbing in a still breeze.

"She brings us all down," the demon leader yelled. "Why are you sheltering her?"

"She's done nothing to you," I answered. "Stay away from her, and your skin stays intact. What is easier than that?"

"That's enough," one of the others bellowed, and marched into the rain of blood, scimitar in hand. But no sooner had he entered Bri's umbra of acid rain than he fell screaming to the pavement, clawing at the burning skin that sloughed off his body like warm wax. As he scratched, skin and sinew separated and fell to dissolve on the road to hell. The road of hell. In seconds nothing remained of the demon's obsidian angst but dull yellow ribs and femurs, clacking and smacking together like ghastly maracas. His remains would be ground to bone-dust for gravebread by morning while he might already have been reborn as an Excre-worm.

None of the other soldiers in hell's army followed. What was the benefit of dying again, and again and again? None of us would ever leave here to go to heaven. So why would we die for hell?

"Come on," I whispered, and led Bri through the barricade. For a while, some stragglers followed us, but soon, the steady patter of red rain was broken only by our footfalls.

I took her to a place I knew far from the center of the Mephistopolis. A place in the country, if boiling craters of molten rock could be called pastoral. I knew of a small passage across the Sea of Obsession that led to an island long abandoned. Once it had housed two sisters, whose mutual hatred had not only destroyed their mortal lives with knives and hatchets, but had led them to be isolated even in hell.

For eons they tortured each other, cutting off arms and heads and puncturing eyeballs with skewers of burning lead. They always recovered -- this was hell after all. But then Satan himself pressed them from isolation into servitude in his war against the Etheress and her sister, and months ago their island of brutal isolation had been abandoned, a refuge for those who could weather the fiery Sea of Obsession to harbor there.

I knew of the island...why, I won't say. But it was a refuge in a hell of hells. I led Rhi to the hidden dock, tied her arms and legs together hog-style and took the boat across the boiling chum-capped waves of the Sea of Obsession to the tiny rock landing. She shivered and screamed beneath the gag as the temptations of the water drew her soul out to hover and shimmer, shrieking above us...but I'd tied the ropes tight for a reason. And when we had set our shelter in the two-room shack there, I eased her down on a wooden chair, untied the last of her binds and told her of the scriptures.

"When the mother of hell descends from the fertile valley of mortals and gives birth to a child conceived in hell, not by demons but by mortal man, then shall the reign of Lucifer end, and the dominion of man begin. A child born in hell will rise to rule, and whether his throne sits in hell or on earth, his kingdom shall rival the Lord God Almighty's. The Morning Star will bow to his glory and his power shall shake the heavens. The kingdom of man will fall under his terrible scepter and the kingdom of hell will bow to his dominion."

She shook her head. "I wasn't pregnant on earth."

"That's the problem," I said. "They fucked you, and before their sperm could do the deed in the mortal realm, they sent you through the deadpass to arrive here. When their seed took root within you, it was after you fell through to live in hell...and that means that your child is neither alive nor dead, human nor demon. And it will be the worst of all."

She rubbed her belly, which protruded beyond the line of her pants. "How can this be?" she moaned. "When they killed me, I wasn't pregnant. And already I'm showing like it's my time?"

"This is hell," I said. It's a lame answer, but that pretty much answers everything here.

IT RAINED blood for 7 days. We stayed in the tiny shack at the island's center, and ate all of the cobwebbed provisions the sisters had left behind. We slept a lot, when the screams from the mainland didn't keep us awake. And when we were alert, I told her of the horrors of eternity, and she reminded me of the indignities and pain of life.

It was the best time I've ever had in hell.

"How did you end up here?" she asked one day, as I ran a long black nail through the flow of her hair. My touch passed through her when I wasn't careful, so I was very careful. I wanted to feel her, to capture her in my memory for eternity. I knew she would not be here to savor long. I laughed softly at her question and hummed a stupid song for a moment.

"Why?" she asked again.

"Because the music didn't move me?"

She looked confused, and shook me with her hands on both shoulders. "Why are you in hell?"

I sighed. "You can sing about the power of love, but that only ends up making you realize how you will never have it. You can talk about passion and possibilities," I said. It was an old, tired explanation for me. "But the songs were lies and the talk got old. You couldn't make me want to live."

She looked genuinely confused.

"They write songs about the power of love and of finding yourself and your soulmate. But the sad fact of the matter is, you can't find yourself in someone else. And no matter how much love someone gives you, if you don't have it already for yourself... forget about it. Nobody can make you want to live, but you. I was happy to take a pass on living. Just wasn't in me. So, I ended it. And now I'm here."

And in that moment, as I looked into Rhi's eyes, I heard a song from my past that I had always mocked. Something in my chest ached then, something that had never ached before and in a wave of bitter irony, I understood.

I looked into Rhi's hopeful eyes and understood that I was truly damned.

IN THAT WEEK, Rhi's belly continued to swell at an alarming rate. And the blood rain accused her presence and ran in crimson rivulets down the tiny windows of our shack, it soon found an exit point inside our refuge as well. When Rhi pulled herself off the human hair-stuffed cushion of the couch on the 7th night of our escape, the burlap beneath her was stained in a dark purplish butterfly. The poor girl had only been in hell for 13 days, and already she was full term with the scourge of Satan.

"Oh shit," she cried. "The baby's coming, isn't it?"

"The prince of hell," I corrected. "He won't be a baby for long."

From outside, a horrible keening wail rose up above the splatter of gore. I went to the window and stared at the bubbling reek of the Sea of Obsession. Now it was my turn:

"Oh shit," I said.

"What is it?" she gasped, while bending over and holding her gut.

Outside, the waters of the Sea had risen higher and higher, fed by the endless blood rain, until the waves lapped just yards away from our doorway. But atop that roiling sea of nightmare and desire, rocked a thousand black boats.

"They're coming for you," I said. Then I shook my head and corrected myself. "They're coming for your child."

"IT WILL GO EASIER for you if you let them take the thing from you," I suggested.

She reacted as I expected. I rubbed the sore spot on my arm, rather than punching her back.

"They'll kill me, and then my baby," she yelled. "You've got to help me get away from here. Send me back home. Do you think I'm fuckin' nuts?"

I shook my head. "No," I said. "But consider this. If you actually make it through the deadpass back to Earth, you will be pursued in the shadows of every night by evil. Satan will not tolerate you suckling his undoing in a place he can barely reach. And make no mistake. It may be hard for him...but he *will* find you. His reach is long. And he will kill your child sooner or later. If he doesn't...well, the result may be even worse."

"How could it be worse?" she screamed.

"Because your child is no human baby," I hissed. I took her by the shoulders, forcing her to look at me. To listen. "Think about it...what baby gestates in 13 days? What baby gathers Satan's most loyal legion to the march to destroy it? You are not harboring a *baby* in your womb Rhi, you are carrying the sword of darkness, the future king of hell."

"Not if I raise him right," she declared, holding both hands across her middle and crying out bravely. "I can teach him to use his power for good."

"And Lucifer could begin healing the sick and sending lost souls to heaven." I shook my head. "He *could*...but it's not bloody likely."

Her eyes were red and she balled up her fists to wipe them free. Then she beat them against my chest, pounding to be free of my grip. "Tell me," she demanded. "Tell me how to go home."

"How badly do you want it?" I asked quietly. Behind me, the walls began to rattle, as the host of hell trudged through the bloody swamp to our tiny hideaway.

"More than anything," she whispered.

I looked at the figures coming towards us through the front windows, and then stared at the empty, angry sea through the pane in the back.

"Then maybe, just maybe, I brought you to the right place."

WHEN THEY BROKE through the door and crashed into the room, Lucifer's army found me alone.

"Where is she?" their leader demanded, and I shrugged.

"Who?"

"The girl you brought here," the Usher snarled. The points of its teeth looked none too friendly, and the horns on its skull shivered with the thirst to impale.

"As you can see, she's gone," I said.

"The blood rain centers here. She can't have gone far."

"Mehitobel!!" screamed a serpentine creature from outside the doorway. "The rain has stopped. The blood is...gone."

A black blade slid across my neck, drawing instant heat in its wake. I felt skin flap like a new mouth against my throat.

"Where?" the demon said again. "Don't toy with us."

I shrugged and pointed towards the back door of the cottage. Towards the water.

"She's gone to find her obsession."

RHI SLID into the warm water like a bath, feet sinking into the liquefied flesh of a million crumbled lives that lined the red sea's bottom. But rather than think about the fingers and rancid, curdled flesh that rippled and tickled her soles as she marched away from the army behind, Rhi only thought about one thing: Planting a shiv right in the balls of that fucking prick Brett and yanking upwards until his balls met his bellybutton. And then she could repeat the trick with his creepy thug friend Charlie. She imagined opening them both up for the crows, and as she let her chin touch and slip under the water, her sole thought was of the joy it would bring her to step back through the muddy hole of the deadpass and into the lost farmhouse. Oh, the blood rain she would bring *there*...

Inside her, a baby writhed in preternatural excitement at the thought.

THE ROOM LAY DEADLY SILENT, but inside, both a mother and a newborn child breathed. Neither stirred. But the baby stared at two men with its dark, intelligent eyes.

Charlie looked up at Brett and shook his head. They'd been standing in the doorway now for several minutes arguing in whispers.

"C'mon, that's ridiculous. She goes to hell for a couple weeks and comes back nine months pregnant…and delivers?"

Charlie stared at the infant, but Brett didn't answer the question. Instead, he pointed. "Hey man, your nose is bleeding."

Charlie wiped his face with a sleeve and gasped when he saw the stain.

"What the fuck?"

Brett laughed. "Shhh…don't swear in front of our baby."

"Yeah, real funny. Damn thing's kinda creepy, isn't it? Hasn't blinked since we walked in here."

Brett stared at the bloody naked creature himself, and then Charlie reached out to touch the side of Brett's head, and returned the observational favor: "Hey man, your ear's bleeding."

"What the fuck?

Sure enough, when Brett brought his hand up to his ear, it came away red as fire engine paint.

"Something's not right here, man."

"No shit. There's a woman on the floor who just gave birth to a baby she wasn't pregnant with two weeks ago, it's staring us down like the fuckin' devil, and we're bleeding for no reason. Time to go, maybe?"

They both began to back away. The infant never took its eyes off them.

"Yeah, I…." Brett doubled over.

"What's the matter man?"

He gasped. "Hurts…in my …gut." He crumpled to the floor. "Oh fuck, fuck fuck!" he cried. "I'm not liking this, Brett."

"I'm… not either…" Brett started to say, but instead of "Either," what came out was a throaty gurgle, followed quickly by a spontaneous stream of blackish red bile. He gasped and choked in surprise. Then Brett heaved, again and again, each spasm coming faster, harder and more painful. Between each loud grunt and liquidy cough, he swore.

Then he cried, as his mouth splattered the floor with chunks of something that did not look like food.

The baby, and its cold, black eyes, did not look away.

But Charlie did. Because suddenly his eyes felt like a swarm of bees had just honed in on him to attack. His pupils burned with pain and he rubbed them...only to find his palms lathered in crimson tears.

"Oh Jesus Christ," he swore, and the baby, for the first time in its earthly life, opened its lungs to cry.

"This...is...not...good," gasped Brett weakly from nearby.

That's when Brett felt the knifing pressure in his guts increase. He started to unhitch his belt, still spewing bloody meat from his mouth, but it was already too late. His pants filled with something hot and acidy as his bowels let go, and he slipped in the mess of his insides and fell for the last time to the floor.

It was just seconds later that Charlie joined him, coughing and crying and feeling the warmth of his own boiling guts streaming down his leg like hot piss. But he knew it wasn't piss, or even shit for that matter. He was dissolving from within. His shoes were already drenched in gore when he fell to the floor next to his gagging friend, a shuddering skeleton wreathed in boiling, desiccating flesh.

RHI OPENED her eyes and stared into the baby's elfin black orbs. They were bottomless, achingly open. A blank slate to build a world in. She gently hugged the infant close and felt her heart surge.

"We did it," she whispered, and struggled to sit up with the baby. That's when she saw the bodies of Charlie and Brett.

"All of it," she grinned. "They got what they deserved. And now we can start a new life. I kinda fucked up mine, but the whole world is open to you."

She kissed the tiny wet pink mouth of the child.

"I'll help you be whatever you want to be."

The baby's dark eyes never left the bodies on the floor. They never blinked at all.

When She Was Ready
By John Everson in collaboration with Honza Vojtíšek

She walked into my studio with the look of a woman possessed. Not by another soul, that's my line of work. She was possessed by an unflinching, unrelenting emotion. It showed in the creases that knit the smooth, high forehead above her wide, pale blue eyes and in the set of her soft, but somehow clearly tense jaw. She looked like a pure and patient innocent, driven by an unsavory desire she did not know how to deny. It wasn't hard for me to make that observation; virtually everyone who comes to me is the same in that sense. The only question is: what is the need that possesses them? And will I agree to be possessed, to fulfill their needs?

There's a price, certainly. But I'm selective. I choose my clients carefully, because I have to live with the memories afterwards. It's not me, in the end, that gets in bed with them. But I still have to watch. And remember. It only took a couple of experiences that I wish that I could forget to inform my selection process.

"Hello, I'm Summer Iris," she said, holding out a pale, long-fingered hand. Her parents must have been flower children. I accepted it as she looked me over carefully. I wasn't the only one in the equation who had reason to be selective. She was here because she wanted to go to bed once more with her husband. The only problem was; her husband was dead.

I would be her gateway to him. But also, her human doll.

"I'm Jake Cutter," I answered her. I gripped her hand warmly as I spoke. It was important to show strength in a first meeting. Women didn't usually want a guy with a wet noodle grip. It said something about personality. Or lack thereof. I forced her to meet my eyes. "We spoke yesterday on the phone."

She nodded, and her hand squeezed back before releasing. Her face was demure, hesitant, troubled. But her hand said she wanted my help.

I gestured for her to sit down in one of the thick cushioned chairs near the fireplace.

"Can I get you something to drink?" I asked. "Maybe one of the three Ws -- Wine, water...whiskey?"

Her voice was surprisingly soft, but she didn't choose the safe course. A good sign.

"Can I get a whiskey?" she asked. "On the rocks?"

"Certainly," I said and poured her two fingers of Black Label from the bar before doing the same for myself. I brought them over and took a spot in the chair next to hers. We shared a small wooden table, and after a sip, I set my glass on a coaster and began our interview.

"So," I said. "You were able to find me, which says something about you in itself. And I know you've lost your husband and want to meet with him one more time.'

She nodded. "I've tried, I really have. But nobody can make me feel the way he did. And I feel so horrible because I never let him do the one thing he really wanted to do to me."

"And what's that?" I asked.

Her face blushed. She struggled to find the words and I reached out to take her hand in mine. "It's okay," I said. "I'm the one that you can tell. I'm the one you have to tell."

"He wanted to make me his slave," she said. Her voice hesitated at first, but then the words came in a torrent. She couldn't wait to release them.

"He wanted me to pierce my nipples and wear chains connected to them, and a collar, and to crawl on the floor like a dog when he commanded. He wanted me to wear a horse's tail and a bridle when I brought him dinner, and he wanted me to kneel and serve as his footrest after dinner when he smoked and drank his bourbon."

I raised an eyebrow at that. "Sounds pretty demeaning," I said. "And intense."

She hung her head. The ivory white of her cheeks had flushed to the color of prickly heat. "I know," she said. "It scared me when he was alive. I always said no."

"But you stayed with him."

She closed her eyes. "I loved him. And he never forced me. He said that if I agreed to his wishes, it had to be unconditional. I would have had to have done anything he asked, no matter how degrading. If he had asked me to take my clothes off in a bar and let everyone look at me, I would have had to do as he said."

"And if you didn't?"

"He would have walked away from me and never let me come home. He was a man who was driven by absolutes. If I agreed to the life he offered me, unconditionally, he promised that I would have more pleasure than I could imagine. But some of that pleasure came from pain, and humiliation. I was too afraid. And he always patted my head and said it was okay. If I changed my mind, he would change my world."

"So, he hoped you would eventually trust him enough to put it all in his hands, to do whatever he said, no matter what."

She nodded. "He had a room in the back of the house. You had to enter a passcode that was hidden in the bookcase in the den to open a hidden door to get there. There were so many erotic things inside. Special wooden frames where you could be handcuffed and chains attached to metal pins in the walls and long couches of red velvet. One side of the room was completely covered in TV screens while another was a giant mirror. There were leather straps and things with feathers and a shelf that had a row of vibrators and beads and other curved and colored sex toys on display. He said he had built it when he was younger for his future wife in the hopes that she would indulge in his deepest desires for domination. If she agreed to use it, then it would be open. Otherwise, it would be forever closed. He showed it to me a few times and promised me that it would be our playroom if I gave my body completely to him, without safe words. Without denial. All I had to do was give myself to him without reservation."

"And you wouldn't do it. Did he whip you or tie you up or anything?"

She shook her head. "Again, with Andreas it was all or nothing. When I agreed to let him own my body, he would flog it, or not, as *he* wished. But if I would not agree to surrender it all, he would only make love to me in the usual ways. And he was so good there," she said. "He made me see stars when he made love to me. When he would turn me on my side and kiss me that way he had while he was still inside me…" Her story halted as her face burned and she took a long sip of her whiskey.

"Did he use the room with other women then, since you would not accommodate him?"

Her eyes blazed. "Oh my god, no," she said. "He wasn't like that. He said I was the only one, and he would wait for me forever. When I was ready, he would be ready, he said. And he never made me feel bad for making him wait. He would show me the room, and say, 'when you are ready. When you are ready, I will make you the happiest slave on earth.'"

"What did you tell him?"

"I laughed and told him he might have picked the wrong bride. But he would just shake his head and say that he had a feeling about me. He knew that in my soul, I wanted to give my body and soul to him. And only him."

She looked at me then with eyes brimming with tears. "He was right," she said. "I did. I always did. I just didn't know how."

"But you do now."

She nodded. "They said that you could let him touch me once more. They said that you're not a fake. And if that's true, I want to give myself to him finally. Completely. So that he can do whatever he wants to me. It's all I have wanted to do since he died."

"Sometimes we only really know what we want when the opportunity is gone," I said.

She looked at me with those wide blue eyes, tears still leaking, and the faintest blonde down weighed with moisture on her upper lip. "They say you can still give the opportunity," she said.

I looked at her with serious, deal-sealing gaze. "I can," I said, "And I will."

I FIRST REALIZED that I could let spirits possess me when I was 15. It was a weird situation. I was in the bathroom of the funeral home that my uncle ran, masturbating to a *Penthouse* magazine that I'd snuck in with me in my backpack. I reached that moment when your hand just can't slow down, and your breath comes in wild gasps even through you're literally just sitting still. The magazine was still clenched in my left hand, with the picture of a brazen, bronzed, very naked and voluptuous fake blonde shivering in my grasp. I was nearly there, when I heard a voice.

Do you mind if I join you?

I wasn't sure if I should be afraid or excited. And at that particular moment in my path to a bathroom stall orgasm, I didn't care. I said "sure," and I couldn't even tell you if I said it in my head or out loud.

But a moment later, there was someone else with me.

And by with me, I mean... inside me.

I don't know what she looked like, because I couldn't see her. But when I said sure, there was suddenly another hand on my cock, stroking and exploring it, as I reached the final moment of my path to quick and furtive ecstasy.

"Your cock feels great," she said, and with that, I felt wet and sticky because when someone tells you that you feel great while you're masturbating, there really is only one reciprocal answer.

In the afterglow, I found out that she was one of the stiffs a couple rooms away. Just a dead girl looking for a last fling before she walked off to wherever dead girls go. Her name was Celine, and she was my first. She was not to be my last. Not by a long shot.

Turns out, while I didn't have that hard of a time gathering live dates, I could really attract the dead. Not, maybe, the revelation most teenage boys want to have. But once Celine slipped her hands into mine and felt... no ... *worked* my cock to a climax... well... other spirits seemed to see me as an open door. It wasn't many days later that I was 'working it' with a different magazine in hand, in the privacy of a forest preserve near my house, when I felt someone else take over my hand like an easy-to-slip-on glove and show me a better way to, let's say... handle things. I was well past the point of resisting and you know what? The spirit within me taught me a few things. His name was Steve, and he thanked me for a last wank before he shuffled off to wherever dead guys go.

Let me be clear here.

Dead people don't come to me when I'm watering my flowers or driving my car.

Dead people find me when I'm naked and threatening to explode with pleasure.

It's a weird thing.

And it took a long time before a use became apparent for this strange ability, but in the end, it created a career.

As it turns out, when I'm aroused, I can allow spirits to take over my body. It sounds weird doesn't it?

Trust me, it is. And my business evolved over a long, strange series of time and events. But in the end, what happened was... I became the prostitute for the dead.

The living come to me, to rekindle their most private moments, with those who are gone.

But nobody's ever completely gone, you know? Maybe you don't. But... they're not. Those who have left this mortal coil are... still in earshot.

Just sayin'.

Watch what you say. They can hear you.

As it turns out, there are a lot of people who would pay big money to have sex with their dead lovers.

Guess who is the perfect person to help?

Yeah. It was me. And it became my business. Not one you'll find in the yellow pages. This kind of thing is advertised in different channels. But it was lucrative. And... I can't say that I didn't enjoy it. Well... most of the time. I learned when it was important to say no.

But when Summer Iris came to me, with her creamy skin and BDSM desires... I didn't say no.

I should have.

"We can try to call him for you," I promised. I was on my second whiskey. She was on her third.

"Can we do it tonight?" she asked.

"I can try," I promised. It was a foolish promise. But she made out a check. And I put I in my desk. And then we went into my private room. There were not a host of floggers and chains there, but there was the promise of privacy, and attention and...

She downed a fourth whiskey and took off all of her clothes in front of me. And together, we called for Andreas to join us. When she unzipped my jeans and reached down and fingered the growing hardness in my revealed briefs to consider whether I could really fill the holes her husband had, I felt him join us. She had whispered his name as she touched me, and I answered her calling with an invitation to Andreas to help me make his wife happy.

He answered.

And he was very interested to help.

As it turned out, maybe too interested. I let him in. And he took over without hesitation. There was a natural feeling as he put my hands on her and slowly traced his fingers over all of her curves. It was loving, and knowing...

And she knew that it was him. She asked him questions, trying to confirm that the man in my eyes was really her former husband with things that only he would know. Her favorite sexual position (missionary), the place they first had sex (the back seat of his car in the parking lot at a football game.)

He answered them all and she looked happier with every response. I had nothing to add because... he owned me in those moments. My body was his. And I allowed him to take me over, so that he could be with his wife once more. He was a slow but very sensual lover, I learned. My body seemed to perform well under his command. When his fingers stroked her breast, I could feel my whole body ignite. She was so soft, so yielding. Her lips met mine with a heat that was explosive. She opened her mouth to me and my tongue was instantly joined with hers, my hands massaging her breasts and waist, eager to feel all of her. He explored her body as if it were the first time, tracing every curve. She was moist for him in seconds, that private thatch turning from a soft brush of faintly wiry hair against my palm to a quickly sticky slick place that rose to meet my palm with every stroke. It was not long before it wasn't my hand, but my penis that was slipping against her secret spot.

Her body yielded to mine like the softest cushion. Her belly kissed mine with a cool smooth caress that quickly turned warm. Her breasts crushed against my chest as her arms slid around my shoulder blades and pulled me tight. It was as if she wanted to hide her body inside my own. She wanted to be a part of me/him, not an outsider. And the closer we got, as my hips ground easily against hers, the more she made small sounds of pleasure. She was like a lamb, bleating her need and the more I filled her, the more those tiny sounds grew until she finally began to cry out in earnest. When her orgasm broke, I thought that she might wake the neighbors.

It was honestly the best sex I've had in months, if not years. My hands knew exactly how to play her, and she was dying to be played.

The problem only came after they were both sated, when she acknowledged what she had done in her desperate longing to be reunited with him.

"I'VE MISSED you so much, and I've felt so bad that I never gave in and became the slave you wanted," she said to Andreas. "That's my deepest regret now, I think."

"If I had had more time, I am sure you would have tried it, and found it was very much to your liking," he answered with my lips. "I am only sorry that you will never experience the anticipation and fulfillment it can bring now."

"That's why I brought you back," she said. "I want to submit to you that way. At least for the time that you can stay."

"I appreciate that," he said. "But if you find it is not what you wanted, I don't want your last memories of me to be colored by something unpleasant."

She shook her head. "I am sure," she said. "Do you remember Martin in our building?"

Andreas nodded my head.

"After you were gone, he took me out a few times, and it turns out that he was very into the bondage scene. I let him tie me up, so I could finally know what it was like. And I completely let go. He told me what to do and I didn't question. Even if I didn't want to do it. I gave in to his will and I finally understood what you had always told me. And…you were right. It was amazing. He said I was a natural. And now I want to feel that with you."

My jaw had started to clench during her confession, and then I felt my fingernails digging into my palms as my fists grew tight.

"You surrendered your body to…to… Martin?" he said softly.

She reached out and stroked my / his face. "Yes," she said. "You were gone and I wanted to understand."

With one hand he gripped her wrist and pushed her arm back down.

"I'm not pleased with this," he said.

Her face instantly turned the color of snow. She knew that she had angered him. And clearly that frightened her.

"I wished the whole time that it was you. I've been kicking myself for not letting you make me your slave every day since," she said. "That's why I sought out Jake, the man you're inside right now. I had heard that he could reunite couples when one was beyond the grave."

"So now both Martin *and* Jake have touched what was supposed to only be mine," my lips said. I didn't like where this was headed.

She shook her head. "No, Andreas," she said. There was a clear edge of fear in her voice. "When you took over Jake, he went away."

"I hope you're right," he said. "But I can feel him near."

"Make me your slave for the night," she whispered. "I want only to serve you."

I felt my head nod. "Anything I ask?"

"Anything," she promised, with one hand cupping her breast. I wasn't sure if it was meant as an invitation, or if she was already reminding herself of what it had been like moments before when my hands were kneading her.

"Get up," he said. When she did, he pointed. "Put your hands on the back of that chair by the desk. And then bend over."

As she did what he asked, I stood up from the bed as well and went over to my pants. With an easy pull, the belt slid out of the loops in the waist and I knew what was going to come next. My hands slid between her damp thighs and pushed for her to spread her feet apart. She started to ask why and he shushed her.

"Speak when I ask you to speak and not any other time," he said.

Seconds later, the room echoed with the sounds of leather meeting flesh. With each snap, she let out a whimper of pain, but otherwise, managed to hold her tongue. It wasn't long before the snow-white skin of her ass was criss-crossed with angry red lines, and her cheeks also reddened with the tracks of tears. He was not going easy on her. And I knew why. You should never pick up a whip or flogger or any instrument of torture when you are mad. And clearly "til death do us part" was not enough of a break for him.

At one point, she jumped from the belt and took her hands off the chair and he immediately demanded that she resume the position. "Five more lashes for that," he said. "You will move when I say to move. Not before."

Eventually, his steady, methodical attack ceased, and he picked up a bottle of lotion I kept on the desk.

"There will be more punishment for what you did," he promised.

"But I am a merciful master. That is enough for now." With one hand, he expertly applied the lotion and she moaned as he applied it to raw and tender spots. She was clearly going to be sore for a couple days.

"Come," he said then, and led her to a couch. He sat down, and she stood before him, naked, with her hands at her sides.

He nodded. "Good. I see at least you learned something from your dalliance with Martin. Hopefully, I will not have to retrain you in anything." He pointed then at his thigh. "Lay your head down here."

She knelt in front of him and turned her head to rest her cheek on his thigh. He stroked her hair softly, gently, back and forth.

"Only mine," he whispered. "You belong to me. Only I can decide what you do and don't do."

She did not say anything and I felt my lips smile.

"Do you understand?" he asked.

"Yes... master," she said.

"Good."

I WON'T BORE you with the other sordid details of that night. She subjugated herself to him fully, and he made use of her in perverse and demeaning and, I suppose, pleasurable ways for both of them. She was footrest and toe cleaner and sex toy and... you name it. I made note of the many places in my house that I would need to use Lysol on the following day.

And finally, she and he were sated and said their goodbyes. He could not maintain his presence here forever and the pull had grown strong for him to return to the other side where he was meant to be. She promised that she would have me call him back soon, for she could not be trusted to roam the world alone without a master. It was typical that one lovemaking session with a deceased spouse was never enough. But I wondered, given the strength of Andreas, how long they would insist on using me as their bridge. I'd take their cash, certainly. And she was easy enough on the eye and body. But these connections were, by their nature, meant to be transitory. I could see this particular one becoming a problem.

After Andreas left me, I covered Summer with a blanket on the couch where she had fallen asleep, and I went to bed. Things got interesting a few hours later, when I awoke to the sound of frying bacon and the scents of onions and eggs.

I pulled on a pair of loose shorts and walked into my kitchen to find Summer there, wearing only a t-shirt as she turned the bacon that looked nearly done in one of my frying pans with a fork. The sight of her bare ivory legs and barely concealed breasts thrusting through the thin cotton fabric with her hair hanging mussed and curled over her shoulders as she cooked was enough to make me want to sit down. She was going to bring back morning wood in about 30 seconds just from the sight of her.

"I thought I owed you something more after last night," she said. "And your fridge was fully stocked. I hope you don't mind."

I laughed. "Not at all. "Most of the time, I'm lucky if I get coffee going on my own. I buy eggs and bacon because it seems like a good idea in the store...and then end up throwing them out half the time because I'm lazy and never cook."

"Sit," she insisted. "I think I might like this service thing."

That was the only comment she made about being a slave the night before. She asked my cream and sugar preferences and then brought me a cup of coffee before spooning a solid helping of eggs and bacon onto one of my plates and sliding that in front of me before sitting down with her own portion.

Nice.

She talked to me that morning about her relationship with Andreas, and how he often had frightened her, but at the same time made her feel loved. A strange dichotomy of pain and pleasure given his propensity for control and anger and yet his equally strong need to shower her with affection and gentleness. She never knew whether she would face the Andreas who slapped her across the face or the Andreas who caressed her like a kitten.

Before she left that morning, she thanked me profusely and set up another meeting for the following week. She couldn't afford to do this more than weekly, she said, but she wished she could hire me every night.

I was happy that she couldn't. I didn't need to face the problem of committing to one client because, while lucrative, eventually that situation would end, and I'd have no fallback clients.

OVER THE NEXT THREE WEEKS, I let Andreas reenter me three more times, and each time, I wondered if I should let it happen again. It was enjoyable to wake the next morning to the smells of homemade breakfast, but I was also aware of the bruises and scabs that covered Summer's body. He did not use her gently. While he made her orgasm, multiple times during every night we lay together, he also made her pay for the time that she had refused his ownership. And the time that she explored the idea of service to another master.

He was a cruel spirit.

But she came back again and again for more. And my bank account grew. My prices for this kind of service were not cheap. Nor should they be. Surrendering your body to another is not something that should be a bargain. I had done it my whole life and I wondered every time if my skin would come back whole. How could you trust someone to care for yourself the way you would? And the dead… what did they care if they put your mortal frame in harm's way?

They were dead. No consequence would come to them if they drove your body off a cliff.

Thankfully, he didn't do that to me. And again and again, I was able to enjoy the luscious flesh that he had left behind. I couldn't foresee putting a limit on Summer's use of me to contact her husband. I was enjoying her touch too much, even if it was meant for another man. A man who used her cruelly.

IT WAS the night before our fourth encounter that I found out how cruel he truly was.

I went to bed looking forward to the following day. I would get up and clean the house, in particular, the pleasure room. Summer would be coming over that afternoon for a long session and I would make sure that everything was ready. There would be red wine and hors d'oerves and a willing bridge to make their union possible. I needed to prepare.

I went to sleep easily, tired from a busy week and anxious for the next day to arrive. I had to admit, I wanted Summer to come. Not for the money. But for me. I tried to ignore the fact that she was a slave for another man... I just happened to be the shell he used to use her.

Things went awry around 12:30 a.m.

The first thing that went wrong was I awoke an hour after having gone to sleep.

The second thing was that I realized I hadn't simply woken up... I'd been awoken. Somebody had entered me and demanded that I wake up.

This had never happened before.

I knew from the cold aura that it was Andreas. He felt a certain way; they all do. He didn't have to say a word and I realized who was possessing me.

I rose from the bed, turned on the light and got dressed. After a bit of searching, he found my keys, and then rummaged through the kitchen cabinets. He held out two of my carving knives side by side, and after comparing the heft of them both, he chose the older wooden handled one over the newer plastic covered base.

A few minutes later, I found myself the ultimate back seat driver as someone else used my hands and feet to navigate my 2008 Honda through the center and eventually outskirts of town.

We pulled up in front of a worn apartment complex that had probably been built in the '50s if I'd had a guess. It reminded me of the way buildings were made then, just after the War. They all had a certain brick and geometrically uninteresting block style to them.

He walked up a handful of concrete steps and entered a narrow lobby that opened onto stairwells on either side. Without hesitation, he turned to the right and walked up three flights. I felt winded at the end, but he didn't seem to mind. He didn't slow. He walked down the dark hallway and arrived at a door with three golden numbers on the door.

322.

He lifted his hand and knocked. Quietly, but with surety. After waiting a minute, he knocked again. Louder and harder this time.

On the third try, the door lock suddenly clicked and the door swung open to reveal a middle-aged white guy in a blue robe, rubbing his eyes. He looked barely awake.

"What is it?" he said. His voice was a slur of sleep and broken dreams.

"I'm sorry to disturb you," my lips said. "But there's been a report of a gas leak in the building and I need to check every apartment."

He looked confused. "I don't smell any gas?" he said.

"That's good," I said. "Let me just take a reading and hopefully it all checks out and you can go back to sleep."

"I don't know..." the guy began to say but that didn't stop Andreas. He pushed right into the room before the guy knew what was happening.

"Hey," he said, realizing that maybe something wasn't quite right.

I pushed the door shut behind me, and flipped the lock closed. Then I pulled out the knife from where it was sheathed in my back jeans pocket.

"Make a sound louder than a whisper and this will be in your throat," my voice said. "I'm not joking. Nod if you understand me."

The guy shook his head up and down. Fast. He wasn't sleepy anymore.

"You're into BDSM from what I understand," Andreas said. "Show me your toys. I'd like to see them."

"I don't know what you..." Martin began to say but before he could finish his sentence, the cold steel of my kitchen carving knife was pressed against his throat.

"Don't bullshit me."

His eyes went wide, and he pointed. "Over there," he whispered.

The knife retreated and he led the way to a back bedroom.

THE WALLS WERE PAINTED BLACK. A light fixture overhead mimicked a hanging basket of candles and its rich light illuminated a blood red ceiling along with the black walls which were littered with chains and implements of torture. There were leather cuffs and floggers and a low wooden horse with a hole in the middle of it that was the perfect size to hold a human neck.

"I understand you entertained Summer Iris here," Andreas said.

Now Martin looked even more worried. This was becoming very personal.

"Don't lie about it," Andreas cautioned. "I want to know which toys she liked the best. I'm her master now and I want to understand what excited her... and frightened her the most."

The frown lines on Martin's face eased somewhat then. Maybe this wasn't going to be as much of a problem as he'd expected. He could understand the need for secrecy, if not the barging in at one in the morning with a knife.

"She liked to be tied up the most," Martin said, pointing to ropes that hung from two metal hooks on one wall. "I think she appreciated having control physically taken from her."

My head nodded. "It's so much easier than having to discipline yourself to give it up," Andreas said.

"So, you tied her up there?" he asked.

Martin nodded.

"Did you fuck her while she was tied up?"

Martin's face looked a little surprised. "Yes," he said. "But I don't know if she liked it there more or over here on the horse."

He pointed to the head and wrist lock device.

"I don't have one of those," Andreas said. "How does it work?"

Martin warmed to that. Showing off your toys was always something that put people at ease. He pointed at how the wrists were cradled and locked into two small round holes between two pieces of wood and how the neck was locked into a hole in the center between them. He showed off the latches that held the structure together and pointed at where the knees were to go, positioned to show off the slave's ass for paddling, whipping or other fondling.

When he lifted the top piece of wood to show how the neck could be placed on the bottom piece where there was a curved slice removed from the wood in the center, Andreas said two words that chilled my heart.

"Kneel down," he said.

When Martin looked as if he would protest, Andreas held the knife out with one hand, as he held the stockade top up with the other.

"Kneel down, now."

Martin complied. For a master, he made a pretty good slave.

The wood slammed down and Andreas flipped the latches that kept it locked together. Martin wasn't getting out of his torture device until Andreas let him.

"There can only be one master of Summer," he said.

"That's fine," Martin quailed. "I haven't had a session with her in a while. I am glad to know she is in firm hands now."

"They are more than firm," Andreas said. He reached out and grabbed a handful of hair to yank Martin's head back. "They are disciplined."

With one hard slap, he hit Martin in the ass. The other man jumped, not expecting it.

"I can see that I have my work cut out for me here," he said. "And the first thing will be to cut you out. Slaves are never dressed in my house."

He cut the sash that held Martin's robe closed, and then used the knife to slash the garment into multiple pieces, peeling it away from the man's trapped arms and neck until Martin was exposed, naked and kneeling in his own playroom.

"That's better," Andreas said. "Now, tell me, was Summer a good slave? Was it difficult to break her in?"

Martin shook his head. "She took to it right away. I only had to remind her to do only as she was told a few times."

"And what was the first thing you demanded that she do."

"I don't know..." Martin said.

Andreas picked up a long wooden paddle from where it rested on a shelf on the wall. He tested the heft with one hand as he walked back to Martin. And then without warning, he raised his hand high and brought the wood down on the other man's bare ass. The room echoed with the sound of the impact. Martin cried out.

"Perhaps you are not as good of a slave as she was. I did not tell you to make noise. What I did tell you to do is to answer my question. What was the first thing Summer did in your service?"

Martin cleared his throat before speaking.

"I made her kneel, unzip my pants, and suck my cock."

Andreas nodded. "And was she good at it?"

"She was very good."

"And what else was she good at?"

"She seemed to enjoy crawling on the floor like a dog," Martin said. "I put a leash on her and she instantly turned into an animal, eager for attention at my feet."

"I see," Andreas said. I felt the edge in his words. "So she made you a good pet."

Martin picked up on the tone. "I only did what she wanted me to do for her," he said. "Her husband was dead and she needed someone."

"Summer can only belong to one master," Andreas said. Then he reached below the other man's belly and grabbed the soft penis dangling there.

"You say she enjoyed sucking on this?"

"Yes," Martin said. His voice was a terrified whisper.

"I'll bring it back for her then."

He pulled the limp shaft of the man's sex as long as it would go before he slid the kitchen knife across its base.

The blood sprayed everywhere as Martin screamed and thrashed, desperate to get out of the stockade.

Andreas held up his trophy and smirked. "Not much to it," he said.

Then he walked across the room and retrieved a leather collar. He drew it around Martin's neck and then pulled the leather tighter and tighter until Martin's face grew beet red and he gasped for air. He fastened it at the last hole and then retrieved a leash to attach to the metal loop in the collar. Only then did he release Martin from the stockade.

The man instantly fell to the floor on his side, drawing his legs up in a fetal position to try to staunch the pain and bleeding. He moaned and cried with every motion.

"On your hands and knees," Andreas demanded. When Martin refused to comply, he yanked hard again and again on the leash, choking the man further. At last, howling in pain, Martin did as he was commanded, and Andreas led him out of the playroom and into the bath. He drew his face close to the toilet, and then pointed.

"Drink, you'll need to replenish your fluids."

Martin's face was now purple, and spittle foamed at the sides of his lips. He glared once at Andreas, but then put his face down in the toilet and put his lips to the water.

"Drink!" Andreas commanded and pushed the man's head under the water. He held it there until Martin stopped struggling. When his body went limp and slid to the floor, Andreas tossed the leash down on the dead man's chest.

"There can be only one master," he said. And then he retrieved the disembodied penis and left the house.

INSIDE, I was more than horrified. Not only had I been forced to witness a brutal murder, but I would pay the price for it as well; Andreas had used my body to kill. It was *my* fingerprints that were left throughout the house. The police would quickly be arresting me and charging me with the killing, and what defense did I have? Would anyone believe that my hands had not been my own, that I had been possessed by a jealous husband?

When we arrived home, Andreas poured himself a tall glass of whiskey and sat in my easy chair and drank as he stared at the clock. The hours slipped by, from 3 to 4 to 5 a.m.

At some point, the liquor and exhaustion conspired, and I lost consciousness.

When I awoke, it was to the sound of a doorbell.

The events of the night came flashing back in a rush and I imagined that the police were at my door, ready to take me in. The feeling in my gut was like nothing I'd ever felt. A cold pit of frightened despair. I wished that I had never seen Summer Iris. Or that I'd been smart and said no to her request. But I couldn't take it back now. I couldn't do anything now but march towards the end of everything I enjoyed about my life.

I turned the knob with a nihilistic acceptance of my fate. But instead of an entourage in blue awaiting me, the pale, wide-eyed face of Summer greeted me.

She looked so different from the first time she had set foot on my threshold. Then, she had presented the demeanor of a conservative, demure housewife. She'd been filled with fear over what she was here to do. Now… she wore a collar around her neck, and the low-cut blouse that she'd pulled on for her trip across town did little to hide the leather bustier beneath it. I could see the lines of garters beneath her jogging shorts, and the black hose that shaped her calves plunged into a pair of black stilettos that were not meant for walking long distances. They were meant for walking proudly in front of a master. As was the rest of her wardrobe.

"Are you ready for me?" she asked. Her voice was breathy in anticipation.

"Yes," I said automatically, but then backpedaled. "Listen," I said, as she stepped past me. "There's been a complication."

The shorts dropped to the floor and she paused on the fourth button of her blouse. "I need Andreas," she said. "Please call him."

"Listen, I don't think that's a good…" I began to say. But before the last word came out, my tongue belonged to another voice.

"I am here, my slave," my voice said. It sounded deeper, fuller, when he used it. "Kneel for me now."

She did as he asked, awaiting his direction. "Unzip my pants," Andreas said. "I want you to take that thing which you ache for between your lips now. Show me that you are *my* slave. Only mine."

If I could have moaned aloud at the pleasure of the next fifteen minutes, the neighbors surely would have pounded on the door demanding my X-rated cries of passion be silenced. Summer knew how to suck a cock, she proved that now, giving attention to every bit of me, blowing soft hot breaths at the tip as her tongue traced my anxious veins. She knew how to draw me to near orgasm and then pulled back, smothering her wet lips against my balls and belly, letting my moment fall back from its crest before sucking me inside her again. Her fingers touched me all over, caressing, no, worshipping me. Well... worshipping Andreas. I have enjoyed a lot of blowjobs over the years from a lot of women... but I think that moment when Summer looked up at me with those huge limpid blue eyes and allowed me to finally explode in wave after wave into her hungry mouth... that had to have been the best.

"Good girl," Andreas said presently, patting her head. With one finger, he wiped a drop of cum from where it had leaked on her chin and absently wiped it into my shirt. Then he retrieved a leash and attached it to her collar. He tugged on it then, demanding that she follow.

"I have something to show you," he said.

Summer dropped to her hands and knees and followed him to the bathroom. He shed his unbuttoned pants then completely, and stood over the porcelain bowl to relieve himself, as she waited nearby, crouched on her knees, with her head hung in supplication.

When he finished, he waved at the toilet bowl and smiled. "I made this water for you," he said. "Drink."

Inside, I quailed, but Summer seemed nonplussed. Without hesitation, she dropped to her hands and crawled across the bathroom tile before dipping her face in the bowl. When it came back up to look at her master for instruction, her lips and chin were dripping.

"Excellent," Andreas said. "You are truly the slave I always knew you could be. Undress yourself now, completely. I will have you without trappings or costumes. Only you."

He walked out of the room and went to my dresser drawer. I don't remember putting it there, but obviously he had last night. The bloody penis of Martin lay amid my underwear. He picked it up and returned to Summer.

She stood waiting for him, naked, hands at her sides. Her breasts hung easy and heavy against her thin frame. Her nipples were erect, even though Andreas had been away. She was so ready for him.

"I brought this for you," he said. Then he held up the shriveled gore-spattered organ.

Her soft face wrinkled in dismay.

"Martin told me that you enjoyed sucking this," he said. "Do you prefer this one, or mine more. Answer me truly."

Her eyes showed her horrible realization that Martin must be dead. And bereft of his manhood to boot.

"Yours, Andreas. You know that," she said. "It has always only been you."

He threw the desiccated flesh in the toilet.

"Good," he said. "Then I will give it to you one last time here, before you join me to be my slave forever." He pointed at the floor. "Hands and knees."

She instantly did as he commanded. She truly was a perfect slave, not asking questions about Martin and not resisting his mean-spirited use of her. When he took her doggy style on the bathroom floor, she not only accepted his cock, she welcomed it, writhing and rising beneath him to draw him as deep as he / I could go. For a woman who just saw the disembodied cock of a former lover, she seemed amazingly horny still.

It was when they both reached their nadir that I saw where things were going. My hand left its driving position on her right rump and reached up to the sink, where the carving knife he'd used on Martin was secreted. When she screamed involuntarily at the crest of her orgasm, and her head bucked back against his face, Andreas brought the knife around and with a fast, hard pull... slit her throat.

"Now it is time to join me," he said as she fell to the floor grasping at the sudden fountain of blood spurting from her throat. "I cannot keep taking over another man's body to have you. I will have you to myself. Now that you have at last given yourself to me unconditionally, you will be my slave for eternity, my love. Die now, so that we can live together forever."

He bent down to kiss her, and I could see a mix of terror and pain and... strangely, hope in her eyes. Love. She wanted this. The taste of iron filled my mouth as her eyelids fluttered and her last breath heated my lips. She let go as she looked into his/my eyes, and I could see that I had truly fulfilled her desires. I only wondered what that meant for me. Now there were two bodies on my hands. I was doomed.

I had done a lot of kinky things over the years for lovers from beyond the grave, but I had never killed. I was somehow now going to have to disappear. There was no way I could escape prison if I didn't. But how? I had never tried to fake my identity my entire life. I did weird and unusual things compared to most, sure, but I had never hidden from them.

I tried to think of people I had helped, who might somehow now be able to help me. This was definitely my hour of need.

That's when Andreas finally spoke again. This time, for the first time, directly to me.

"I have to thank you," his voice said, in the back of my head. It was like hearing someone talking to you from the back of a theater. Hidden, behind the velvet curtains. Unseen, and yet, so close at hand.

"You gave her back to me. I thought that I would never see her, be with her, again. And you made it happen."

I guess I felt good about that. Andreas seemed like a bit of a dick, but... clearly, he was a dick that Summer wanted. And I'd made it happen. Still... her blood was warm right now on my hands. How could I feel happy about that?

As it happened, I couldn't.

"I am pleased that you brought her to me, but I cannot allow another man who has touched her perfect flesh to live," the voice said. "She can only belong to one master. As long as there is another..."

I didn't like the sound of that. A moment later, I liked it less.

My hand still held the knife that had killed Summer. Her blood still dripped from the edge of the blade.

That blade began to rise.

"I only tried to help," I protested. My voice sounded weak in the echo of the empty and really, nonexistent room of our shared mind. I don't think my rationale mattered to him. Jealousy defied logic.

"You touched her breasts," Andreas said simply. "You put your cock inside her. I won't have you remember those things. I won't have any man live with those visions. I won't have you fantasize about the secret places that only I should know. While I appreciate the fact that you brought us back together, you must not go on."

The blade rose to my throat.

"Wait," I begged. "I just did what she hired me to do! I understand why you're upset, but it simply is not possible for me to leave my body *completely* while you're inside. Trust me, sometimes I'd rather be completely gone, but it just doesn't work like that! It's not my fault."

I tried my best to control my fingers again, to change the direction of the knife, to no avail. I was a passenger in my own body and Andreas was driving.

Recklessly.

For he had absolutely nothing to lose. He did not need to come to this realm ever again. He'd taken what he wanted from it.

Just before the blade touched my neck, my hand stopped. And not because I was *trying* to stop it. My fingers simply... relaxed, let go, and the knife fell free, tumbling over my leg and hitting the floor with a metallic *ping*.

Andreas had let go of his weapon. *Why?* Why had he released the knife? Had he listened to, and *heard* what I'd said finally? Understood that none of this was my fault?

I held my breath – I honestly couldn't tell you whether that translated physically, or just mentally. But when nothing happened for a minute... I let it out. And I know *that* action was physical.

My relief resonated with a sigh throughout the room. But I felt the awareness of Andreas still, floating near at hand. Considering?

Despite the dropping of the knife, the realistic part of me knew that there was only one ending possible to this story outside of a life in prison.

I should never have agreed to help Summer Iris. There were so many women to whom I'd said no. Because I had recognized the risk.

Those big blue eyes had blinded me. Her breasts had tantalized me.

Sex with her brought me to the brink of doom.

The key to life was knowing when to say no.

Sadly, I'd said yes.

I don't know if he "heard" my thoughts or made his own determination but suddenly my legs started to move, stepping past the bloody knife and Summer's tragically still body. They carried me out of the apartment, through a quiet, dark stairway, past the door to the uneven sidewalk beyond. And then, straight to the road.

"Goodbye, Mr. Jake," that stage curtain voice said in my head. And at that moment I noticed the huge, dark, and loud blur barreling straight at me from the right.

Maybe the knife had been a ploy, a tease all along and his real goal was this. It didn't matter in the end, because my moment of relief was shattered. Andreas had led me right in front of a semi-truck, whose massive cargo now approached at a dizzying speed. There was no escape, but somehow time slowed and I was forced to fully comprehend the danger and the inevitable outcome. Perhaps Andreas stopped time so I could appreciate my doom as his inescapable punishment. After all... punishment was what Andreas existed to dole out.

I wanted to stop, to jump back to the curb. I tried my best to halt my own body. But my legs didn't belong to me anymore. At that moment, my consciousness huddled somewhere in the abyss, no longer in any control. I was a spectator of my own demise; a small, defenseless, frightened schoolboy.

The truck did not slow. It roared and rumbled like an apocalyptic meteorite rushing to planet Earth.

"Goodbye, world," I thought, remembering the joy of Summer's body. The last positive memory of my life.

But the beauty of that memory quickly faded as the dark of death loomed over me. For one brief moment, I was alone in the void. Never again would I cling to a woman as beautiful as Summer. Never again would I have the chance to let a dead soul take over my body. Because my body was about to be dead.

The inescapable shadow of the truck obscured the sun and enveloped my whole world in that final second in darkness. The scream of its brakes tore my mind in two but could not possibly stop the tons it towed in time. Reality hung in stasis for a second, long enough for me to understand every millisecond of my death. While time seemed to halt, Andreas didn't even have time to blink my eyelids before the truck crashed into me at full screeching speed. And faster than the eye could blink, Andreas and the truck erased me from earthly life. I saw more than felt that final moment, and then I saw something else entirely.

There were things suddenly begging for my eyes to see, just beyond the bounds of my vision. I knew that I had to let go to understand. To see my new reality.

"Goodbye Summer," my throat gurgled as my life slipped out on the hot, unyielding asphalt. And then I let the things waiting in the dark wash her memory... and me... away.

The Last Word

Be careful what you read.

Be careful what you say.

You might not believe this. You might not believe me. But…

Words are powerful things.

You don't think about it, because you use them all day, every day, without thinking much about it. You hear others use them all day long – the idle chatter of co-workers, the nagging cajoling of spouses, the vacant conversations of friends speaking just to pass the time. The fake banter of television and radio ads, the passionate lyrics of songs playing throughout the day from your computer speakers on Spotify. We're surrounded by words, and most of them are not only lacking in meaning, but intentionally, or, more often unintentionally, false. Deceptive. Misleading. Words are misused and malformed all day, every day. There are billions of them, most of them vacuous, released into the world every day. But don't be deceived.

Words are powerful things. Certain words. Said at certain times. In certain ways.

Some words can kill.

I WISH I had never opened that thin, dusty book. The words I read inside it changed my life. Threatened my life. And so I leave this warning. I only hope that there is someone left to read it.

I HAD DRIVEN over a hundred miles to escape words. I didn't want to hear any more of the empty promises and gaslighting stories designed to guilt me into doing things to save someone else from their own inadequate skills and planning. My girlfriend Aimee had backed out of coming along at the last minute and to be honest, while I was initially annoyed at the fact that my backwoods escape would now not include sex with another human, I was also somewhat relieved. I wouldn't have to endure her words. "Why *don't* you... "Why *do* you... "Why *aren't* you..."

I pulled my backpack and tightly rolled tent out of the trunk of my tiny Mazda and slung both across my shoulders. I filled my pockets with my phone, a lighter, a pocketknife and other minor implements and slammed the door in a gesture of finality. Goodbye.

The woods were just steps away from my car. A twig-laden trail led from the small parking lot into the copse of trees that included specimens hundreds of years old. These were old woods. While there was a parking lot and a trail entry, this was not a place that many people visited. Remote, and undeveloped. I had no doubt that many of the trees here predated the signing of our Constitution. This land had resisted the hand of man, and I longed to disappear within it. With one glance at the broken asphalt of the parking lot, I said my goodbyes to "today" and stepped onto the trail that led into the heart of yesterday.

The forest knew. The forest remembered. The forest was not eternal... but it was close.

The first hour or so of my hike was uneventful. Eventually, the trail grew wild. And soon, there was no trail at all. I threaded my way through wild brambles and empty spaces between trees that had grown so tall that their lowest branches were yards above my head.

I was moving steadily downhill, through clearings and dense cover.

There would be a river or large creek bed when I reached the bottom, and that is where I intended to set up camp.

I heard the water before I saw it. A gentle gurgle and drip through the brush. With the hum of insects and the call of birds, it made for a perfect backdrop of non-human sound. My soul felt at perfect peace for the first time in weeks. Maybe months.

And then, just as I reached a clearing and saw the outline of a narrow but deep riverbed ahead, I saw the grey outline of something that was not of the forest.

Something human.

A small grey, weathered cabin.

I approached it slowly; I didn't want to be shot at for trespassing. But by the time I reached the door, I knew I was safe; this cabin had not been tenanted in a long, long time. The windows were opaque with dust and spiderwebs, and the wood of the small porch had rotted through in several spots. The door made a horrible rusty creak when I turned the knob and forced it open.

Somehow, it had maintained its integrity against the elements, despite decades of neglect. The furnishings inside were spartan – a couple of wooden chairs tucked against a square wooden table. Two small tables with candle holders and half melted candles on top. A fireplace with a rough-hewn mantle where there were more candles, and a row of handmade dolls. Everything was grey with years of slowly accumulated dust. I couldn't imagine how long it had been since anyone had lived here.

Beyond the front room was a small kitchen with another table and chairs, and a wood-burning stove. No old refrigerator or microwave or anything like that... no electricity out here.

One of the doors in the kitchen opened into a pantry. I grimaced at the jars that still lined the shelves there. How old were those canned jams ... or pickles? The jars were so dark I couldn't tell what was preserved inside.

Another door opened to a small bedroom. It was as minimalistic as the rest of the house. A twin bed with a hand-stuffed mattress, draped in yellowed sheets. A thin chest of drawers. I pulled out the top two and found a collection of small trinkets and jewelry. The next held socks, panties and bras.

There were outer clothes in the next drawer, and all of them feminine.

So… a woman had lived out here a long time ago. Alone. From the clear tracks of my footsteps across the floor, no man or animal had been inside here in years.

I walked back and forth between the three rooms and found no evidence of animals having infiltrated the confines…which was a miracle. I had planned on camping in the woods but now reconsidered. There was no running water or power here, but there was shelter. And as I forced open the back door that exited the kitchen into an overgrown clearing behind the house, I heard more than the complaint of a weathered, warped door.

The rumble of thunder threatened overhead.

A small wooden structure was visible a few yards away from the house, nearly hidden by bushes and tall grass. An outhouse.

I raised an eyebrow at that. I might set up camp in the house, but I'd make other arrangements for the facilities.

The thunder peeled again, louder this time, and I nodded. After taking a leak near a tree out back, I lit the candles in the front room and kitchen and eased my way into one of the chairs. It looked as if someone had fashioned it by hand, and I worried that it would be old and brittle, but it held my weight.

I pulled out a bottle of Jack Daniels and prepared myself to weather the storm.

THERE WAS a small stack of towels in the pantry, and when the rain began, I took a couple pots outside and let them fill with water. After an hour and another drink, I brought them in and saved one for drinking, while the other became my wash bucket. I didn't mind roughing it, but I was not going to spend a week in here breathing in dust bunnies. I started with the table and chairs and then wiped down the mantle, the tables and the spiderwebbed front windows. It was a miracle they still held out the elements; the wood was clearly dry rotted.

Over the course of the night and several trips to the outdoors to gather fresh rainwater, I managed to wipe everything down in the front room and then got down on my hands and knees and washed down the old wood floors as well. By the time I unrolled my sleeping bag and slipped inside, I was feeling pretty good about my candlelit palace in the woods. Maybe tomorrow, I'd see about lighting the fireplace.

MY HEAD HURT the next morning, but when the sun burned its way through the newly cleaned windows to shine a spotlight on my face, I couldn't ignore it. The warmth on my neck and the fullness of my bladder and the unpleasantly hard base of the wooden floor beneath my sleeping bag insisted: Rise and shine.

I surveyed the room and nodded. For a place that had been abandoned in the woods for god knows how many years, it looked pretty homey. I stumbled through the kitchen and out the back door, walking towards the outhouse. I wouldn't go inside, but... it was as good a place as any to mark my new territory.

After eating a couple granola bars and wishing for something hot with lots of caffeine instead of canteen water, I decided to scope out my surroundings.

The river was just a few yards away, and after last night's rain, running fast. But while there was still a clearing around the house, really, everything else was thick with bushes and brush and trees. The house was enclosed by the forest. I felt as if I'd truly pushed open the gate and walked into the middle of nowhere.

And that was all right with me. When my phone buzzed with a notification from work, I shook my head and turned the device completely off without reading it. No words from the outside world. Not here.

That afternoon I spent cleaning the kitchen with water I lugged up from the river and eventually started on the bedroom. I washed some old sheets out in the river and laid them on the grass out back to dry. I'd decided to see if I could make the bed sleepable, and dragged the mattress (I was right, it was hand stuffed with feathers) out to the back to pound the dust out of it. The first couple hand claps brought out such a cloud that I ended up in a gagging coughing spasm. Eventually, when the dust clouds diminished, I dragged it back inside and covered it with three sheets to make sure whatever crap was still inside couldn't creep or seep out.

It was while I was shimmying the bed base back and forth to tuck the sheets in that I discovered the book.

The wooden frame had moved across the floor a few inches and I saw the old edge of the leather volume poking out. I knelt down and looked underneath. There was just bare floor... some dust bunnies... and the book. I pulled it out from beneath, and sat down on the newly made bed to take a look.

It was a diary.

The Diary of Gwyneth Piermont, Last Keeper of the Word, according to the inscription on the first page. There was a date on the page too, and the numbers made my eyes widen.

June 13, 1957, it said. Almost 65 years ago.

Her first entry set the stage for everything that was to follow.

"I have arrived at The Keep. Agatha trained me for this moment many years ago, and when I received her letter, I tried my best to follow her directions and get here before it was too late. But alas, when I arrived, Agatha was no more. It was unpleasant, but I was able to get her body out of the small house, and buried near an old Sycamore out back. She had mentioned the tree to me in her letters, and it was easy to find, towering above so many others in a knoll near the river. A tree of strength and protection. The ancient book which contains the Last Word, handed down for generations, and now handed from Agatha to myself, was still lying on a table next to her bed. I wondered if she had read it in those last hours before she died. I put it away in my cupboard. I don't want to be tempted to read it. Because in reading, one is primed to action, and the one action I must never do, is to speak The Word. Better to put it away, and stand guard, as so many sisters have over the years.

For now, I must settle into my new life here in the wilderness. Alone."

A FEW DAYS LATER, she wrote again, this time talking about her days of cleaning the house and tending the overgrown garden Agatha had left behind. I read a couple more entries, largely dealing with her domestic pursuits and finally set the book down. I needed to perform some domestic pursuits myself, or I was going to be starving out here soon. I had stuffed some mac and cheese and a pack of dried vegetables in the bottom of my backpack, and now it was time to get a fire going so that I could boil some water. The real question was... could I use the fireplace without burning the whole shack down?

The answer turned out to be... yes!

Something, probably a bird nest, caught fire briefly up in the flue and some things fell down from the shaft and into the logs... but after a half hour or so, I stood outside and saw a steady flow of smoke escaping the top of the chimney. A half hour after that, I had one of Gwyneth's old pots sitting on an iron rack above the logs, boiling water, and bits of dehydrated meat and vegetables. Later, I would add the rice. While it cooked, I explored the clearing behind the house. I found what I thought was the old sycamore tree that Gwyneth had written about, and was careful not to walk too close. There was pile of rocks in front of it which I assumed was a marker; I did not want to step on Agatha's grave.

Eventually, I stumbled over another rock marker – an embankment that I soon realized had once been the border of Agatha's vegetable garden. Somehow, her plants had continued to propagate over the years –squash vines wound into the weeds and stands of green onion and garlic chives stood strong their own, fending off the grass. When I pulled some of the weeds near the garlic, the strong smell of herbs filled the air, and I realized that there was still a stand of basil and thyme interspersed with the grass. I found a few stalks, plucked some garlic and took it back for my stew.

That night, by the light of a low fire and candles, I sat in the front room and read more of Gwyneth's diary.

"*I can hear them out there in the night,*" she had written in June of 1958.

"*They are always near, but especially now at the solstice. They know the book is here. I have never spoken one word of power here, but they remain nearby. Waiting. Sometimes at night, I hear their footsteps on the roof. I can feel them watching me in the daytime.*

Agatha called them. She said it got lonely all those years, and sometimes it made her feel better to see their eyes outside in the night. Small orbs of power waiting in the forest. Standing by, listening for a Word.

There is more than one Word of power. There is the Last Word, of course, and we have guarded that word with our lives since the dawn of the written word. There may be a day when the word is needed. But until then, it must never be said.

But there are other Words. Syllables that speak to the primordial. To the creatures that can traverse worlds; those who lived before us, and will remain when we are dust.

Those Words are also in the book we guard. And those are the Words Agatha used sometimes. She invoked them for food... and comfort. I wonder if those words did her in, at the end. The sisterhood swears to never speak the words, even the weakest of them. For the Words hold power. The Words are power.

And we are sworn to protect and assume no power at all.

Agatha strayed some. But I will stay true. I will not speak any of the Words."

SOMETHING CREAKED ABOVE MY HEAD.

I jumped at the sound, slamming the journal shut. Then I sat rock still and listened.

I could hear the beat of my heart, but nothing more.

Just as I began to relax, there was another creak. My eyes stared at the rough-hewn ceiling as if something might jump out of the wood itself.

Nothing did. But the creak sounded again. And again. It was travelling across my head... across the roof.

I was alone in the forest, in an ancient cabin, and something was walking across my roof. There was nobody I could call, and I had no gun. I prayed it wasn't a bear that had smelled my stew cooking and would decide to paw through one of the dry rotted windows to get at it.

The sweat began to roll down my ribs.

I didn't dare go outside to see what it was. I just prayed it didn't come inside.

Then there was another creak, at the far end of the roof. Something rattled outside, on the ground. I had images of a grizzly casing the joint, a few feet and a thin wall away.

After a few minutes with no noise, I peered outside. The stars were alive with summer energy above the dark tree line. I couldn't see anything on the porch. I scanned the area between the house and the line of the forest and saw only shifting shadows, grass moving in the wind. Then I looked deeper into the shadows of the tree line, and saw the eyes.

Yellow orbs. Dozens of them. Watching the cabin. Rarely blinking.

The hair on the back of my neck stood up.

And I shook my head.

"Power of suggestion," I whispered to myself. "You just read about eyes, so now you're seeing them. They're not eyes. Get real. They're fireflies."

I looked outside again and stared at a pair that seemed closer than the rest. They blinked and stared right back.

I didn't believe a word I was saying.

Fireflies.

Sure they were.

I didn't sleep well. The creaking didn't repeat itself, but as I lay in bed, I knew the forest was alive with eyes. Watching. Waiting.

When I got up the next morning, I turned the cabin upside down. Gwyneth's diary talked about the book she guarded, but the diary was not the book. She said she had put it in a cupboard in an early post, so I searched those first. Nothing. I emptied the few books stacked on a shelf in the bedroom and searched in the bottoms of every drawer. I moved all the furniture and even pulled the blackened canned goods off the pantry shelf.

I found nothing resembling a book of ancient words. The only books here were a couple of cookbooks and a handful of crumbling paperback novels.

Eventually I gave up the search and decided to go for a walk in the woods surrounding the house. That's why I was out here, after all. To enjoy the forest. Without the endless interruption of texts and emails and calls.

Without words.

Ironically, a book of words is what I'd wasted half the day searching for. I walked down to the river, and explored the banks, looking for tracks. Whatever roamed the forest at night would also roam the edge of the water, right?

I slapped away clouds of gnats, and jumped at the splash of a couple fish that leapt out of the water for a second before plunging back in.

There were no tracks.

I couldn't shake the feeling that I was being watched from the shadows of the trees. I turned my head quickly several times, sure that I was going to spot someone or something nearby, but all I saw were the gently waving blades of grass in the summer breeze.

Eventually, I returned to the cabin. On a whim, I decided to explore the old garden. I found the herbs again and started to pull out the unknown weeds and grass that they struggled to rise above. After an hour or so, I was rewarded with a five-foot swatch of chives and basil and silver sage. I also discovered some squash vines. Most didn't have fruit, but I did stumble over one plant that had a half dozen crookneck squash. I picked a couple and stood up to admire my work. I hadn't done much hiking today, but I had tended an herb garden. Somehow, I felt accomplished for that.

I added the squash and basil to the leftover stew from last night. I'd kept it in a covered pot near the fire and added water in the morning to keep it from drying out. At this point, it was largely mush. The squash would give it some texture.

After dinner, I poured myself a drink and sat back to watch the fire. It wasn't long before I drifted to sleep... but not for long.

I jerked awake when something above my head creaked. Paused. And creaked again.

Steps.

On the roof. Slow and steady. Moving from one side to the other.

My eyes shed their drowsiness quickly.

Creak. Click. Creak. Click. Creak.

Something moved just a few feet above my head.

Slowly, I rose from the chair. It was dark outside now, the only light from the low flame above the embers of my fireplace.

Crack.

I jerked backwards at the sound, knocking over the rest of my glass of bourbon. It rolled off the table and hit the floor with a telltale snap. Broken glass. I didn't care. I was staring at the ceiling, wondering if whatever was on the roof was now inside an eave.

The noise didn't repeat, and I walked slowly to the window to peer outside. Maybe it had jumped off the roof?

As I stared out at the old porch, there was nothing but the reflection of the moon on the rotted planks. The tree line was ominous. Pitch black and silent.

And then something blinked.

And again.

Small points of light. Orange, intelligent light.

Soon, the tree line was alive with eyes, all of them looking right back at me.

I shifted away from the window and bent to pick up the shards of broken glass before I stepped on them.

As I did, I noticed the line of bourbon on the floor. It had fled the ruined glass and ran right up to the old wood paneling behind the small table. I got down on my hands and knees to pick up the glass beneath the table. But then I stopped.

There was a latch at the bottom of the paneling, right where the liquid disappeared underneath the board.

I traced an almost invisible line that ran in the crease of the paneling. Now that I knew it was there, I could see where the line cut across the grain.

I crawled backwards, moved the table and chair and found a second latch that had been hidden.

Then I understood why there was a low indentation in the floor. So you could slip a finger beneath the edge to pry it open. There was no knob, which helped keep the door's existence hidden from casual sight. I slid my finger into the indentation and pulled… and the small door – maybe only two feet by two feet – squeaked outward. Inside the hidden cabinet was a stack of candles. And dolls. And a small black wooden case.

I ignored the rest and pulled that out into the light of the room. And opened the lid.

Inside, as I'd instantly suspected, was a thin book. It looked ancient. Weathered and cracked brown leather. I was afraid to open it, but slowly, carefully, I did. When I saw the intricately drawn script inside, I forgot all about the eyes in the forest and the creature over my head.

This was, without a doubt, The Book.

The beginning pages were difficult to understand. The letters were drawn like art, and the words were archaic. English… but old English. They spoke of doorways and power and gifts and retribution. I wasn't terribly clear on any of it, but I decided to flip forward.

That's when I found the first Word.

It was written in black, block letters, accentuated with gold and red ink. The Word was large and ornate and all alone in the center of the page. It was 13 letters long.

On the borders of all four sides of the page were tiny words written in a thin and almost invisible script. I turned the book slowly around as I struggled to read them. They said,

With a Word they will Feed you,
With a Word they will Come,
With a Word they will Stop you
from being Undone.

I sounded out the Word in my head. It was strange. Not English, though represented in the English alphabet. Did I dare to speak it aloud?

I pondered this thought for a moment and then laughed. An old book of magic words. Seriously?

I opened my mouth and said it, as best I could.

I waited. The air seemed pregnant with anticipation.

Nothing happened.

What did I expect? I laughed and then opened my mouth and said it again, this time louder. Almost a yell.

The house remained still. No explosions of smoke or fairy appearances. I smiled to myself and closed the book. After another swig of bourbon, I looked outside. The forest was dark. I chided myself. Imagination running wild. After a bit, I went to bed, and almost instantly fell into a deep and dreamless sleep.

THE DEMANDING RAYS of a summer sun woke me in the morning. The room was bright with the promise of a gorgeous day. I sat up, stretched and then walked through the sitting room.

When I opened the front door to let in some air, I almost stepped on my breakfast.

There were four large white eggs sitting on the rotten wood of the porch.

I frowned and looked around the clearing. Nobody was around. Who would have brought me eggs?

I bent down and picked one up, rolled it around in my hand. It seemed like a normal chicken egg. Looking around once more and seeing no one, I took the eggs into the kitchen. I cracked them open in a small bowl, and yellow yolks slid out. They were fresh.

Shrugging, I stirred them up. They smelled and looked good. I wasn't going to look a gift horse in the mouth. I was making scrambled eggs for breakfast.

After adding wood to the fire and cooking my unexpected breakfast over it, I settled back to look at the book of Words again. I read the page from last night once more. *With a Word they will Feed you, With a Word they will Come, With a Word they will Stop you from being Undone.*

Had I really received breakfast because of speaking an ancient word? The idea was preposterous. But... there was nobody else in these woods from what I could tell.

My phone vibrated then, and I glanced at it, but shook my head. Work. I knew if I answered it, I'd be drawn into some pointless drama. So, I thumbed the notification away. I was on vacation, damnit. I would spare no words for work.

That afternoon, I walked for a mile or more through the trees and long undisturbed forest floor and found no evidence of other campers or hikers or habitation.

WHEN I RETURNED to the cabin, there was a deer laid out on the porch, and a handful of potatoes.

The hair rose on the back of my neck.

Again... the clearing was empty. But there was no question in my mind now that the Word had invoked the glowing eyes to feed me.

Luckily, there was still a large supply of salt in the cabin's kitchen. It was hard as a rock, but I knew that it would work to brine the venison and keep me in meat for a few days. Refusing to think of the why, I dragged the deer out back and got the sharpest knife I could find from the kitchen. I didn't have the means to properly preserve all of the meat, but I could preserve a good bit of it in large pots of brine until I could fashion some kind of smokehouse.

That night I ate fresh wood-fire cooked venison and baked potatoes, with spinach and mushrooms I found growing out back near the garden and tree line. Gourmet camping.

After dinner, the eyes glowed bright in the forest.

I pulled out Gwyneth's journal and read more.

"Agatha's influence remains long after her death. They feed me and comfort me in the night. I remain cautious of their influence, however. They are not human. They are not even lost souls. They are something else. They have no morals. Whatever is wished...I must control my thoughts. The wrong desire could be deadly. But they provide some relief from my life-long sentence here. Someone must guard the Words. And somehow, I must eventually find my own successor. The book cannot be discovered by the uninitiated. And it is too valuable to be destroyed. Someday, somebody may have need of it. Agatha considered using it during the World War. I know this from her training so many years ago. And maybe she did... maybe that's why the tide turned and the carnage ended. I don't know. But someday, we may need the Last Word of power. I will guard it with my life, all my life."

I closed the diary and pulled out the Book. Bits of yellowed paper flaked off every time I turned a page. There were many words inside, each alone in the center of a page, with some description written on the four edges around it. But now I was curious. What was the "Word of Power" exactly? I skipped the middle and opened the final page of the book.

The Word was written alone on the page. There was nothing surrounding it in the margins. Only the Word itself. It was long. Seemingly seven syllables.

I raised an eyebrow as I tried to fathom the meaning and pronunciation of its 21 letters. My throat constricted as I considered that women had sat here in this cabin for years, solely to guard this page from being seen by the likes of me.

My phone buzzed in my pocket then, and I pulled it out to see another notification from work. I thumbed it away angrily. "On vacation," I murmured. Then, on a hunch, I pulled up Google and searched for the Word.

The webpage turned white for a moment and then refreshed.

No Results. Did you mean...

Google offered a completely different word.

"No," I said. "I meant..." and without thinking, I spoke the word that I'd been pronouncing in my head.

Something thumped hard on the roof. The scramble of feet moved above my head and disappeared over the other side.

My heart jumped, but just as it did, my phone buzzed again in my hand. I looked down. Another text from work.

"Oh my God," I whispered, "I wish the world would just go away and leave me alone already!"

Something slammed at the window and I saw a pair of yellow eyes staring in. Close. Not out in the forest. I jumped up, but the eyes vanished as soon as I moved.

I approached the window and looked out. The forest was black. I walked out into the clearing and peered at the roof. I could see nothing up there. Shrugging, I returned to the cabin.

THE NEXT MORNING, there were no eggs on my porch. I had to admit slight disappointment, but you couldn't expect magical creatures to feed you breakfast every day. I focused on the practical, and with some basic tools from the cabin, I pulled apart the remains of the outhouse out back, added some logs and refashioned the wood as a smokehouse. I dug a pit and lined it with rock, and then doused the wood with river water. Then I hung some of my brined venison from a metal rod I'd found in the cabin's storage closet and built a fire beneath it.

My phone did not go off that day. Or the next. I let the battery die.

It was blissful. And the smoked meat was plentiful and amazing. Several times, I silently thanked whatever powers had brought the deer, but the eyes did not reappear.

I read more of Gwyneth's journal and studied some of the book's other Words of power. She had apparently gotten ill, and towards the end wrote that she must ask Agatha's friends for help for she felt at her end. There were no more entries.

What had she asked? What had they done for her?

I charged my phone from a battery and decided I should probably check in with Aimee, but I got no response. There seemed to be a cell signal, but... my text went unanswered. And when I checked my Facebook page, there had been no activity from anyone all week.

After a couple more days of complete silence, I got worried and decided that my solitude had reached its natural end. I had eaten all the venison I dared, and the bourbon was gone. I packed my backpack and closed the door to the cabin after ensuring the fire was completely out in the hearth.

"You were just what I needed," I said to the silent structure. And then I began the trek back up the hillside to find the trail back to my car.

Only... as I left the clearing and began to walk through the woods, the trees seemed to thin out. I don't mean that there were fewer trees. Just... the trees grew insubstantial. With every step, the woods in front of me faded. It was as if everything turned to fog.

After a few more steps, I reached out to touch one of the hazy trees and... my hand passed right through the three-foot wide trunk.

What the hell?

I hurried forward but found that I couldn't go much farther. Because the world in front of me soon stretched out in an endless cloud of empty white. I walked forward a bit, but when I turned and could barely see the trees behind me, I headed back. I did not want to lose my way in the nothingness.

My heart grew cold with the realization of what I had done.

I had spoken the Last Word of power. I had wished the world away.

And it had gone.

My wish granted.

THE FOREST EYES eventually came back when I used the Word. They feed me. Perhaps they kept me *"from being Undone"* as the Book promised. They are not of this world, I realized, and so they remain. But no matter how many times I say the Last Word and wish for the world to return, the emptiness beyond the cabin remains unfilled. And so, I write this at the end of Gwyneth's journal, in case somehow, someday, the World returns and finds me gone, but this book remaining. I only hope that this is what will happen.

WORDS CAN HAVE POWER. Sometimes, far too much power.

I pray that there is someone left to read these words I leave behind. And heed my warning.

Be careful of the words you choose to say.

Words can be more powerful than you might imagine.

Especially... the Last Word.

Triggered

Ava woke in a fog. The room kind of... swam into focus when she opened her eyes. It took a moment for things to become clear enough that she realized she was not in her house.

Not in her bed.

She had to concentrate hard to remember what had happened the night before. She'd been at a wine bar, enjoying the warmth of the grapes in her throat as she read a new Harlan Topes novel on her Kindle. And then a woman had sat near her and struck up a conversation about reading. Books were Ava's favorite subject, so she was easily distracted from her Kindle. Topes was a newbie and she was already keeping notes on his inadequacies. She enjoyed posting reviews and she already had a feeling that Topes was a pedophile. You could just tell from the way he wrote about kids. Skeezy.

The woman... her name was Beth and she seemed kind of mousy – limp shoulder-length hair and a tendency to look down when she spoke – said she hadn't read Topes yet, and Ava had laughed. "Based on what I'm seeing, you might want to take a pass. I think he's a pedophile."

"Ew," Beth had said. "Are you sure?"

"You can just tell."

"Can you?"

Ava had gone on to explain in depth what kinds of things tipped her off. The other woman had nodded, her eyes intent, as if she were taking internal notes.

"Did you ever read Frank Milton?" Beth had asked later.

Ava had just laughed. "Oh, hell yes," she had. She was proud of the fact that her reviews and Internet fist-waving had crucified that creep. When he'd tried to excuse what she insisted were misogyny and racism and strong hints of pedophilia in his novel, she'd led a shitstorm of social against him that got his book dropped. She was proud to have gotten him cancelled because he was a creep. When she told Beth all this, the other woman frowned.

"Did you ever meet him?"

"No. Thank God."

They'd talked more. Comparing favorite authors and films and even politics. But then after another glass or two of wine, Ava had gotten suddenly lightheaded. Beth had helped her down from her high top chair, and that's when things grew foggy. She remembered the girl's arm around her, steering her out of the bar. And that's... pretty much where her memory ended.

AVA SAT up in the bed and realized two things.

This wasn't a bedroom and she wasn't on a bed. She was lying on an air mattress. And she was naked beneath the sheet.

She looked around. The room was large – maybe 50 feet long. It seemed like a warehouse space, with white cement floors and corrugated outer walls. There were harsh florescent lights 20 feet above her, and a series of doors in front of her.

And that was it. There was nothing else in the room.

"Hello?" she called.

She stood up, holding the sheet around her as she stared further around the room. There were several doors in front of her, but only one on the wall behind. Guessing that might be the entry to this place, she walked over and tried her hand on the knob.

It was locked.

"Is anybody here?" she called again. This time, there was an answer from overhead.

"Ah, you're awake I see."

The voice was female and emanated from speakers two stories up in the ceiling.

"Is that... Beth?" Ava asked.

"It is."

"Why am I naked?"

"Because I took your clothes off. You won't be needing them here."

"Wait... did you... did we..."

"Fuck?" The voice laughed. "Of course, you'd assume I'm a lesbian if I took your clothes off. You make far too many assumptions."

"Where are we? Why am I here?"

"We're going to play a little game," Beth said. "Today we're going to explore some of your triggers."

"What?" Ava's fear was quickly cycling to anger. "What is this bullshit? Give me my clothes and let me go home. I've got a lot to do today."

"I don't think so," the ceiling said. "You can hide behind your avatar and your computer screen online. But not here. Here you will face your fears head-on. No protection."

"What *are* you talking about?"

"I want you to face your triggers today," Beth said. "I want you to understand that by defanging stories that have difficult scenes, by demanding authors have their work sanitized by so-called sensitivity readers and crucifying those who don't hold the same world-view as you do on social media, that you are doing the exact opposite of what you claim. You say that you want to promote unique voices and diversity. But then in the same breath you set the lynch mobs on anything you don't like under the guise of "protecting others."

The voice was silent for a moment, and then suddenly it was right behind her.

"Well, I'm here to take your protection away."

The sheet suddenly yanked out of her hand, and Ava turned to see Beth standing there in jeans and an old t-shirt, balling the sheet up in her hands.

"Give that back," Ava demanded, and reached out to grab it.

Beth jumped backwards and pulled out a boxcutter from her back pocket. She held it out in front of her, and thumbed the red button on its side until the razor extended an inch from the base.

"The good news about being naked is, if I cut you, I won't ruin any of your designer clothes," Beth said.

It occurred to Ava that the other woman no longer looked sheepish and shy as she had last night. The predator had revealed its teeth.

Ava feinted to her right, and then jumped to her left, grabbing at the sheet in Beth's hand. But even as her fingers gripped the cotton, a plume of red flowers blossomed on its folds. The ice of pain shot up her arm. Ava retreated fast, staring at the two-inch long gash in the pale underside of her arm. Blood was dripping like a loose faucet on the white floor.

"It hurts when there is nothing to hide behind, doesn't it," Beth said. "No Internet anonymity. No shield of righteous indignation."

"Oh my god, it hurts," Ava cried. She stared at the blood leaking steadily out of the slash and began to feel a little faint. "I need a doctor."

Beth laughed. "Nah, you need a thicker skin. You know, like you expect authors to have."

"I'm losing a lot of blood," she complained.

"You've got plenty to spare," Beth said. Then she put the blade to the sheet and slashed a long cut along the edge. She chopped it at either end and threw a long strip of cloth at Ava.

"Tie that around it. You'll be fine."

Ava took the cloth and clumsily wrapped it around her arm. A moan of dismay escaped her as she watched the white material turn first pink, then red. She wrapped two more revolutions of cloth around it and then quickly realized she couldn't tie it one-handed.

Beth shrugged. "Tuck the loose end under," she advised. "Suck it up, isn't that what you'd say to someone who complained about one of your mean-spirited little reviews?"

"What is your deal?" Ava snapped back. "What do you care about my reviews?"

"I care about the people you hurt."

"My reviews don't hurt anyone. Maybe some of those authors I critique will use what I tell them to write better stories."

"Your reviews do hurt people," Ava said. "Because you don't simply review the stories. You attack the people behind them."

"I do not," Ava argued. "I just say what I think."

"So... critiquing an author's sex scene by saying you pity his wife because he clearly knows nothing about sex is sticking to the merits or deficiencies of the story?"

"Oh please," Ava said. "I know the review you're talking about, and I do pity his wife."

"Accusing an author of racism because she doesn't include minorities in her novel is just about the story?"

"Clearly she has an issue with diversity."

"Or perhaps she was simply telling a story that didn't call for it?"

"Whatever. I don't understand what you want from me."

"I want you to understand that the things you say are wrong. I want you to know that you're stifling artists and human expression out of a misguided sense of righteousness. But most of all, I want you to understand that your personal attacks and assumptions have truly hurt people."

"They just need to get a ..."

"... thicker skin," Beth laughed. "Yeah. Just like you."

She pointed to the doors. "Behind each of these doors, you will learn something. But since you always insist that books have trigger warnings, I've listed the triggers on the doors. It's up to you which door you choose. But once you're inside, you have to review all of the material before you can leave. The door will remain locked until you do."

"You're fucking crazy," Ava yelled and tensed to lunge. But Beth held up the boxcutter in front of her and asked, "How much blood do you want to lose today?"

Slowly Beth began to retreat, the weapon still held out in front of her.

Suddenly feeling exposed, Ava hugged her bare breasts with the wounded arm, while holding her other hand awkwardly over her crotch. "Why are you doing this?" she whined.

"Choose a door," Beth said. And then she turned and swiped a key card that she'd had in her pocket above the door handle. In a flash, she opened the door and slipped through. By the time Ava realized what was happening, the door was closing. She vaulted forward but her hands slapped on the metal just as it snapped shut.

"Let me out of here," she screamed, pounding with her fists on the door. The sound echoed throughout the room, but Beth did not return. Her hands began to hurt after a bit, so she stopped her fruitless attack on the door.

Ava paced back and forth, calling again and again for Beth to open the door and let her out. But there was no response. Finally, she decided to take a look at the doors on the other side of the room from the exit.

They all looked the same from ten feet away. A white door with a silver handle. But a little above and to the right of each handle was a piece of paper with notes on it.

She walked to the first one. It said:

TRIGGERS:
Human Sacrifice
Animal Sacrifice
Child cannibalism
Incest
Genocide
Stoning
Burning

SHE WALKED to the next one, and the list was shorter:

TRIGGERS:
Cannibalism
Child killing
Pedophilia
Incest
Slavery
Torture

THE NEXT HAD EVEN FEWER:

TRIGGERS
Animal killing/sacrifice
Natural disaster

FINALLY, she arrived at the last door, which said simply:

TRIGGERS
None

Ava looked back at all of the doors and shook her head. She wanted nothing to do with cannibalism or animal cruelty or incest or any of the rest. She had campaigned on the Internet to make sure that there were warnings of all these kinds of things placed on books so that she could avoid being surprised by any plot twists that included them.

At the end of the day, "None" was exactly what she wanted. She opened that door and stepped inside.

The lock clicked behind her, as she looked around the room.

It was... completely empty.

The walls and floor and ceiling were all painted white, so much so that she could barely tell where the floor ended and a wall began. In the center of the room, there was a white vinyl chair. It looked comfortable, and there was nothing more that she wanted to do at the moment more than sit and think.

She collapsed into the soft vinyl covering of the chair and brought her legs up Indian-style. She wrapped her arms around her chest, and leaned forward, completely covering the "naked" bits of her body with her stance.

This was all completely, utterly, ridiculous.

Who would go to these lengths to make a point? And why?

She sat there in silence for what seemed like a long time. And then finally, the voice came once again from overhead.

"Are you enjoying the silence?" Beth's disembodied voice asked. "Somehow, I figured that you'd end up in that room. Though it's a shame really. There was so much to learn in the other rooms. Things that might have made you understand why I brought you here in the first place, honestly."

"Why are you doing this?" Ava yelled. "Just let me out already."

"Do you remember Frank Milton?" Beth asked.

"The pedophile? Yeah, what about him?"

"He was my brother. And he wasn't a pedophile. He was the sweetest man you might ever meet."

"Well, his book was badly written and super skeezy. I'd still bet he touches kids. You'd never know."

"And you base this on what... fiction?"

"Yeah," Ava answered. "I'm sorry, but if it's on the page, it was in his head."

"Thoughts are not actions," Beth said. "Imagination – even dark imagination – is not reality."

"Whatever," Ava said. "What does that have to do with any of this?"

"You killed my brother."

Ava laughed. "I killed his fiction career maybe. But that would have died without my help."

"You killed HIM," Beth answered. Her voice cracked over the speaker. "Thanks to you, he lost his job."

"What?"

"Your little Internet lynch mob made the school board where he worked nervous, and they fired him."

"That isn't killing him. Guess he should have been more careful about what he wrote."

"Because he was fired, and his marriage was already on the rocks, his wife left him," Beth said. "Neighbors just took that to be more evidence that he was a pedophile – the false rumor YOU started. He couldn't get another job because everyone heard the rumors. So, in short order, he lost his job, his family and then his house. He killed himself because he couldn't take it anymore."

"What does any of this have to do with trigger warnings and you kidnapping me?"

"I want you to understand what you did. How your false accusations spun up an Internet lynch mob that ultimately took my brother's life. And for what? Because he chose to write something dark from his imagination that you didn't like? One of your complaints was that there were no trigger warnings on that book. Well, I've got news for you. Trigger warnings and Internet lynch mobs are the death of free speech and free expression. If you'd chosen any other room, you'd have seen that the stories that have meant the most to human empathy and understanding are those that included horrible things happening. Things that people wouldn't read if they'd been "warned" about them in advance. The element of surprise is part of what makes them powerful. And the culture that you have helped create not only stops authors from exploring those kinds of things, but it runs them out of town on a rail. Your warnings and lemming mobs of do-gooder, politically correct chest-thumpers are just as destructive as the fascists and neo-Nazis, and more dangerous than any idea or situation in a book. You should be dead, not my brother."

"I have a right to my opinion," Ava said. "And I have a right to express it."

"You don't have a right to burn people at the stake who you've never even met just because they *seem* like witches to you. You don't have a right to cancel people when you don't know the whole story. And you sure as hell will never get the whole story from the clueless echo-chambers on the Internet."

"Look, I'm sorry about your brother," Ava said. "I didn't mean to destroy his life; I just wanted to save anyone from reading his books."

"You still don't get it, do you?"

"I said I'm sorry. Now would you let me out of here?"

Beth didn't reply.

In the outer room, she went to each door and took down the signs, after removing the items from inside the rooms. She took the Bible from the first room, and book of Greek Mythology from another. Shakespeare came out of another room. In the animal death/killing room she turned off a small laptop that was set to play *Charlotte's Web*, *Bambi* and *Old Yeller*. In the distance, she heard Ava's screams of anger. After a couple trips to her car to drop the books and laptop and other equipment, she went back to her "control room," a second story manager's office in the abandoned industrial park building that overlooked the white room. Ava stood naked in the center of the room below, hands on her hips in visible indignation.

"You fancy yourself an arbiter of taste," Ava said into the microphone. "You love it that all the little lemmings pat you on the back and prop up whatever you support and stomp all over whatever you denigrate. You are the dream crusher of everyone you feel is beneath you."

"Okay, you've made your point," Ava said. "When do I get out of here?"

"You chose the room where there is nothing to learn. Nothing to be surprised at. The room that has been sanitized of everything that is human. The room stripped of everything good and bad."

"Right. Whatever. When do I get out?"

"Never. Because you'll never learn anything with no triggers."

Ava switched the mic off and walked back downstairs. She locked the doors behind her, and just before reaching her car, dropped the keys in a sewer grate.

The screams from inside the building reached a hysterical pitch that echoed through the parking lot. She called Beth a host of foul names, but this time, there was nobody around to hear her negative review.

"Sorry, bitch," Beth whispered as she started the car. "But you've just been cancelled."

About the Author

JOHN EVERSON IS a staunch advocate for the culinary joys of the jalapeno and an unabashed fan of 1970s European horror cinema. He is also the Bram Stoker Award-winning author of *Covenant* and its sequels *Sacrifice* and *Redemption*, as well as a dozen other novels, including the erotic horror tour de force and Bram Stoker Award finalist *NightWhere*, the haunting thriller *Voodoo Heart* and his latest giallo homage, *The Bloodstained Doll*. Other novels include *Five Deaths for Seven Songbirds*, *The Pumpkin Man*, *Siren*, *The 13th* and the spider-driven *Violet Eyes*.

Over the past 30 years, his short fiction has appeared in more than 75 magazines and anthologies and received a number of critical accolades, including frequent Honorable Mentions in the *Year's Best Fantasy & Horror* anthology series. His story "Letting Go" was a Bram Stoker Award finalist in 2007 and "The Pumpkin Man" was included in the anthology *All American Horror: The Best of the First Decade of the 21st Century*. He has written licensed tie-in stories for *The Green Hornet* and *Kolchak The Night Stalker* and novelettes for *The Vampire Diaries* and Jonathan Maberry's *V-Wars* universe (Books 1 and 3). *V-Wars* was turned into a 10-episode Netflix series in 2019 that included two of Everson's characters, Danika and Mila Dubov.

His short story collections include *Cage of Bones & Other Deadly Obsessions*, *Needles & Sins*, *Vigilantes of Love* and *Sacrificing Virgins*. To catch up on his blog, join his newsletter or get information on his fiction, art and music, visit www.johneverson.com.

Made in the USA
Middletown, DE
22 June 2025